This is a work of fiction. Names, ch... ncidents are either a product of the a... d ficti- tiously, and any res... ead, events, or locales is ... nse may have been take... better serve the p... ovel.

ISBN: ...6700872911
*The Love of Her Life*
All Rights Reserved.
Copyright © 2020 Rebecca Ruger
Written by Rebecca Ruger

Cover Design by Kim Killion @ The Killion Group

All rights reserved. No part of this publication may be reproduced, distributed or transmitted in any form or by any means, or stored in a database or retrieval system, without the prior written permission of the publisher.
Disclaimer: The material in this book is for mature audiences only and may contain graphic content. It is intended only for those aged 18 and older.

# The Love of Her Life

**Highlander Heroes, Volume 6**

Rebecca Ruger

Published by Rebecca Ruger, 2020.

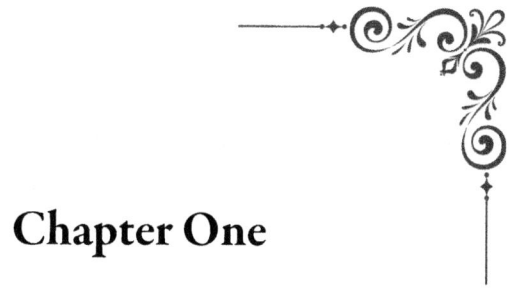

# Chapter One

*Chester Castle Prison*
*Northern England*
*1298*

HE WAS VERY GOOD AT waiting. Very good at sitting perfectly still for up to an hour now, could ignore the pins and needles in his legs while he waited on his haunches. Sometimes, he didn't blink for many minutes, staring at that small gap between the damp stone wall and the cold hard floor. Other times, the lines betwixt those spaces blurred, that he was forced to blink, to dispel what wasn't real. He'd caught many mice already, his reflexes honed daily and lightning quick.

And then they stopped coming.

Mayhap they'd been warned to avoid this means of entry, mayhap they'd caught the scent of the previous deaths. No more came through, not for a long time.

But there must be more. There had to be, Alec was sure.

*Jesu, Alec, give up already*, someone whispered behind him.

*What's he about?* asked the other.

There were only the three of them in this farthest corner of the dank dungeon. After the first few days, it had become apparent that neither he nor Iain nor Lachlan would go easily, that they'd scrape and claw for each and any tiny triumph against their captors. The other prisoners had separated themselves, keeping to the lighted areas, putting distance between themselves and these three, where any trouble usually began.

*Alec, what are you doing?* Iain asked again.

His voice was starting to grate on Alec's nerves, the same noise again and again, that harsh murmur, infused partly with surrender, seeming to ask instead, *Why do you bother?*

Alec ignored him.

Finally, his prey showed himself. Alec's eyes brightened but he did not move. Not yet. He waited, let the intruder acclimate himself, let him imagine safety and move further inside. When he was but a foot away, Alec struck, swiping his hand swiftly from left to right, snagging his prey on the first pass.

He could not call out the fierce joy he knew just then with his success. They would come and he would lose his prey.

*Alec—*

*Leave off, Iain,* he hissed darkly. *I'm working on a wee critical something*

Lachlan Maitland groaned, prone on the ground, as he had been for two days, since they'd lit his face on fire.

Alec stared at the wall when he broke the intruder's neck. After a moment, when it moved not at all, he opened his hand and stared at the small brown mouse.

At least he would eat today.

Iain, and now Lachlan too, continued to call his name, over and over that his lip curled, and he squeezed his eyes closed hard, willing them away, or quiet, or dead already.

# THE LOVE OF HER LIFE

*Northwest of Edinburgh*
*1307*

WHEN HE OPENED HIS eyes, a blinding light shone upon him.

They called his name yet, louder now.

*Alec!*

"Alec!"

He came to quickly, a great burst of air exploding from him, as if he'd held his breath while he'd dreamed.

"Alec."

He swiped a hand at the one that reached for him as he sat up.

"Bluidy fireballs!" Aymer's voice. "Sulfur and coal and God knows what."

That would have been the burst of fire that had dropped out of nowhere in front of his horse, that had seen him thrown and momentarily disoriented. His ears rang yet, which was why Aymer sounded as if he shouted his words into a barrel between them.

He was lifted to his feet, dazed, but spun around to see a bit of charred and smoldering earth some distance away. He'd been thrown several yards.

"Let's go, then," Simon urged. "They're falling back, all the armies. We need to get help for Malcolm."

This pulled Alec from the last of his haziness. "Malcolm?" His captain had been close. He searched his mind for his last recollection of Malcolm before the fireball had sent him through the air, but he could recover nothing, no memory.

Simon came close, handed the reins of Alec's big black to him. "He's in bad shape. C'mon."

Alec gained the saddle and immediately was at ease. A horse under him always put him to rights in a battle. He took a quick inventory of his unit, saw Aymer and Simon were close yet and further ahead were Nigel and Ranald and William and the others.

He followed, as opposed to led, as however few or many minutes he'd been out, had put him behind in the knowing, in the discerning of the situation. The lads would know though, would lead for now.

*Bluidy English!*

IT WAS A SHAME THAT such charming weather really did not see any more game brought to their table, or at least a better variety. One might think that as much as she longed to be out of doors when the weather allowed, so too might the animals.

She stirred the few pieces of meat around in the kettle, supposing she should be happy for even the substance of one hare she was able to add to the stew. Truly, it only was afforded the name *stew* because she'd been able to add one carrot and one leek and a very tiny bit of garlic. When all the chunks were gone, tomorrow possibly, she'd toss in the pile of bones she'd hoarded of late and boil these for a full day. At least they'd have a good bone broth for several days after that.

Mayhap tomorrow someone might call, might need her aid. Mayhap she'd be paid with food—bread, she hoped, thinking

Henry ate any bread or oat cake so much more agreeably than any pitiful thing Katie might put to the kettle. She supposed it was not very charitable of her to wish illness on another so that she might eat, even if she were imbued with plenty of faith in her healing capabilities.

Straightening, she tossed a glance over her shoulder, found her son still seated at the small table where they took their meals, busy yet with the needle and thread and his own tattered hose. He was young yet, only seven, and a lad at that. He shouldn't then ever have to learn such domestic chores, but she was only one person and couldn't possibly do everything. Actually, they were two, Katie and Henry—a good pair, he'd said—which had put her in a mind that he was indeed old enough to start helping out. Turning fully, she watched as he scrunched up his brow and showed just the tip of his tongue, as he did often when he concentrated, pushing and pulling the needle and coarse thread through the hole in the toe of his hose.

"That's very well done, Henry," she said, and meant it. His stitches, learned only in the last month, improved with each attempt. "Mayhap I'll have you begin mending my things as well."

He turned his disappointment toward her. "Aw. You said I'd only have to fix these."

"Fair enough," she said.

It had been just the two of them for so long that she supposed she often treated him more as a friend and companion than her son because she thought him much older than his years. Possibly a harsh life demanded that a child grow quickly. She thought she had, for certain.

Their hound, Boswell, larger than Henry yet, his coat wiry and three shades of brown, lifted his head. He tipped it toward the right, the gray snout and whiskers moving as he sniffed the air. Of course, this was not uncommon, as their cottage sat well away from the Dalserf castle, tucked between a small forest of trees and a narrow stream, that so many critters scurried around and through their immediate yard. Until, apparently, she stepped outside with any intent to catch one for their supper.

Boswell did not settle, as was normally the case, but growled low and got to his feet. The hair along the ridge of his spine stood straight, prickled with some awareness that Katie was not privy to, despite her own stillness.

She stepped softly to the front window, moving aside the linen covering, just an inch or so, to peer out into the yard. It was empty and the landscape of trees beyond, some hundred yards away, showed no one, of two feet or four, approaching.

The hound continued to growl, moving again, around the table, now facing the backside of the cottage. There was no window that faced the stream, so she could not peek to find what had spooked the normally unflustered Boswell. And when he began to bark in earnest, the hair on her own neck stood on end, and she said calmly, "Henry, get under the bed. Now. Dinna come out for nothing."

Her son obeyed, not terribly accustomed to such a command, but then sadly it was not completely foreign to him either. No sooner had the boy scrambled from the table and slid under the low mattress in the far corner of the room, than the noise came.

Katie froze, knowing full well what dozens of mounted riders sounded like. But it couldn't be that swine, Farquhar, from the castle, not coming 'round the back, from the stream and from the south. She took up the lone knife she possessed, which had

# THE LOVE OF HER LIFE

remained on the table after she'd sliced the sparse vegetables, and hid it within the folds of her skirt.

As one, she and Boswell turned, their gazes following the noise outside, from the back wall, around the side, and then to the front.

And then it stopped. No hooves pounded the earth. No harnesses jangled. No words were called. Everything was quiet.

Breathing quickly now, Katie stared at the handle of the door, watching, waiting for it to turn, imagining it probably wouldn't have done her any good anyway to have set the bolt in place.

The handle did not turn.

The entire door crashed in, swinging fully around, slamming into the small cupboard behind it.

Boswell charged and Katie shrieked, jumping back.

A goliath entered, having to duck under the door frame, having to twist and turn as his arms were laden with yet another mammoth man.

He growled at the charging hound, but otherwise ignored him and laid the man unceremoniously upon the table, setting him atop the carrot and leek parings and knocking over Katie's only jug of ale. It crashed to the packed earth floor as several more giants entered the small cottage, each and every one of them having to duck as neither Katie nor her husband had ever needed to do.

Sadly, Boswell was forever the proverbial more-bark-than-bite hound that this was the only defense he offered just now.

"You are the healer?" Asked the man gruffly over Boswell's dislike of this circumstance.

Katie nodded, transfixed and aghast at the same time.

"Call off your hound."

She shook her head, not persuaded to remove whatever little defense Boswell might provide for her, against this horde.

"Call off your hound or Aymer there will happily snap his neck."

She made a face at him, for giving her no choice, hating this man instantly.

"Aye," she said. "Boswell. Corner," she instructed. The hound knew this command, as it came his way often when people in need came calling. He went, but not quickly, and not without more low growling.

She swallowed as the man approached her, strode 'round the table and bore down on her. Every instinct, every fiber inside her screamed *run*, but she held her ground as he came close and towered over her, held her breath as well, lest he see how frightened she was.

"Boswell, stay," she instructed while the man appeared interested only in intimidating her. She'd sensed that the hound was getting to his feet again, in the far corner, near the bed where Henry hid.

Leaning over her, that she was forced to tip her head back, the man spoke slowly, infusing great menace into each word, "You fix him now," he said, pointing his hand behind him, to where he'd laid his friend. "If he dies, then so shall you."

She didn't move, continued to hold her breath, her fright immobilizing her.

The giant lifted a brow at her until she nodded shakily.

With that he pivoted, and Katie released a whimper of breath and then a greater puff of air. Sadly, it was only now that she recalled the knife in her hand. Little good the blade might do against this horde of goliaths. She sent a critical glance over the warriors, their presence shrinking the size of the very tiny cottage.

"Out. Everybody out. I need light and space and you're taking up all of it." She'd meant to sound imperative, but it emerged more as wretched begging.

The big man who'd just threatened her sat in the very chair Henry had only seconds ago. He inclined his head toward the rest of them, and they departed, one at a time, leaving the door open.

"I'll be sitting right here," the man said, "make sure you dinna carve him up yet more."

Katie sighed nervously and tucked the knife into the pocket of her gown and then exchanged her house apron for her work apron and washed her hands at the small cupboard near the hearth. She approached the table and the unconscious man with the bright orange hair and the barrel chest, possibly larger than the one sitting in the chair, terrifying her with the very essence of savagery that surrounded him.

"All this needs to come off," she said, indicating the bloodied leather breastplate and his sliced and charred tunic. "And I'll preface any treatment with an initial estimation that there's a lot of blood, likely worsened by you moving him and carrying him so recklessly. Hence, if he dies, I'd say the fault lies with you."

"And yet you will be the one who pays for it."

Narrowing her eyes at him, so that there was no confusion about what she thought of him, she tried to move around him in the chair. He grabbed at her, his fingers circling her upper arm almost completely.

"The patient is here," he said, pointing at his friend. His eyes were as black as pitch, the same color as his hair and the stubble on his cheeks and jaw and chin. Likely the same color as his soul, she thought uncharitably.

"And my tools and remedies are there," she said heatedly, indicating the counter along the far exterior wall, under the only other window.

ALEC RELEASED HER AND watched for just a moment as she strode to that counter and began pulling items from all the different shelves and crocks and jar. She walked by again, going to the hearth and dropping several utensils into one of the two kettles over the low burning fire. Satisfied that she would get about the work of saving Malcolm quickly then, he stood and began to remove the captain's gear, slicing his knife through the leather and then the linen, pulling everything open, baring the entire trunk of his body, and showing three wounds, all bleeding still.

Alec grimaced, not at the unpleasantness of the wounds, but for the seeming severity of them.

The woman returned, her hands full, and stood across the table from him. Biting her lip, she considered the wounds as well, blindly setting all her implements down next to Malcolm's head, the only space yet available on the table. She lifted her blue-eyed gaze to Alec but briefly, though did not manage to suppress her negative opinion quick enough that Alec's heart dropped to his stomach.

"I can clean them and sew what needs repair," she said, "but I...I can promise nothing else."

The first words she'd spoken to him only minutes earlier had been harsh and without any emotion save perhaps her anger at Alec's threat. These words were given with some sympathy, a healer's tone, which offered no hope.

Nevertheless, he maintained his fierceness with her. "I dinna think you want to die, woman."

Nae, she did not, as told by the seething in her gaze, and something deeper, as yet unknown to Alec. He watched her work then, addressing the largest and bloodiest puncture first, not wincing at all when she opened it further to gauge the damage within.

"Cracked his rib but doesn't appear to have punctured his lung. Next time, leave the entire shaft and arrow intact until it can be treated. Keeps the blood from flowing freely."

"Aye, but you'll have to repeat that to him when he wakes. He's the arse that yanked it out."

With a swift scowl, possibly for his language, she asked, "Will you fetch the pliers?" She gestured vaguely behind her while peering inside the wound. "On that cupboard?"

He hesitated, not entirely trusting her.

"Or we can sew up the tip of the blade that broke off in his rib and only hope it doesn't become infected."

With that, and the brutal look she leveled upon him, Alec did as requested and returned with the tool, expecting to hand it to her.

She shook her head. "I'll hold everything out of the way. You pluck it out."

*Bluidy hell.* He did grimace now but bent over Malcolm's chest and stared inside the wound, blood and tissue and torn muscle staring back at him.

"See it? That glint of metal?"

"Aye."

"Do not yank too hard," she instructed, "or you're likely to cause more damage to the muscle and skin. Clutch at the metal and wiggle it back and forth, gently, to cause no other harm."

Alec nodded and used one hand upon the tool, his head touching hers as they both bent so close over the hole. He managed quite easily to clamp the pliers around the piece of metal, but it was embedded fairly deep, and he was afraid to cause more harm as she'd said, that it took several minutes to wrest it free.

"Very good," she said when he did. "Now, behind me, fetch the two spoons I dropped into the boiling water."

He did this and returned to the table, opposite her, holding the hot metal gingerly.

"You're going to hold open the skin flaps with the spoons while I stitch up the inside." Without waiting a response, which was yet another twisting of his features, this time indeed for the gore, she retrieved a needle made of bone and threaded it with two strands of string that looked like silk.

She set this down on Malcolm's chest and took the spoons from him, both their hands and fingers bloodied now. She pressed the spoons inside, taking her time to wedge them against the skin and not the muscle. When they were set to her liking, she inclined her head to Alec that he should take them. He set his hands over hers, and she pulled hers out from underneath when his fingers had control of the spoons.

Straightening so that she might be able to lean in further, he stared at the top of her head while she sewed, saw not much more of her face than the thick fringe of lashes and her nose, slim and straight. He hadn't met many healers in his life, and while all the ones he had were women, he didn't think he'd ever met one like this. The ones he'd known were ancient and bent crooked with age, their manner abrupt and often surly.

This one was...she was beautiful. Her manner was indeed abrupt, but that might have been wrought by their barging in, and his threatening her life. Might have been, he wouldn't know. She was certainly not ancient and not at all crooked with age but was young and lean and crowned with a wealth of dark blonde hair that might actually be very blonde outside this dim cottage. Her eyes, when she'd faced him earlier so breathlessly, were true blue, light and dark and brimming with more a show than a reality of fearlessness, he'd understood at the time.

While she worked, he held his hands and the spoons still, even as her fingers so often brushed against or rested upon his. He passed his gaze around the cottage, making judgments about her based on the evidence around him. The meal he'd spied inside the second kettle had been sparse, more broth than anything else; the bed in the corner next to the cupboard was covered in a blanket of coarse wool, the color as drab as the ground beneath his feet; linen curtains, such as they were, hung over the two windows but seemed to serve no purpose but to keep out the light and mayhap the summer flies; a vase of wilted wild flowers sat on the cupboard near the hearth, next to a crude ewer and basin. Alec's brow lifted and then lowered darkly as his gaze landed on two pairs of boots to the left of the door. He frowned, considering the different sizes of the footwear. The woman was tiny, relatively speaking, but that smallest pair of boots there by the door would likely not fit her. Above that, hung on pegs hammered into the wooden wall, was what Alec assumed to be a cloak of wool, which matched the drab bed covering and next to that, a wee jacket of earthen brown.

Alec sent his gaze around again, studying everything with a fresh eye now. The hound—useless as protection, Alec had already decided—lay sleeping now between the bed and the counter where he'd fetched the pliers, his snout pointed under the raised mattress. On the mantle above the hearth, beyond the woman's head, were stacked two wooden bowls and two wooden cups.

"You can move your hands now," she said, standing straight for a moment, while she threaded the needle again.

Alec pulled his hands away and inspected her work. Of course, he had no idea what it should look like at this point, but he was pleased to see that it didn't bleed so much now.

She bent again over the remaining puncture marks, quiet and efficient, cleaning the other wounds and then sewing, these apparently requiring only external stitching that his assistance was not needed.

Alec sat in the small chair again and when she was done, she surveyed her own work while wiping her bloodied hands on her previously clean apron. She set her palm against Malcolm's forehead but declared it too soon for a fever if there was to be one. Then she dipped her fingers into a bowl and drew them out, covered in a gooey yellowish substance, which was thicker than liquid and did not drip, and was speckled with bits of whatever seeds and plants she'd ground earlier. She laved this all over the three wounds and applied more to a wide scrape on Malcolm's forehead. Her fingers were long and thin, her nails short but neatly trimmed, though dirtied now with all this business.

"If that doesn't become infected, it should cause him no trouble at all. Change the bandage every third day. I'll send you off with the mixture to smother over the wound to stave off infection."

So now she stood, her hands on her hips, staring across Malcolm's inert form with her pretty blue eyes, waiting it seemed, as if she thought he might just scoop up Malcolm and be on his way.

"What is your circumstance here?" Alec asked.

She blinked. "My circumstance?"

"Aye. We were given your direction in a village called Rutherglen." It hadn't been given kindly. Aymer had crept up on a lad moving sheep from pasture to meadow and held a knife to the lad's throat, inquiring of the nearest healer, threatening to come back and carve up the lad if he breathed even one word about Aymer's visit. *Lad said to follow the stream to find the witch's cottage*, Aymer had reported upon his return to where Alec and the others had hidden.

*Witch, was she?*

"Healing seems to bear no fruit," he said. "The coffers appear empty—or rather, the kettle."

She was only befuddled by his questioning, his suppositions.

"I get by," she said, with some hint of annoyance, "obviously." She shrugged then. "The poorer I am, the richer they are in health."

"Who are they? Who do you minister to?"

"To Rutherglen, and sometimes Eastfield, and to the castle, Dalserf."

Alec frowned. "Dalserf? Is that Thomas de Dalziel?" Alec did not know him personally, but he kept in good memory the names of any Scots' families in these Highlands who had sworn allegiance to Edward I.

"Aye." Her frown was deepening.

Holding her nervous gaze, he asked evenly, "And where is your son just now?"

She went completely still, unbreathing again it seemed, as she tried very hard to give nothing away.

"I have no son."

Ah, the lass was no liar, was torn up inside to denounce her own flesh and blood, even if it had been done to protect him.

"You sure about that, lass? You sure there's no' a lad under that bed?"

She whimpered and shook her head, her gaze pleading now.

"Come on out, lad," Alec instructed, holding her now tortured gaze. No one and nothing moved. "Dinna make me say it twice."

A shuffling was heard behind him. He thought the hound might have risen as well as the lad crawled out from under the bed.

Her blue eyes watered with her fright, her lips trembled. Her gaze left him, found the boy instead, and told Alec of the lad's position by the movement of her gaze. And when her eyes widened frantically and the hound barked, he knew a wee attack was coming. He turned his head, saw a scrawny arm raised, and caught the hand before any damage was inflicted. He dragged the boy to his side, his skinny arm held firmly in Alec's hand, the weapon seeming to be only his woeful fist. The hound continued to shout his distress.

Sensing movement over Malcolm, he turned and found that the lass had lifted her hands above the lifeless man, her skinny knife facing downward, her expression fierce.

"Let him go."

"You dinna want his neck snapped."

"You dinna want his heart pierced," she returned, her tone just as dangerous.

Alec pushed the boy away, saw him scramble around the table to his mother, who immediately put him behind her and lowered her knife. The hound followed, whining to his mistress.

"I've fixed your man," she said. "Take him and go."

Alec sighed, still seated, rubbing his hands up and down his thighs. He gave his regard to the lad, met a now familiar intense blue gaze, narrowed in a fashion remarkably like his mother's, his blond hair short but unkempt.

"Now, lass, you ken how these things work," he said, indicating the sewn wounds upon Malcolm. "Fever, infection, all sorts of peril imaginable. We'll be staying right here until my man is well out of danger."

# Chapter Two

Having been advised that she might simply carry on with her day as if there had been no intrusion—as if that were possible, with these two men taking up so much space in her tiny cottage—Katie sent Henry off to the bed, where he sat with his legs crossed, eyeing the big man suspiciously. They would be required to stay close to the dwelling, she'd been told, would not be allowed to go up to the castle, or into any village or town.

She filled a bowl for him, and one for herself and joined her son, likewise crossing her legs under her, while they supped, their table otherwise occupied.

The man stood and left the cottage, but only briefly, leaving the door open, calling out for someone named Simon, and returning soon enough with several flat pieces of bread, which he tossed onto the end of the bed.

"Of course, there's coin for you, when Malcolm is well again," he said, "but we can share our bread until then."

Two things crossed her mind. First, that she was so rarely paid in coin, she wasn't sure she would know what to do with it, what to purchase first, their needs many. Next, she wondered if she were expected to offer a share of her pitiful stew to the man. He hadn't returned with bread for himself, that he seemed not of a mind to sup just now.

# THE LOVE OF HER LIFE

To her dismay, he turned the chair a bit, facing her and Henry.

"What's your name, lad?"

Katie spoke up before Henry might have. "I understand your desire to remain here, in my home, but let's not pretend we have any desire for conversation. There is no reason that we need to know any more about you than already established. The reverse is true as well: you don't need to know anything about us."

He flexed his lips a bit, looked as if he might be torn between good humor and anger. "Lass, you keep acting irritable toward me, I'm going to lose all my charity and kindness."

More than once, she'd been scolded that too often, she spoke before she thought better of it. "I am no more a lass, and I have seen no evidence of the latter." She would not denounce the sharing of bread, however.

"You're both still breathing, so there's that kindness," he retorted smoothly, lifting a brow at her, a challenge.

Every word uttered, every smug look that crossed his face, she only hated him more.

He tried again, "Your name, lad?"

Henry consulted his mother first, and at Katie's tight-lipped nod, he answered, "Henry Oliver."

"Where is your father?"

"Heaven."

"And what is your mother's name?"

"Katie."

"How old are you?"

"Seven."

"Is your mam a good cook?"

Henry giggled, surprised by the question. He shrugged. "I dinna ken. I guess so."

"Is she always so fierce?"

"What's that?"

The man raised his gaze from Henry to consider her. Let him have his fun, she thought. He must think I don't know scorn or ridicule or haven't been interrogated like this before. Must think as well that no other man had ever befriended her son, thinking somehow Henry's attitude affected her own toward a person, as if a seven year old could see duplicity or an ugly soul or nefarious intentions.

This one seemed only to want to rile her. She would do well, she decided, to make sure that going forward, he was regularly disappointed.

"Fierce, with that scowling brow and those wary eyes, like someone just trod upon her foot for no reason."

Henry grinned again, turning to consider Katie. "She's nice to me."

Katie smiled at Henry, letting all her features soften for his benefit.

"Which way is Dalserf Keep?"

Henry pointed to the wall across from them, north. "Through the trees and over the small hill, no' the big one."

"How far?" The man asked of Katie.

Likely he expected some reply measured in distance, but she had no idea about such things. "Three quarters of an hour, by foot."

"Do people come to you, call on this house?"

She nodded. "If their need is urgent, otherwise I—we—go into the village or over to Rutherglen two or three times a week, to see the long-suffering or bed-ridden."

He nodded at this and left the cottage once again but stayed close that Katie could see half of him through the open door. He spoke to someone for several minutes, maybe two or three persons, Katie decided, hearing different but muffled voices reply, and when he returned, he left the door open.

He sat again and Katie was aware of movement outside, in front of her cottage. She stared through the opening, horrified as she watched so many people move past. Possibly there were forty or fifty of them, all mounted, one bigger than the next, riding away. They didn't want to be found, she surmised, sensing by the noise that the entire horde had moved to the rear of the cottage, where the woods beyond the stream would afford them little chance of detection if anyone should come calling.

"Dalserf has an army of hundreds," she said, pleased to deliver this news. "They train daily, always outside the walls of the castle. And they hunt often, in all of these woods." She hoped this might hurry along his departure.

He was unperturbed and unimpressed, mayhap saw through her motivations for saying as much. With a lift of his huge shoulders, he said evenly, while his gaze fixed on her with some taunting, "Better hope they dinna come 'round, lass. That'll be one hell of a clash, with your snug little cottage smack in the middle."

The man on the table moaned then, drawing all attention.

Katie jumped up, taking her empty bowl with her. She approached the wounded man just as the other man stood and leaned over him as well.

"Malcolm," prodded the one at her side.

The man spoke, or tried to, but nothing intelligible was ascertained. He had no fever still, she determined and went to the hearth once again, filling her bowl with just broth. To this she added a bit of powdered mandrake root and cloves, hoping to fight off fever from the inside.

"Lift him to drink," she instructed when she neared the table again, standing opposite the big man once more.

He eyed her and the bowl suspiciously. Katie rolled her eyes and sipped from the bowl herself, letting him see her swallow. Only then did he nod and move to the end of the table and Malcolm's head, lifting him by the shoulders. The red-haired man groaned again but did sip at the bowl when it was pressed to his lips. But not much before he seemed to sleep again or lose consciousness. She slapped softly at his cheek, forcing more down his throat when he opened his mouth at the disturbance. They did this for several minutes, slowly, until the bowl was empty, and thankfully not more than a quarter of it dribbled down his chin and into his darker orange and brown beard.

Katie was encouraged that he had roused at all, truly having no idea if he would wake, having no sense of exactly how much blood he might have lost. He was huge and appeared fit, and likely his age, not more than forty she guessed, would assist in his recovery. She wanted him mended and well, and soon, so that they might exit her life as quickly as they'd entered it.

When she sat again with Henry, her son asked of the big man sitting in his chair, "Are you giants then?"

Katie grinned before she might have held it back.

The man was amused as well, though he kept it in check. His eyes shone a bit, but he allowed no grin. "Aye, lad. Giants we are, from the northernmost reaches of the Highlands, where you ken all giants are bred."

"I dinna ken that," Henry said, holding the empty bowl between his crossed legs. "You've come from a battle then?"

"Aye, but only a wee one," said the man, not adverse to entertaining Henry, it seemed.

"Guess you dinna win."

The man shook his head, chewed the inside of his cheek for a moment. "We dinna. But we will. One day, all the English will be driven from Scotland."

"Farquhar says any Scots who fight the English are traitors," Henry repeated.

The man's countenance turned harsh once more as he narrowed his eyes at Henry. Katie expected some retaliation just now, even if only verbally.

"And who is this Farquhar?"

"The captain of the Dalserf army," Katie supplied.

The man addressed her son again, "You'd do well, lad, to ken that Scotland bows to none. She's her own, belongs to no king but a Scot's king."

Unmoved by this, Henry asked, "What's your name?"

"Alec MacBriar."

"How old are you?"

One corner of his mouth lifted. The man answered, "Saw my thirtieth year this past spring."

"Is your mam a good cook?"

"She might be, but I dinna ken she does. Her cook makes all the meals."

"Do you have a hound?"

"Several," the man—Alec—answered. He met Katie's gaze. "And they're a wee bit better at protecting the valuables."

"Are they giants, too?" Henry wondered.

The man shrugged. "Bigger than your hound, aye."

"Do they—"

"That's enough, Henry," Katie interrupted. "The man likely wants to sit quietly and prayerfully over his friend."

ALEC LEFT THE COTTAGE early in the evening, having no sense that the woman was foolish enough to bring harm to Malcolm while he was gone but a few minutes. He crossed the stream behind the house and gave a short whistle, which brought Simon out of hiding.

"Watch the front door, make sure she and her boy dinna run," he said.

"Boy?" Simon had helped carry Malcolm inside initially, had seen only the woman.

"Aye, hiding under the bed," Alec told him, then moved into the woods, relieving himself first and then finding the MacBriars camped in a small clearing some fifty yards inside the tall pines.

His officers gathered to him when they realized his presence, Aymer, William, Nigel, and Elle.

He updated them about Malcolm's condition, heartened that his captain had awakened enough to take sustenance and whatever medicine the healer had forced down his throat.

"Might be a few days though," he said. "I'll stay inside. Keep two posted at all times—put one on the west side as well. Send someone back to Rutherglen in a day or two, buy or steal a cart. He will no' be able to ride when we leave."

They discussed their return route, what roads they might travel and through which counties—and more specifically, which friendly clan lands—to finally get home to Swordmair. Ranald interrupted to offer Alec more bread, which he ate while they talked. When they were done, Alec collected his flask and saddlebags from his horse and returned to the cottage, pausing just a moment to wash up a bit at the creek.

He spied Simon close and inclined his head to send him back into the woods and then returned to the tiny cottage, wondering how she could stand living under that small roof—the thatch in dire need of repair, he noticed—and in only that one room.

They were, mother and son, as he'd left them, huddled together on the bed, this time sitting and facing each other, a task between them, mending he thought.

He wasn't returned more than ten minutes when a voice called out, "Katie Oliver!"

Alec jumped up. He hadn't heard a horse approach. Standing beside the small window, he peered through the linen to see a gangly man walking across the field in front of her house, his hands tucked primly behind his back.

When he turned, he found Katie and her son watching him, their eyes wide.

"Who comes?"

"Gordon Killen."

"What does he want?"

"He's courting Mam," Henry supplied helpfully.

Katie's cheeks pinkened while she returned Alec's hard frown. Something must have shown in his gaze just then that she leapt from the mattress and came very close to him.

"Please don't kill him. He's a very nice man. He hasn't done anything to you."

"Get rid of him," he said, his jaw tight for her assumption that he randomly killed people without provocation. He tipped his head toward the door.

She nodded shakily, her hands wringing, and passed a quick glance over her son before stepping outside, closing the door behind her.

"He's verra old," Alec commented absently, spying through the window, shifting so that the man and Katie were both in sight. They stood facing each other, a good six feet separating them, and many yards from the front door.

"He's the steward up at the castle," Henry said.

The boy had not left the bed, was busy with a thread and needle. Alec scowled at him, for both having no interest in what his mother was about and for his industry—*bluidy Hades*, the lad was sewing.

Alec returned his gaze to the pair outside.

"I wasn't expecting you to call today, Gordon," Katie Oliver said, sounding uneasy.

The old man—honest to God, Alec thought he might be more than sixty years of age—chuckled softly and replied, "Hence my shout. Dinna want to startle you by rapping on the door."

"Is there a need up at the castle?" She wondered.

The man shook his balding head, showing about as much hair as Alec had on one leg. "Nae, ma'am. All are well. I was thinking, that is, I'd been told, well sometimes I hear that..." he brought his hands from around his back, shoved a messy bouquet of wild flowers at Katie Oliver but added no more words to his presentation.

Och, but he was pitiful, Alec thought, snarling. To reach that age and not be able to put sentences together in front of a lass. *God love him.*

"He come around often?" Alec asked of Henry, his gaze constant on the pair, reading well the body language: the steward, not much bigger than the lass herself, shuffled his feet and wouldn't, or couldn't, meet her gaze; the lass only seemed anxious, wringing her hands, and then appeared awkward at the sight of the gift, stepping forward to retrieve the bouquet when the man seemed only rooted to the ground. She took the flowers and backed away, resuming their initial distance.

All very peculiar, Alec thought.

"More than most, 'cept Farquhar," Henry said, still more interested in his work than Alec's questions or his mother's visitor. "Mam dinna like Farquhar, though. We hide under the bed a lot when he comes 'round."

This turned Alec's face from the window. "Why dinna she like him?"

Henry shrugged. "I dinna ken. Told me no' to get friendly with him, said he was only using me."

Returning his regard to the window and beyond, Alec said absently, "Your mam's right. You should be careful who you befriend, lad. Always ken the why of it."

"He was kissing her once, I saw, when I came back from the creek. It was gross. My mam dinna like it either, I ken. She was hitting him. That's when we started hiding under the bed."

Alec's scowl returned. *Farquhar*, he catalogued.

She was vulnerable, Alec realized, and not merely to him and his party crashing in. She was bonny, and likely drew plenty of attention, those willing to overlook the witch part, to have her. Her vulnerability made her a greater target even than her beauty, he supposed. Neither Henry nor the hound were fit to protect her.

Wasn't his problem, yet he felt a little remorse for the fright he'd visited upon her. Obviously, she had her hands full with her suitors, kind and otherwise. Mayhap when he finally returned to Swordmair, he'd send down one of his hounds, for added protection. Those beasts, part wolf, would rip a man's hand off if he dared touch the lass. He'd consider it additional payment for the disruption caused to her just now, for the aide she'd given.

He couldn't hear much of what was said, but at no time did the little bald man lift any worried gaze to the cottage, as if she'd tried to alert him of the soldiers in and around it. He hadn't suspected she would have dared; self-preservation made all her decisions. She wouldn't risk her son's life with any pitiful hope that this slight man might save her.

Alec squinted out, focusing more, wondering what they were saying now that Katie Oliver raised her hand toward the man, still many feet away. Her entire posture, dropped shoulders and tilted head, seen in profile by Alec, hinted at sympathy. She curled the fingers of her raised hand and returned her fist to her skirts.

And then he very clearly heard her say to the bowed-head of the steward, her tone suddenly high-pitched with her disquiet. "I'm sorry, Gordon. I didn't expect...I couldn't. I've...I've had already my life's love. I haven't more to give beyond Henry. It would be unfair to you...." She let that drift away.

The man mumbled something, and Katie said again that she was sorry and a minute later, the steward turned and walked away, trudging listlessly through the tall grass of the meadow.

Very strange and very interesting, Alec concluded, taking the chair again when the lass turned to enter the cottage. Out of the corner of his eye, pretending no great interest in her return, he watched her stride to the small cupboard where a previous bunch of flowers sat wilted and dead inside a short and narrow crock. She only stood there, though, her back to Alec, did not remove the old and replace with the new. Her head was bent, mayhap staring at the man's gift, mayhap rethinking her refusal.

His curiosity was piqued enough he almost suggested that a husband, even an old and fragile one, might provide some security to her. He didn't though, just watched her struggle with it, saw that one hand was white-knuckled around the edge of the cupboard.

And then she turned, her face devoid of any expression and said, her voice only hopefully bright but barely that, "Come along, Henry. We'll wash up at the creek for the night."

Henry lifted his attention from his chore and scrunched up his face. "It's early yet. And we haven't had our walk."

"We won't be allowed to walk tonight, I fear."

"Walk where?" Alec asked.

"Up and back," Henry answered, which was no answer at all.

Alec lifted a brow to Katie Oliver.

She waved a hand with some residual weariness. "Up and back, along the stream. We collect the roots and plants."

Industry and exercise, he guessed, getting her work done and tiring out the lad before bedtime. "Go on, then," he said. He stood and opened the door again, stepping outside. Another sharp whistle showed Robert now, closest to the house. "Sit inside with Malcolm. She needs to gather plants and such. I'll take her up along the stream."

He turned, expecting the woman and her son to have followed. Stepping back upon the threshold showed both of them, sitting at the side of the bed, changing from their shoes to their taller and heavier boots. The lad jumped up first, grinning back at his mother, suggesting it had been some race tying the laces of their boots. He annoyed her then, as lads were wont to do, Alec supposed, stepping on the toes of her boots while she laced them. In retaliation, the woman yanked at one of her son's laces, pulling it loose.

"Argh!" Growled Henry playfully, going onto one knee to fix this.

Katie stood and proclaimed with a glorious smile, "I win!"

"You cheat!" Henry accused, but he was smiling.

Alec caught himself before he might have grinned, stepping back outside, not sure why he should have liked that little scene so much. But he did. Henry was very comfortable with himself for a seven year old, and Alec appreciated this small snippet of interaction between mother and son. And if he were honest with himself, he was very appreciative of how playful she'd just been with the lad—he'd not seen anything thus far in her personality that would have hinted at such ease within her—and then there was her smile, which was fascinating in that it transformed her wholly, erasing every furrow and frown, beautifying her yet more.

Mayhap she'd smiled once at that old steward, mayhap that had been what had entrapped and enchanted him, that he'd come courting—though that seemed to have ended today, Alec reminded himself.

Katie and Henry withdrew from the cottage, a wide and shallow basket now slung over her arm, and without waiting him, walked around the side of the house toward the stream. Alec followed leisurely while Henry bounded ahead. The hound raced past Alec as well.

He kept his distance, telling himself that he had no interest in this pair, in their daily lives, what they might get about, the charm of their routine, how quickly Henry had acclimated to the strange army essentially holding them hostage, and the half-dead man on the table in the middle of his home. Alec certainly had no interest in Katie Oliver of the splendid smile and those moody blue eyes. He took barely any notice that out of doors her hair was indeed much lighter, the very light brown streaked liberally with true blonde, matching her son's wayward locks. She was very thin, likely more a product of her circumstance, constant labor and hunger, than anything else. She was a nervous person, regularly casting glances over her shoulder to gauge his position. He thought this was done not with any hope to catch him unawares and grab her child and flee, but rather with a desire not to be alarmed by his closeness, if he dared to encroach further.

Alec was surprised that they were out for almost an hour. Henry darted all around the creek and all the area on either side of it, and now Alec understood the need to don his sturdier boots. The lad splashed with the hound and lifted rocks in the creek bed to inspect beneath. At one point he picked up a broken limb, bare of leaves, dead for quite some time, and twirled himself until he was dizzy, letting the short and chunky branch fly away from his hands indiscriminately that it sailed close enough to his mother and she was forced to duck to avoid being clubbed by it. As soon as he saw it's trajectory, Henry clapped his hands over his mouth, his head sinking into his shoulders, expecting a calamity. Even Alec winced, seeing where it was headed. When she moved, barely in time, she slapped one hand on her hip and gave her son a meaningful glare.

"Sorry!" called Henry.

Alec recognized the laugh that wanted to burst from the boy and decided he was rarely punished, certainly not severely, that he had no fear of his mother.

They must know some predetermined spot, and only walked that far every evening, as Henry crossed the creek and began walking back without having to be told. And his mother, bent with her knife attacking some plant and root, turned and followed him when she stood again.

He let them catch up to him. Henry bounced to a stop in front of Alec and pointed upward, lifting Alec's gaze into the nearby conifers.

"That's where the goshawk screams from. She must be gone now, or she'd be yapping to everyone that we're here."

"She nests up there?"

Henry nodded. "Four chicks this year, but we found one down here, dead."

"Must've fallen out of the nest," Alec guessed.

Henry shrugged and darted away. Boswell followed, coming from nowhere, disappearing again into the trees on the south side of the creek.

Katie Oliver trailed after them along the stony bank of the creek. Alec fell into step beside her.

"That's quite a lad you've got there," he said to her.

She jerked so abruptly, narrowing her eyes at him, that Alec was instantly put in mind of what Henry had said earlier, sharing some hint that men might try to get close to her by way of her son.

While he'd been sincere, he'd rather not be lumped into any lot that would use a boy to get to his mother. Alec had no designs on Katie Oliver.

He said, "Of course, you're ruining him."

## Chapter Three

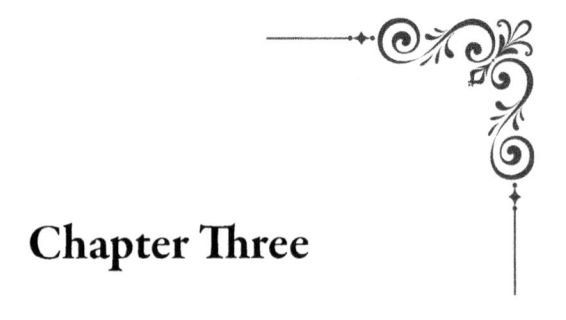

She stopped suddenly and appeared about to question this. She didn't though, only clamped her lips and began moving again, marching stridently now, her arm swinging.

"He's coddled too much, you ken. Nice mam he has, but sewing and mending? You'll no' make a man of him that way." Alec walked behind her, easily keeping pace with her, not sure why he felt the desire to rile her.

She continued to ignore him, marching on.

"Does he spend time with anyone but you? Lad needs to be around other boys at least, men at times as well. Do you ever let him out of your sight?"

"He's seven," she said, her voice as harsh as her walk.

"Hell, at seven I could already peg a squirrel from twenty paces. He ever go hunting? Fishing? Practice swordplay?"

She whirled on him so quickly that he stopped abruptly as angry strides carried her back to him. She stared him down as she approached but gave no words immediately to accompany what he supposed was to be her intimidating glare.

He dared yet more. "I'm right, aren't I? He's never out of your sight."

She barked a surprised laugh. "Do you have children, sir?"

He shook his head, not surprised by this query. Her eyes, in natural light, were absurdly blue.

"Aside from the fact that you were once a boy, have you any experience at all raising a child?"

He shook his head again, enjoying the fire that lit her gaze now.

"Were you born to privilege?" She asked. "I think you must have been, to so readily be able to tell others how to live their lives."

"I'm only thinking that it must be—"

"Are you a single woman, living in a shack in the woods? Was your husband killed before your child was even born? Do you ever wonder where your next meal will come from?" With each question, her thin brows rose further into her forehead and her voice grew angrier. "Do you worry that you won't be able to keep your child from freezing to death on a cold winter night? Have you ever been nearly raped in front of your child?"

Alec's brows drew together at this last query.

"I didn't think so. Do not judge me. Do not presume to lecture me about the correct way to raise my child. You don't know me, and I certainly don't want to know you. Let's not pretend otherwise."

Well and truly chastised—and more, rightly made to feel like a really huge arse—he watched her walk away, still unsure why he had provoked her. He knew nothing about the woman, but he could read people, and her face so readily displayed every single emotion that played across it. Thus, he understood her intent, that such marvelous revelations had not been slung at him to garner sympathy, but to show him that she would survive him, survive what trauma he now brought to her. She'd done it before, she'd just revealed, had slogged through more suffering than he might ever bring to her; she'd do it again.

He dismissed Robert upon their return, saw his man give the two Olivers a quick and apprising glance before ducking out of the cottage.

Malcolm remained as he was, but the woman said they must force him to ingest more of the medicinal broth, and they spent the next several minutes doing this.

Hours later, the house was dark and quiet, the only noise the gentle snoring of both the hound and Malcolm. The woman and her child had both climbed into that narrow cot, fully clothed, and exchanged many minutes of dialogue, whispered and secret, its content hidden from him. They'd been silent now for some time, presumably asleep.

Alec laid his plaid on the floor, against the door, and stretched out, grimacing a bit as he was made to feel evidence of today's battle, his back and shoulder aching. He sighed, hoping Malcolm showed more progress on the morrow, hoping to be on the road soon. He was too long gone from home.

He'd been tempted recently by some idea that they might actually return to more warring, could have stayed embedded with those armies involved in today's fight. But he'd given his notice to the MacKenna when he'd joined up with them last spring that he was bound for home soon. Jamie MacKenna, himself, had said the same, had said no man should be expected to be removed from his own home too long at one time.

"Until we bring these nobles to the same side of the table," MacKenna had said, "the war isn't going anywhere."

And, too, Alec had promised his army they were destined to be home before the summer ended. He would keep to that plan.

When he'd been very still for quite some time, another noise joined that of the rhythmic snoring. His brows lowering, he realized that the healer was crying. Seemed only one louder sob had escaped and gained his notice. Listening intently, he imagined the rest were being forced into her pillow or that rough blanket, the sound barely perceptible, muffled almost successfully.

*I've had already my life's love. I haven't more to give.*

Henry's father, then, must have been one hell of a man.

Alec supposed this might explain her regular pinched-face expressions. Sadness was so often joined with bitterness, in his experience.

---

KATIE MIGHT HAVE SUNG her joy when she was awakened by the injured man, Malcolm, just as the sun began its ascent. She climbed quickly from the bed she shared with Henry at Malcolm's low moan and stood beside the table, laying her palm against his forehead. No fever, or any that concerned her. He moaned a bit and Katie bent over the wounds, evaluating them. They could be wrapped today, she decided, pleased to have left them to the air for so many hours. She was satisfied thus far that no angry redness showed around any of the marks.

The man woke further and just as Katie straightened away from her inspection, his huge paw struck out, circling tightly around her neck. She could do naught but squeak, pulling at his hand, as she was lifted onto her toes. She abandoned her efforts to wrest his strong hands away and reached for him, pulling at his hair with all her might as her feet were lifted completely off the earth.

The rude man, Alec, was awakened and came quickly to her aid, wrenching Malcolm's hand away at the same time he jammed an elbow onto Malcolm's arm.

"*Jesu*! Malcolm, what the—"

Katie was freed, dropped really, that she released the tufts of hair she'd yanked and fell to the ground, clutching her neck.

"Bluidy hell, Malcolm!" The one called Alec cursed, crouching at her side. "Och, lass, are you harmed?"

Katie lifted her hand between them, closing her eyes, willing him away.

He hesitated, but did back away, standing at Malcolm's side. "Bluidy arse, that's the healer!" He growled at his friend.

"That's no healer," Malcolm mumbled, his voice rusty.

"Knock it off. Do you ken the battle yesterday, the fireballs they hurled?"

"Aye."

Katie took a deep breath, shifting to stand. A hand appeared before her, the rude man extending his to help her rise. She ignored this and stood on her own. But she wasn't completely foolish, that she remained at his side, using his broad shoulders as a shield, as she peeked at Malcolm.

"He's definitely feeling better," Alec surmised. "More broth?"

"Aye. And today I'll bind the cuts."

Alec MacBriar punched lightly at Malcolm's shoulder. "And he'll behave himself, showing thanks to the woman who saved him," he ground out a warning to his friend.

"What?" Groused Malcolm, his eyes closed again. "Healers ain't bonny. Thought she was the cause of all the pain. Beautiful creatures usually are." He tried to sit up.

Katie stepped forward, instinctively pressing him back down on the table. "Are you daft?"

Alec added his hand to the effort, pressing down on Malcolm's chest. "Dinna get up yet. No' until she says."

Katie allowed. "You certainly can sit up, but not straight away, using all your abdomen muscles to rise. Let him pull you up, but be warned, it's going to hurt, the hacked rib."

He seemed then disinclined to move, that Katie stepped around the table and prepared another bowl of broth and medicine.

Alec lifted him once more, Malcolm winced now with his consciousness, and Katie persuaded him to drink from the bowl.

He fussed with every swallow, making faces and rolling his tongue out with distaste.

"Stop with that," Katie chastised, much as she might her own son. "I'm not pouring fire down your throat." She felt Alec MacBriar's gaze on her but dared not meet his eyes to know if he disapproved or not of her scolding.

Henry came to the table then, roused by their talk, sleepy and curious. Katie was sorry that she missed their morning chat, as it was nearly as lovely as their nighttime ones. Normally, they would remain abed, upon first waking—Henry was at his loveliest then, groggy and sweet, and so very innocent—and their talks then were some of her favorite, hushed and still as the sun rose, his thoughts and questions so endearing and sweet. That's when they spoke of his father, and her own life as a child, and often events that had happened the day before, for the questions that had come through the night.

An hour later, Katie and Henry had seen to their morning ablutions, and had broken their fast with more of the thin stew.

She did begrudgingly offer some to the two men, but this was politely declined by Alec.

"Today is wash day," she told him, indicating the tall standing basket of soiled clothing between the bed and her work counter. "And I'll need to get about to check my traps." Hopefully, any of the dozen or so contraptions she'd set around the nearby woods would have yielded more than the lone hare she'd snagged yesterday.

"You launder out in the creek?"

Katie nodded.

"Go on then," he allowed. "I'll have my men scout the traps."

When he wasn't scowling at her, or instigating trouble with her, she thought him quite handsome. She didn't dwell on it though, had some impression that he thought himself handsome as well. His hair was very dark, almost black, and chopped unevenly, as if he'd cut it himself or had allowed someone else without know-how to do so. At the creek yesterday, when he'd harassed her so effortlessly, she'd noticed that it was thick, and she thought it might want to curl if it were longer. She'd been wrong about his eyes though, or the dimness of the cottage had lied to her. They were not black at all, but a very dark hazel, with golden flecks near their centers.

She wondered if he ever smiled, speculated if such a thing, coupled with that square jaw and indeed the very aura of power and vitality that oozed like honey from a hive, brought many females boldly to his side. Mayhap the braver ones would stay there, undeterred by the simmering fury, kept in check often, but always so near, just under the surface. Realizing she was glowering at him for all this conjecture, she shook herself and collected the basket and the precious ash lye soap—payment from the fletcher's wife for delivering her of a healthy bairn, but sadly, near its end after several months of use—and tipped her head toward Henry, so that he came along with her.

The big man smacked at Malcom's shoulder. "Behave yourself for a bit, will you?" And he followed them out of the cottage.

Katie set up her chore at the creek's edge, as she did every week. If they owned more pieces of clothing than their pitiful collection, she might only be required to do this every other week. As it was, they regularly stretched the wearing of each garment to two days, or three when necessary or allowed by some rare cleanliness.

If she lived nearer the village, she might enjoy the company of other women, about the same chore, mayhap also once a week. But she did not, and they weren't a kindly group, those women. She knew they considered her a witch. Yet, they never hesitated to call upon her for her skill and weren't they astonished when she'd managed to save the life of the young lad, Ewan, when he'd taken with the sweating sickness in her first year here? Sadly, that had not helped them see her any differently, had not pierced the general perception that any person who practiced healing must also practice some magic as well. As if she'd the time for such nonsense. As if she'd not miraculously put herself in some greater and safer circumstance if she had such capabilities.

She used the washing paddle on her gowns and kirtles and Henry's small tunics, letting the badly soiled aprons and breeches soak while she worked from cleanest to dirtiest.

The man, Alec, was speaking with Henry. They stood many feet away, and Katie could not hear what was being said. She imagined her son was once again quizzing the man about this, that, and the other thing, as was his way, his mind ever whirring with curiosity.

A soldier stepped through the trees after a while and spoke with Alec. Henry stood between them, his head tipped back and moving left and right, unabashedly listening before he steadied his gaze on the newcomer with fantastic awe.

Katie pursed her lips and lowered her head to the laundry task. Likely, she'd have no help from her son while these men remained near.

When a shadow fell over her hands and her work, she lifted her face to find the newcomer standing very close, having crossed the three-feet wide creek. His face was shadowed and outlined by the sun being directly behind his head.

"The MacBriar says you're no' to cook today," the soldier said. "We've plenty to share."

*Good heavens.* "You're a woman."

The lady warrior snorted, leveling a distasteful look upon Katie.

And owning as much amiability as that other one, Alec MacBriar, Katie decided, her shoulders slumping for this fresh hostility. Mayhap it was warranted, as her comment had likely come off as ignorant.

"Sorry," Katie mumbled. "I was...just shocked, that's all." She had to imagine the woman was accustomed to such reactions.

Her voice as snarly as it had first been, the woman asked with some hesitation, "The captain—Malcolm—he's going to be well, aye?"

She'd known her literally but seconds but assumed concern was not a regularly used tool in her repertoire. Mayhap, it was Katie's slight hesitation in answering that persuaded the woman to say, quite gruffly, "He's holding us back. We need to get on the road."

That made more sense.

"Aye. If there's no fever today or tomorrow, I'm convinced he'll recover well."

Katie stood, finished with two more pieces, walking over to set them with the others in the grass, away from the mud and muck of the water's edge. Returning to the creek, she saw Henry perched on his haunches across from her, his gaze rapt upon the woman, his mouth still slack.

Alec was gone now. The woman crossed the creek again and seemed to have no other purpose but to watch Katie and Henry, slapping her hand on her hip and tilting her head, giving some indication she did not cherish the duty.

Katie planned on ignoring her then, the laundry in need of her attention, but this was not so simple. And when the woman turned her head, staring off upstream, Katie looked her over. She was remarkable, the sheer size of her as daunting as it was shocking. Equally astounding was the harshness about her. Plenty of miserable females Katie had known in her life, but none with this...manly severity—it must be manufactured, Katie decided, must be necessary, living in a man's world as she so obviously did. Yet, she set herself apart, purposefully it must be assumed, as her costume was more striking than that of any man.

Across her shoulders, under the straps of her leather breastplate, she wore a caplet of fur, which seemed only a nod to singularity or design as the piece could not be expected to provide any warmth, covering only the top of her shoulders. Otherwise her arms were bare, colored by the sun and honed into solid, muscled limbs. At her waist, she wore a leather belt, which supported her scabbard and several other hanging pouches, the narrow aged hide decorated with grommets of silver metal, the likes of which Katie had never seen. Incredibly, she wore breeches, which showed that her legs were long and well-proportioned to her great size, which meant they were not small. Her boots also were adorned, the tall brown leather festooned with tassels of black and blue threads, six or so on each shoe, scattered in random fashion about the laces. She was possessed of what Katie could only assume might have been a striking mane of dark brown, but Katie couldn't exactly be sure. She only supposed at one time the woman had twisted the extreme length of it into many braids, not only one or two, but that she had not unraveled them in quite a long time; mayhap, she only bathed them as a whole, that they were just now solid and chunky streamers, matted and stiff.

But all the accoutrements of her garb might as well have been invisible, as it remained that the most striking thing about her was her eyes. Even as she did not directly regard Katie now, she could see that they were large and round and showing so much white and were the palest and prettiest blue Katie had ever seen, a perfect summer sky, made lighter and brighter by the contrast of her deeply tanned skin. The lids of her eyes were oversized, which only served to make the entire eye so much larger in her face, not at all unattractive, save that they were set under brows that were almost too thick and, Katie had to believe, permanently crinkled.

"Ye done with your gawking?" The woman asked of Katie. She'd not turned her face to catch her staring, but somehow was still aware of Katie's overlong regard.

"Most likely not," Katie answered, which was truth—and, she somehow knew, not at all detested, despite the woman's sour tone. Why else would she have decorated herself so garishly but to draw attention? "Are there other women?" She wondered.

The woman ignored her now, but Katie noticed Henry coming to his feet, idling over toward her. *I'd like to see her ignore Henry.* He didn't ever make it easy. Katie almost grinned when Henry worked up the nerve to speak to the behemoth.

"Were you always a woman?"

Katie's eyes widened, but she was quick to duck her head, hopefully secreting the bit of laughter that burst forth with her son's unexpected query.

"What kind of question is that?"

Henry shrugged, likely not comprehending her exact question, that he pressed on. "Do you kill many people? You look like you do."

*Good grief.* Henry would get *them* killed if he kept that up.

Surprisingly, the woman replied to this innocent query. "What's a person look like when they've killed others?"

"Mean. Angry."

"That what I look like, lad?"

Henry nodded, Katie noticed. Her head was lowered, but her watchful regard was lifted to the woman and her son.

"Aye. Do you have any sons?"

The woman snorted. "Nae. I dinna like bairns."

"Can I hold your sword?"

"You'd no' be able to lift it."

"Can I touch it?"

The woman shook her head. "Get on with ye. I'm busy."

"Doing what?" Henry asked with that scrunched up face of his.

"Making sure your mam dinna run off."

Henry turned and regarded his mother. "Run off where?"

"Screaming for help."

Completely misunderstanding her statement, Henry said, "For the washing?"

The woman warrior leveled Henry with an impatient, be-off-with-you glare that was not well read by the boy.

Katie was vastly amused.

And then the man, Alec, returned, and dismissed the woman with a bare inclination of his head. But Henry was apparently not done with her and made to follow her into the woods.

Katie jumped up quickly, calling out, "Henry. Stay here."

"He's fine," the MacBriar said, stopping directly across the creek from her while Henry ignored her.

"I don't want him traipsing about with..." she stopped and bit her lip.

Alec MacBriar raised a brow.

"With Eleanor?" He frowned. "She'll no' harm him. He can meet the whole unit then. Give you a break."

Katie harrumphed and slapped her hands onto her hips. "I don't want or need a break from my son." Recalling his accusations of last evening, she added with some snap to her voice. "I need him to help with the wringing." He stared at her, his expression inscrutable, that Katie found herself explaining, "We have a system, and it works better with the two of us."

He sent a frowning glance to the pile of cleaned but sopping wet clothing. "A system for wringing?"

Obviously, the man had never been accountable for his own laundry, or if he was, suffered no aggravation that his hands were too small to effectively twist and squeeze all the water away.

"Never mind," she said. Ignoring him, she began the chore herself.

The laird was still curious. "Two people can only make it better by cutting the time in half. But I canna imagine that your lad can be so helpful with this particular chore."

With her back to him now, she twisted her hose, and water dripped and fell onto the ground. "As I said, we have a system."

"Show me."

Katie turned, her brow furrowing.

"C'mon, then. I'll do Henry's part."

She hesitated.

He argued, as terse and gruff as she'd known as of yet, "I dinna imagine you want to spend too many hours on your laundering."

It *would* make for better and quicker drying. And since he'd yet to give her the promised coin.... "Very well." She laid aside her hose and scooped up her best gown, which was only notable in that it was the least frayed and worn. But she was wary yet and stepped hesitantly toward him, squinting at the sun behind his head. He seemed only curious about her methods, taking the bottom end she handed to him. She walked backwards until the piece was stretched between them, Katie holding the neckline and shoulders of the heavy linen.

"You twist," she instructed, "and keep twisting until all the excess water is removed."

He nodded. "Aye, that's a good system indeed for the bigger pieces."

He did as directed, taking so much less time than Henry normally did to turn the whole thing until the curls reached Katie's end. Katie turned her end in the opposite direction and the water was quickly expelled. She couldn't then argue with his assistance and had every intention of making good use of his strong hands, quickly shoving another gown at him when the first was done and laid out behind the house.

In the midst of wringing out the second one, she said, "I'm thinking I should wash all the bed linens today and take better advantage of your help."

"No' too late," he said, by way of an offer of further aid. "I've naught to do but wait for Malcolm to get better."

Somehow this struck her as odd, this huge and fierce warrior, with the massive sword at his hip, proposing to help with her laundry. The offer was incompatible with so much of his previous snarly behavior, and certainly it disagreed with how he'd chastised her about the manner in which she was raising her son.

This time, Alec walked over and laid out the gown to dry and Katie grabbed next one of her aprons. Boswell came loping through the woods, rather sedately until he saw the tug-of-war between Alec and Katie when they'd begun wringing the apron. He darted across the creek with some excitement and joined in, ignoring Katie's cry of "Don't you dare!"

The hound clamped his teeth just in the middle and yanked so hard that she lost her grip.

"Get away, you mangy brute!" She lunged for the apron but missed as he danced out of her reach, being invested in a serious fight for the apron with Alec. He moved in a circle as he tugged, turning the big man around as well, not in the least intimidated by Alec's deeper voice.

"Release!" This was followed by more commands, though he found it less humorous than Katie did.

Katie huffed with exasperation, chasing round in circles the playful Boswell, acting nearly half his age. "You are the worst hound ever," she said, allowing a rare laugh, imagining they looked like fools, Alec MacBriar spinning and yanking and Katie circling him, trying to catch the hound.

Alec stopped so suddenly, giving a powerful and swift tug that the apron was finally freed but at the same time, his elbow connected with the side of Katie's head, sending her reeling. She landed with a thud on her backside, and Boswell jumped, just as startled as Katie.

"Aw, shite!"

He was at her side immediately, on his haunches, his countenance severe with his concern. He touched her arm. "Lass, are you—sweet St. Andrew, I'm sorry."

Nodding, she held the side of her head. The instant dizziness had been brief and everything was promptly returned to clear focus. She decided fairly quickly then that much could be ascertained about a person in circumstances such as these. He felt awful, she could well see on his face, a grimace remaining, his brow crooked while he checked her out, even put his hand on her face, turning the walloped side of her head toward him while his other hand held her steady at her arm.

It was so...gentle, something she would do without hesitation to Henry but that she wouldn't have thought this man capable of, that Katie was made to feel extremely awkward with this close contact, his huge hands so tender on her. And since awkwardness and Katie never did sit well together, she said lightly, "If you did not after all want to help, a simple leave-taking would have sufficed."

He went completely still, his gaze found hers. She decided he was only judging her tone, the attitude behind the words.

Katie shrugged with a nervous grin, which wrought some relief on his face. But this was still tremendously uncomfortable that Katie lifted her hands between them, latching softly onto his forearms, pushing him away.

# Chapter Four

When all the laundry had been laid out to dry about the shrubs and bushes directly behind the house, Katie walked around to the front of the cottage, the empty basket propped against her hip, clamping her jaw to keep from calling out to her son to follow. She didn't want him spending time with any of them, certainly not some horrible warrior woman who might only ever show him how to be unpleasant and condescending. But he'd been mightily intrigued by the woman, that Katie wasn't entirely sure he would heed her call, if he were still close enough to hear her.

A deafening noise of charging destriers reached her then. Confused she glanced behind her, toward the creek, knowing this camped army were within the woods. But charging?

*Sweet Mother of God!* Lifting the hem of her skirt, she dashed around to the front of the cottage just as Farquhar, captain of the Dalserf, rode up to her front door—the front door that had been left wide open. Her mind spun quickly, anxiously, and she purposefully slowed her steps, raising her hand in a bare wave as she assumed a position in front of the door.

Farquhar was the bane of her existence, the sole reason she so often wondered how she might ever escape Dalserf and live without fear, also one of the reasons she'd even considered Gordon Killen's suit. He'd brought a dozen men with him, seemed to rarely travel without a retinue. Katie gulped, not wishing a war right here at her doorstep, if the soldiers all around were discovered.

He wasted no words, obviously having spied the huge form lying atop her table. He dismounted quickly and strode past her without a word.

Katie followed him inside.

"What is this? Who is this?" He spun on Katie.

She pressed her hand to her heart, taken aback by his harshness, unusual for him, in that he preferred oilier methods.

"Sir, what is amiss?" She asked, stalling with this ridiculous question, pretending a fright for his manner.

He frowned darkly at her. "This is amiss!" He shouted, throwing a hand out to indicate Malcolm's inert form.

"'Tis but my brother," she said, as innocently as she could manage, tilting her head with some befuddlement.

His black eyes narrowed. "You said your brother was dead. Felled at Glen Trool."

"As I'd been told. You were the one who delivered the report, sir," she reminded him. "Alas, it wasn't true. And praise the Lord." She set down the basket and stood at Malcolm's side, brushing the orange hair away from his forehead, a great loving gesture. "I cannot even imagine how he'd found his way here. Day by day, mile by mile, is all I can guess. But thankfully, he found me and now you, sir, can finally meet him, as you have ever been plagued by my constant gushing about him."

The actual truth of the matter was this: Katie had no family, none that lived yet, and had never had a brother. When her husband had died almost eight years ago, they had only just established themselves at Dalserf. Farquhar had only come on the scene in the past year or so and when he first began pushing his intentions upon her, she'd invented a brother, one she'd been happy to report might arrive any day, one she called William. She talked about him endlessly to Farquhar, imagined tales of his bravery, and his travels, hoping that the very idea that her sibling might one day arrive at Dalserf would hold Farquhar at bay, keep him from pursuing her. So imagine her surprise when Farquhar rode up upon her one day and informed her the castle had received a roll call, listing the names of all those dead in the last month. He'd previously asked her from whence she hailed, who her father might be, and thus was able to give her fictional brother a surname, saying to her that William Merton was listed as killed in action with the Scottish rebels. At the time, she'd imagined it dumb luck, that a man of the same name had existed. She'd soon begun to believe that Farquhar had lied to her, same as she had to him, either to test her lies or to have her understand there was none to protect her.

"When did he arrive?"

"Only yesterday." As much of the truth as possible when inventing tales was a good practice.

"Arrived on foot? No mount? No weapon?"

Katie nodded and gave her attention to Malcolm, feigning more sisterly affection. She was more likely to have convinced Farquhar that the warrior woman was her sister than to expect him to believe Malcolm could possibly be her brother. He was huge and she was not. He wore a shock of orange hair and she possessed not one freckle. His face was wide and bitten by the pocked scars of youthful skin disease while her cheeks were unblemished. Likely he was a good ten years her senior, as Katie had just passed her twenty-sixth year.

"Dear William," she cooed. Thankfully, Malcolm remained near comatose once again that he could not rise and refute any of her lies.

Farquhar, likewise sensing the man yet posed no threat, sidled near Katie. She stiffened, being drawn away from Malcolm by the heavy hand on her arm.

His voice lowered, was meant to be seductive she thought, but it only made her want to gag. "I'd told ye, when last we met," he said against her hair, "that you would be mine. My patience wears thin."

She remembered well his last threats and his assault, had thought that only the army taking leave of the castle for so many weeks had kept him away.

"And I've told you," she said, yanking to have her arm released, to no avail, "that I have no aim to become some man's plaything." She turned her face and met his gaze, let all her bitterness show. "And I won't be forced."

"No child or hound to save ye this time, Katie Oliver," he taunted.

"Would you commit rape, then, while my brother lies just here?"

He seethed at her, "I dinna want to force you..."

Oh, but he did. That was much of the appeal, she believed.

Malcolm moaned beside them.

Panicked, Katie wrenched her arm free and attended him, grateful for his timely waking, but fretful that he might inadvertently give up her lies. Malcolm did not open his eyes, but groaned more, that Katie said to Farquhar, "I must see to him," hoping this might see his departure.

It did. Farquhar sent a scathing glance over Malcolm and one shorter, angry gaze to Katie, which she ignored, and pretended she was about some industry, fussing with the nearby linen strips and her small knife, hacking them into even smaller strips over the chest of her supposed brother.

When he left and was gone from the view of the open door, Katie pushed out her held breath and whimpered a cry. She dropped her head and closed her eyes, hating her weakness, her very helplessness. When she opened her eyes and drew a deep breath, she found that Malcolm was staring at her, his eyes clear and wakeful.

She returned his regard, not sure what to make of his stoniness just now. Her lips trembled, as fear had not abandoned her quickly, but she could do nothing about it.

"He's gone now, lass," Malcom said quietly, attempting to calm her.

She nodded and turned away, took the hacked up linen and her knife. She retreated to her work counter and stared out the window. She'd been a fool to refuse Gordon Killen, thinking she didn't want to be bound for the rest of her life to Dalserf, knowing she could never be happy here. It wasn't about happiness. It was about survival. She needed to find Gordon, needed to tell him she would wed him after all, if he would still have her. True, he was neither young nor strong enough to protect her, but he was the steward of a great castle, likely had the gratitude of the laird. No one would dare harm the steward's wife, or her son.

Would they?

"Brother, eh?"

Closing her eyes, she dropped her head to her chest. When she opened her eyes and turned, she found Malcolm sitting up, his feet upon the floor, seeming none the worse for wear for this action. She set her hands on the edge of the counter behind her and met his measuring gaze.

"It's a long story," she said weakly.

"Aye, I got the spirit of it."

Katie said nothing.

Malcolm wondered, "And what happens when your *brother* leaves, lass? And he's still here?"

Farquhar and the contingent of Dalserf soldiers had barely gained the trees at the far side of the meadow before Alec and that woman, Eleanor, came rushing into the cottage.

"Who was that?" Alec wanted to know, his tone severe. "What the hell happened?" His stormy gaze swung back and forth between Katie and Malcolm.

"Farquhar," Katie answered reflexively, "the captain of the Dalserf guard."

"Sealed her fate, is what just happened," Malcolm said evenly, holding Katie's gaze.

Pointedly, Katie said to Malcolm, "My fate is my own." Feeling all the harsh regard aimed her way, she pushed away from the counter and left the cottage.

---

ALEC WAS CONFUSED, by the look exchanged between Malcolm and Katie Oliver, by Malcolm's strange statement, and now by Katie Oliver's abrupt departure.

"I dinna ken that lass, save for what she's done for me," Malcolm said. "Likely, that was done at your bidding, promising brutality to her if she refused."

Alec gave a spare nod, allowing this was true.

"But she canna stay here. Whoever he is, he's coming back for her. I get the sense she's the prize and he dinna take losing too kindly."

"That's no' our concern," Eleanor said, with her habitual surliness. To Alec, she said, "He's well now. Let's go, let's get out of here. We'll get the cart tonight."

"Quit with your posturing, Elle!" Malcolm barked. "She done us a favor, willing or no'. We canna leave her." To Alec again, "She's got no man?"

Alec shook his head. "Plenty beating a path to her door, it seems." He almost grinned. "One a day, by my reckoning." But Elle was right. Malcolm was ready, and Katie Oliver wasn't his problem.

"Swordmair could use her," Malcolm persisted.

Elle threw up her hands. "Swordmair has a healer, more advanced than her!"

Malcolm harrumphed. "Morven's got a foot in the grave, getting dotty now."

Alec could not argue this.

"She could have given me up, which might've seen me impaled to the table permanently, but she dinna," Malcolm argued.

"For her own good," Elle scoffed.

Malcolm sneered at Eleanor but addressed his next words to Alec. "You owe me still."

Alec sent a dark look to Malcolm. "You calling that in for *her*?"

"What else am I gonna use it on?"

"You're a bloody fool," Elle seethed at Malcolm. "You canna pass off a life-debt to someone else."

As if there were actual rules.

Malcolm ignored her now and addressed Alec. "I saved your arse at Methven. You'd be strung up next to Niall Bruce, with your innards on the ground beneath ye, and you bluidy ken it! Aye, I'm claiming the debt now."

Alec shrugged. "You can claim all you want. Lass'll never go with us."

Bushy orange brows rose into his thick forehead. "Guess you'll have to talk her into it."

Alec considered his longtime friend. Malcolm was many things—loyal beyond description, ferocious in battle, a surprisingly smooth diplomat on occasion, and the funniest drunk you'd ever meet—but he was, with annoying regularity, entirely too soft when it came to those less fortunate.

"We canna fix everyone," Alec reminded him, not for the first time.

Malcolm stared at Alec. "You owe me, mate." And then he showed a smug, gap-toothed grin. "Off she goes," he said, pointing through the open door. "Better catch her."

Alec whirled, and saw the healer stomping across the meadow, her son in tow, walking so fast the lad had to skip to keep up with her.

"Bluidy hell!" Alec cursed and left the cottage, jogging after her, Malcom's hearty laughter chasing him away. He called out to her but of course she didn't stop. Henry turned at the sound of Alec's voice, his face not showing fear for whatever upset his mother knew, but some confusion for their mad dash across the field. "Whoa! Whoa!" Alec said, grabbing at her free arm.

She jerked so suddenly, so violently, she won the freedom of her arm. "What?" She hollered at him. "What do you want?"

Trying to keep himself calm, he asked levelly, "Where you off to?"

"Up to the castle," she said, her tone still angry. "I have business with the steward that is not any of yours. I didn't give up your presence here, when I very well might have, so you can have no fear that I aim to do so now."

"Business with the steward?" He asked, lifting a brow. "That wasn't addressed yesterday when he called?"

She was surprised that he knew that Gordon Killen was the castle steward. Certainly that's what her frown suggested. She shook this off. "*My* business and not yours," she reiterated. "Your man is well, sitting up even. Be gone, already." She turned again, began marching away. Henry sent Alec another confused look.

"He won't be able to protect you," Alec called out to her. It was clear now, the whole of it. She continued walking. "Old man like that is no match for the likes of Farquhar."

Likely she wouldn't have stopped, might have kept right on marching to Dalserf. But Henry cried out, having lost his shoe with all the scurrying to keep up with his mother. Katie let go of his hand and turned around while he dashed back for it. To her chagrin and Alec's amusement, Henry did not merely fetch the shoe and rejoin his mother. He sat on the ground, only his head and shoulders visible in the tall grass, and took his time tying the laces.

Alec walked forward. And while he wondered what his next words might be—more assurance that wedding the steward would not gain her the security she imagined, or forging ahead with an invitation to Swordmair—she said first, "Why do you care?"

He didn't. Or he didn't think he did.

But she was rather pathetic, her stance and her constant anger, and not least of all her circumstance, that her options presently made even Alec's stomach turn.

"You saved Malcolm, and for that I owe you."

"You said there'd be coin. I cannot buy necessities with your dubious concern."

He grimaced at this, for how tart she was, for what truth he must give her now. "Aye, about that. See, lass, we've been on the road now more than a year. Might be, the coin is gone."

She smirked at him, her derision evident. "Let's go, Henry."

While Henry still sat, Alec said, "I've no plans to shirk the debt, lass. But mayhap you come up to Swordmair with us—we need a healer. More friendly there, safer. We dinna take to those who mistreat women."

She stared at him as if he'd sprouted a second head. "Why would I do that?"

"Get away from here, is all I can think of," Alec answered, his hands on his hips, shifting his weight onto his left hip.

"But I don't...I don't even like any of you."

He wasn't quite sure why her brutal honesty put a crease into his forehead. He countered with, "And how do you feel about Farquhar?"

"Henry," she urged through gritted teeth, her gaze locked with Alec's.

"Aye," Alec said, "but you ken it's no' about liking. It's about living." He glanced back at the tiny cottage, at the vast meadow and the forest and the mountains behind her home. "You're naught but a target here, lass." He had some sense that at this point Henry was only sitting in the tall grass, his shoe well-secured, watching them. Honestly, Alec didn't understand her reluctance. He'd said she'd be safe, he hadn't harmed a hair on her head. "I'm offering you something better. What keeps you here? Would you refuse the offer for your pride? You'd sacrifice your son's safety and a chance at something better—for your own pride? Are you that selfish?"

Her blue eyes widened, but only briefly before she narrowed them contemptuously at him. "Be out of my house by the time I return," she said, her tone clipped, "or I swear to God, I will alert the Dalserf army of your presence."

Alec ignored the baseless threat, having some idea just now that she would never see the Dalserf castle again. But he prodded her still, his own anger a bit muddled, "Lass, I'm offering you something better. You got other options here? Should we expect more grunts come sniffing after you tomorrow?"

And that was the last straw apparently. He thought she might have cursed under her breath, was quite sure that's what he heard just before she moved and yanked Henry to his feet.

Alec might have reached the boy sooner, quicker, but it truly wasn't his intent to terrorize her. He let her collect her son and begin marching again toward Dalserf.

Damn. He wasn't sure why he did suddenly care, why he felt confident that she and the lad at Swordmair would be for the best. And he still owed Malcolm.

He called out after a moment, "His wound is bleeding again. Mayhap look at that first, afore you run off to your next husband."

She stopped, the healer in her unable to ignore a man's need as easily as she could ignore Alec. She didn't turn immediately. She lifted her face and squared her shoulders first, and then she swiveled and faced him, turning Henry around as well.

"Might you have led with that? The injured man's pressing need?"

"Aye, I might have."

*Jesu*, but the lass was sharp. Like fine steel, shiny and beautiful but so willing to cut.

She retraced her steps, her gait no less angry, and returned to the cottage.

Alec allowed a rare grin, well pleased. He was going to enjoy having her around, he decided.

---

KATIE STOMPED INSIDE the little cottage just as that woman, Eleanor, departed, giving her a curl of her lip but nothing more. She left Henry outside with that damnable Alec MacBriar. She could do nothing just now about his infatuation with these giants, had too much to think about.

The gall of the man!

Upon the table still, Malcolm was yet bare chested, the binding showing no signs of bleeding through.

Katie sighed.

"He said there was bleeding," she accused belligerently, as if the patient were in on the scam.

Malcolm shook his head slowly, watching her.

She acknowledged that she'd been tricked into abandoning her trek to Dalserf for the moment. Ignoring Malcolm then, she began to pace the short length of the single room, her mind whirring, wondering what she might—or should—do. Pivoting at her counter, she slapped her hands onto her hips and strode across the floor again and again. It was unlikely she would be able to outwit them or outrun them to get away, running toward Dalserf and Gordon Killen, as had been her intent. She wished she were brave enough to have slapped him—Alec MacBriar—for his high-handedness, for his absolute and infuriating certainty that she might do as he bid.

As if he knew best what—

"Which part is causing you the most grief right now?"

Katie startled at Malcolm's voice. She'd reached her work counter once again, had just turned when he spoke. He'd been prone, but rose now, sitting up slowly and not without a harsh grimace. Instinctively, Katie rushed to his side to assist him in his effort to sit upright on the table.

"You're going to tear all my careful stitches if you persist with the up and down," she scolded.

"And you're going to wear tracks in the earth beneath you if you persist with the back and forth," he said when he was settled firmly.

Katie gave a prim little snort. "Your man—Alec—is infuriating."

"But tell me true," he said, his color pleasing for its healthiness, "if it's his overbearing manner that offends you, aye but that's a small price to be paid for security."

Katie narrowed her eyes upon the man. He must have known of the MacBriar's intent, this incredulous idea that she should go with them when they left. "First," she said, punching her fists once more onto her hips, "his manner is atrocious, nearly unbearable. Second, he has no right to command or demand anything of me, certainly not when he—and you as well—are indebted to me. Next, I've lived here at Dalserf for years and have managed just fine on my own. And," she added smartly, "this is the only home Henry has ever known. Who is he to say I must take my son away from that?"

"You want that I address them individually?" Malcolm asked, the hint of a grin showing. "Or, can I enfold everything into one answer? Lass, it's no' safe here. You'll come to no harm by any at Swordmair, no' ever. We dinna bear mistreatment of any. No fear, no' for you or your boy."

Holding his clear gaze, Katie tried to read him. She imagined he seemed genuine, concerned even, but she knew him not at all.

"I can't just pack up all my life and...go," she argued.

"Aye, you can."

"Why should I trust you? Or him? Any of you?"

"Guess you've no cause to," He answered with a shrug. "But we've done you no harm and you ken we could. Easily." He waited while she digested this and added slowly. "Leap of faith, I ken they call it. Landing somewhere better."

Her lips trembled as she admitted, "I couldn't. It would be too...risky."

Malcolm nodded. "I'd think you a fool if you thought otherwise." Leveling her with a piercing gaze, he said, "I ken the tending this"—he waved a big paw across his bandaged midsection—"was done at Alec's behest. I ken you had no choice. But that man come here today, and you could have screamed for help of him, but you dinna. I am indebted to you, healer. I put out the invitation. Aye, so I can vow to you that no harm will come to you or your lad, no' ever by a MacBriar hand." His bushy orange brows lifted. "And I can promise you a better life than what you've got here."

Katie chewed her lip a moment. "Thus it would be you I would hold accountable for any mistreatment or harm—" No! She stopped herself from even considering it.

"How long do you think you can hold him off, that one from the castle?" Malcolm asked.

Katie winced and groaned, knowing well the answer.

"It's no' weakness to run from this," Malcolm insisted sagely. "It's just good sense to move toward something better."

"Something better is merely your assumption, but you—"

"It's no' a theory, lass. That's a promise." While she considered this, considered him and the weight of his assurance, he added, "Life will always be hard, you ken. But safety brings a lot of peace, aye?"

"I will poison you if you prove false," she vowed, hardly able to believe she was actually considering this. She felt only, as always, a certain helplessness. She was naught but a dried leaf upon the ground, taken by the wind, moved here and there at its discretion and not her own. The only truth she knew just now was that if nothing changed, it was only a matter of time before Farquhar had his way. But to live without fear....

"I ken you will," he said, a grin coming. "Be disappointed if you dinna. But there'll be no need."

"If you prove false, if it's naught but a trap, what...?" She couldn't even imagine all the questions that needed to be asked and answered.

"Lass, if we meant you harm, we wouldn't be asking, we'd just be taking."

She supposed that was true. "Honestly, it would be safer?"

Malcolm leaned downward, giving a deep-throated groan and surprising Katie by withdrawing a large dagger from his tall boot. He straightened and flipped it over in his hand, presenting the hilt to Katie.

"Take this. I give you leave to use it on me, on Alec, on any one of us, at any time, if I prove false."

Hesitantly, she extended her hand at the same time Malcolm did, until the hilt was pressed into her palm. It was heavy, as long as her entire forearm mayhap, and likely would be naught but a futile nuisance to any MacBriar, but she was not immune to the gesture, understanding it carried some weight. She didn't know very much about a soldier's life, but she understood they didn't give up their weapons easily.

A nervous laugh spilled out. "How would I even carry this thing?"

"Aye, I'll get you a sheath and a belt. You wear it around your waist."

She met his kind gaze. "You want to turn me into that woman, Eleanor?" She teased, though was still decidedly nervous.

Malcolm's face screwed up. "She's got her charm, that one," he said, a grin hovering still. "Yet, you dinna want to aspire to that, lass. But you keep yourself safe, aye?"

After another long pause, she said with a heavy sigh. "I'm Katie, by the way." She watched him closely still, waiting for some shrewd bit of malevolence to color his face now that she'd essentially agreed to go to some place called Swordmair.

"Malcolm, as you ken." He pointed a finger at her. "I'm indebted still. Taking you to Swordmair dinna erase the debt, I ken."

"How angry is he going to be for how long it will take me to pack up my entire household?"

Malcom snorted. "No patience, that one. But then you travel with an army, those lads come in handy, lifting and lugging and all that."

Katie smiled, but felt no peace for her decision, was already thinking she wouldn't—couldn't—leave Dalserf. Oh, God, what to do!

Vaguely, her brain still churning, her belly equally unsettled, she said, "I'd need my entire home packed, all my roots and plants and seeds and—"

A voice from the doorway turned Katie around with a start.

"That's no' going to happen," said Alec MacBriar, standing at the threshold with Henry, his hand comfortably set on her son's shoulder.

Straightening her spine, she declared, "A healer is useless without her medicine. Would be silly to drive us halfway across the country, if I can serve no purpose once arrived." She realized that with those words, likely spouted merely to thwart him, she had made her decision.

God help her.

Alec snorted derisively. "Lass, I can simply scoop you up and toss you over the back of a horse."

"Please do. And then pray you never are injured or become ill. I vow the remedy will be worse than the need for it." She continued then, as if she had not just threatened his life so casually. "If you want to have an effective healer, then every seed and plant and leaf is necessary."

He curled his lip at her, while she lifted a brow, challenging him. "And Boswell comes with us."

Holding her gaze, Alec ground out, "Start packing."

## Chapter Five

"Won't see Swordmair until tomorrow," Eleanor said gruffly.

No, they would not. Alec shook his head, not wanting to have this conversation yet again with her. She'd already made her displeasure known many times over the last several hours. Eleanor had groused about the number of things the healer expected to take with her, had been decidedly vocal in her dissention with the choice to pilfer yet another cart to accommodate the household and inhabitants, and had grumbled and murmured almost non-stop in the last hour since they'd actually gotten on the road.

"Elle, give it a rest, aye?" He begged wearily. *Jesu*, but when she got her dander up, it was a long time coming down. Alec couldn't imagine why she cared, what all her fuss was about. To his mind, they were on the road sooner than expected. Initially, he's supposed they might have been holed up for many more days waiting on Malcom's recovery. Having given it some thought over the last many miles, he could make no sense of Eleanor's blatant dislike of the healer and these plans to bring her to Swordmair.

Eleanor pinched her lips and moved a bit ahead of Alec, to ride side by side with Aymer instead.

With a sigh, Alec threw a glance over his shoulder, which showed the two wagons plodding along. The cart directly behind him was driven by John and was filled beyond the brim with most of the Oliver possessions and, as she'd insisted, every last kernel and plant from her work counter. She'd wanted to uproot the garden as well, which Aymer and Simon had actually begun to do, when Alec got wind of it. He hadn't touched her, but he'd wanted to, wanted to shake her forcefully until she understood she would not be able to dictate to any of them.

"Only digging they'll be about is your own grave," he'd snarled at her, "you keep up with this."

She'd given up so easily, with naught but a negligent shrug, Alec had been forced to wonder if she'd made the ridiculous request simply to provoke him.

From his vantage point, Alec could now see just the top of Malcolm's head, the bright orange hair bouncing rhythmically beyond Fergus, driving the second cart. Malcolm was not yet well enough to ride himself. Alec could hear Henry, or rather muted words from the lad as he spoke almost ceaselessly to Malcolm, sitting in the bed of the wagon as well. Alec grinned at this and thought 'twas the least Malcolm deserved for insisting on transporting the boy and his mother.

Likely, Malcolm minded little; he was infused with an inordinate amount of patience, something Alec often found sorely lacking in himself. As it was, it was hard not to like the lad. He was neither troublesome nor whiny, had pulled his relative weight—under his mother's direction—during the packing with nary a complaint, made conversation fairly easily with any and all, and had proven already to be a rather adaptable boy.

Loping happily alongside the moving army, Boswell had impressed him that he kept up so well with the moving horses, disappearing here and there but always returning to canter near his mistress's vehicle.

Sitting at the end of the wagon's bed, with her arm thrown up over the side rail, Katie Oliver stared only at the passing scenery. She did not look ahead, to what might come, but allowed her gaze to stay only on that which was in her line of vision as she sat sideways. Her bonny face was still and drawn. She barely blinked, it seemed, and Alec had to imagine she was allowing all sorts of terrible scenarios and outcomes to plague her just now for this drastic change in her circumstance. As he'd realized already, her face only softened when addressing or looking at her son. No sooner had he thought this than she turned at Henry's bidding and smiled at something he said. Once again, she was transformed, every line easing, her mouth losing its pinch, her eyes brightening momentarily.

And then she discovered Alec turned and watching her and her expression shuttered and tightened once more. Alec allowed her the hostility, couldn't blame her actually. Truthfully, he considered it Malcolm's chore to rid her of her reservations, as he'd been the force behind the drastic change in her life.

Alec faced forward again.

Wasn't his problem.

And when they reached Swordmair, it would be less his concern. His mother would likely embrace her and her boy, as was her way, would make sure one and all welcomed her properly, would set her up nicely in one of the nearby cottages. Possibly, Alec would have very little to do with her.

BY EARLY EVENING, LONG past the time she'd thought they might have stopped for the day, Katie's bum was sore from the hard boards of the wagon bed. The sun had yet to set and she could barely keep her eyes open. As she was accustomed to laboring from sunrise until sunset, she had to imagine that only the constant and even rumbling of the cart was lulling her into sleepiness.

Even Henry had succumbed to a rare nap, having talked himself out. He curled up next to Malcolm, making use of their stacked linens as a bed and pillow. Malcolm remained wakeful, seeming to take up so much space inside the small vehicle, his legs stretched out so that the bottom of his boots nearly touched Katie's thigh at the end of the cart. She supposed it was the soldier in him that had made him so alert, his head continually turning, his eyes scanning all the scenery—not, Katie thought, with any interest in the late summer greenery or all the marvelous colors presented by the hills and mountains and lochs, but with an eye toward vigilance, wary of who else might be on the road with them.

They rode somewhere in the middle of the line of soldiers, their trek neither too fast nor too slow. She'd met the eye of the chief but once, caught him shifted in his saddle and staring at her actually. She wasn't sure why he bothered her more than any of these MacBriars—save for Eleanor, mayhap—but she found his regard both unnerving and unwanted. She couldn't say for sure, at any given time, what she read in those piercing hazel eyes.

# THE LOVE OF HER LIFE

A man rode up close to the rear wheel of the wagon, opposite where Katie sat, and smiled at her. Instinctively, she returned the gesture, though with some wariness.

"Big changes ahead for ye, aye?"

She recognized him only as one of the soldiers who'd begun to tackle the removal of her garden—until that hard-bitten Alec MacBriar had put a stop to that—and allowed, "It appears so." *Not that I was given much choice in the matter*, she thought but kept to herself, mostly since it wasn't entirely true. She was still petulant though, her nerves doing dastardly things to her innards.

"We've got ol' Morven up at Swordmair, of course," the man continued, "but he's seen all his best years, and those were a long time ago. Will be good to have a fresh faced healer, mayhap with fresh ideas. The old goat likes to hack things off and hope for the best."

Katie's eyes widened at this worrisome bit. *Dear Lord.*

"Aye now, dinna ye fuss, ma'am," the man was quick to insist. "Morven's tired, likely will cheer your coming."

She nodded uneasily and tried to smile for this awkward conversation. The man, about her own age, she would guess, was possibly one of the smaller of the MacBriar soldiers, with a softness about him that seemed ill-suited to his occupation. His brown eyes were heavy-lidded and wide-set, the brown almost as liquid as a pup's; his hand, one upon the reins and the other rested on the hilt of his sword, were without scars and appeared clean and well-groomed, almost childlike; his shoulders were neither broad nor square, but slumped and curved; and even at his midsection, rolling over the belt at his waist, his belly was soft.

"I'd be Aymer, ma'am, and hope you find Swordmair to your liking."

"Katie," she introduced herself formally. "Thank you for your help with the garden earlier, or your attempt at any rate—"

"Hush."

Katie startled and jerked toward Malcolm. He sat as he was, but now with his hand held up for quiet. Stiffening, Katie realized immediately that the posture of the entire party had shifted. They slowed and only tiptoed along, making almost no noise at all. Malcolm—all the soldiers—scanned the area, moving only their eyes. They were crossing a large stretch of flatland, a narrow glen set low between a steep hill on one side and a gentler rise of pines on the other.

Anxiously, Katie sent her gaze around the area as well, wondering what had caught Malcolm's attention.

"Northwest," he said, only loud enough to be heard by those closest.

Katie heard or sensed nothing and was only confused by the reaction of Malcolm and all the others.

She heard then Alec MacBriar's voice. "Get those carts into the trees."

"What is it?" She begged of Malcolm as Fergus turned the cart left and encouraged the palfreys to a swifter pace. "Malcolm—"

He leaned forward and collected his sword from where it had lain near his feet. "No' to worry, lass," he said. "Bandits or English or some other, intent on concealing their presence—which never means anything good, you ken?"

"I *dinna ken*," she cried, hanging on stiffly to the side rail as the wagon gained speed. "Are we being attacked?"

"About to be," Malcolm said, as calmly as if they were not.

Katie whimpered just as Henry woke, roused by the change in momentum. He was groggy and confused and Malcolm addressed the sleepy question in his gaze before Katie might have.

"Gonna have a wee little skirmish, lad. Look lively."

This woke Henry but quick. He sat up promptly, bouncing onto his knees to look back at the soldiers left behind. "Will Eleanor fight?" He wanted to know.

"She'll be the first to make contact, mark my words," Malcolm advised, showing the large space between his top row of teeth with his grin. "She looks sweet, I ken, but she ain't," he said with a grin for what Katie had to assume was a jest, as Eleanor looked anything but sweet.

They entered the hillside of trees but did not go very deep within. Fergus maneuvered the cart efficiently through the tall pines, turning it around so that it was poised to leave the woods quickly if need be.

"But why would someone attack a moving army?" Katie wanted to know.

Malcolm shrugged, standing inside the wagon when it stopped. "English, you ken, will make war with almost any Scots. If they be regular bandits, they're looking for gold or goods." He shrugged as he walked to the end of the wagon bed. "Sometimes people fight to eat, might hope we've livestock or food to pilfer."

"But to kill for—" Katie began.

"Kill or be killed, lass." And with that he leaped over the rails and onto the ground, his sword held loosely, comfortably in one hand as he walked back to the edge of the trees to watch the spectacle, if there truly was to be one.

Katie rolled her eyes for Malcolm's gadding about, hopping out of wagons as if he hadn't even one stitch in his body. But she followed, leaving the wagon as well, admonishing Henry to stay within.

Fergus gainsaid this as he, too, disembarked. "Nay, ma'am. We've all to be afoot, should the need to run arise."

"Dear Lord," she murmured, and then grumbled with no small amount of nervous frustration, "Didn't have these problems in Dalserf."

Possibly Malcolm heard this but chose to ignore it. "C'mon then, sidle up near behind a tree. Keep out of sight. Nay, lad, go there with your mam. I need my hands free."

Katie gathered Henry to her, and they did as Malcolm suggested, concealed themselves behind a thick trunked pine, with Malcolm and Fergus on either side of them, hidden as well behind other trees. John, who'd parked the second wagon, appeared as well, tucking himself behind the same tree as Fergus, on his haunches, his sword also at the ready.

"But where's the battle?" Henry wanted to know.

Katie wondered the same thing. The MacBriars, minus the two carts that had been moved into the woods, only continued to move forward along the open meadow, their pace unhurried.

"Wait for it," Malcolm instructed.

He'd barely given these words when arrows began to fly, coming from the same woods much further ahead. They sliced through the air with great menace toward the MacBriars. Katie covered her mouth and her cry with her hand when she saw immediately two MacBriars fall. Absently, she tried to turn Henry's head toward her, away from the sight. He would have none of it, removing her hand from his head to watch, his fascinated reaction so different from Katie's horrified one. She shrieked against her hand when Alec MacBriar himself was struck by a flying and deadly missile, nicking his side just as he'd lifted his sword to engage his men to charge the hidden villains.

He seemed to pay no heed to the wound but gave a savage cry and led his army toward the woods just as the enemy finally showed themselves, spilling out of the trees to clash with their prey.

Katie didn't know where to look, tried only to keep her eye on the black and blue and tan tartan worn by almost every MacBriar soldier. Eleanor was easy to find, mighty upon her steed, her hair flying out in clumps behind her as she hacked and cleaved her way through the bandits.

The foot soldiers of the attackers were joined quickly by mounted men, their numbers not terribly greater than those of the MacBriars.

"Are they English?" Henry wondered.

Katie shrugged, having no idea.

"Aye," said Malcolm, seething, likely itching to be anywhere but here, so far away from it. "Scouting party, mayhap, no banners."

"But how can you tell?"

"Their weapons," Malcolm answered. "The English are too tiny to lift any heavy halberds or war hammers. See how thin the blades of their swords are?"

Katie could not discern the difference between the swords of either side, as both looked equally frightening when drenched in blood. Anxiously, she watched the melee, which after the initial flight of arrows, seemed woefully one-sided, the walking Englishmen falling like raindrops under the defense of the MacBriars.

Her gaze found Alec MacBriar once again and her eyes widened as she watched him fight. He had no fear, only continued to push forward, employing a weapon in each hand. She wasn't sure how his big brown destrier understood when or where to move, but the animal only paused when his master was engaged. The attackers were swiftly incapacitated by either his sword or the long-handled axe in his left hand, his proficiency with his left hand as great as his right.

Dismayed by both the easy violence of this battle, risen from nowhere it seemed, and by the recklessness of the MacBriar, who was both daring and tireless, Katie stared gape-jawed. And then her gaze caught movement straight ahead, not north toward the skirmish.

"Malcolm!" She cried out, her finger lifted to point where her wide eyes watched.

Shifting against the tree, Malcolm cursed roundly as he spied what Katie had, a dozen riders coming out of the trees from the steep hill across the glen, headed directly toward them.

"You have the dagger, lass?"

"Aye." Her voice quavered.

He lifted a fist next to his face and rammed it downward with a striking motion. "Anyone comes near you, you put that dagger right in his eye."

Katie nodded, even as she knew she could do no such thing.

Malcolm met Katie's terrified gaze and instructed tersely, "Run. You and the boy." He pointed further into the trees, past the wagons. "Run that way. Straight. Dinna look back. We'll find you. If we dinna, keep running."

# THE LOVE OF HER LIFE

Her stomach dropping, Katie nodded jerkily and grabbed Henry's hand, wasting no time darting away from the trees. They raced over the soft needle-strewn ground, deeper into the woods, quite a chore even though the incline was slight. She pulled Henry along with her, never having moved so fast in her life, she was sure. She glanced back only once, when she heard Boswell's bark. A cry escaped, fearful for her hound but knowing he would give them away if he followed them.

Daylight grew dimmer and dimmer the deeper into the woods they went. She heard a clash of swords far behind her, knew that Malcolm and Fergus and John had met the enemy. And then, horrifically, she picked up what sounded like horses charging through the woods after her and Henry.

She paused behind a tree, pulling Henry close, catching her breath. Straight ahead sat a broken birch tree, cracked and bent near the base. The trunk had tipped over but was still attached so that a small triangular void was created before the upper portion of the tree touched the ground. The fat limb was draped with moss and vines and leaves.

Moving quickly, Katie dragged Henry to that tree, pushing him onto the ground and into the gap.

"Hide under there," she said quickly. "Dinna come out until me or a MacBriar call for you."

"Mam—" he started to protest, his voice quaking.

"Henry, please. I will lead them away from you. You will be safe here." She pressed him further under the dropped tree and arranged the moss around him. She couldn't right now address his fear or the pitiful look he'd given her. She needed to draw them away. "Not a sound," she commanded and straightened and began running again, far away from where Henry was hidden.

"There!" she heard called out as her pursuers rediscovered her. Katie tripped and fell but leapt up quickly, determined that she get as far away from Henry as possible, racing further into the darkness. If she were bound to die, she did not want her son to witness it. Tears fell unchecked down her cheeks as they came even closer. And then more swords clashed, the clanging sound close, that she thought perhaps a MacBriar had followed as well and now engaged her pursuers. Ducking behind another tree, Katie dared to glance behind her.

She could see little, the gloom heavy under a thick canopy of pines. A glint of steel flashed, a man groaned, and horses moved again. Katie whimpered and turned, needing to be further away but suddenly unable to move, her fear immobilizing her. She lowered her head and let more tears fall.

A man appeared, coming around the tree, cloaked in the shadows of the woods. She drew in breath to scream just as her mouth was covered by a huge hand.

"Dinna move."

Alec MacBriar.

Katie cried into his hand and sagged against the tree with relief, closing her eyes.

Lowering his hand, he stood very close to her so that both of them were invisible behind the tree.

"Where is Henry?" His voice was close to her bent head, his breath at her ear.

Her lips trembled. "I hid him, under some brush." She lifted her gaze to him, terrified anew, thinking she'd made the wrong decision to separate from her son.

Alec nodded, possibly sensing her returning panic that he assured her in a low voice, "He'll be fine. He's a clever lad, kens no' to move."

"Yes." More tears fell even as she squeezed her eyes so tight against fear.

She gave some thought that Alec had used both hands on her, one to haul her against the tree and one to cover her mouth. Empty hands.

Katie opened her eyes. "Where is your sword?" She whispered in a panic, her question spoken nearly into his neck as he leaned close again, peering around the tree.

He didn't move away or give up his watchfulness as he answered. "Embedded in a man. In a tree."

"Malcolm's dagger is on my waist," she whispered back at him.

She felt his hands move, reach down, skim her waist, as he claimed it for himself from the leather sheath Malcolm had procured for her as well.

Still, she couldn't stop every limb and bone and nerve from quivering.

Shifting his head back, Alec lowered his face again, his dark eyes glittering in the eerie daytime darkness of the wood.

"Shh."

Katie nodded instantly, her head bobbing wildly.

"Shh," he said again, to soothe her. He set the fingers of one hand around her hip and moved his body closer so that she felt the massive and solid wall of his protection. "You're safe, Katie."

She settled immediately and closed her eyes again. The warmth of his body, the enormous confidence in his tone, the weapon in his hand put her at ease. She concentrated on breathing evenly and hopefully not giving up their position because she was hysterical.

Sounds penetrated still. Riders moved closer, slowly, searching for them. Skirmishes carried on, but not very near, shouts and cries and the clink of steel muted and further away. They stayed completely still, Katie squeezing her eyes shut, as one rider moved past them, only yards away but unaware of their presence. He continued on, soon invisible when he'd put some distance and some trees between them.

Hearing nothing in their immediate proximity for several long seconds, Katie opened her eyes and lifted her face.

Alec MacBriar was staring down at her. Shadows concealed his features, but she was aware of his gleaming eyes trained on her and his breath hot against her cheek. He said nothing and gave no indication what he was thinking so that she was left to read his close and intense scrutiny for herself.

She didn't know what to make of it, why he was staring at her and not watching their surroundings. His breathing sharpened, she thought, and his gaze moved from her eyes to her lips, but otherwise his countenance was mysterious.

And yet....

Despite the fact that she had been wed, and had borne a child, she lacked so much experience with interactions between men and women, but God help her if she didn't believe just now that Alec MacBriar wanted to kiss her. Why else would he stare so boldly and heatedly at her?

"Jasper!" Came a shriek, garbled and pitiful, and the rider who'd moments ago walked past them, charged back in their direction at the cry for help from his mate.

Alec pushed away from Katie just as the man came into view. He leapt directly at the side of the horse, halting its forward progress as he managed to grab hold of the raider's sword arm, bending back his wrist until the sword was dropped. Katie grimaced and skittered around the tree as Alec ripped the man from the saddle and slapped him onto the ground with such force that the man let out a long moan. Alec knelt over him and sliced the sharp dagger across the man's throat.

Katie clapped her hand over her mouth at the sight.

But then Alec's name was called, in what Katie thought might be Malcolm's voice. Whoever it was, the tone of it suggested only a search and not anything more dire.

Alec jumped to his feet and grabbed Katie's hand, pulling her along behind him as he dashed toward the greater light at the edge of the wood.

"Henry!" She cried when she spied the fallen tree directly ahead.

The moss and leaves moved at the sound of her voice, and a bit of blond hair began to show. Alec, reaching him first, scooped Henry off the forest floor as he crawled out of hiding, and took him into his strong arms.

"Well done, lad," he commended, allowing Katie only a moment to smile at her son and run her hand over his cheek. "C'mon," Alec said, holding Henry with one arm and taking Katie's hand again to direct them back to the wagons. Henry wound his arms around the MacBriar's neck, finding comfort in this man's strength just as Katie had. Over Alec's shoulder, Henry's watery gaze was trained on Katie.

She tried to appear at ease for her son, but Alec's swift pace meant that she had to hike up her skirts and keep careful watch on the uneven ground, even as she was trying to look ahead, to see what the situation was. Running only a pace behind and almost to the side of Alec MacBriar, Katie finally noticed Malcolm, coming into view, unharmed and standing, waiting them. Eleanor and Aymer stood close and others moved about around them.

The fighting was done.

Katie breathed easier at their near-casual stances, if one could say that Eleanor, with the hilt of her long sword held at her hip and tilted upward so that the bloodied blade lay over her shoulder was indeed a casual pose.

They had almost reached them when a shout rang out. "Incoming!"

All those before them stiffened and struck battle poses, swords swung high and forward, turning their backs to the trio coming from the woods to face this new threat.

"Son of a—" Alec began, only to be stopped as Katie felt a stinging bite at the same time her hand was snatched from his.

She was heaved backward by the force of the blow and thrown onto her back with a thump.

"Cover them!" she heard Alec shout, his voice brutal, just before he appeared at her side. He pressed Henry onto the ground at her hip and used his own body as a shield over both of them.

Katie lay still, confused about what had flung her backward, vaguely aware of pain above her right breast.

"Mam!" Henry cried with fright, but the sound was muffled, as if he were under water.

Above her, holding himself up on his arms even as she felt so much of him pressed along the length of her, Alec MacBriar swore and pushed the hair away from her face. "You're hit."

"Oh." It was then she saw the shaft of an arrow rising upward, leaning against Alec's shoulder. It was fletched with three feathers—of a goose, she thought unnecessarily. She blinked, confused, wondering why it didn't hurt more.

"Mam!" Her son continued to cry.

"She's fine, Henry," Alec told him, though she detected a wee bit of worry in his tone. "I promise you she will be fine."

Her son had grabbed her hand, was holding it tight with both of his. She squeezed hard and tried to smile, though Henry likely couldn't see this.

His face only inches from hers once again, Katie thought that Alec MacBriar's eyes really were a remarkable color. So much intensity as he scanned her face, his worry evident there, inside the depths of the piercing hazel.

The fighting continued at the edge of the woods, she understood, brutal noises penetrating her consciousness. She was in no serious peril just now, she knew, either from the arrow jutting out from her shoulder or the brigands making war with them. Alec wouldn't be lying atop her if he were needed elsewhere, within that fight. Yet, she felt as if she were enveloped in rather a haze of wanting to sleep and a cloud of numbness.

Shock, she thought it might be.

"Open your eyes," Alec commanded in a harsh voice. "Damn it, Katie. Open your eyes."

She did and met his, dark orbs under heavily furrowed brows.

"You should have kissed me," she whispered.

## Chapter Six

She closed her eyes again.

His entire body was pressed against hers, though he tried to keep so much of his weight off her. One elbow dug into the ground at her side, the other arm was flung across Henry, curled up in terror against his mother.

Malcolm and Eleanor and the others addressed the current attack. The very sound of it suggested no hardship. When Malcolm had either the time or inclination to spout slurs at the enemy, Alec knew that victory was nigh.

"I'll gut you like the pig that you are!" His captain charged. This was followed by noises suggesting Malcolm had suited action to words. "And that's for clipping our healer, you belly-crawlin' bastard!"

Alec was right pissed about the attack, though not entirely surprised. Still, he'd have words for his unit for giving the all-clear call when they'd obviously not scoured the area for stragglers.

The fingers of his right hand, laid along Katie's cheek, having moved her tangled hair away from her face, were covered in blood. Behind them, Eleanor let loose a guttural cry, likely the preface to running her sword through some poor bastard. Katie Oliver lay beneath him with an arrow protruding from her shoulder. Her son was a ball of pudding, his tremors shaking his mother even...and all Alec could think just now was: how the hell did she know I'd been thinking about kissing her? And then, more intriguing: why, in the name of all that was holy, had she just hinted that she might have welcomed it?

Quiet descended around them. Only Malcolm's frustration was vocal, equal to Alec's and for the same reason.

"Bluidy hell! Elle! Aymer! Who the hell was charged with clearing the hills and the woods? Take ten into those hills and make sure we'll no' be surprised again." His voice lowered to grumbling but drew nearer to Alec. "Bluidy simpletons, acting like it's their first fight."

Alec shifted off Katie, settling on his knees beside her. With his movement, Henry sat up as well.

The lad wailed anew. "Is she dead?" was asked just as Malcolm, standing over Alec's shoulder, breathed, "Shite."

Katie's long lashes fluttered.

"Mam. Oh, mam," Henry sobbed and threw himself at her, lying over her midsection, hugging her tight.

"I'm fine," she murmured weakly. "Just shocked, that's all. Fetch my pouches, Henry."

"C'mon, lad," Malcolm said, his voice kindly. "I'll take you back to the wagons. You ken what she wants?"

Henry removed himself from his mother, received her slight but encouraging smile and went off with Malcolm.

"Tell me what to do." Alec said. His anger intensified, that she should have been injured while under his protection.

She took a deep breath, which came with a wince, and met his gaze. "'Tis not your fault."

"Everything that happens within this unit is my responsibility."

No further argument came, though he sensed more inside her. But it wasn't on her to relieve him of guilt.

Lifting her hand, she grabbed hold of the shaft and moved it cautiously and so very slightly, testing its depth, eliciting a wrenching expression of pain that effectively twisted Alec's gut.

"It's in the bone," she told him, dropping her hand back to the ground at her side, as if she hadn't the strength to hold it aloft any longer. "So it cannot be pushed through, needs to be pulled out."

Fergus and John appeared then, hovering over the pair.

"Bluidy hell, lass," Fergus said. And then to Alec, "Who fixes the healer?"

Alec held Katie's gaze while she answered for him. "He will."

Alec nodded. He speculated briefly if this was to be his penance.

"But then, who's going to patch up everyone else?" John wanted to know.

"Me first," Katie said evenly. "Get this out and I'll be fine—"

"You'll no' be running around tending others," Alec interjected hotly.

Ignoring him, Katie continued, "You've been hit as well."

"'Tis but a scratch. One thing at a time," Alec argued just as Malcolm and Henry returned.

Henry placed the pouch on his mother's belly, which for some reason made her smile slightly. Curiously, as she appeared mostly calm, a tear slipped away from the corner of her eye.

Another deep breath and she instructed evenly, her eyes closed now, "Try first to remove the entire thing. Likely, the tip will remain embedded in the bone and you'll have to address that separately. But you might get lucky and the tip will come out with the shaft."

Shuddering inwardly for his own ineptness, but buoyed by her calmness, Alec shifted onto one knee and leaned over her. "Should I wiggle it?" He asked, having taken a firm grip of the shaft.

"You can try that," she answered without opening her eyes.

"Do I need to hold her down?" Fergus wondered.

"That won't be necessary," she said, waiting.

Alec mumbled a curse and began to move the shaft gingerly back and forth. It was wedged firmly, he could feel, and wondered if firm but even pressure to pull it out would be successful. He worked with singular attention, trying his best to not be made weak by her changing expressions. First, her closed eyes tightened, forming many creases at the corners, then her lips rolled inward, clamping down against the pain he brought to her.

He wriggled it, slowly and with control, but to no avail. A firmer tug with more pressure only proved what she'd expected, the shaft breaking away from the tip.

Those hovering gasped, and then a collective groan was heard when it was realized the arrowhead was no longer attached to the shaft. He didn't turn around, but it appeared a larger crowd had gathered.

"Well, that dinna work," someone said needlessly.

"Now he's got to dig around in there." John's voice. "That'll bring some mighty pain."

Malcolm grumbled to the watchers, "I ken about forty things need being done right now and yet, you're all standing here."

Katie opened her eyes as some, not all, departed, ignoring all the fuss around her, and met Alec's tortured gaze. "It's fine. That was unlikely to work anyway. You'll have to go in and fetch it, and possibly I might lose consciousness if the pain is too great."

Alec rolled his head back, wishing to dear God she hadn't said that.

She continued, "So I'll give all the instructions now and my apologies if I do pass out, as you and the others will have to await my—"

"Will ye stop worrying about the others?" Malcolm growled above Alec.

"Henry can mix the salve," she went on. "He knows about that. Fish out the tip, apply the salve and all will be well. I'll bind it myself later. Very simple," she said.

Alec couldn't believe she was trying to make *him* feel better. Obviously the tension he felt just now was not well disguised, though he couldn't imagine that his face moved at all, his jaw being clamped so tight. He managed a nod.

With a grimace, as if afraid to deliver the rest of her instruction, she added, "And...if it gets too messy, it will need stitching."

Alec cursed under his breath.

"Sounds awful, and I'm pleased it's not me," Malcolm said unhelpfully, and finished, "but we gotta move this along. We canna stay here much longer, too vulnerable right now."

Henry jumped up then, uncinching the pouch on Katie's belly and then taking off, saying as he ran, "I forgot the honey."

Turning his head, Alec requested of Malcolm, "Send someone into the woods to retrieve my sword and axe. They're holding bodies against trees, about sixty yards straight in."

# THE LOVE OF HER LIFE

Alec withdrew the knife he'd earlier borrowed from Katie and wiped it on the forest floor, removing as much blood as he could, and once again leaned over Katie, gently lifting away the fabric of her gown, about to slice it open.

"Wait," she said, curtailing his intentions. "Could you not shred my gown?" At Alec's incredulous look, she added feebly, "I'm sorry. It's just that I haven't many frocks and..."

"I'll get you a new frock," he said crossly and cut away at the wool. He was forced to cut away the strap of her undergarment also, supposing he might provide her with a new kirtle as well once they reached Swordmair.

He swallowed hard then and considered the exposed skin and wound. It looked so small, too small for his fingers or any tool to get in there to find the arrowhead. Chewing the inside of his cheek, he touched only one finger to the bloody gap in her skin, upon the curved line of her collarbone. Immediately, he sent his gaze to hers, measuring the depth of pain from that small touch.

"Are you hoping I do pass out?" She asked.

"Aye—for your sake and mine. At least close your eyes, lass. You're making me all kinds of uneasy."

"Sir, I saw you earlier hack off a man's arm with one stroke of your blade." Her voice was slower, weaker, he thought. "And apparently you applied such force in the last strike of your sword that even now it is still impaled inside a tree. This here seems rather simple an act, all things considered."

"It's no'...this is verra different. I dinna ken how to be...soft."

"But you cannot be soft, as this requires strength. Same as when you retrieved the tip of that blade from Malcolm."

"I dinna have the spoons to hold the—"

"They would not be helpful. This is very near the surface, as you can see. You might have to slice more of the skin to get to it."

Alec lanced her with a disbelieving scowl. "Are you jesting? You want me to cut you?"

She stared hard at him. "Will you get to it, already?" Her voice had returned to that angry one he was familiar with.

He ground out, "I dinna want to hurt you."

"It hurts now and there stands no chance of that ever lessening if you do not get the tip out," she informed him, her own tone heated.

Furious at both the godawful tension and anger at this wretched circumstance, Alec curled his lip and finally plunged his finger into the hole of her creamy skin. His eyes lit up almost instantly, his finger quickly landing upon the arrowhead. He dipped his other hand into the pouch on her belly and withdrew her small pliers just as Henry returned. It took some doing, and the incision was inadvertently made larger, but he managed to pinch the tip of the arrow with the pliers.

And Katie Oliver did indeed pass out while he wrestled with removing the metal from her bone. He was convinced it was embedded deeper and more firmly than the one he'd removed from Malcolm's rib. Twice, while he struggled with it, he heard Malcolm drawing in a hissed breath between his teeth behind him.

"Henry, the salve," he said then, when the offensive piece was finally removed. But the boy only handed a small crock to him, did not himself apply the ointment.

Alec swabbed her collarbone with the honey mixture and spared a few seconds to consider her now peaceful expression. More tears had come, traced a crooked pattern down into the hair at her temple, nearly undoing him. Otherwise, she appeared

# THE LOVE OF HER LIFE

as bonny as ever, perhaps more so with the serenity that came with oblivion.

By now, all tasks having been completed, a crowd formed around again.

They concurred with Alec's conjecture, unanimously deciding that the process had indeed enlarged the originally tiny laceration and would now require stitches. With that, Alec pulled one long silk thread and the bone needle from another of Katie's pouches and tried to recall exactly how she'd sewn up Malcolm so efficiently and expertly two days earlier.

Despite her slumber, the sewing of the lass's smooth and otherwise unblemished skin was not a chore he was keen to assume, the undertaking made more unbearable by the fairly universal opinions of those watching that he was doing it wrong.

"Smaller seams, I would think," Aymer had suggested, peering over his shoulder.

"Dinna crisscross them," John advised, "or the removal of the threads will be made worse."

"Get that end there," Malcolm said.

"I'm getting it," Alec hissed through a tight mouth. "*Jesu*, back off!"

They did, but only for a moment.

"Should you space them closer together?" Ranald wondered then.

Alec stopped sewing, letting his fingers rest against her warm skin, and glowered up at Ranald. The glower had turned to exasperation when Henry, opposite Alec and watching, had chimed in.

"He's right, though. Mam's stitches are closer." When all eyes had turned toward the lad, he only shrugged and added quietly, "And neater."

When finally he was done, and happy to remove any prospect of more recriminations from his own men—and now Henry!—Alec gently lifted the still sleeping Katie into his arms and followed Malcolm's pointing to where the wagons had been brought nearer.

"And that's that, lads," Malcolm called out. "We ride in five!"

Alec passed a silent Eleanor, near the wagon and watchful upon her steed. She'd not been party to the ogling crowd that had gathered 'round Alec as he'd tended Katie, and now gave him only a hard, unfathomable glare as he walked by her. She spared not one glance to the woman in his arms.

Henry bounded up in the wagon bed just as Alec reached it. The lad scrambled around on his knees, moving items out of the way to make room for his mother's prone form. Malcolm climbed up as well, reaching down for Katie as there was no way for Alec to take such a high step onto the bed with Katie in his arms. He acknowledged but did not examine the slight hesitation that made him withhold her from Malcolm for the space of a second.

When she was settled on some of her own linens from her cottage, still sleeping, Malcolm said, "Henry and I'll take care of her now," which also did not sit well with Alec, though he couldn't have said why.

His brow still wrinkled, Alec nodded. And, left with no other options, he searched out his abandoned horse and led the small army once again along the road, leaving all the dead English where they had fallen.

He spent the first quarter hour making internal notes of improvements to this unit's training, that so many proper and necessary procedures seemed to have been neglected in and after the fray. He began to give further thought to Elle's most recent aggression and whatever that seething resentment was that she donned as a cloak but then dismissed Elle completely, considering any conjecture in that regard not worth his time or energy. Let her have her snit; he'd advise Malcolm to straighten her out if she didn't come around in the next few days, certainly if she remained hostile once they reached Swordmair.

The next hour of the steady but slow drive was mostly spent trying not to think, or overthink, the whole situation that was Katie Oliver. Yet twice he circled back from his lead position to check on her, only to be told each time that she slept still. The second time, Malcolm showed some concern for her lengthy slumber, his orange brows knit.

For a while, he managed to convince himself that any ridiculous thought he *may* have had about kissing Katie Oliver was borne of circumstance—hearts pumping, danger seething, the enemy threatening, and all that—and had nothing to do with any actual desire for her. After all, she wasn't exactly the sort of female he would normally be attracted to. Too lean, too severe, too anxious and angry for his tastes.

*I've had already my life's love.*

Too...unavailable?

Alec shook himself. *Enough!*

She's nobody and means nothing.

A light bark sounded near, reminding Alec of that damn hound, who apparently had survived the skirmish and trudged along still with them.

*What a bluidy day!*

Eight hours ago, he was scolding Boswell for trying to steal the laundry. Before he'd so clumsily knocked Katie onto the ground, she'd been laughing, chasing the fool of a hound around him, her hand at his waist while she'd circled him. Mayhap, it was only his complete infatuation with the sound of her laughter, and her hand so innocently but familiarly upon him, that had rendered him senseless momentarily, that he'd yanked at the apron and had inadvertently struck her.

Farquhar had come then, stealing any time for reflection over his reaction to her happiness. Her merriment had been exhilarating, in that he somehow knew she might so rarely have cause to be so engaged. Not like that, not that full and lustrous sound, which came from the belly, and with no sense of impropriety, no call to hold herself back as he was sure she regularly did.

When the fight had come to them today, he'd easily dispatched the first aggressors, believing it would end as quickly as it had begun, and they'd be on their way again within minutes. But then he'd caught sight of a band of English charging into the trees where Malcolm, Katie, and the others had hidden. He gave chase immediately, shouting out to Elle and Aymer to take charge there, and had raced headlong into the woods after them. Malcolm, Fergus, and John were holding their own, as the English had split up, some taking on Alec's men at the edge of the trees while others continued into the woods.

Alec had joined the fight eagerly, his frustration rising to fury when Malcolm had called out to him amid the fray, "They're chasing her and the boy into the woods."

His blood had run cold and he'd wasted no time, pressing his heels to the destrier's flanks with a loud snarl for his rising wrath, and had gone deep into the woods in furious pursuit. Two of the five English chasing Katie and Henry were easily and swiftly destroyed, though he'd been forced to abandon first his horse and then his sword when his fury saw it struck so far into the man and the tree into which he'd skewered him. His axe had been left inside some man's head, Alec not even daring to waste mere seconds to wrest it free. Bereft of weapons then, he'd employed stealth and thankfully had found Katie before the English might have.

But then...

Well then, proximity was a dastardly thing.

Possibly she was not even aware that her fingers had curled into the sleeves of his tunic, that she held him close. She'd been so small and terrified but then so readily calmed with only his presence, her body soft and warm, pressed against the length of him. *Jesu*, and her lips were...so close, so damn tempting.

It was her faith in him that had stirred him primarily, he realized. When he'd first wrested her back against the tree, sorry for the fright he'd caused her, she'd lost a substantial amount of fear at recognizing it was he who'd accosted her. She didn't like him, didn't truly want to be traveling to Swordmair, thought him a tyrant in all probability, but she believed he would keep her safe.

That had elicited some powerful emotions inside him. Proximity had done the rest, bringing the scent of her to him—not fear, but woman. Her briefly trembling lips had beckoned him, their shape tempting, their promise unknown but stirring him to curiosity.

*Stop!* He reproached himself, not allowing any further recollection, denying it each time it begged to resurface.

When the sun had been gone for some time and all the light of day disappeared, he reined in the entire party at the base of the Clachan Hills, near a long and narrow loch that he thought might be Loch Kern. If so, they could conceivably make Swordmair on the morrow, late, if they rode hard. As it was, the condition of the group suggested a slower pace would need to be set and they would spend yet another night camped under the stars before finding home.

It was a busy camp then, as there were still wounded men that needed attention and some sort of sustenance to be prepared and consumed; horses needed tending and Alec spent some private time with Malcolm, in heated discussion over their disappointment in today's behavior of this portion of their army.

When the camp settled down, Alec found sleep near the Olivers, making a pallet for himself directly beneath the wagon in which they slept, wanting to be close should she wake.

She did, but much later. As Alec had yet to sleep, he was aware of a creaking of the boards, suggesting some movement above him. He listened for a moment to determine if this were only ordinary nighttime adjustments or if Katie might be awake.

"Henry?" He heard her call softly.

Alec made to move just as the lad answered, immediately and with nary a hint of grogginess that Alec wondered if he'd slept yet at all either.

"Does it hurt?" Henry wanted to know.

"It does, but not too much," Katie said.

Alec remained still and listened.

"I'm sorry if you were made afraid," she said to her son.

"I was no' afraid for me, Mam. I was safe with all of them."

"Aye, that is good."

"Alec said you'd no' die, so I just felt bad that...it looked like it should hurt a lot."

"Did you help with the sewing?"

"Alec did that," Henry informed her, adding, "but you're no' going to like his stitches. They're kind of sloppy."

Alec rolled his eyes at the little traitor but pictured Katie showing a grin.

"He did his best, I'm sure."

"I guess. He should practice more though."

She let out a quiet chuckle. "Let's hope he has no further need, aye?"

"Mam?" Henry had whispered.

"Hmm?"

"Why are we going with them? I...I thought you dinna like them."

There was a great pause before she answered.

"I do not *dis*like them." A small sigh preceded the rest of her answer. "Truth be known, Henry, it wasn't safe for us at Dalserf. And you know as well as I, the people were not especially friendly."

"They call you a witch," her son said, his tone laced with confusion. The fact that he didn't negate her statement about their safety suggested he understood this as well.

"Aye, they do. Be that as it may, we've been promised something better at Swordmair—"

"I like that name."

"It's nice, I guess. I'm sure there is some meaning behind it. Won't it be nice, though, to have full bellies and warm beds and...and maybe some friends?"

"Will you still be the healer, though? Will we have to live far away from everyone?"

"I will still be the healer, they've said they need one. I'm not sure though where we might live, mayhap close enough to the castle or village that you can make friends, close enough to feel some security." She paused and then added, "Henry, if I'm...wrong about these men, if they mean us harm, we will have to get away from them."

"I dinna think they will," Henry said, his tone suggesting he was or had given it some thought. "I think they like us."

"I'm sure they like *you*, love. How could they not?"

Alec liked her nighttime voice, liked how sweet and smooth it was, imagined her face worry free and soft as well. He was sorry, though, that she was still suspicious of their motives or their intentions.

They were quiet for a while until Henry spoke again.

"Would Father have saved us? If he'd been here today."

"Aye, he would have. He could handle a sword as well as any of the MacBriars, better mayhap. He'd have slayed each and every one of those English, mayhap all by himself."

"Aye, and you'd no' have been shot by an arrow if he'd been here?"

"Almost certainly not," Katie answered, her voice wavering. "He would have kept us safe. He'd not ever allow another to harm a hair on either my head or yours."

They were quiet after the small exchange, and Alec mulled it over a wee bit, deciding he truly didn't know what to make of her continued adoration for a man who had been gone for seven years.

# Chapter Seven

Katie rose with the sun, stiff and sore, from both being prone for so many hours and for the hole in her shoulder.

While Henry slept still, she scooted out of the wagon, sorry to leave the warmth of the provided furs, and headed off into the thicker brush away from the camp. A quick glance around a nearly dead fire showed the MacBriars had made their own beds on the ground, some bunched together, others singular, mayhap cold now.

When she'd taken care of her private business, not without difficulty, she continued up a small slope and discovered a loch of fresh blue-gray water. Not wanting to be gone too long, for fear that Henry might wake and worry, Katie quickly washed her hands and face. She did the best she could, unable to use both hands to scoop up the water, her shoulder being very sore just now. She used her good arm to pull the tie from her hair so that it fell over her shoulder as she dragged the band away. She would task Henry with helping her do something with the mass of it when he woke.

She meant to find her cloak, as her slashed and drooping gown exposed all of her shoulder. The MacBriar had sliced the fabric from its neckline and downward several inches that it gaped away from her skin, showing all of her shoulder and the top of her arm. The kirtle beneath, its strap cut as well, hung loosely, almost uselessly, dropping lower under her gown with even her careful movements this morning.

Soon enough she returned to the wagon, tiptoeing as she drew nearer, for all the sleeping bodies.

Alec MacBriar stood beside the vehicle.

"Dinna go off without telling someone."

It took a moment for his words to register. She might have understood them sooner but that he stood beside the wagon bare-chested. He must have just washed up himself, as his chest and arms and face were wet yet, while he used his plaid to dry himself. Wordlessly, having yet to respond to his suggestion, her transfixed gazed followed his hands as they moved the plaid up and down his heavily muscled arms and across wide shoulders, perfectly square and large enough to encroach into his neck. His naked chest was as thick and well-honed, sculpted to rock hardness, and her thoughts carried her back to when he'd pressed himself against her behind that tree yesterday. All that virile beauty had been within her reach then.

Her lips parted just as his hands stopped moving. Katie stared at his fingers, clutching folds of the plaid and she wondered—

He'd stopped moving. This dawned on her.

*Sweet Jesus.* Startled, she lifted her gaze to his and her cheeks heated instantly. She'd just been caught nearly drooling over his magnificent form. She waited—prayed—for the ground to open beneath her. It did not, that she blinked several times and clamped her lips, trying to recall what he'd said.

He lifted a brow at her, the only indication that he might give her grief for gawking at him so...ravenously.

Before he might have spoken, she realized what words he'd used to greet her this morn and feigned a bristle. "Am I to request a partner when seeing to my needs?"

He let a moment pass before he responded, let his compelling and curious eyes disturb her a bit more. "Just tell someone you're heading away from camp, that's all."

She nodded tightly, made sour by her inexcusable gaffe, yet felt duty-bound to say, "Thank you for...what you did yesterday. For...all your help." She shifted a wee bit, so that he and his naked chest weren't directly in front of her. She wished he'd return his tunic to his gorgeous body.

"Sore now?" He wondered.

She nodded. "But no more than expected." Against her will, as if she physically couldn't prevent it, her regard was drawn again to him.

He inclined his head but offered nothing else. He was staring at her hair, making her very self-conscious about it, having it loose. It fell nearly to her waist, great tangles of hair and dirt and whatever else she'd picked up from the forest floor yesterday. Her cheeks pinkening, she felt obliged to explain, "I cannot put it back up." She lifted her right arm until pain made her stop, indicating her dilemma.

He shook his head and moved his lips, jerking his gaze from her hair, meeting her eye with some awkwardness, she thought.

"It's fine, aye," he murmured. Finally he tossed the plaid on the siderail of the cart and pulled his tunic over his head.

He continued to hold her in his gaze, his expression inscrutable. The morning light cast the whole of him in shades of gray, darkening his eyes.

Katie shifted, muttering a getaway excuse, uncomfortable with his prolonged and silent regard. "I should see if—"

He spoke at the same time, as soon as she made to move around him. She lifted her face again, not hearing what he'd just said. "What?"

"I should have kissed you."

Katie blinked. Her lips parted.

"What?"

"You said so yourself."

"I...I did?" Inwardly, she winced. She might have some vague and dastardly recollection of that.

He didn't grin or show any sign of overconfidence but was matter-of-fact when he confirmed this. "Aye, you did."

"Mayhap I was delirious?" *Wretched, rising blush!*

"I dinna think so. Those were fairly clear and explicit instructions on wound care."

"Were they?" No other part of her body moved, save her lips. She could not even force her gaze away from his, 'twas like watching the battle yesterday: it was shocking and gut-wrenching, but she couldn't look away, had to see what happened.

"Aye."

She nodded, too quickly mayhap, too shakily. "I suppose it must have been rather coherent for you to have done such a fine job with my care. It bleeds not—"

"You're changing the subject," he accused, his voice steady and low, all of him so...intense.

"I am trying."

*Do I want him to kiss me?* Ignoring her statement to him, as she had throughout the night, meant that this question remained unanswered.

Alec MacBriar stepped forward.

Katie held up her hand, breathing a wee bit raggedly, and stepped back. She gave all her attention to the ground.

"Changing your mind now?"

"I am...I do not want to be kissed," she decided.

"Perhaps you will no' ken for certain until I actually do kiss you."

"I do not think it works like that." She recognized that her voice had risen an octave.

"Let's find out."

"Why—why would you want to kiss me? I was under the impression you didn't like me at all."

She sensed, rather than saw, his head shake. "I dinna understand it either. Yet...something draws me to you."

"Maybe too long away from home and...female company?" She was proud of herself, having lifted her gaze as high as his arm.

"Lass, that's no' the—"

"Bluidy hell. Either kiss the lass or cease with the yapping."

Katie startled, recognizing Malcolm's voice. More heat rose in her cheeks, coloring them blood red, no doubt.

"Ye ken some people are trying to get their last winks in?"

That was Aymer, Katie thought, her mortification expanding immeasurably.

"Who does that?" This voice clearly belonged to Fergus. "Talks about kissing before actually kissing?"

With a whimper of humiliation, Katie finally met Alec's dark eyes again, sending him a pleading look, begging him to alleviate this embarrassment.

He was smiling at her now, beautifully if maddeningly, apparently not at all shamed by this situation.

"Mayhap you lads can help her decide," he suggested, calling over his shoulder.

His smile, wide and natural, the first she'd known from him, was absolutely mesmerizing.

And yet...'twas but a game, it seemed.

*Oh.* She lifted her hand and covered her mouth, as understanding dawned.

He was but toying with her.

How foolish she was.

How awful *he* was!

Without a backward glance, she stomped away from him, from the entire camp, stalking into the trees closest to the wagon.

*I hate him. I knew I did.*

She could not say if it were the degradation or the disappointment that misted her eyes. She snarled with ill humor when she was smacked in the face by a low-hanging pine bough. "Argh!"

But she marched on, wanting to be as far away as possible, thinking it would serve him—all of them—right if she were gone for hours and held up their leave-taking.

A yip of dread emerged when she heard him, Alec, calling her name. She would swear to God she detected laughter still in his tone. She moved faster, pushing through the brush, holding her arm gingerly at her chest, and then tripping over a hidden root that she went flying forward.

Strong hands saved her, seizing her around her waist from behind, righting her. She stumbled backward now against his hard body. When her feet were solid beneath her, she swiveled and pushed off him, crying, "Get your hands off me." Facing him, she slapped him across his cheek. But she'd had to use her left hand, and the slap was awkward, glancing off his chin. He barely flinched, his face wasn't thrown to the side. Huffing and seething, she railed at him. "You are despicable. You can unhitch those wagons. I'm not going anywhere with you. I don't want my son within spitting distance of the likes of you."

"Will you listen? Can I explain?"

"You cannot! There is no justification for such a shameful hoax." Why—why!—could she not have raged at him without sobbing like a forlorn child? Through quivering lips, she accused in a small voice, "You are a wretch. A miserable wretch." And she hated herself just then, for her weakness, for letting him see it. But then she was pleased that she recognized it quickly enough to put a stop to it. Purposefully, she gathered strength from every corner of her body. She straightened her back and lifted her chin.

He lowered his brows. "That was no' a hoax!"

"I meant what I said. Either unhitch those wagons and leave us be or return us to Dalserf." Her voice was calm and clear.

"Cease!" He said curtly. "I'm sorry the whole damn thing was overheard. I never meant that—"

"You understand I will believe nothing you say? And I will care even less?"

"Aye, but you're the wretch then, that you'll no' even let a man defend himself."

"There is no defense. I understand exactly what just happened." If her wound would have allowed it, she'd have crossed her arms over her chest, would have closed him out completely.

And now she was calm, and he was yelling.

"You dinna understand! You are embarrassed by their taunting and you're taking it out on me. You think I'd have wanted an audience when the chances of rejection were so high?"

Katie barked an unholy snort of disbelief for this weak, likely just-invented argument. "I didn't even know that you were capable of smiling, so sullen are you, and the first one I see is attached to that despicable game. You are a heartless person."

Neither of them moved.

Until finally the silence lengthened that she closed her eyes against his piercing gaze, wishing him away.

"I'd no' lie to you. I thought they slept still...and then I thought to make light of it, thought—I dinna ken, I thought that might make you less embarrassed."

Wanting only to end this conversation, wanting nothing more than to be away from him, she conceded tersely, "Fine. Thank you for that." She started to walk away.

"I dinna like when you do that."

He was following her, his pace even, though he did not try to stop her.

"When I do what?" She snapped.

"When you close up like that, bottle it all inside."

"Not every battle is worth the fight."

"A man who wants to kiss you no' worth the effort? Your time?"

She whirled on him, surprising him so that he jerked to a halt and she was forced to tilt her head back to address him and his ridiculousness. "You can stop now. The jest has been played. You show your dishonor by persisting."

His face hardened. "Lass, you accuse me of almost anything else, I'm no' going to fuss at you. But dinna question my honor."

She was only curious, not anything else, about his suddenly implacable tone.

But then he asked, "Why the tears then?" He lifted his shoulders. "If you—"

"Why won't you let this go?"

His lips curled before he admitted, with no small amount of reluctance, it seemed, "Because I still want to kiss you."

From a distance not too great, there rose a voice. Aymer again. "They're still only talking about it!"

"Hush up!" Katie hollered in the general direction of the camp at the same time Alec snarled loudly, "Shut the bluidy hell up!"

Her breath came unevenly and sharply still, facing him again. "Then do it. Get it over with. And then send me and my son home."

Alec didn't move. Seeming to find the very idea disagreeable, he conceded harshly, "Something tells me if I kiss you, lass, I'll no' be wanting to send you away."

Inexplicably more breathless, unable to stave off the rapid and nervous blinking, she reasoned, "You cannot possibly know that." She pinched her eyes closed and prayed for deliverance from this most awkward scene. "I suggest we just forget all about—"

His mouth crashed into hers. Instinctively, instantly, she stiffened, even as her lashes fluttered open with her shock. He was upon her, his hands at her cheeks, his firm and warm lips melting against hers. Katie's heart beat in double time, and somehow, she found herself less shocked than fascinated that her eyes drifted closed again. He persisted, gentling the kiss, his actions studied and deliberate, neither too forceful nor too slow. Hardly able to believe her own audacity, she responded, her mind woozy while her rigidity slowly evaporated. She found herself tilting her face to receive him better when he angled his head and leaned over her, his fingers tightening on her cheeks and in her hair as the kiss intensified. It seemed only natural, as kissing was not unknown to her, to open for him and take more from him. His tongue was delicious, delving into her with slick expertise, raising gooseflesh on her arms. Heat rose, from him, in her, enveloping them.

And yet, the delight of the kiss didn't make anything right, didn't somehow erase the ugly prelude to said kiss. Katie groaned and splayed her fingers against his solid midsection and pushed him away, lowering her face.

They were motionless, her head bent toward his chest, unable to face him, her hands still pressed against his hard body.

"And now that's done," she said, finally, breathlessly, the huskiness of her voice surprising her.

He allowed her to keep her chin to her chest.

"Nae, lass."

"I want to go home."

"You can no'. No' now. I did warn you."

Stepping backward, so that his hands slid out of her hair, she said. "No more."

And here was the arrogance she might have expected sooner from him. He was well-pleased with himself, regarding her with glittering eyes, even as his square jaw might have been clenched, hardening so much of his handsome face.

Still, he surprised her by nodding his agreement, even offered, "I will no' kiss you again."

Before she could determine if the sudden tightness in her chest was wrought by disappointment or joy for the reprieve, he added, "I will wait for you to ask for it."

She sputtered a bit. "F-for a kiss?"

"Aye."

"I can assure you that will not happen." She breathed raggedly with relief.

"Time will reveal to us if that is true."

"I-I cannot ever see myself *asking* you to..." she trailed off and gave a shaky laugh. No, she would never. She knew herself well.

---

THE ENTIRE DAY WAS simply miserable. It began to rain when they were not twenty minutes into their drive. Malcolm, once again sitting in the back of the wagon with Katie and Henry, seemed unperturbed by the stinging wet barbs, barely blinking as it poured over him, spiking his lashes and dripping down his face.

Thankfully, and bless him, he'd made no comment about the way the day had started, said nothing to Katie at all, gave her no sly glance that she wondered if Alec had cautioned him to leave off teasing her.

By midday, she and Henry were soaked through and her shoulder was throbbing that she briefly bared it to Malcolm, asking if her flesh was bright red, unable to see as it was so close under her chin. It was not, he thought. Even Henry was made melancholy by the rain, his earlier conversation with Malcolm, when they'd first set out, quiet and quick.

"Malcolm, where will Mam and me live when we get to Swordmair?"

The big man shrugged. "Haven't thought about that. Morven dinna live inside the castle walls, nor even in the village. We haven't been home in almost a year, I'm no' sure what cottages—if any—might be vacant. Aye, but the mistress will take good care of you."

"Who's the mistress?" Henry asked.

"Alec's mam. Nice lady. A coddler, you ken."

Henry had nodded and tucked his head more deeply against his mother, away from the cold rain.

Sometime later, when she'd been tortured enough inside her own head for that kiss, when she could resist no more, she asked quietly of Malcolm, "What happens if we reach Swordmair, and...perhaps it's not a good fit, either for Me and Henry, or for Swordmair? What happens then?"

Malcolm showed her a scowl, his thick brows bunching together while his lips pursed. But his answer did give her some relief. "I'll return ye myself to Dalserf or take ye anywhere ye want to go. Ye give the word, and I'll get ye out of Swordmair."

They stopped only once all day, and Katie and Henry dashed through the rain to find relief in the trees and when she returned, Alec MacBriar sat atop his huge destrier beside the wagon, talking to Malcolm.

"If no' for the rain, we might have made good time, might've pushed to reach Swordmair tonight," Alec was saying, "but we've lost time, will have to camp out one more night."

Malcolm stood on the ground at the rear of the wagon, where they'd left him after he'd helped Katie and Henry alight. He shrugged and responded to Alec, "Makes no difference if we get home before dark or before the sun rises tomorrow. I say we push on."

"We'd need to stop at least an hour tonight to rest the horses," Alec argued. His hazel eyes rested on Katie as she neared, even as he continued speaking to Malcolm. "Canna think they can walk twenty hours, no rest."

"Aye, give 'em an hour. We can move in the dark up here, safer now closer to home. To Swordmair by sunrise." Malcolm turned and lifted Katie by her waist to set her back into the wagon bed.

She settled herself first before meeting Alec's gaze again. He watched her still, said nothing more to Malcolm, seemed content to disturb her with the power of his regard.

"Can I ride with you, Alec?" Henry asked, having not followed Katie up into the vehicle.

Still, his gaze kept with Katie. "If your mam says aye."

She nodded quickly. She didn't give consent to earn his favor, but to please her son, and because there really was no reason to say no. If Alec didn't object, she had no cause to deny her son.

They took to the road again, or rather to the never-ending patchwork landscape, moving from meadow to hill and through woods and across streams, the sullen rain their constant companion.

With naught to do but huddle inside her cloak and the fur, trying to stay warm, Katie was left with little choice but to address the entire circumstance of this morning. Sighing with some weariness at the very thought, she was not entirely sure that a sunny sky would have colored her deliberations about that kiss this morning any differently, but she decided this was not the way she'd have chosen to begin her new life.

*Something draws me to you.*

Aye, that she understood, might have said something similar—if questioned at knifepoint, mayhap.

What was it about Alec MacBriar that intrigued her so, despite her previous certainty that she really didn't like him? True, the very essence of the man was appealing. Beyond handsome, built for war and shelter and apparently bewitching kisses, he had much to recommend him. Was it only then, residual wariness or resentfulness over the first few minutes of their very first meeting that distorted the whole picture of the man?

And, more importantly, was it all truly and simply merely a game to him?

Having no answers, having only an ache about her temple for all the unknowns, Katie resolved that she would do well to avoid Alec MacBriar and his magnificent kiss altogether.

---

"AND WHEN WE STOP IN a bit, you first make sure your mam needs no help with anything before you get your grub, aye?"

Henry nodded in front of him. "Mam dinna need a lot of help. She got better already faster than Malcolm. He dinna wake for a long time."

"Aye, she's verra strong," Alec readily agreed. "Still, you ask her, aye?"

"Yes, sir. Will there be another battle before we get to Swordmair?"

"Nae, lad. We'll find no English this far north, God willing, and we'll no' travel any unfriendly clan lands."

"Can I be a soldier?"

"When you're older," Alec answered, "and if your mam allows you."

"She will," Henry assured him. "She dinna like to be scared. I can save her when I'm bigger."

"Aye, that's a good lad. Was your da' a soldier?"

"He must've been," Henry allowed, which was not quite a definitive answer. "He could slay ten men all by himself. His sword was the mightiest sword in all the world, and Mam says he was as clever as he was brave."

Alec was sorry he asked. The man couldn't have been that great, or he'd not have died and left her alone. *Jesu*. Catching himself, he rolled his eyes at his own perverse thinking.

Mercifully, the heavy rain had finally exhausted itself, though a persistent mist seemed to hang thickly in the air. They paused along a rolling stream just before dark and Henry did indeed run straight for his mother. Alec gave his horse to Simon as Henry stood on tiptoe over the rails of the cart. His mother smiled at whatever he said to her and alighted from the wagon, taking Henry's hand to find some privacy.

They were gone long enough that Alec's brow furrowed and eventually he made to follow them, his hand on the hilt of his sword. While the horses were fed and watered, Alec walked upstream, relaxing when he spied Katie and Henry huddled together much further ahead. Actually Katie was sat upon a flat-topped rock, as tall as Henry's knees, and Henry stood very close. As her back faced Alec, he realized that she'd pulled her arm completely free of the sleeve, likely easy to do since the gown had been cut so drastically.

Henry was attempting to wrap her wound with a long strip of linen.

Moving around to her front, Alec perused her arm and shoulder but briefly, taking note of the creamy paleness.

Henry had already begun the binding that Alec was afforded no view of his inept handiwork with needle and thread.

Katie didn't fuss at his arrival, seemed only weary and cold, her shoulders slumped. She lifted her arm each time Henry made to pass the linen underneath and gave her silent enigmatic regard to Alec.

Shrugging a bit, he offered only, "I did the best I could."

"It's cleaned and closed," she allowed dully. "No worries."

"We'll share some bread and feed the horses, but then we're off again."

Henry asked, "Can I ride with Eleanor now?"

Alec made a face. "You can ask." His gaze stayed with Katie.

Katie tilted her head at him. "How is it that when you are in the midst of a battle, using two hands on two weapons, your horse knows what to do?"

He didn't answer immediately, his attention caught for a moment—once again—with how beautiful she was. Injured, bedraggled, drenched with rain, her hair flattened against her head and molded to her shoulder and chest, she was still remarkably lovely. Her blue eyes were clear, showed only curiosity, not any of her usual angst, and he was sure he knew not one person with skin as milky soft as hers.

"At the beginning of the fight, when they first came from the trees?" She prodded when his answer was delayed by his gawking.

Distraction, he thought. She was uncomfortable with his stare.

"Aye," he said and shook himself mentally. "You ken the legs then do all the work. The horse kens a knee pressed hard on the right says move left, kens two legs squeezed around him means stop, a quick kick of the heels jumps him forward. Long, steady pressure of the heels tells him to canter."

"How long does that take, to train a horse to know and do all that?"

"Many months, actually. At Swordmair, we've three men, the horse trainers, and that's all they do, constantly training war horses, from foal to full-grown. A soldier is nothing without a shrewd and powerful destrier beneath him."

"How old is your horse?" Henry asked without lifting his face from his chore.

"He's three now, almost four mayhap."

"How do I tie this, Mam?"

He'd come to the end of the linen, the strip having been wrapped many times around Katie's narrow shoulder. She turned and considered the end of the fabric held in Henry's small hands.

"Take the end and rip it straight up, trying to score it right up the middle."

He tried, likely having recalled that he'd seen his mother do the very same thing time and again, that his method was correct, but that he was young yet and not strong enough to actually tear the fabric.

"Here," Alec said, stepping forward. He went to one knee beside her, which put them eye level and took the linen from Henry. With one tug, he stripped the end into two pieces and passed one part under her arm to tie it at the top.

She swallowed visibly, a reaction to his proximity, he imagined, but otherwise held herself very still.

Alec lifted the cut end of the strap of her kirtle. "Shall I knot this together as well?"

She nodded, dropping her face from him that a quick glance showed her lashes sweeping low on her cheeks.

He was an arse, he knew, didn't know why he always felt the need to irk her, but couldn't resist asking, "Are you thinking about offering that invitation just now?" He took his time joining the two ends of her kirtle strap, letting his fingers touch the bare and cool skin of her upper arm.

To her credit, she didn't jerk her gaze to him, showing the irritation he surely courted, but stayed very still and wondered, "How did I know you might suggest that very thing?"

"Och, lass, dinna tell me I've become predictable so soon."

"Are you done?"

"Aye. For now." He raised himself off his knee, only then becoming aware of her fists, clenched so severely in her lap. This, he understood, all that coiled...whatever it was, whenever she was near.

# Chapter Eight

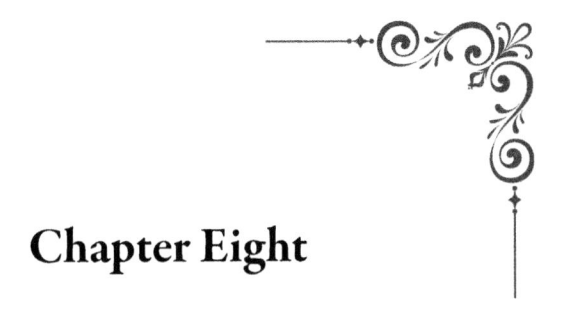

They rode then through the night, something they certainly could not have done if they'd been further south. Still, the wet paths and trails made for a slow go that the sun was risen several hours before they stepped foot onto MacBriar land.

By this time, since Henry had woken much earlier, Alec was sure the boy had made conversation with each and every MacBriar along the way, though most of his attention was usually given to Elle, who proved more stalwart than most in her ability to ignore the boy, and who did, as suspected, deny him a ride. When Malcolm had abandoned the wagon and returned to his steed this morning, declaring himself fit, Henry had begged to ride with him, which had left Katie Oliver mostly to the mercy and conversation of Fergus, driving the wagon. After a while though, Fergus was forced to slow as Boswell was following close enough to suggest he was tired of loping about. The hound joined Katie inside the bed of the wagon, stretching out on his belly, likely sleeping almost instantly.

Having tried his powerful best to avoid Katie Oliver throughout the night and this morning, Alec was then not witness to her reaction at seeing Swordmair for the first time. Alec had traveled to a number of great cities and even to the northern reaches of England on occasion, but he thought there wasn't a more magnificent sight than Swordmair with its four tall towers and expansive courtyard rising above the mist of Loch Choire. Its backdrop was the mountains of Beinn Clìbric, shrouded in a dozen shades of green, the gray sky kneeling upon its peak. Before the castle, beyond a great field of rock and thistle, dotted only sparsely with a half dozen cottages, a long bridge sat atop four arched piers of stone, wide enough to accommodate horses six abreast, stretched over the shallow loch. Never was the water so blue than here, he thought, filled suddenly with a wistfulness for home, glad to have finally arrived.

Shouts from the crenellated wall heralded their arrival that by the time they'd crossed the bridge and entered the courtyard through the lifted gate, the door to the keep had been thrown open and his parents waited his return. Others gathered as well, come from the keep or the outbuildings, the stables and the bakehouse, that a grand cheer greeted them.

Alec crossed the wide bailey quickly, reining in sharply and leaping off his horse to stand before both his mother and father.

"Oh, but there's my prayers answered," his mother cried, taking his hand, touching his midsection.

His father, the great Alexander MacBriar, stood as tall as his son and circled his arms around both Alec and his wife. "Bluidy bollocks, but ye've made my day, lad!" His voice boomed. Always. In sorrow or joy, in contemplation or when sour, Alexander MacBriar's deep voice rumbled about the air as if God himself were speaking.

Magdalena MacBriar pushed her husband's arms away from her, getting her first look at her son in almost a year. "No holes anywhere," she noted, her little blue eyes watery, "all your limbs yet attached. Oh, what a marvelous day." She reached her hand up to Alec's cheek. "Are you hungry, dear?" Her voice was scratchy and thin, wispy even, always had been.

Alec smiled down at her. "We're all hungry, ma'am, and hoping you'll provide a feast as we haven't seen in months."

"We can," she assured him with delight. "We will."

Alexander MacBriar took his son by the shoulders then, meeting him eye to eye, measuring his well-being with a steady gaze into hazel eyes so like his own. He asked no questions, found all the answers he needed in Alec's happy grin. "I missed you, lad."

"Aye, sir. But home now, no plans to leave anytime soon."

"Your mother will be pleased."

Alec nodded and he and his father watched Magdalena MacBriar greet all the soldiers individually while others inside the bailey made welcome to their friends and family as well, so long gone.

Malcolm approached and was embraced by the elder MacBriar, Malcolm having been Alexander's personal pick for Alec's captain years ago, having fought beside his father in more battles than Alec and Malcolm had yet seen.

Alec took in all the reunions, proud to have delivered this unit wholly intact, if a bit roughed up. With his hands on his hips, his smile unbroken, he scanned the yard, seeing the kitchen maid, Elsa, rush into Aymer's arms and the smithy, Kyle, greet his son, Fergus. People rushed in through the gate on foot, coming from the village or the closer group of cottages to greet the group.

In two corners of the yard, two women stood, one contentedly aloof, the other biting her lip and holding her son's hand. Eleanor was Eleanor and had no need of succor, but Alec supposed he should introduce Katie and Henry to his mother, at least. He began moving that way, across the wide bailey but saw that his mother had already spied the newcomers and was headed toward them. He arrived behind her, just in time to hear his mam say, "But you're not a soldier, a wee bit short on the years, I should say." She tweaked Henry's cheek.

Henry showed a hopeful grin. "No, ma'am."

"And's who's this pretty lass you've brought with you?"

"It's my mam, she's a healer. Are you Alec's mom?"

"I am," she answered, folding her hands over her thick middle. "The laird's wife, Maddie. It's Magdalena properly, of course, but what a millstone to hang 'round my neck, a name like that."

She'd lifted her button gaze to Katie, including her in the introduction.

"Katie Oliver, ma'am, and this is Henry. I'm pleased to meet you and I think Magdalena is a very fine name."

"For a horse, mayhap," his mother quipped.

Quite sure that Katie Oliver was aware of his approach but politely kept her attention with his mother, Alec placed his hands on his mother's shoulders and said, "Katie lent her aid to Malcolm, ma'am, that it seemed only right to invite her to Swordmair, as her situation down near Rutherglen needed improvement." He thought to ask, "Is ol' Morven still practicing?"

"Morven? Oh, but Alec, he passed last winter," she said over her shoulder. Then, to Henry, in a manner to which they would swiftly grow accustomed, she expounded, "Hard as a rock, he was, frozen in his cart just outside the village." She shrugged under Alec's hands. "Might've been dead a day, mayhap more, no one seems to ken. Or care. One foot'd been chewed off by a—"

Katie's eyes widened dramatically.

"Aye, ma'am," Alec cut in, "then Katie's coming is fortunate, indeed."

"What? Oh, yes. Do you ken about the healing, lass?" His mother asked, a wee hint of doubt in her airy tone. "You seem fairly young, a mite too bonny for all that blood and gore."

Katie smiled. "I am older than I look. I've been healing for more than a decade now, trained by a great woman."

Alec listened, realizing he knew so little about her. She'd been healing then, mayhap, before she was wed. He suddenly wondered what her life's tale was, how she came upon her occupation so early in life.

"Very well, and have you a husband to go with this lad?" The mistress of Swordmair asked.

"My husband is dead." Katie answered, apparently unoffended by his mother's bluntness.

"Mayhap that's why Alec picked you up, then. He always liked the bonny ones." Before Alec could express any indignation to this, his mam grabbed up Henry's hand. "Come along, Henry, you can help me in the kitchens while my son figures out what he's going to do with you and your mam. We've a feast to prepare."

The pair walked away, Henry nearly bouncing on his feet with excitement, not too many inches shorter than Magdalena. Alec gave Katie an apologetic grimace while she showed a hint of a grin, possibly charmed by his mother's habit of saying whatever came to mind.

"She's..." he began, but recalled he never knew quite how to explain his mam to strangers.

"Delightful," Katie surprised him by supplying.

Somehow, he might have suspected that she gave praise neither often nor so openly.

"What shall I do?" She asked then. "Will I take over Morven's cottage? Shall I start unpacking?"

Throwing a rueful glance toward the keep, where his mother had disappeared, having hoped she'd have dealt with just this issue, he said with a sigh, "I dinna want you at Morven's old place. It's too far and, in all likelihood, derelict. C'mon inside the keep. I'll need to see what's available."

---

KATIE WAITED JUST INSIDE the hall, while Alec went to find someone named Edric. She'd been inside Dalserf Castle on a few occasions, had been awed by the splendor of the main hall even while she'd wondered if English loyalties or good old fashioned hard work had decorated that keep with so much finery.

Swordmair's main hall was possibly longer and wider than that of Dalserf, and mayhap grander for its simplicity. Slim windows, high upon the two story walls, were clean and without glass but offered a sufficient amount of morning light to brighten the room. The farthest wall was white-washed and decorated with family crests and shields and a variety of weapons. There was no decoration aside from those implements and the grouping was haphazard at best, and yet there was a charm to how simply the MacBriar pride was displayed, neither framed in gold nor cased in glass. The wide planks of the floor were clean and surprisingly bereft of the rushes that hid so much dirt and odors. The hall was large enough to accommodate three rows of trestle tables and boasted two huge hearths. The tables were matched only by the uniformly faded wood as each had its own design.

Some were surrounded by mismatched chairs and stools and others flanked by low and crude benches. Tempering the patchwork atmosphere of the room were a few well-placed, soft and womanly touches; atop each table, a strip of tattered lace stretched from one end to the other; there was no massive chandelier suspended from the cavernous planked ceiling, but upon every table sat a round metal trencher, each holding two or three candles, of different widths and heights; no great and ancient tapestries hung on any of the walls, but over the doorways and in one corner of the room, long gauzy swags of linen softened the starkness; one table, sitting solitary at the far end of the room, was draped with a crisp white cotton cloth, and upon the metal where sat those candles, little sprigs of thistles and greens had been set.

'Twas all very pretty, with an eye for charm and not ostentation.

Katie removed her threadbare cloak then, hoping the day improved and that she might be warm again. She folded it over her good arm just as Eleanor stepped into the hall from somewhere deeper inside the keep.

The woman's expression showed yet no hint of thawing, and her greeting, such as it was, hinted that a melting might never come.

"Just idling? Ye have no work to be getting at? Or have ye smiled pretty and the lads are managing your affairs again?"

Supposing her lack of surprise spoke more about what she'd learned about Eleanor's manner than anything else, Katie sighed and dared to stride closer to the giant woman, effectively stepping into her path as she crossed the hall. Eleanor halted, seeming to understand her own hostility must receive some form of retaliation.

"Eleanor, I'm thinking we'll have very little need for any interaction now so that I don't care that you do not like me, but do you really have to behave so boorishly? Just ignore me, and I'll do the same. There's no need to assert your dominance at every meeting."

Eleanor only smirked with no small amount of nastiness and stepped around Katie.

"But, Eleanor," Katie called after her, "If you ever mistreat my son, I will slit your throat."

Eleanor hadn't turned back around, kept right on walking away, shouting out a bark of laughter in answer to Katie's threat.

Katie watched her disappear through the door and out into the courtyard and shook her head with lingering frustration. "I might better poison her slowly," Katie decided.

"Poison who?"

Katie whirled and found Alec striding from the same corridor through which Eleanor had come.

With a sigh and nothing to hide, she confessed, "Eleanor."

He blew out a short and humorless chuckle. "You dinna wanna poke that beast, lass."

"She's impossibly sullen. But to only me? Or is she like that with everyone?"

Alec stopped when he reached her. Casually, he plucked at a thin little twig that had fastened onto her cloak. He did not discard it carelessly onto the clean floor but walked over to the hearth and tossed it within, saying, "She's actually no' usually verra crusty. No' sure what's eating at her, but she'll get over it." When he returned, he slid his hand into the bend of Katie's elbow and led her outside. "Edric said one of the nearby cottages is empty."

"But Henry...?"

"Is happily eating his fill in the kitchens, charming one and all. We'll be back 'fore he misses you."

The two wagons that had carted the Olivers and all their belongings had been abandoned inside the bailey. Alec helped Katie to climb up into the one which held their personal items, directing her onto the seat rather than the wagon bed. He perched next to her and snapped the reins against the palfrey's back, circling in the yard to turn the vehicle around and then passing through the gate and along the well-worn road until they came upon six similar houses, all neatly thatched with white-washed walls. They stopped at the fourth one.

Locking the brake and stowing the reins, Alec hopped down and turned to fetch Katie. She didn't need assistance, truly, as she had one good arm and might have used the seat to push off from, but thought there was no need to be rude and ignore his outstretched hand.

When her two feet hit the ground, she followed him as far as the door. They might have gone right in, but that the door was wedged and refused to respond to Alec's persuasion until he was forced to put his shoulder into it. It gave way with a loud groan, spewing a cloud of dust at them.

They were immediately assaulted with an unpleasant odor, the likes of which suggested more than poor housekeeping and something closer to decomposition.

"Whew!" Alec exclaimed, waving his hand in front of his face.

"Good heavens," Katie said, her eyes watering almost instantly. The first thing she noticed after the smell was the shaft of light spilling onto the middle of the floor. "Oh, my," she said, regarding the large irregular hole in the roof, and the thatch that hung in or had fallen down to the floor.

When Alec blew out a disgruntled breath and sent her an apologetic grimace, Katie sought to be optimistic and said, "Nothing a good scrubbing cannot fix. Once the roof is repaired, I'm sure it will be...just fine." Glancing around showed that the former tenants had left the cottage in shambles. Household items lay all around the floor, two timbers at the far end were dropped from the roof and leaned across the width of the house, and a great portion of the wattle and daub of the wall at the rear was missing. Biting her lip, she decided it would take her several days at least just to make it livable. "It will be fine," she said again, not wanting to be or sound ungrateful. On the bright side, "It's certainly much larger than where we've come from."

She tried to smile at Alec.

He shook his head and grabbed her hand, turning her around, leading her outside. "You're no' living there."

She was shuttled back in to the wagon and they drove across the picturesque bridge by which they'd come into Swordmair, but now turned right at the far side of the loch and followed a narrow trail into a beautiful grove of silver birch trees.

Alec explained, "The village is beyond the trees. Two empty cottages there. I'd wanted you closer to the castle." At Katie's speculative glance, he clarified, "Thought you might feel safer if your house were closer."

"Oh." She was just about to ask if the village was very far when the trees thinned and were left behind. The village lay just ahead. With some excitement for this happy circumstance, she announced, "Oh, it's so close!" She'd not have to trek so long in inclement weather if needed at the castle. How lovely. She counted mayhap twenty different cottages, rather grouped upon a few meandering roads, forming somewhat of a circle, the outskirts of the village being barren fields, harvest gone now, and a bright green meadow where sheep and goats lazed.

Alec steered the wagon around the first wide corner and halted in front of a cottage tucked between several others, the door curiously painted a bright blue. Katie glanced around but saw no persons milling about. She hoped her neighbors were friendly, her stomach suddenly knotting.

"I'll have words for Edric if this one proves to be anywhere near as awful as the first," Alec said as he helped her alight once again.

It was not awful at all. Dark and dusty, true, but the roof and walls were intact, the entire home empty of any remnants of the previous residents, save for a few pieces of useful furniture. It was easily twice the size of the home Katie had known for nearly a decade. The hearth stood against the middle of the long back wall, flanked by uneven but secure stones.

Alec, in front of her, assessing the cottage as well, turned with some expectation at her.

She smiled happily, not adverse to allowing her excitement to show.

He seemed to relax then and walked back outside while Katie spun around and considered all that she might do with so much space. Alec returned shortly, bearing baskets and crates of her belongings, stacked and crowded in his strong arms.

This prompted Katie to move. Ten minutes later, the wagon was empty, and her new home was filled with most of her meager possessions, stacked along the front wall until she settled them properly.

Alec straightened, having set down the last bit of goods, and pointed to the far end of the room. "Mayhap we can build a few walls, make two bedchambers here at this end."

"Two bedchambers?" She stepped forward, considering.

"Henry won't be seven forever, lass."

There wasn't any part of her that liked to admit when he was right, but the truth was, she'd had similar thoughts not too long ago. "Aye," she said with some dejection. She didn't want Henry to grow up.

With a melancholy sigh for this thought, Katie bent and plucked something from the hard earth floor. 'Twas only a large stone, she realized, and then took one step to remove another, which had come loose from the packed earth. When she straightened and turned, she nearly bumped into Alec.

She went completely still, closing her mouth against the quick breath that wanted to come. He seemed in no hurry to move himself out of her way, seemed quite pleased to trouble her with such closeness. She wished he wouldn't, couldn't imagine she'd done anything to warrant it, to attract his notice. She hadn't stared overlong at his gorgeous mouth, she was sure, or looked longingly upon his plaid and tunic, recalling what beauty was hidden beneath. She hadn't set her gaze on him with any admiration, none that was visible, that she recollected. She hadn't even—

"Do I disturb you, lass?"

She swallowed and nodded, whispered, "You bring...chaos." And he knew he did. It twirled in her belly and lodged in her chest and he liked doing that to her, she somehow knew.

"Chaos is good though, aye?"

"Is it?" She thought not.

"Aye. It is. It forces you to think and be in a way you secretly find splendid. Be honest, lass. You like my chaos."

"I do not—cannot—trust it."

"Dinna trust *it*? Or its purpose? Or...dinna trust me?"

"Aye. All of it." She closed her eyes for just a moment, reveled in the feel of his hot breath on her cheek, let it linger, and then she forced herself away. Raising her face, she took several steps out of his reach and turned on him, sorry that there was nothing she could do about her hands, nervously tripping over each other at her waist. In a stronger voice, she told him, "I simply do not understand your motives. What's the point of all this?"

"All this?"

"You are either attempting to seduce me or frighten me, and I appreciate neither."

His expression, the intensity of it, didn't change. "I dinna want to frighten you."

"I think you do."

He inclined his head almost imperceptibly, accepting this, or at the very least, not refuting this. Turning, he kicked out the stool from the table that had remained with the cottage and sat, facing her. He rubbed his hands along his thighs. She'd seen him do that before.

"I dinna mean to frighten you. If I tell you precisely what's going on in my head"—here he gave a sheepish, somehow still humorless smirk—"whenever I seem to be within arm's reach of you, will you consider it? I'll tell no lies."

"I-I am willing to listen."

"Fair enough. First, let me ask: trust aside, why dinna you want to be seduced?"

She bristled, but only because she didn't want to be questioned. Not about anything. She gave the most expedient answer, which also happened to be closest to the truth, though she hadn't really thought long and thoroughly over this, she knew. Of late—since he had kissed her—she'd spent too much time considering how to keep herself *from* being seduced. "I'm not...that is, I don't—I mean, mayhap you are familiar with women who like to be...seduced simply for the sake of being seduced, but I'm not...made like that."

He rather winced. "You're telling me that you've no liking for the end product of seduction."

Katie frowned in response. "I did not say that. I just don't...do it for the sake of doing it." Frustrated by this monumentally unseemly conversation, she said, "You are supposed to be telling me what's in your head."

"Aye, but you've answered so many questions just there that it won't be necessary."

Her jaw fell. And then she figured it out. "You want to couple with me, but only for the sake of coupling."

For the space of a second, he appeared as if he would—at least wanted to—deny it. "I dinna ken you well enough to want more."

*More.*

His delivery was unfortunate, his honesty rather brutal, but she had to appreciate the truth, anyhow.

"Well, I'm pleased to have that settled then."

Alec lifted a brow in question.

Stymied by his confusion, Katie explained in a curt voice that made her proud, "You want something I'm not willing to give. I do not know you very well, but I believe you'd not ever force it, so that I consider the entire matter at an end."

He nodded, slowly. Ruefully? After a moment, he said, "You have so much anger, lass."

She did. She knew that. Or rather, she'd lived with worry and fear for so long, which often manifested itself as hostility, that she wasn't sure it wasn't who she truly was, or if she simply couldn't recall how to behave without anger.

She only shrugged, not sure what he expected her to say. She shifted uncomfortably on her feet, left off claiming she might have said the same about him. But then, what would be the point?

Alec stood. "I'll bring the other wagon down in a bit and send 'round lads tomorrow, use them for what help you need to get settled. They can erect a counter there at that end for your needs." He walked to the open door. His hand rested on the jamb for a moment before he turned and faced her again. "I'll leave you to it." He watched her a moment before adding, "I hope that Swordmair pleases you, Katie Oliver, that you ken it's a better life here, mayhap find some joy." Another pause. "Mayhap some peace as well."

She cried when he left, when his footfalls could no longer be heard moving further away. It started slowly, just a whimper, heat pooling in her chest, until it grew, spilling out that she clapped her hand over her mouth.

She didn't cry for Alec MacBriar or because he might quit his nebulous pursuit, but for the pattern it represented in her life.

"Ol' Maybeth willna let me near ye 'cept if I am willing to wed with ye," her husband had said so many years ago. "If that's what I've got to do...." Hindsight had shown that those words, in effect, had been his proposal.

There had been others before Farquhar. Boswell had run off Eagan Tonny when he'd made loose with his hands after she'd stitched up his father's leg. She'd been invited to wed by persons with whom she'd spent even less time than Alec MacBriar, their intentions as clear as her husband's had been. Older and wiser, she had understood them better.

And then Farquhar.

Possibly Gordon Killen had been unique in his pursuit, as he'd not ever tried so much as to hold her hand.

Katie fell gracelessly into the chair Alec had vacated and gave herself the same speech she'd used so many times before. She didn't need to find love. She didn't need a man. She didn't crave the physicality of a marriage great enough to become chattel once again. She wouldn't barter her body for whatever fleeting but surely meaningless benefit it might bring her.

Her son was her life.

She needed nothing else.

# Chapter Nine

Katie spared one last glance at what progress she'd made—very little, on the whole—but was excited about the unexpected delight she found in her new cottage. She been busy over the last hour, industrious enough to have dispelled her tears and nearly all thoughts of Alec MacBriar. She closed the door behind her and made her way back to the castle, intent on collecting Henry. She didn't want him getting underfoot or becoming bored with whatever kitchen task the mistress had set him.

While she indeed appreciated the short walk up to the keep, she chewed her lip outside the door, which had been closed, wondering if she were allowed to simply walk right in.

"Staring at the door dinna open it, lass. You need to push it."

Turning, grinning already at Malcolm's words, she found him walking toward her from what appeared to be the stables, the first of many low-roofed buildings that made up the northern wall of the keep.

She admitted willingly to him, "I didn't know if I—"

"The hall is open to visitors always," Malcolm explained, stepping past her to open the door. "Alec said he found you a place. It'll do?" He asked, preceding her inside the hall.

"It's wonderful, so spacious," she said. "I've come to collect Henry. Where are the kitchens?"

"Through here," he answered, leading her to the archway at the corner of the white-washed wall. He was forced to duck a wee bit inside the dark corridor, which twisted and turned toward the very rear of the keep.

Katie thought to say, "You should stop by tomorrow, Malcolm. I should give one last look to your injuries."

"Aye, I'll do that."

The corridor widened and lightened and finally opened into a tall and wide room, crowded with at least a dozen industrious people, filled with smoke and steam and laughter.

Malcolm walked her straight to where Henry sat upon a tall stool at the long counter in the middle of the room, next to Magdalena MacBriar, both of them pinching all the stems and leaves from a pile of blueberries. Malcolm helped himself to three bannocks, stacked high upon a plate in the middle of the counter, as he passed.

"Henry lad, your fun is done. Here comes Mam." With that, he flashed his charming grin at Katie and walked out a rear door.

"Aw," her son grumbled, though was excited to see her, Katie thought.

"I hope he hasn't been any trouble," Katie said to the mistress.

"Trouble?" Magdalena frowned and smiled at the same time at Katie. "The lad's a gem, good company."

Relieved, Katie addressed Henry. "We've quite a bit of work ahead of us, Henry. We have a new cottage."

His eyes lit up at this news, even as he didn't necessarily look as if he was happy to leave the kitchen and Magdalena.

"You'll join us for the feast tonight, aye, Katie Oliver?" The mistress wondered, plopping sometimes almost every other pruned blueberry into her mouth.

"Oh, no, but thank you."

"But what will you eat? You cannot have settled your kitchen so soon, aye?"

"Mam, please," Henry begged, folding his hands pleadingly at his chest, showing what he assumed was an irresistible grin.

"Canna say no to that face," Magdalena MacBriar chortled, her cheeks easily reddened. "Ye come up when you hear the bell peal, lad. Bring your mam with ye." She winked at Katie and then innocently returned her attention to her blueberry stash.

Not yet committing, Katie gave her thanks to the mistress and extended her hand to Henry, who jumped off the stool and left the kitchen with her.

Inside the corridor, Henry began eagerly, "Maddie said—"

"Henry, I dinna care what permission she gives, but you're to address her properly."

"Mam, I did. Called her mistress all the time until she said she would no' talk to me any more if I kept it up."

This struck Katie somehow as rather funny that she laughed a bit. "She's very sweet, I think."

"I like her," Henry agreed.

---

BY THE TIME THE BELL sounded from Swordmair, three long and slow gongs, Katie noted, she and Henry had not only set up their bed and linens and arranged most of her sparse kitchen items, but they had fetched water from the creek and washed up, though sadly she hadn't any fire wood yet to warm the water or the cottage. They'd changed into their cleanest garments, ones washed with Alec MacBriar's help, and were ready when the supper call came. Katie had decided that her cloak was unusable until she laundered it and wrapped herself instead in the old woolen shawl, which she'd acquired from Maybeth, who had been the only mother she had ever known, who had taught her the healing arts.

Henry didn't hold her hand as he normally might but bounced and bounded along the trail, jumping and scraping his hands against low hanging leaves, so much livelier than she'd seen him in recent memory. He talked non-stop as well, though Katie could only hear some of what he said.

"...And Maddie said she was going to mix cream and sugar into the blueberries and I dinna ken what that's gonna taste like, but it sounded good. The one girl, I think her name was..." he carried on, further ahead now that Katie heard him not at all. But she smiled anyhow.

Guards stood atop the gate and along the curtain wall, nodding pleasantly as Katie and Henry passed beneath. The courtyard of the keep was lit with wall-hung torches, though the sun wouldn't set for hours yet, and many people and groups of families walked ahead and behind them, all gathering for the feast.

And what a feast it was. Not once in her life had she ever dined in the hall of a castle, not ever anywhere outside whatever her home was. She didn't know if there was any protocol to follow, if there were an ascendancy order to the trestle tables, or if people just sat anywhere. But the seats were empty as of yet, all the folks milling about, making jolly conversation with their neighbors and friends. Standing just inside, having only moved out of the way of the door, Katie held Henry's hand tightly, unsure, uneasy, biting her lip and looking around for any familiar face.

Her awkwardness was thankfully short-lived, as the laird and mistress appeared and took their seats and the entire room moved about to claim their own. Aymer came bounding through the door then, spotting Katie and Henry.

"Aye, c'mon now," he said, taking Katie's elbow. "Canna stand and eat."

Bless him.

He directed her to a table in the middle left aisle, where Fergus and a lass were seated—whom Katie was sure she'd spied in the kitchens earlier when she'd fetched Henry—their four hands joined across the table. Aymer climbed over the back of the bench and sat next to Henry while Katie sat opposite, next to Fergus. Aymer quipped to Fergus, "She'll need at least one paw to eat, lad. Let her be."

In the next moment, Simon joined them and then the laird stood and banged his tankard on the table, which effectively quieted the hall rather all at once. Katie straightened and glanced up at the head table, seeing that the laird stood in front of a large ornate chair, with carved arms that depicted the head of a wolf. Seated next to him was his wife on his left and Alec on his right. Next to Alec sat Malcolm, his head angled, his lips moving that Alec nodded at whatever he said. On Magdalena's left sat a man Katie did not recognize, about the laird's age, but slimmer, neatly dressed, his gray hair cropped close, very distinguished looking. Katie wondered if he were a guest.

"Aye now. Welcome! Welcome! Aye, and God bless us all, it's good to have a full house again." He opened his hand toward his son. "Favored by God yet again, for look who He's returned to us once more."

His voice was ideal for this, for any occasion that required speech to carry far and wide, and to so many ears. Deep and resonant, the laird's voice suited him perfectly, as large and imposing as was the man, the richness of it filling the hall.

Cups and tankards were banged on the trestle tables and choruses of "Aye, aye!" followed. Someone whistled and Katie smiled softly at this warm response. Alec nodded slightly at this praise, seeming to stare at no one in particular, mayhap only the edge of the table upon which one hand sat. At his side, Malcolm gamely raised his tankard, inducing a louder cheer.

The laird continued, which silenced the room again. "Gone and back, and no the worse for wear, battling for honor and tradition and our blessed freedom. Your future laird proudly reports that Robert the Bruce, our true king, fights bravely and steadfastly, gaining ground"—he winced a bit here— "slowly, but certainly. We can do no more just now, until Bruce builds his own army stronger, greater in number, and as thirsty for English blood as any true and honorable Scotsman."

Another cheer rang out while the laird bent and said something low to his son. Alec glanced up and replied, his voice unheard as well, and then surprised Katie by lifting his striking gaze to meet hers directly. Embarrassed to have been caught staring at him, she lowered her eyes to the hands in her lap.

And then she was startled to hear the laird say, "And where is Katie Oliver?"

Gasping, she raised her eyes again, finding the laird, watching him search about the room.

"Katie Oliver!" He called again.

Laughing, Aymer said, "Up, lass. Stand up."

Horrified, she did so, slowly, haltingly.

The laird noticed her movement, the only person standing aside from himself. and his bright eyes lit on her. "Och, and isn't she a bonny one? *Jesu*! So here she is, folks. Ministered well to Malcolm here, like as no' a still-breathing man because of her fine handiwork. Now, dinna get excited, there's no saving all the rest of Malcolm—God bless him."

Laughter rang out. Malcolm lifted his hands and pinched his face comically at this jesting, moving his smiling gaze around the room.

"Aye, Katie Oliver will tend all your aches and pains and sew up your troubles, I ken. Morven, God save him, left us in a wee bit of a dither. Aye, but now we've Katie Oliver in our midst, here to stay, and kind enough to be so young that it seems she'll be with us long after I'm gone. Will ye no' welcome her kindly to Swordmair?"

More cheers sounded and more tankards lifted, the noise thrumming in her ears and her chest.

She'd never received such recognition—any recognition!—in all her life. Truth be known, it was as warm and lovely as a smile from Henry, one of those sweet ones he gave when he was in awe of her cleverness or pleased with her teasing or such. But her cheeks were red, nonetheless, the singular attention unsettling. She bobbed her head a bit at all the curious regard settled upon her and quickly retook her seat. Aymer, across from her, was grinning and saluting her with his tankard.

And then supper.

Katie and Henry pursued no effort to keep their eyes from widening as so many generous platters were laid about every table. Henry actually shifted on the bench, folding his legs under him to make himself higher, that he might see and reach every bit. One entire platter was piled high, with some endeavor at a pleasing presentation, with cheese and sweet breads and fruits. Another long dish with curved ends offered cutlets of meat, smothered in a thick sauce showing mushrooms and onions. The blueberries Magdalena and Henry had pared made their presence inside a shallow and hammered silver bowl, mixed with the cream and chunks of sugared cakes. Garlic seasoned beans and two-bite individual pork pies completed the meal.

Every bite was divine and, Katie was sure, never to be forgotten. At some point, though, she had to caution herself—and then Henry as well—to not overeat lest they be made sick by bursting bellies.

Mostly, Katie and Henry only listened to the constant and pleasant conversation at their table, too invested in the fare and too new to Swordmair to contribute much. When all the tables had been cleared, people seemed only to linger, chatting still, the din merry. Music was strummed from some corner of the room, lifting Katie's gaze to find its source, though she could not. Occasionally some folks left their seats, greeting others at different tables. Katie was happy to sit and watch.

She hadn't paid too much attention to the soldiers on their journey, her mind fairly preoccupied with any combination of dread and hope and possibly so many other negative, energy-wasting things—and of course, Alec MacBriar. But she observed much throughout the evening, noting that Aymer and Simon seemed to be quite a pair, moving as one unit from table to table, chortling and guffawing louder and louder as the evening wore on. Malcolm never moved from his seat, kept in constant conversation with Alec, and then John and Ranald who stood before the head table. Fergus was never far away from the pretty lass, whose name was Margaret, she'd since learned. The elder MacBriar, likewise, stayed seated, though was rarely without company, some person seeking his attention; sometimes the meeting appeared quite serious, others showed the huge and aged man chuckling easily and loudly. Always, though, there was a hardness about his wide features. Magdalena MacBriar was up and out of her chair as soon as she'd eaten her supper, making her way to each and every table, talking cheerily to everyone.

The music seemed to grow louder then, almost as an inducement to move along with it, that soon people began to dance wherever they might find space to do so. A group at the front of the room, in the space between the head table and the rows of trestle tables, was particularly lively, their shouts and laughter sometimes drowning out the notes of the harp and the cithara.

"I think this is the happiest place on earth," Henry commented.

"I think you might be right," she said, leaning toward her son. "This is our new life, Henry. I'm very excited."

His bright eyes lit on her face. "I hope we stay here forever."

Nodding, she acknowledged, "Me, too."

"Can I go now, to see what they're about in the corner?"

Katie swiveled her head, following Henry's gaze. In the far corner, opposite the kitchen end of the keep, several young boys were bent on their knees, rather tightly in a circle. Two or three of the lads appeared around Henry's age.

She turned and nodded. "Have fun," she said with a smile, heartened by his willingness to engage with strangers, something she found so very difficult to do. He scooted quickly from the bench, his little face lit with no trifling amount of excitement.

He approached and only stood behind the circle of lads for a few seconds, until one boy lifted his head. The lad said something to Henry, at which her son shrugged. But then the two directly in front of Henry each moved over, just enough to make space for Henry to join their circle.

Her regard so happily consumed by Henry, Katie was startled by a voice very near to her ear.

"They say you're a fine healer."

Whirling, her jaw gaped briefly to find the elder MacBriar bent over her, his hand on the back of her chair.

"I am. Katie Oliver, sir," she said, by way of introduction. "You are very kind to welcome me—"

He disappeared, moving to her other side, swinging Katie around as he took the chair next to her.

He was huge, a big bear of a man, too large for the tragic chair, disappeared now completely from view. His eyes were a light and familiar hazel inside his ruddy cheeks. His hair was thick and rather long, mostly gray but for the near black ends, falling over his shoulder as he leaned forward.

"My son said you're competent, so I'll be asking you what we're going to do about my knees."

"Your knees, sir?"

"Aye, aching something fierce, have been for years."

"Have you prior injuries?"

"Hundreds," he answered, giving her a look that rather hinted, *what kind of man would I be if I hadn't?* "But none directly on my knees, but aye how they ache." Between them, he began to dig into his tall boots, yanking up his hose from near his ankle.

"Oh, we're going to address it right now," Katie said, bemused.

He proceeded to roll up his breeches from beneath his knee as well.

"Da'! What are ye about?" Alec appeared across the table, his outrage not feigned at all. "You will no' be showing the lass your knees just here in the hall."

"What? She's no' busy at the moment." Alec's father appeared truly perplexed by the fuss.

Alec waved his hand at his father's leg. "Cover that up. Ask Katie to come by tomorrow and discuss your bluidy knees with you."

"It's fine," Katie insisted, made merry by the old man. The fierce mien about the man had suggested he'd sooner have lopped off her head with one of his ceremonial swords than have sat beside her and bared his thick legs.

"Nae," Alec said, his countenance as grim as usual. "Mother will put a knife through his eye if she finds out."

"Perhaps I should return to the keep tomorrow afternoon," Katie said to Alec's father. "Will that suit?"

With a pursed-lip glare at his son, he nodded. "Aye, that'll do." He stood then, with a bit of a huff, and walked away.

Alec took a sip from his tankard, the vessel being quite ornate, possibly made of pewter or a dull silver but cast with a repeating pattern of thistles and wolves and swords. Over the rim he kept his hazel eyes on Katie, his brows yet drawn low.

Shifting, having too swiftly been put in a mind of their conversation only hours ago, Katie lowered her attention to the precious lace upon the table and the centerpiece of candles. She saw

Alec set his tankard down with a pronounced slowness, as if he wanted her to see it, to lift her gaze again.

She did.

And he sat down across from her, setting his elbows on the table, crossing his forearms over each other as he leaned toward her.

She recognized the look he gave her, that devilish one that brightened his hazel eyes and caused her heart to thud unnaturally. She refused to allow him to have any fun at her expense.

"So, you are the son of the laird, and one day a laird yourself," she rushed out, before he might have begun to goad her again.

He grinned, which properly expressed to her that he knew well her ploy, the distraction. But he allowed it, leaning back a bit. "Aye, no' anytime soon, though. I'd rather keep the old man around for many more years."

"But where does all your fierceness come from? Your parents are wonderfully agreeable."

The grin became more pronounced while his eyes darkened, as she'd essentially just told him that he was not at all pleasant.

"Da' was no' always like this. Was brutal in his day, greater than I'll ever be."

"Is that...is that a requirement? Brutality? To fight so recklessly, to rule so large a clan?"

"Aye. And to see the end of southern aggression. England will no' be sent packing if we welcome them with cheery smiles and trenchers of sweet breads."

"And when they're gone? *If* they are."

The grin faded, replaced by a ruthless frown. "They'll be gone," he vowed. "For good one day. Scotland will be free."

"And that is your sole desire in life? To soldier? To make war?"

He stared at her as if she'd given these words in another language. "To live free," he corrected. "What else is there?"

Katie's eyes widened. In spite of herself, and his steady, probing gaze, she laughed. "There *is* more to life. Family, children, laughter, joy."

"Won't mean a thing, if we're no' free."

"So....you'll have none of it, until war is done?"

"You letting yourself have any of that, lass?"

Swallowing thickly, she defended, "My circumstances are different. I haven't this fine keep, or a loving family or...or other opportunities."

"Aye, you do now," he countered. "Opportunities. Are you going to chase them, Katie Oliver? Embrace them?"

"I've come here, haven't I? I'd be a fool to..."

His lifted brow and the returned smirk gave her pause. He would challenge this, turn it around and accuse her of not truly embracing all that was offered to her.

She couldn't help but wonder: if his rare grins and smiles ever reached his eyes, would she react differently to him? Would she be made more susceptible?

"Very clever," she said stiffly. "Well done, and we're back to where we were this afternoon."

"It's a fine subject to address again."

"It's a closed subject."

Alec glanced toward the front of the room and the rowdy dancers and then back at Katie, inclining his head at her. She thought his teeth might be clenched now, his jaw shifting from

# THE LOVE OF HER LIFE 149

left to right. Again, he tossed his gaze at the dancers and then back at her.

Her cheeks colored at what she thought was happening, what he might be thinking. His expression was returned to that blustery darkness that was so maddeningly indecipherable, so that it was hard to tell if he were about to ask her to dance.

Malcolm, merry and mayhap slightly inebriated, suddenly appeared, bending low over the end of the table, his elbows smacking down on the wood, his face close to Katie's.

"Katie, lass! Come dance with me!"

Her breath rushed out. Much safer, dancing with Malcolm as opposed to Alec, she decided.

If she danced at all.

"I've never danced before," she confessed. "I dinna know the steps."

Malcolm didn't seem to care. He pulled her to her feet. "There are no steps, lass! We just move."

She was dragged away but quick, about to panic, unable to throw even a fleeting backward glance at Alec MacBriar. Thankfully, Malcolm had been right. There were no steps, which meant that Katie was spared any larger discomfort. People only moved and swayed and bounced, no rhyme or reason, until arms began to join, slapped onto the nearest shoulder and a circle began to move.

Katie couldn't yet lift her arm very high, forced then to swing it around Malcolm's lower back as he made a face of absurd horror when he had almost plopped his heavy forearm onto her sore shoulder. Catching himself, he did as she had, and set his big hand in the middle of her back. Simon was at her left and thankfully his hold was sloppy that the hand he'd dropped across her neck caused her no pain.

They spun round and round, two of the women in the circle trying to actually perform some steps, which slowed down the revolving circle. A cheer rose up as several children ducked between the adults, appearing in the empty center, making up their own dance. Henry was with the small group, both lads and lasses, completely at ease and game, and Katie's heart soared.

Suddenly a loud ruckus sounded from the front of the room, near the head table. The twirling stopped. All heads swiveled. Katie followed the noise and then the pointing fingers, singling out and shouting cheerily at the MacBriar soldier, John, who stood with slumped shoulders, nodding with a disgruntled smirk as he received all the notice and good-humored censure.

"What has happened?"

"He messed the floor," Simon slurred into her ear.

He had. While he held in his hand his tankard, it was tipped sideways, the contents on the wooden planked floor at his feet.

"See you in the morning, dear," Katie heard Magdalena MacBriar call out and the hall erupted in laughter.

Katie was enormously confused and sent her questioning gaze to Malcolm.

"Mistress dinna like the rushes," Malcolm explained, "says they hold more dirt and debris than they hide. She likes the clean floor and works hard to keep it that way. If you make a mess, that's you standing next to her, bright and early come morn, mopping and sloshing aside her."

Katie's eyes and mouth widened at this. "That is the most marvelously wicked and ingenious thing I've ever heard."

"Aye? She's a rascal, is the mistress."

"She's amazing."

She couldn't remember the last time she'd had such fun. Upon reflection, she wasn't sure she ever had. She danced for quite a while, until Aymer inadvertently smacked her shoulder and she excused herself. Still, she didn't want to leave, didn't want to take Henry from all this merriment.

Eventually, nearly an hour later, she was approached by a young woman she'd seen throughout the evening but that she hadn't met. Lifting her gaze to the woman showed Alec standing near as well, his unfathomable gaze upon her once more.

"I'd be Ann, ma'am," said the woman. "I wanted to tell you we're leaving." At Katie's blank stare, she explained. "We all head back together, all of us from the village, so no one gets lost or silly."

Oh, she liked that idea very much. She stood then to follow Ann, and despite her best efforts, found her eyes straying again to Alec MacBriar.

He didn't move, said nothing as she followed Ann, who passed directly in front of him. Katie lowered her gaze as she walked by him, holding her breath lest he was made aware of what his probing and heated regard did to her.

Katie and Henry joined all the families of the village and walked through the dark night and the dark trees, the group recollecting about the evening already, talking over one another, their gaiety yet curtailed.

They said goodnight to each person or family who stepped inside their home and Katie was sure she'd never known such a warm and lovely feeling in her life when the last of the group called after her and Henry when they turned at the walkway to their blue door.

"Goodnight now, ma'am. Goodnight, lad."

## Chapter Ten

She was up with the sun, but then pleased to linger inside her bed a wee bit, bringing to mind all the wondrous fun that was last night. But then the day called, she had much to do yet, and she rose quick enough, tickling Henry's nose that he might rise as well.

They were dressed, thankfully, when a sharp rap sounded at their door, though Katie had yet to attend her hair. Exchanging a curious face with Henry, she pulled open the short, blue-painted door.

A woman, shorter and rounder than Katie, but possibly having seen many more years, stood close.

"Well, here I am, your first customer, aye?" Said the woman with some cheer, despite the bloodied cloth she held wrapped around her left hand. She stepped forward, not exactly waiting an invitation, though Katie had begun to pull the door open.

She hoped the woman wouldn't judge her too harshly for the sparse furniture and remaining general clutter, since her unpacking was not yet done. She ushered her over to the stool at the table, and the woman began to unravel the cloth she'd turned round and round her hand, revealing a deep slice running diagonally across her palm.

"Oh, my," Katie said and left her there, pivoting to fetch her pouches.

With no other preamble or explanation for the hideous slice across her palm, the woman called over her shoulder to Katie. "Ye ken why the door is painted blue? The only one, you see."

"I did find it curious," Katie mused.

"Aye, but was only Martha and Callum lived here, nigh on twenty years. She were sweet, but Callum liked the ale more than I and dinna he have a fine habit of stumbling into different homes each night, too soused to ken which was his own? So the laird heard enough grousing 'bout it every month at the court sessions, he finally says aye, paint the door so the bugger'll ken where he lives."

Katie found this equally amusing and concerning, giving a spare and charitable thought to poor Martha.

"But then one day, Callum dinna find the blue door, nor any other. Unearthed him a few days later, in the low spots out in the pasture, blue and bloated. And so Martha took her bairns back down near Glasgow, had a sister there, if I recall." And with that, apparently the end of the tale, the woman promptly asked, "And how do ye like your payment? Morven, goat that he was, only ever wanted food. Sweets were his favorite. I gave birth seven times and it only ever cost me five puddings and some sweet breads." She cackled then, her laughter loud and scratchy, but somehow very charming for its hardiness.

"Well, I'm willing to trade for anything that my son or I might need," Katie said when she'd returned and sat next to the woman on the long bench. "Presently, I have no kindling or firewood."

## THE LOVE OF HER LIFE

"Och, that's an easy one. You sew this pretty and I'll send down my oldest with your fire-making stuff, and I'm getting the better deal, I ken, so mayhap I'll send down some ale as well."

"Is that your occupation then? Are you the alewife?"

"Och, nae. But I sure do like it, so I keep plenty on hand."

Katie smiled and introduced herself. "And my son is Henry."

The woman slapped her forehead with her uninjured hand. "Bluidy—och, sorry, lass. Been sitting here working my jaw all this time, dinna tell you my name. Agnes, I am. And even I canna remember all my bairns' names, so I won't bother ye with that yet. The loud, always bellowing ones, those are mine."

Her smile never left, seemed just to be permanently fixed in place. Her hair was gray and orange and wiry and her gown tattered but clean, the buttoned front stretching a bit, filled with her soft belly. Katie liked her instantly and they chatted long after her wound was sewn.

The door hadn't been closed but a few minutes after Agnes's departing figure when another knock came. Swinging the door open once more, she found Eleanor at her stoop. As ever, her expression was filled with that simmering aggression.

Holding the door with one hand, Katie lifted a brow at the woman.

Eleanor stood with her left hand covering the top of her bare right arm, just under that ridiculous fur. At Katie's silent question, she pulled her hand away, showing a deep gash across the tanned and muscled skin of her arm.

"Good heavens, Eleanor," Katie exclaimed, throwing the door wide. "Come in."

Henry, having lost interest eventually in Agnes, perked up when he saw Eleanor.

And then wasn't he a dear, when his jaw dropped and his eyes widened, reaching for Eleanor's gaze, when he saw the trouble, his concern so endearing.

Katie handed a strip of linen to Eleanor. "Hold that over it while I fetch my supplies."

"Dinna fuss, lad," Eleanor said, less snarly than any tone she might have used with Katie. "I've seen worse."

He stood next to Eleanor when she sat where Agnes had. He put his hands at the edge of the table, his thumbs underneath, his gaze moving between Eleanor's striking blue eyes and the terrific gash in her arm. "Was there another battle?" He asked.

The woman warrior shook her head. "Nae, there was no'. There was that bugger, Fergus, who dinna ken when to temper his swing during training."

Katie returned to the table and laid out her needles and thread, realizing she would need a fire soon, to boil so many of her implements before they were used again. This was her last clean needle.

First, she addressed the slash, deep enough to bleed but hopefully not carved too deep that any muscle was damaged. She sat close and manipulated the opening as needed to assess it.

"Any pain other than right there, at the cut?"

Eleanor shook her head. "It dinna need anything but Alec ordered that I see ye."

"It does need to be sewn, Eleanor," Katie advised. "Will take but a moment and will heal so much quicker."

"Aye."

"I dinna suppose I need to warn you, this will sting."

Eleanor rolled her eyes at her but remained otherwise motionless, did not flinch at all as Katie pushed the bone needle through her skin. As she sewed, aware of Henry's drawn face, managing enough flinching for both himself and Eleanor, Katie sent him about a chore. "Fetch the honey, Henry, and the smallest green pouch."

She continued running thread and needle back and forth across the three inch gash. Only the middle of it truly needed any stitching, but since she was already about the chore, she closed the entire wound.

"Eleanor," Katie said as she worked, having some sense that the woman purposefully did not watch the process, "I've just managed to secure some firewood and kindling from a neighbor—believe it or don't, you're not even my first patient today—but I was wondering about our food situation. Am I allowed to trap and fish around and about as needed, and forage for what roots and seeds I need, or are there—"

"Ye sup up at the hall."

Katie heard a frown in her reply but did not remove her attention from her work.

"But certainly, we shouldn't expect to sup there every night."

A shrug moved the arm Katie was holding. "Ye can, none would gainsay ye. Others do."

"Still, there's other meals, breakfast and whatnot. And I would feel...less a burden if I could prepare our meals myself. Also, the roots and that are for medicinal purposes, but I wouldn't want to overstep any bounds, if, well, if there were any."

"You've a job here, so you have some worth," Eleanor said, with her usual gruffness. "Take the meals in the hall. And no one is going to give you grief for procuring the wares you need to minister well, so dig up your plants and roots as you need. The fishing, I dinna ken. Best ask the mistress or the steward."

Though she'd asked the question, it had been more for conversation that Katie was surprised to find herself satisfied with the answers. "Very well. Thank you."

She finished shortly thereafter, using her teeth to trim the end of the thread, giving a critical eye to her stitches, pleased that the wound openly bled no more. "Of course, you cannot return to training for several days," she said and was forced to insist, when Elanor gave her a look suggesting she'd do as she pleased, "or you'll find yourself in this very chair again right quick."

"Aye." The consent came grudgingly. She watched as Katie mixed the honey with the dried and ground plants and applied this liberally to the sewn mark. "What do I owe you?"

Oh, how she hated to ask that question, Katie understood.

"You owe me nothing, Eleanor." She gathered all her supplies and finally met the woman's hard glare.

"I will no' be in your debt."

"You will not. Now we're even, for you putting up with us during the drive to Swordmair."

Pushing her lips out, Eleanor held Katie's gaze as she said pointedly, "He's no trouble at all."

*But Katie was*, Katie understood she was supposed to glean from her statement. She smiled at Eleanor, determined that this woman was not going to spoil her new and bright situation at Swordmair.

Henry, having heard Eleanor's vague praise, pushed his advantage. "Elle, do you want to come with me to the loch? I'm going to catch frogs. Fergus said the loch is filled to the brim with them."

Katie's grin stayed. His mother would have—had on occasion—done that very thing with him. He hadn't any idea that she'd participated in the icky fun only for his amusement, his benefit; likely he imagined that other people, other women, might also like to catch frogs in ponds.

Katie lifted her brow, daring Eleanor to refuse the smitten boy, giving no thought that somehow she trusted the woman to keep her son safe, in some way also understanding that Eleanor actually might like Henry.

Eleanor stood from the table. "Nae, lad. I dinna like frogs, too slimy. But ye can come up with me to the meadow. I've got work to do with my horse."

"He doesn't ride—" Katie was quick to interject, even as she was almost as pleased as Henry for this invitation.

"He'll no' ride alone, maybe no' at all. Gotta learn sometime though."

"Very well. Stay up at the castle then, Henry. I'll be up shortly to see the laird."

Eleanor amazed her by turning a funny smirk on her. "The old man got you looking at his knees?"

Katie laughed before she might have caught herself. "He does."

---

SHE HAD TO SUPPOSE that every time she walked up to the castle, she might well worry that she stood a chance of running into Alec. With this in mind, she decided that if so, she would behave cordially but coolly, the brief and perplexing part of their relationship now done. He was the laird's son, and she would treat him accordingly, polite but not overly friendly. She nodded as she walked, pleased with her sound plan.

There was some benefit, then, to his usually fierce mien, in that it didn't often invite dialogue, let alone friendly conversation. And really, how often would she find herself having to step foot inside the keep? Like as not, if she managed the laird's knees well today, she wouldn't often be called for her healing. And she'd already determined, despite Elanor's assurance, that she and Henry would not take all their meals in the hall. Mayhap once in a while, for Henry's benefit, but she didn't want to make a habit of it.

Truthfully, she was excited to get about her work and meet people in the village. She'd been so heartened by their general affability last night, she couldn't wait to pursue more with them.

She spied Aymer atop the wall when she walked through the gate and gave a wave to him, and was happy to find the laird in the courtyard, as she' hadn't been sure how she might have found him inside the keep, had only thought she might find the mistress in the kitchen and seek out her husband's direction.

He was speaking to the tall and handsome man, about the age of the laird, who'd sat at the family table last night. The man and the laird were perusing a ledger in the man's hands, before shifting their gazes to the roofs over the stables.

She waited until either they were done, or she was noticed.

The latter occurred first, the laird turning—pivoting awkwardly upon an apparently sore knee—and finding her standing near.

"Aye, lass. Verra kind of ye to come up so early." He addressed the man once more. "Find me later, Edric. Alec says the ol' Norrie cottage is in disrepair."

"Aye, chief," said the man, inclining his head briefly, politely at Katie.

"C'mon then, lass, we'll go on up to my bride's solar." He led the way, walking stiffly toward the keep. "I've been warned to refrain from undressing unless I'm up in the family rooms," he said over his shoulder as he passed through the door.

The hall was empty, save for a young lad cleaning out the furthest hearth of ashes.

Climbing the stairs was a painstaking task for the laird and Katie found herself wincing behind him with each step, but then hopeful that she might be able to offer him some relief.

"I'll get to a certain point, I'm thinking," he said, "either I go up or down these stairs, I'll be forced to remain there all the day."

"You won't get there yet," Katie felt confident assuring him. "We're going to take away much of that pain."

Pulling himself along with a heavy hand upon the carved railing, his voice was cheery through his pant when he said, "You do that Katie lass, and anything you want is yours. I'll make it happen."

Upon the second floor, he strode down the darkened hall and pushed open the second door, indicating that Katie should precede him. She stepped inside the most charming room she had ever seen. The entire frame, walls and floor and ceiling, had been white-washed. The lone thin window was hung with creamy, lace edged linen and the furniture was neither crude nor too fussy, but showed turned legs and upholstered seats, the round table set between two arm chairs covered with yet another lace doily.

It was like stepping into another place or another home, so vastly different from all the dark wood and exposed timber in the rest of the keep.

"It's so beautiful," she said, her voice tinted with both awe and envy.

"My bride, she brought her English ways up here with her, and what do I care if it makes her happy?"

Katie absolutely adored that he called her his bride, though they must have been wed by now more than thirty years. "The mistress is English?" She certainly neither sounded nor looked so.

"Used to be," the laird said, plopping down with a great puffed breath into one of the two chairs.

Katie set down her larger, all-purpose treatment bag on the table. "Can you simply disavow your heritage?" She asked with a grin.

"Half-English, to be precise," the laird explained, emitting a grimace as he lifted one leg up onto the small, tufted ottoman at his feet. When it was set there securely, he winked at Katie. "I cured her of that."

Katie went to her knees upon the timber at his feet and teased him, "She is a very lucky woman then, aye?"

He latched onto this, smacking his hand upon the arm of the chair. "That's what I've been telling her. Everyday. For thirty years."

"So very kind of you to remind her so regularly."

Laird MacBriar chuckled easily, his rounded belly jiggling with his laugh. "Now you get it, lass."

"Let's look at those knees then, sir."

---

OUTSIDE THE DOOR, ALEC shamelessly eavesdropped. He might have entered, announced his presence. His father wouldn't have minded, mayhap Katie not either. But she would stiffen in his presence, guard her words and withhold smiles, he was sure.

He'd known—had seen some evidence of it—that away from him, in more agreeable company, she was very natural and charming and easy to make smile, even made her own fun here and there. She'd been a marvel inside the hall at supper last night. First, so bewitchingly shy when his father had singled her out to introduce her to all of Swordmair's people, and then, so adorable upon the dance floor. It had been Malcolm's urging of course—she'd not ever of her own volition go willingly, Alec was sure. But she'd been game, moving at first nervously, self-consciously, until the general merriment simply could not be ignored, that she was soon bobbing around as gaily as the rest of them.

But this—her ability to blend well, if slowly, with others, but not with him—suggested that he might consider either leaving her alone altogether, as he'd said he would but was already struggling with, or that he might spend more time in her company, that she became just as cozy with him as she so easily might with everybody else. Aye, excepting Eleanor, of course.

Listening as intently as he was, by the time he realized someone was coming toward him, he'd effectively been caught. He turned, relieved to find only his mother, who was walking on her toes with some effort to be quiet, obviously having surmised what her son was about.

At his side, while Alec tried to appear casual, she whispered, "Careful what ye listen for, love, might not always like what ye hear through doors."

And yet she pressed her ear to the thick timber, jerking back quickly when she recognized the voices within. Sending a merry grin to Alec, who couldn't remember the last time he had actually blushed, she whispered, "Aw now lad, just stop scowling at her at every turn and she'll smile at ye."

Alec clenched his jaw and strode away just as his mother pushed open the door.

---

"GOOD MORN TO YE, KATIE Oliver," called out her neighbor, Agnes.

Katie smiled and returned the greeting as she closed the blue door behind her. Agnes's hand was bandage-free now, a week gone from cutting it. "Flower picking?" She asked, as Agnes was approaching her own door, carrying a sloppy bunch of late summer wildflowers in muted colors of pale pink and dusky mauve.

Agnes nodded, squishing up her nose. "My oldest, Mary, was a great help over the last week. I've naught to give her but my thanks and these silly things."

"How sweet," Katie said, smitten with the very idea. "I bet she won't think they're silly."

Agnes shrugged and waved and entered her home.

With that, Katie headed up to the castle, folding her arms across her chest against the biting wind, cataloguing her plans for the day. She'd been at Swordmair for almost a week now, having learned fairly quickly that she simply hadn't enough hours in her day of late. It would get better, she knew, but over the past many days, she'd had the setting up of the cottage to contend with, and the general ministering to the people of Swordmair, who'd not had a proper healer in nigh on a year. She begrudged it not at all, gratified by the warm welcome and the instant trust they placed in her, but she was struggling, truthfully, to keep up with her personal chores and her own household. As it was, they had indeed supped each night in the hall, as she had yet to provide one item of food in her own home.

Henry was barely at her side the last few days, which she normally would have found unnerving. However, between her delight that he'd made friends, her own busyness, and her certainty that he was safe all around Swordmair, she was more pleased than not for his current lifestyle, which saw him—like the lads he made friends with—getting his chores done first thing in the morning that he might get out of doors while the weather allowed. He'd left several hours ago, when the young lads, Ronald and Martin, had called. She'd barely had time to call after him to be safe and home for supper, so quick did he dash away.

She saw very little of Alec, or even Malcolm or Eleanor, for that matter. When she did spy Alec, he seemed always to be about some chore, as if he didn't idle well, needed constantly to be moving and working and busy. She'd come across him repairing the thatch of the Norrie cottage himself, had walked past without drawing his notice while he'd been busy up on that roof. Next she saw him in the distance, helping two young lads bring in their sheep from the pasture; he'd been but a silhouette on the horizon, the setting sun at his back when she'd walked up to the keep at supper. Another time, she'd spied him inside the smithy's shed. He'd been talking with the blacksmith but had noticed her crossing the bailey, had neither called *good day* nor sought her out, had simply watched her with that dark and searching glare of his, that on this occasion Katie had thought that his chiseled handsomeness and even his unforgettable body were wasted on one so surly. She noticed that he was usually the first person to depart the hall after dinner. Watching him—though she wished she did not feel the confounding desire to!—she took note that when his trencher was empty, he stayed only long enough to finish the ale in his tankard. When that was done, he gave a few words to first his father and then his mother and took his leave, always going outside, into the night, and not above stairs, to where surely his own chambers were housed. The last time she'd seen him, aside from those suppers of course, was yesterday morn. He'd been riding through the gate as she neared it, followed by a dozen soldiers; his mien had been fierce and while he'd stiffly inclined his head at seeing her—a greeting, she supposed—his expression had remained dark and brutal.

She was honest enough with herself to admit that she was torn with their present circumstance. Aye, she'd begged him leave her be. And now he did, pursued her not in the least, lazily or otherwise, that Katie found herself again and again seeking him out, if only with her eyes, and aye, sometimes wishing he'd kiss her anyway. It was his eyes, she knew, sensing there was so much hidden behind what he allowed people to see, so much depth and turbulence. Part of her, mayhap the healer in her, wanted to peel away the layers, remove that intense façade and discover what lay beneath.

Swordmair's courtyard was quiet today, as she crossed from the gate to the keep and entered through the hall.

"There she is!" Shouted the laird across the room when he spied her. He sat at the head table with Malcolm, their conversation at first glance seeming to be serious. But no more. The laird lightly backhanded Malcolm on his upper arm, drawing his attention. "She says no more wine, less ale, and makes me drink the most godawful tea you'd ever want to ken, and I dinna care—do it ten times a day if she says I must. Naught but a twinge in my knees just now and if it wouldn't have scared my bonny bride, I'd be bouncing up and down the steps all day."

Malcolm smiled at this and then at Katie when she stood before the table.

She wiggled a small pouch she'd prepared for him. "More tea, sir. Keep up the good work," she said, pleased that her diagnosis of the aging stiffness and her recipe of a mixture of nine different plants and seeds and roots had brought him some relief. "It's all pulverized, but remind cook to knead it with honey before adding the steaming water. Oh, and same as last week, the rowan berries must be cooked."

The elder MacBriar leaned forward across the table. "Runs right through me, lass. Is that the way of it?"

"Aye," she acknowledged sadly, "hence cooking the rowan berries, lest it run even quicker."

Alexander MacBriar nodded vigorously and addressed Malcolm once more. "Lass kens everything, aye?"

"Aye, she's a clever one, is Katie." He winked at her.

As that had been her only purpose inside the keep, Katie bid them good day and departed, adjusting her shawl immediately as the wind greeted her so forcefully just outside the door.

She was halfway across the bailey when shouts and cries reached her.

Someone was calling Aymer's name. She saw him race along the battlements to stand above the gate, his back to Katie, while someone spoke to him from outside the wall. Katie continued, moving toward the open gate that she spied Ronald and Martin, with their heads tipped upward.

Her brow crinkling, Katie sped up, looking further, around the lads standing in the opening. Where was Henry?

She began to hear Ronald's words. "...And we made swords—just from sticks, not real ones—and we had to—"

"Where is Henry?" She asked, not frantic, but close, the high-pitched nervous tone of the lad alarming her. She rushed outside the gate, grabbing Ronald by the arm. "Where is Henry?"

He shook his head, looking about to cry.

Aymer called down, "Dinna fret, lass. He's no' far, I'm sure, and we'll get him back straightaway."

"Who's no' far?"

Katie whirled to find Malcolm striding up to her, the laird not far behind.

"Henry is missing. They cannot find Henry," She said now, latching onto Malcolm's arm.

"Sound the alarm!" Called the laird.

Katie spun again, the chief on her other side. She almost didn't recognize his voice. Gone the cheery and silly laird, replaced now by a sternness that should have been a regular feature of this man, to match his naturally harsh countenance.

This gave her no great ease, but plenty of hope that actions were being taken so quickly.

"Malcolm, get what ye can out of them," Alexander MacBriar directed, pointing to the lads just as the horn began to blast overhead, the noise low and eerie, so very different from the bright notes of the supper call. "Gilbert!" The laird hollered toward the stables. "Bring 'em out mounted!" Several soldiers gathered 'round, come from the wall and from other places inside. "Groups of four!" Laird MacBriar continued to command.

# THE LOVE OF HER LIFE

"Work in patterns, inside sections. Aymer, start splitting them up. Someone fetch the hounds!"

The blare of the horn continued. Katie turned her attention back to the lads, and Malcolm's interrogation of them. The big man had gone down to one knee, assured the boys, "You're no' in trouble, ye ken, but we'll find Henry sooner, you tell me exactly what happened."

They took turns, picking up where the other left off, but after nearly a minute of the disjointed telling, a story unfolded.

Mounted soldiers appeared further out, gaining the bridge, the alarm having brought them, their pace furious. Katie spied Alec at the lead, Eleanor at his side, a dozen behind them.

Alec would find Henry—if only to thwart fate or prove somehow that the world was meant to do his bidding. She began to move toward the coming army unit, meeting Alec's eyes, heavy under his dark frown.

"Henry is missing!" She said before he'd even left the saddle.

"Aye, we'll find him," he said without hesitation, dismounting quickly and taking her arm, leading her back to his father and Malcolm. As expected, his own instant certainty was a balm to Katie's fright.

Malcolm explained what they knew.

"Lads were playing battle down by the gulch, running, hiding on each other. Henry leapt across, went up into the woods there. They lost him."

"How long?" Alec asked, his solid and warm hand now at Katie's back.

Eleanor joined them, giving Katie a rare sympathetic nod.

"They canna say. Sounds like quite a bit, more than an hour," Malcolm said, with a worried look toward Katie.

Alec's father said, "Aymer's divvying up the troops, lad. You and each of your officers lead a unit."

Alec nodded while Katie declared, "I want to go with you."

"Nae, lass," said the laird. "You stay here now with me. Let them get to it."

With that, Alec glanced down at her and said sternly, "We'll find him, and we'll no' return until we do."

Tears threatened but did not fall. She nodded again, having no choice but to believe this. Alec took off, Malcolm following, running back inside to claim a destrier put out by the stable hands. Eleanor remained a moment more, drawing Katie's watery gaze.

"We'll find him."

"Please," was all Katie said.

# Chapter Eleven

The next many hours were unbearable. Morning turned to afternoon and afternoon to evening. The wind carried on, whistling throughout the keep, throwing leaves and dust about outside. The hall was eerily empty, the quiet doing Katie no favors.

"Aye now, that's enough, lass," called the laird, returned to the family's table some time ago, drumming his fingers upon the wood. "You're bringing on heartache here, watching ye pace like that."

The supper hour had come and gone. Even in her state, Katie had thought to ask where everyone was, why none had come to dine. Magdalena MacBriar, putting out a single dish before her husband and then another upon the head table for Katie, had informed her, "All gone looking, lass. They'd have heard the horn sound, would have met up with the searchers, joined the hunt." Her face was soft, her eyes filled with compassion as she took Katie's hand. "Now come and eat. I'll be up in a bit with my own stew. Sit right there, next to our laird. He dinna bite, as well you know."

Katie sat as the mistress returned to the kitchen once more.

The laird reached over and patted her hand, awkward but kind.

"It'll be fine."

She couldn't eat, of course, just stared at the trencher, her brain not even allowing her to make sense of what it was, not caring.

Maddie returned shortly, sitting on her husband's other side, setting her own supper before her. "Eat now, lass, or you'll see me lose my temper."

"Och, but leave her alone," the laird spoke up, though his voice was not raised above its normal hugeness. "She's worried, ye ken? Same as ye would be."

"Aye, but Laird MacBriar," said his wife, who regularly referred to him so formally, "Alec will bring him back. Being sweet on the lass here, he's not about to let her down."

Even this, from Alec's own mother, wrought not much more than a blank stare from Katie.

"Well, it's true," Maddie said, shrugging, before she dug into her stew.

Minutes later, while the laird and mistress ate in silence and Katie sat very still, Maddie leaned across her husband and said to Katie, "Did you know my son went missing once?"

"Did he?" Katie asked, without great interest, as quite obviously, he'd been found.

"Was gone for more than seven months," Maddie said casually.

This turned Katie's head and lowered her brow. "Seven months?"

Alexander MacBriar sat back swiftly, shoving his hands against the rim of the table. "Now dinna be telling that tale, woman. That's no' yours to be spilling."

# THE LOVE OF HER LIFE 173

With her usual and genuine innocence, his wife wondered, "Is it to be a secret?" She continued to eat, moving the spoon slowly from trencher to mouth. When next she swallowed, she said, "Wasn't precisely lost. Was taken by the English. Naturally, we had no idea—of either his whereabouts, his capture, or what he was suffering." To her husband, "But aye, how we fretted when we'd gotten word, aye?"

Her husband nodded, his jaw clenched, so very like his son. He kept his head down, aimed at his lap or the table or food, Katie wasn't sure.

"Lord knows what entirely he suffered," the mistress mused with a little shrug. "But not any of it was good. I often wonder what might have become of him if not for the fact that he was imprisoned with his friends, Lachlan and Iain. Their horrors were equal to his," she said and then amended, "maybe not poor Lachlan, he had it worst, I always thought."

"Is...is that why he is so often...why he smiles so little?"

"Like as no," answered his father. "He dinna—"

"I don't think that's the reason," Maddie said.

"Ye dinna?" Her husband asked. "What ye mean?"

"I mean what I mean, Laird." She shrugged. "He's not unhealthy or unhappy or unloved. The lad always had so much pent up...everything, never knew what to do with too much joy or too much fear or too much pain."

"Aye, I will no' argue that," said Alexander. "Face used to turn radish red, I'd say, holding in whatever it was that overwhelmed him. But," he argued further to his wife, "he'd outgrown all that by the time he left."

His wife shrugged at him. "And then it returned. I wasn't surprised."

Alexander MacBriar said to Katie with some sadness, "He dinna talk about it, not ever. I'd seen enough that I...I had an idea."

"You had seen what?" Katie asked.

"It was his father that brought him out of those dungeons," Maddie said, nodding an affirmation.

"You did? You discovered where he was being held and charged in after him?"

The laird harrumphed. "Nae." A short pause, while memories assailed him. "I could no' ever find him, was only a message come to my camp—I was searching, we were set up near the border, had a dozen or so English prisoners myself. So they want a trade and ye ken, I said aye right quick."

"He dinna trade, though." Maddie said, pursing her lips sadly, shaking her head.

"You didn't?"

"I meant to, but they sent one out, showed me some still lived. I sent one over as well, as whole as the day he was taken. Not so what they shuffled over to me."

"They were to trade the next morning," Maddie said, taking over telling when her husband seemed lost in his thoughts, grieved by memories. "Aye, but our laird couldn't stand it, dinna want his son one more second with that kind of evil. Stormed the house in which they were held, carried his son out of there in his own arms, brought a half dozen more out as well—so many less than those English had originally taken." She whispered to Katie, as if her husband might not hear what was said, seated between them, "Killed more than twenty, tortured to death."

"Holds onto anger, and all, mad at himself for not effecting his own rescue."

"But that's absurd," Katie argued against Alec's self-loathing.

"You tell him that, lass," said Maddie. "He dinna want to hear it from me. And so ye have it, the lad's bent on being fierce, never showing weakness, nor fear, nor empathy—God save us all—or anything he might consider soft. Laughter, apparently, would be a softness. A smile for his mother." She whimpered. "An embrace."

Katie's heart broke. The mother in her wondered, "Do you miss your son then?"

"Every bluidy day," the laird answered instead.

"Does he...improve when he's home for any length of time?" She wondered. Was there no saving him?

The laird shook his head even as his wife answered, "He's a good lad, ye ken, just won't allow himself to be happy."

"A weakness," Katie surmised. How tragic.

When no more of the tale seemed to be forthcoming, no more insight offered about the man that was Alec MacBriar, Katie went to the door again, as she had a dozen times today, standing in the threshold, waiting.

Full night had come, the sky clear and milky black around a bright showing of stars. The wind had died away, left swirled piles of leaves and debris in various spots about the yard. The torches, high on the bailey walls, lit by the laird himself earlier, bathed the yard in a golden haze.

She listened carefully, wanting so badly to hear the sound of horses, of cheery people, anyone, returning with her son. She couldn't panic, mustn't panic, must stay strong, but oh how frightened she was.

A lone tear slid away, her ears sensing nothing. But she waited still.

More long minutes passed.

Finally, sounds came to her.

Not jolly, but muted, that she could claim no immediate joy.

Dashing toward the gate, the noise grew louder, not voices, just the sound of hooves clip-clopping over the bridge. Hanging onto the wooden frame of the gate, Katie scanned all those coming toward her, looking for only one face.

He wasn't there!

Alec rode in the lead, alone upon his horse. There was Malcolm and Aymer.

Henry wasn't there.

Her hand slid down the wood as she sank to her knees and sobbed forlornly into her chest.

Malcolm called out, "He's here. He's safe, Katie!"

She lifted her face—but where?

Eleanor showed herself, moving her large steed around Malcolm and Alec. Henry sat before her, sleepy and untidy, but safe.

Covering her mouth with both her hands, she howled silently her relief. And then leapt to her feet and ran to them, ignoring every other person, her gaze seizing on her son, whom Eleanor easily lowered to the ground, to Katie's waiting arms.

He wrapped his arms just as tightly around her as she did him, showing her exactly what a fright he'd had as well. When finally she loosened her hold enough to scan his face, taking his hands in hers, holding them wide, checking out every part of him for injuries, he grinned at her and said, "Eleanor saved me."

---

THEY RETURNED TO THE hall, let Magdalena and even the laird fuss over the boy, the laird saying with some feigned sternness, "And that'll be the last time you cause your dear mam fits, aye, lad?"

"Yes, sir." No small amount of contrition attended his reply, but Henry was otherwise only tired and, as ever, besotted with Eleanor, staying close to her, while so many others convened in the room.

"How do I thank you?" Katie wondered. "All of you?" She let her gaze fall on each and every person in attendance, all those who had done this service for her.

"Aye now," answered the laird, "ye give and ye receive, aye folks?"

Her hand found her chest, her heart full.

"It's late," Alec said, near to her. "I'll walk you home."

"Eleanor, too!" Henry insisted, threading his fingers through hers.

No smile accompanied her agreement, but Henry was thrilled, nonetheless.

The four left then, stepping out into the dark night, Henry keeping hold of Eleanor's hand, a spring in his step. He talked continually of course, bound to make good use of this precious time with his hero.

While her gaze mostly stayed with Henry, Katie was especially aware of Alec at her side, and finally, now, gave more thought to the unfortunate tale his parents had told her earlier. She wondered when this had taken place, when he'd been taken captive, but thought this moment not the time to ask. Mayhap she never would, mayhap he only wished to let it rest.

At one point he rubbed his hand along the back of his head and said in a low voice. "You've seen a wee bit of troubles since we took you from Dalserf. Mayhap you're wishing you were there still."

She jerked her gaze to him. "Good grief, no," she was quick to assert.

At his quizzical stare, she explained, "If Henry had gone missing in Dalserf, I'd have been forced to comb the woods and creeks and lochs by myself." Her throat tightened. "None would have helped. None would have offered." When he remained silent, she said with forced lightness, "You said I did him no favors by smothering him. He's getting a right nice life education this last week, aye?"

"Mayhap you'd rather it came not at the price of your own terror."

Her newfound knowledge of his own circumstances caused her to ponder if this were said with some awareness of his own mother's horror, when he'd gone missing.

Funny, she thought, how the loss of fear and worry—with Henry's return—thrust thoughts of Alec MacBriar back to the fore. Katie was aware of each step he took, knew that he'd plucked at some leaf as they stepped into the trees, twirled it idly around between his thumb and forefinger. Something nipped at her, telling her to make conversation with him, that she said, "I like Swordmair very much. I-I suppose I should thank you for...insisting we come away from Dalserf."

"Aye," was all he said.

They were quiet then, letting Henry's voice be the only sound for a moment, until he asked, "What changed your mind—about coming to Swordmair? What had you say *aye* in the end?"

"Mostly, I suppose it was Malcolm who persuaded me," she said truthfully, though was compelled to admit, "And...and because of those few minutes when you accidentally struck me to the ground when you helped with the laundry."

He turned a curious eye to her.

Though he asked for no clarification, Katie said anyway. "It was your reaction, actually. You were...immediately remorseful, felt awful I thought."

"Aye, I did." There seemed to be a question yet in his tone.

Shrugging, watching her footfalls and not him, she told him, "I thought a man who feels so poorly for a mere mishap wouldn't ever wish harm upon me, or bring harm to me."

"Hm."

Which was barely a response at all, that she felt the need to defend her reasoning. But she did not, left it at that.

Inside the small village, Henry and Eleanor entered the house first. It was cold and dark and Alec bent almost immediately to the small hearth to light a fire when they'd followed.

Eleanor said to Henry, "You'll sleep well tonight, lad."

"I'm no' tired at all," he said, indeed wide-eyed and bright.

"Aye, but us old folk are. Climb in there, give your mam some peace tonight." She pointed to the narrow bed in the far corner of the room. "Get lost again, I'll no' speak to you for a fortnight, aye?"

"Aye," he agreed readily enough. He removed his short coat and jumped up to hang it on the hook beside his mother's cloak and then sat and removed his shoes, saying to no one in particular, "I dinna wash my face yet though."

"A little dirt overnight will do you no harm," Katie assured him. She held back, did not approach him or the bed when he climbed into it, supposing he might ask for Eleanor to tuck him in even.

He did not, just laid there on his back, his hand settled over the coverlet on his belly, and stared at the three adults watching him.

Katie added, "If you do not sleep, I'll be forced to give you a wee talking-to for the scare you gave me."

He frowned, "But Eleanor already scolded me."

Katie's mouth opened but she said nothing. Inwardly, she smiled. *I knew she cared for Henry.*

Eleanor said gruffly, "Close the peeps. Canna sleep with 'em open."

He did, but so tightly that Katie grinned in truth now. She turned to Alec and Eleanor. "I cannot thank you enough. I am forever in your—"

"Let's no' get fussy about it," Eleanor cut her off. "We dinna suppose you aren't grateful."

Unsurprised by her opposition to praise, Katie nodded and folded her hands at her waist.

Alec spoke up, having passed his gaze a bit around the single room. "I'll keep you company then," he said, adding almost as an afterthought, "until the lad falls asleep."

"I'll stay with her," Eleanor said, her tone one that seemed likely to accept no argument.

Katie gave a wan but appreciative smile to Alec as he didn't argue against this. With a nod, he turned and left, closing the door softly behind him.

"Sit," Katie invited, throwing out her hand to the table and stools.

Eleanor did, taking the stool which faced the bed. "You're no' going to get all funny with the lad then, are ye? Keep him underfoot that ye dinna lose him again?" When Katie lifted her weary face to her, Eleanor furthered, "He was no' in any real danger, ye ken? Just turned around in the wood. He'll get used to it."

She considered this, hadn't thought that far ahead, hadn't thought of much but that Henry was safe. And that Alec MacBriar was somewhat awkward in his skin tonight. Yet, Katie knew that she didn't want to curtail Henry's freedom, his joy. "It is generally safe here at Swordmair? There's none who live about that would bring him harm? No beasts outside the gates to cause him injury?"

Eleanor sighed. "Generally safe, aye. And, I canna think of a soul who would dare to harm another, no' any who live on MacBriar land. Beasts? Animals? Aye now, that's another matter."

Katie screwed up her face a bit. "So close to giving me all the perfect answers."

Eleanor smirked. "Ye ken yourself, you've seen it enough I'm sure, a lad's got to own some bumps and bruises to get through life."

"Aye, I do know that. Hopefully, he'll give me a wee bit of time to recover from this scare first."

Eleanor sighed then, looked to have no further conversation in mind, even shifted in her chair as if she might depart now.

"Eleanor, where did you learn to fight? How did you become a warrior?"

She harrumphed. "It's complicated." Her lips twisted while Katie let her know with lifted brows that this answer didn't satisfy, so she said, "Only daughter, wanting to be noticed"—she shrugged— "by anyone. Seemed the best way to garner attention in my household. But then they never did notice. We—the keep, the village—were put to a siege by the English, and everyone was...they're all gone. Four brothers, da', my mother."

Aghast, Katie put her hand to her chest. "But how did you survive?"

Her shoulders lifted and fell again, as if she spoke of some lesser tragedy. "Lord Edmund Campion, who laid the siege, thought he'd have some sport, dragged me above stairs, tossed me down on my own bed. I knifed the bastard in his neck while he was raping me. Snuck out through the tunnels."

Her mouth gaped. What did one say to that? *Sorry* seemed impossibly inadequate. She lifted her hand but then did not suppose Eleanor would tolerate any touch from Katie that she laid it on the table again.

"There was a woman with that army," Eleanor continued, her gaze unblinking and set upon the table. "She were dressed fine, no' a soldier, just traveling with them, I guess. Servicing them, I assumed later. But she ken everything that happened, ken verra well what Edmund Campion was doing to me and she did nothing. Laughed at it, shouted insults at me and encouragement at him while he pulled me up the stairs." She shook her head, "Women are awful creatures."

"You realize you are one yourself."

"No' a normal one."

"What's normal, Eleanor? Who's to say?"

"I really hate Eleanor, ye ken."

"I know, but as I don't even think I've ever heard you say *my* name that I must retaliate."

And that was how Katie earned her first true smile from the woman warrior.

"Like I said, women are awful," she said, with some accusation pointed at Katie. But the grin remained a moment more. "Give me a man any day, uncomplicated, their needs fairly basic—feed 'em, house 'em, swive 'em—so easy."

"Good grief, Eleanor, you make them sound like animals—"

"Which they are, but at least ye can understand them. They're all pretty easy to figure out."

"I can think of several, right here at Swordmair, that are not at all uncomplicated."

"Ye canna think of several," Elle accused. "You're thinking of that one, just out the door."

Katie held her breath and stared at Eleanor, wondering what the woman might know or suspect about whatever it was that had been a wobbly beginning and now seemed to be done.

Eleanor rolled her eyes. "Ye ken the lads are all fairly decent ones, the MacBriars—but they yap more than most women, clucking hens they are. So, aye, everyone kens all about the kiss, or whatever that whole calamity was."

Katie groaned, but defended promptly. "It was nothing, of course—a farce that's done, him testing me mayhap. I still don't quite know what to make of it. But it's done. It won't happen again."

Eleanor slanted a dubious look at her but was kind enough to push it no further. With some insight, she told Katie, "He's no' complicated, either. Wants peace and obedience and a good harvest," she said, and then laughed, "and a woman who will challenge him but no' too much, and an army that respects him but also fears him to some degree, and mayhap some notion how to lose all that anger he carries around, and likely, he'd no' squawk at any idea that would somehow make apples grow all year long."

"I see. Not complicated at all." Katie gasped then with a horrible thought, one she could not believe hadn't occurred to her until just now. "Sweet St. Andrew! Eleanor, are you...do you...are you and Alec...?"

Eleanor's instant dark frown answered well enough before she sneered, "Bluidy hell, no!" And then, with a familiar disgruntled tone, she allowed, "He's all yours."

And now it was Katie's turn to scoff.

# Chapter Twelve

If not for Eleanor, Katie might well have done just as the woman had feared, smothered Henry with her worry, keeping him close, refusing to allow him out of her sight. He was only permitted any freedom from his mother because Henry wanted nothing more than to be with Eleanor, and strangely enough, Eleanor didn't seem to mind.

Left then with some time to herself, no patients to see, no one come to her door for an urgent need, her laundry finally attended this morning with her son's help before he disappeared with Eleanor, Katie was determined to spend a good amount of time about the nearby woods. She needed desperately to replenish her supply of roots and plants, simply not having the time of late to restock.

She gathered her shallow basket and her cloak and headed up toward the castle, turning off into the trees before she might have reached the bridge. Soon, she would likely have to tread further, but was not yet very familiar with the land and area that she felt confident enough to stray too far from Swordmair.

She was about her chore for almost an hour, keeping either the village or the castle in view through the trees at any given time. Her basket was quite full, happily so. At one point, she was able to sit right down next to a rotted stump, crossing her legs, collecting a goodly number of mushrooms and lichen in just that one area.

When she was done, she stopped at her cottage but just to relieve herself of the basket, and claim the only other one she possessed. She went in search of Maddie, who was usually easy to find as she was often about some chore inside the keep.

"You've recovered well enough, my dear?" The mistress asked, as she had every day since Henry had been lost and then found.

"Aye, thank you." She stood across the counter in the kitchen from Maddie, while the older woman was busy trimming peas. "Maddie, I am in need of sea kelp."

"Sea-what?"

"Sea kelp. Are you familiar with it? The green algae that grows and lives in the sea, or its relatives that possibly grow in some of the larger lochs?" At the woman's blank look, Katie expounded, "It's rather like a slimy green plant." Still nothing. "At any rate, I'm not sure where the sea is from Swordmair, and I wondered if I might have your permission to have the castle steward procure some sea kelp for me. At Dalserf, the steward had seaweed sent over from Arran Isle, simply for my practice. It has many medicinal qualities." It had taken some doing, Gordon Killen having to send out many inquiries before a positive response had come, and subsequently, the sought after seaweed.

"Aye, Edric might do that for you, lass," Maddie offered encouragingly, but then said in an offhanded manner, "Of course, you could walk to Loch Oykill in less than an hour. Always something slimy there."

"Loch Oykill? Is it very large, the loch?"

The cook, a woman whom Katie knew from all those times she fetched Henry directly from the kitchens, whose name was Corliss, turned from the hearth and answered, "Verra large, lass. And aye, very slimy stuff. I grew up near there. Three quarters hour, gone and back before we sup."

She thought she just might. But then hesitated, "Is it wise, though, to...wander about in that direction?" She understood that Swordmair was safe, but she'd heard numerous tales of the relentless and fierce clan wars up here in the Highlands.

Almost as if she were offended by the question, the cook turned and straightened, leveling Katie with an *are-you-daft* glare. "Aye, it's safe. Unless your sea kelp bits are the biting kind." And with that she chuckled and turned her back again, the kettles receiving her chortling.

Katie looked to Maddie, who only shrugged, sending her own funny glance to the cook. To Katie, she said, "Middle of the day, lass. Gone and back so quick. Seems harmless enough. Aye, and when the lad comes in, I'll bid him remain at the keep until we sup."

She decided right then she would do it, would strike out to Loch Oykill and collect her own sea kelp. She needn't then bother the castle steward or be indebted to anyone.

She had to disturb Corliss once more for the direction, who snorted a bit but did take Katie out into the yard directly from the kitchen and point toward the west.

"Beyond the trees, see the lass's cleavage?"

*Lass's cleavage?* Oh, the slight dip in the mounded hills beyond the narrow forest of pines.

"Aye, I see it."

"Head straight for that, loch's on the far side. Ye return same way, through the bosom."

Katie smiled at this unfamiliar landscape language and thanked the woman for her time.

The sky was clear and the sun warm upon her. She spent a wee bit of time searching for Boswell, thinking he'd make a fine companion for her brief journey. He wasn't in the bailey or inside the stables, where he liked to spend a fair amount of time. He wasn't at home, though she'd bothered to walk back to her cottage to check. He was not seen anywhere in or around the village that Katie left off searching before it was then too late to set out.

Thus, she walked away from Swordmair, quite proud of herself for this undertaking. She was not averse to seeking help, but she so much preferred to manage her own occupation, and the things she needed to perform well.

---

HE WASN'T SURE WHY he should care. She was a grown woman, could do as she pleased, even if that did mean making some bluidy hare-brained decisions.

Still, his jaw ached from the tightness that had come with the news he only happened to overhear as he passed through the kitchens, seeking Edric. He'd not found Edric and then his business with the steward had been swiftly forgotten when threads of the conversation between his mother and Corliss, the castle's cook, penetrated.

"Haven't been over to Oykill way in years," Corliss had said. "Hope I dinna steer the lass wrong."

His mother had responded, "Nor I. Seems I'm thinking now it's more of a hike than I'd led the lass to believe."

At his mother's wavering tone, Corliss had gestured with the long wooden spoon in her hand. "Aye, but I'm sure she'll still be there and back...well, mayhap before dark."

With worry now coloring her voice, his mother had said, "If she dinna get lost, of course."

That was when they'd noticed Alec, neither reacting to the frown he eased only to lift his brow to inquire, "Which lass has gone to Loch Oykill?"

"Katie has," his mother answered haltingly, the severity of his voice causing her alarm.

Alec used every ounce of strength in his body to control himself and ask calmly, "Why did she go there?"

"Sea...something, she was after," his mother said, her fingers unmoving inside a wide bowl of dough she'd apparently been kneading.

"Slimy stuff," Corliss added in a small voice, sensing his rising ire.

"And when did she leave?"

The women consulted each other uneasily.

"More than an hour ago? Mayhap two?" His mother said, which emerged as a question, fearing his response.

Alec said nothing more but spun on his heel and left the kitchen. He'd mounted and left the castle immediately but had yet to overtake her—and he'd been searching now for nigh on an hour that Loch Oykill was just ahead.

*Gone to Loch Oykill? Was she daft?* He wondered for the hundredth time. It was naught but three days ago that her own son had gone missing! Had she forgotten so soon? He was going to blister her hide within inches of needing a healer's attention when he found her.

As he descended the far side of the hills, he was greeted by the faded yellow gorse blooms, which claimed nearly all the land until it was overtaken by the loch itself, mottled navy and turquoise. Alec directed his steed carefully through the shrubs, some which stood taller than he atop his huge destrier until he'd traversed all of it and stood before the water. The loch itself on this eastern side was ringed for hundreds of yards by a flat and rocky beach that chasing footprints was not an option. A quick glance up and down the stretch showed no lean figure about the chore of collecting anything from either the water's edge or the uneven shore.

He mumbled a curse and then said aloud, "I'm going to wring her beautiful neck." He yanked on the reins, turning the horse, intent on gaining high ground again that he might better peruse the area. Facing the tall and prickly gorse, he saw Katie Oliver standing directly upon the path he'd taken, exactly at the spot where the rocky beach began.

She was staring directly at him from a distance of several yards, biting her bottom lip that he supposed she'd overheard his heated words and was aware of his fury.

The next thing that struck him, he put to words, "Were you hiding yourself?"

She nodded. "I couldn't see who came."

There was that, at least. He wasn't sure how, but he managed to again command an even tone. "Which part of this—this foolish scheme—seemed like a good idea to you?"

She countered with a frown and, "Why are you here?"

He was accustomed to people wilting under the weight of his sometimes robust fury. She did not. Of course she did not! Alec raised both brows sharply. "Why am *I* here?"

She nodded.

"Aye, I thought I'd take a leisurely ride through the countryside," he answered, his sarcasm biting, his voice deepening to a dangerous level as he continued. "I've naught to do but chase around a simple-minded lass who believed it a fine day to stroll so far away from home all by herself!" This, the last, was shouted into the air between them.

Katie was undaunted, or equally as peeved. "Did I ask you to?"

"You dinna have to ask! You can no' be venturing so far afield all by yourself! Do you have any idea of the dangers that you might encounter even in this friendly land? Do you?"

"But your mother—"

"My mother hasn't left the castle in twenty years!" He roared. "And even she's no' dimwitted enough to undertake a march like this on her own!"

She'd snapped her lips together when he'd interrupted her, but now drew a quick breath to offer up more of her pitiable defense. "Corliss said—"

He shouted over her, drowning her out, "I'd given you credit as a fairly intelligent lass, Katie Oliver, but I promise you now, I'm rethinking—"

"You've just called me dimwitted and simpleminded and...something else in a span of thirty seconds," she cut in, her voice equally forceful, her scowl as severe, "so pardon me while I challenge the first part of your spewing. But more importantly,

I do not take orders from you. I am free to come and go as I please."

He'd had enough. He swung his leg over the saddle and dismounted smoothly, quickly, striding angrily toward her. "There'll be no coming or going, you bluidy fool," he ground out, "if you're dead—drowned or set upon by either man or beast or lost—" He cut himself short, taken aback by her changed expression. *Bluidy fool* had hit home, seemed to sap all the fight right out of her. Or his bearing down on her had, that she was completely still, unblinking even.

He'd seen it before, all her passion and rage and emotion evaporating to nothing as she composed herself. She was as inscrutable as any gray rock hereabouts just now, her expression bland and unremarkable, her shoulders squared and chin angled upward.

"I am not a fool." Underneath her attempt at coolness, Alec sensed that she was absolutely awash in her own seething rage. "I did not invite you or ask you to mind me. I am my own person, and not a bird to be caged."

Aye, but there was something there, he surmised, wildly intrigued by whatever had just happened, whatever had chased the storminess and replaced it with this deliberate frostiness.

Or...was this more defense? Against him? His closeness?

Alec took one more step, closing the distance to less than a foot between them.

The narrow chin lifted yet more. She held his gaze with her stormy blue eyes, all her emotions convened there. "I am neither ready to return or in need of an escort," she hurried out, her voice starchy. "I have only just arrived." This came not without some

# THE LOVE OF HER LIFE

trepidation as he noted that one of her hands was folded into her skirts, showing him little else but her white knuckles.

He inched closer, his boot meeting the hem of her gown, his own gaze riveted upon her.

Ah, but his Katie Oliver was a fierce soul, so brave. Didn't even flinch, didn't bat an eye. If not for her mouth pressed so tight, forcing her rapid breaths out through her nose, he'd have guessed her completely unaffected.

Alec lowered his eye to her chest, watched the faded blue wool of her gown heave and settle again as she struggled to breathe evenly. When he lifted his face, he found her regard now given to his mouth. He quirked one corner and reminded her, "Aye, but lass, you have to ask for it."

That jerked her gaze from his lips, her fiery eyes meeting his, so much willpower shown, silently promising him she'd do no such thing.

But then, he'd have thought that Katie would have verbalized her refusal, would have vowed with great vehemence once more that would never happen. Yet, she did not, was unmoving still, that Alec had to wonder if she were too afraid to say anything, too afraid to open her mouth at all.

He leaned down toward her and caught the quiver in the movement of her chest, as if she held back a whimper. Still, she didn't move, didn't run.

"Two words, that's all you need," he whispered, heartened, enflamed by the struggle she fought with herself. "Kiss me," he said, reminding her of the words. He set his hand on her hip, warm and familiar.

Katie closed her eyes. She rolled her lips inward.

*Jesu*, but she was exquisite. Long and thick lashes swept across her cheeks; milky blue veins marbled over her eyelids, her skin so pure and white; a beautiful blush stained her cheeks; the column of her neck was exposed, heightened by the proud lift of her chin and her rigidity.

So fragile under all that strength.

"I'll no' throw it back in your face, Katie. I want it—Christ, how I want to kiss you." He lifted the hand from her hip to push a stray tendril of her blonde hair away from her cheek.

"Please," she begged. She opened her eyes, but could not meet his, stared only at his neck.

"Please...? Please go? Please stay? Please kiss me? Tell me what you want, Katie."

She nodded, but said nothing, only closed her eyes again.

It wasn't a lack of courage that kept the words inside her, he imagined, but pride. Pride was a curious creature, so often keeping you from getting what you truly wanted. But Alec had given his word, had said he'd not kiss her unless she asked.

Dropping his fingers away from her face, he shifted to step away.

"Kiss me," she said, breathless, her voice small. Startled mayhap as well, by her own daring.

He didn't smile outright, wouldn't taunt her in such a manner, but oh, how he was filled with pleasure just then.

"There's that fearless Katie Oliver I ken," he said and lowered his head to her.

He let the first touch be light, gave her one last chance to push him away, to come to her senses. He wanted to devour her, truth be told, but held himself in check. But then Katie Oliver tipped her face up to him and sought his lips, reached up for more of him, and from him. Alec growled low in his chest and swept her into his embrace, arms encircling her, hands digging into fabric and flesh while their tongues met and teased and tasted.

Their first kiss had shown him that she was possessed of so much passion so that he was not surprised when her hands rather made free with his body. She'd allowed this much, asked for it, that she wasn't about to sit back and let it happen to her. She wanted to live it, to breathe and feel and be a party to it. Her slim hands ran up his arms and over his shoulders and wound around his neck, holding him tight and close, clinging to him. Her fingers rose up, into his hair, content there, or forgotten when he began to move his own hands, sliding one up her side, over her ribs and above, to cover her breast. She made a sound in the back of her throat, encouragement enough that Alec began tugging at the neckline of her gown.

He broke their kiss when her shoulder was exposed and pressed his lips to that familiar sloppy scar. Dragging the gown and chemise lower, his lips followed, touching each inch of bare skin until it settled with divine delight upon her rosy tipped nipple. All of Katie was lean and trim that she was not generously endowed or even curvy, but damn, how she provoked him. Her bosom was modest, rounded to perfection, pale and eager for his touch. He fondled them possessively with his fingers and his mouth. Katie held him close, tipping back her head, her fingers yet entwined in his hair.

He returned to her lips, the kiss demanding now, while one hand began to lift her skirts. His hand touched the smooth warmth of her thigh before skimming around and cupping her bottom, crushing her to him, to his own growing need.

Some demon reared its head, made him say, "Stop me now, or I'll just keep taking." It was for her own good.

She whimpered. He couldn't discern if it were a cry of need or wretchedness.

Yet, she still held him tightly, did not push him away. Her eyes were firmly closed.

"Katie," he warned, his voice thick.

Her lips trembled. She wanted to push him away, wanted to deny them, and this. Possibly her need, her desire was stronger though, that she was completely still, leaving the decision—to stop now or to continue—to him.

Alec growled. He didn't want her like that, to come to him in some hopeful yet ambiguous haze, letting the choice be only his. "Aye, and then you'll rage at me when it's done? Say I forced you, I gave you no choice. Hating yourself but taking it out on me."

Dropping her face forward against his chin, she shook her head so starkly, so minimally he'd have missed it if she weren't pressed against him, her hair moving along his chin.

Damn her.

---

WHY DID HE HAVE TO speak? Why did he have to throw those things out there?

Of course, she knew why, but had chosen to disavow the reasons, had let his kiss and his touch realign all her previous indifferent convictions.

She kept her head bowed against him, but he'd stopped touching and teasing her so gloriously, had dropped her skirts and lifted the bodice of the woolen fabric to cover her breasts.

Just now, she was so very sad that he'd stopped, even as she realized that he'd spoken truth: later, soon, she would be very sorry for what she had done. These emotions—whatever they were regarding Alec—were so useless. 'Twas naught but a physical need actually, one she'd not ever imagined lived inside her, and something she considered quite impractical. It was foolish to make decisions and be guided by such folly as this, mere minutes of pleasure stacked against all the trouble it would cause, not least of which would take up residence in her head.

Eventually, he shifted, his hands falling away from her completely that Katie had no choice but to raise her face to him and take her hands from him.

His extraordinary eyes blazed with some unfathomable darkness. For a brief second, she tried to let an apology show in her own tortured gaze.

"You are right," she admitted. "I would hate myself."

"Why?" This came with some anger. When she didn't answer, he asked, "You ken you are your own worst enemy?"

Her brows lowered. She stepped back. "What does that mean?"

"Means you dinna ken when to feel and no' think."

Spoken like a man bent on seduction but lacking any proper emotion to attach to it. Katie rubbed her temples for a moment and then pivoted, about to collect the basket she'd dropped.

"And let's go now, back to the keep," he called after her. "I've wasted enough of my time."

She bristled at this. Possibly the words were merely off-handed, possibly laced yet with his own residual frustration, but they raked over her, nonetheless. She whirled and challenged, "Is it that you *want* me to hate you? Have you no goal, no agenda, but to see me loathe you?"

"I dinna think that was loathing kissing me a moment ago."

She couldn't resist throwing back at him, "*I dinna think* there'll be any more kissing." Childish, she recognized, but blamed him, that this is what he'd reduced her to.

Ugh. She would never win. She could rage at him, call him names, but it was all for naught. The man was a stone. He felt nothing. Not for anyone. Katie sighed, more resigned to a lifetime of occasions such as this—pushed and prodded and wrecked by him—than she was filled with any hatred or animosity toward him. It was simply too exhausting. She turned once more, headed for the shoreline, calling over her shoulder a dismissive, "You needn't wait. I'll be returned to Swordmair before supper."

His voice reached her, bereft of that huskiness that had so aroused her only moments ago, overtaken by that harshness, that need for control. "We're leaving, Katie. Now."

"Leave me be! I found my way here. I'll find my way back."

"Your stubbornness might see you killed."

"If your hate doesn't do me in first," she mumbled to herself and kept right on walking.

"It's no' *my* hate, lass."

Katie rolled her eyes, not having known he'd followed, that he might hear her.

But she ignored him, until he said, "I'm sorry."

This halted her, drew her brows together.

She faced him again. He stopped, leaving several feet between them. The bare wind, which had throughout the day hastened to disrupt things, lifted the hair off his forehead and pushed it away to the left.

"Sorry for what?" She couldn't imagine he was about to apologize for trying to seduce her again.

"For whatever was done to you that you will no' let yourself feel any personal joy."

It dawned on her then, the difference between them. He'd had this fantastic catastrophe happen to him, had been held prisoner by the English, and while he put out that aura of ruthlessness and invulnerability, he'd really just closed himself off to any deep or great emotion. He would not feel pain, would allow pain no chance to claim him, had closed himself off to even his parents, to some degree. His idea of personal joy might only be wrapped up in physical gratification.

Katie hadn't ever been hurt or harmed, truly. However, there had been no warmth or joy in her youth and no emotion tied to her brief marriage. She'd not known love, save from and for her son. It just wasn't something she went out searching for. Another insight emerged just then, as she realized that her refusal to lay with Alec might actually be her seeking, and not accepting anything that wasn't love, not subjecting herself to more of the same.

"There was nothing done to me," she finally told him. "This is just who I am."

## Chapter Thirteen

The next morning, Katie was standing in front of her cottage, chatting with Ann and Agnes, listening with fascinated delight as Agnes recounted the tale of how just last night the entire family of nine had chased around a mouse inside their cottage.

Grinning, Katie acknowledged, "That would explain the shrieks heard then." She'd been alarmed initially when she'd heard the first cry in the dark and otherwise quiet night but had settled soon enough as those loud cries had been followed with so much laughter, drifting down to her own home.

Agnes rolled her eyes. "More harm done by the lads chasing it than the poor little mite would have managed. The lads tore up the place, flinging everything away from the walls as it scurried around."

"After the first scream," Ann said, "I thought, *well, this is it*, she's finally fulfilling that promise to skin her dear Niall after all these years of threatening."

Niall, Agnes's husband, was as quiet as his wife was not, but then his inability to be roused to excitement, over anything, often had his wife regularly hollering at him, in any small or large calamity, to *Do something!*

"He'll be spared, ye ken, for the next few days," Agnes allowed, "since he was the only one makin' use of his noggin'—opened the door that the thing was finally chased outside."

She went on, giving more detail of the upset to her home, and how much time it would take to set it to rights.

Henry was near, at the end of the lane with Ronald and Martin and another lad, while they amused themselves with Boswell, throwing short, fat sticks that the hound happily returned to them.

It was cold today, the sky gray and the wind mean. Katie had already planned that she must devote some time to her cloak, in need of general repair, and now a way to keep it secure about her, as the threads of the frog closure had finally frayed enough to have given way completely. Katie tucked her left hand under her right arm and held her shawl closed at her neck while she enjoyed the company of these two women.

"Oh, he's coming fast," Ann said then, watching over Katie's shoulder.

Glancing behind her, Katie saw that indeed he was.

It was Alec, flying from the trees on his big horse, turning down their lane. Even before he'd come very close, Katie could see that his gaze was set on her. What now? She wondered, with some residual harshness for yesterday's awfulness with him. Honestly though, as she'd discovered yesterday with the unavoidable deliberation that had come when finally they'd parted, her emotions regarding that confrontation with Alec at Loch Oykill were infuriatingly mixed. She was caused no wee amount of vexation that his kiss was so intoxicating, that his hands brought so much pleasure, but that he was so often ornery and confounding.

In the end, after that wild interlude at Loch Oykill, he'd allowed her "twenty minutes and not one more," to collect the algae that was indeed quite prevalent at that spot in the valley. When they'd ridden back to Swordmair, she'd been chastised, "And if you even set foot outside Swordmair to anywhere that takes you farther away than the eye can see, I'll task Eleanor as your personal guard—she'll no' ever leave your side."

Sitting before him, she'd ignored his scolding. She'd closed her eyes and leaned her back against him, reveling in his arm around her, allowing herself just for a moment to wish that they were made differently. She wished she might actually allow herself to be seduced, and only for the sake of knowing the sure joy he would bring to her. Nothing else. She wished he were capable of feeling something for her, other than what he did, naught but physical desire.

Katie could not yet understand, though she'd certainly given it thought of late, how it had come to be that she knew she wanted more than just to lay with a man. Possibly the want had been borne in her subconscious, during any or all of the perfunctory, cold couplings with her husband. Mayhap she'd come to resent being only a vessel to his needs. Mayhap she wasn't as strong as she'd always hoped she could be, that she did crave affection and emotion. Even as she wondered this, she chastised herself for even considering that such sentimentality should be something she might desire. How silly and nebulous and useless must be love between a man and woman.

She'd snorted yesterday when these thoughts had come, quietly and inelegantly. Mayhap she was only bitter that life had not allowed her the chance to discover what all the fuss was about.

Now, Alec reined in sharply and didn't bother to greet either Agnes or Ann. His gaze was hard—not unusual—but then didn't seemed to be so for her personally.

"Word from the Listers over near Spotswood," he said to Katie. "Bring what you need for a birthing."

She reacted instantly, the speed at which he'd come spurring her to move quickly.

"I'll keep the lad here, Katie," Agnes called as Katie dashed inside her cottage. "Dinna ye worry."

When she'd gathered her supplies, she returned to Alec, who had dismounted and awaited her. He received the many different sized pouches and bags and tucked them into his saddlebags before lifting Katie up into the saddle and pulling himself up behind her.

And they were off, Alec's arm secure around her waist that she wasn't caused too much consternation for the swift pace he set.

When they were away from the village, heading west over the barren fields, he explained what he knew.

"Lad rode up all the way from Spotswood, said Avrel Lister's been laboring since early this morn."

"Oh, my. But who are the Listers and where is Spotswood." She had to lift her voice and turn her face toward him, that he might hear over the noise of the wind and pounding hoofbeats.

"Edge of Swordmair. Tom Lister manages most the logging, felling of trees for all our lumber, sells some off down in Glasgow as well."

She nodded. She needed to know nothing else.

They rode hard the entire way, more than half an hour, until a huge but simple two story building came into view. The vista was amazing, as the building sat at the base of a heavily treed beinn, the trees rising behind it displaying so many different colors, autumn's orange and red and yellow, though there was plenty of green yet, the forest filled with so many pines as well. The sky above, angry yet, sat atop that forest, adding yet more color, the thick clouds purple and gray and white.

As they neared, Katie saw that indeed a lumbering operation took place here, as stacks of huge felled and limbless trees lay behind the building. Several carts and long wagons were lined up near the structure, and saws and tools, appearing to have been dropped quickly, were scattered around the ground. A lone horse idled, tethered to the back of one cart.

Alec dismounted first, pulling Katie to the ground with hands at her waist. The door, the only opening on this huge side of the building was pulled open before they reached it.

She let her gaze wander only briefly over the interior, a cavernous shed which showed more production capabilities, larger saws and tools and half-finished wood products taking up more than half of it. Against one wall leaned a stack of doors, thick and arched, not yet fitted with hardware, the wood pale but carved well.

Alec ruffled the hair of the lad who'd pulled the door open. "You did good, lad. Rode the old mare well."

The lad, only a few years older than Henry, nodded and twitched his lips. "She's back there." He tipped his head toward the back of the building where two walls of long red wood planks had been erected, enclosing one corner of the building.

Alec led Katie there, slowly pushing open another door.

Katie realized immediately this enclosure served as the home inside the spacious workshop.

A man, as long as he was lean, was bent over one of the cots inside, but turned at their entrance, rising quickly to his feet.

"Here's Katie Oliver," Alec said. "She's in good hands."

Katie nodded and smiled only briefly at him, already letting her gaze fall on the young and pale and writhing woman inside the bed, moving toward her instinctively. There was always time, when all was said and done, for pleasantries and introductions.

Tom Lister said to her as she passed him, "It's no' like the others. They was easy."

She met the woman's gaze, tortured and near frantic and skipping every other second to her husband. Another pair of eyes peeked at Katie from the opposite side of the bed, another lad, maybe only three or four. Somewhere inside this chamber a baby wailed.

Rolling up her sleeves, Katie said, "Alec, take the bairn and the lads into a far corner, or out completely. Tom Lister, come and hold Avrel's hand." She bent over Avrel just as her husband appeared and took the hand stretched out to him. Katie touched all around her distended belly, realizing fairly quickly what the trouble was. She smiled kindly at Avrel. "Sometimes the bairns like to come bouncing out, feet first. But we cannot have that, so we'll be turning him around inside."

She pivoted away from the bed, collecting the pouch with the flaxseed oil and caught site of Alec, gingerly lifting the youngest child, barely more than a year old, from a low cradle and into his arms. He held the bawling child at arm's length, keeping that distance even as he began to move, saying to the older children, "C'mon then, lads," leading them out of the room. His lips, twisted and pursed, displayed well his unease, at which Katie grinned.

It was many hours later, long after Katie had spread the flaxseed oil about Avrel's belly and had worked so tirelessly to manipulate the fetus into the proper position, that the bairn came wailing into the world. When the cord which attached the babe to his mam had been cut, Katie swept him away in a warm cotton blanket to clean him, making note that this was now the fifty-seventh birth she'd attended.

Avrel was exhausted, her lids drifting down even as she received first, Katie's praise for how well she'd managed the hard labor, and then her child, her fourth son, into her arms. Tom Lister hovered over the pair while Katie tidied up and washed her own hands thoroughly.

When Avrel had wept with joy over her healthy child for a few minutes, Katie stepped in and collected the infant, rocking him gently in her arms, that his mother might rest for a while. "I don't think you'll be able to hold them off much more," she said to the very relieved Tom Lister, nodding her head toward the door, where two of his sons had many times peeked in, having to be shooed away.

"Aye," he said, his smile large, leaving his wife but briefly to usher in his other children.

Katie returned her attention to the new babe, so tiny and precious, cooing over him. "Look at you," she said, "so beautiful and new." He blinked, barely and slowly, his eyes unable to focus yet. "Oh, but aren't you handsome." She lifted him higher in her arms, inhaling the clean and pure scent of a newborn babe, before turning as the two boys burst into the room.

Alec followed and they faced each other, each of them holding a babe that she smiled at him for this circumstance, and for how blessed this family was. Smiled at him as well for how comfortable he was with the toddler now, after so many hours. The babe was tiny in Alec's huge arm, his bottom nestled into the crook of Alec's elbow, leaned against his broad chest. His little face was tipped up to Alec's, the lad's bright brown eyes rapt as they stared at the big man holding him.

Alec returned her smile. She wasn't as startled by the smile itself, though she'd seen them rarely upon him, but for the way it reached his eyes, crinkling the tanned and weathered skin at the corners. Inside the depths of those remarkable hazel orbs, he seemed well pleased, and Katie thought it was lovely to see true joy in him.

They stayed for yet another hour, with Alec keeping those active lads well-entertained and Katie fussing over Avrel and her new bairn. The older boys were more excited for Alec's presence, Katie was sure, than the arrival of their new sibling, pouting and fretting when Alec said they must return to Swordmair.

"If you need anything at all," Katie told Avrel just before they'd left, "please send the lad again to Swordmair. I can be here within an hour."

None of the urgency employed during their ride to Spotswood was needed upon their return to Swordmair that Alec only set the steed into a leisurely jog. Katie sat before him, grinning yet over the scene they'd left behind, that happy family in that cozy home.

"How blessed they are," she said, yesterday's unfortunate episode with Alec forgotten now as they had this experience to share.

"Aye, and rightly so. Tom is a good man, solid as any."

"He's so patient with those boys—as were you," she said.

"Aye, but I dinna mind telling you, Katie, that was no' a good time, trying to get the wee one to settle."

She turned her face into this chest, grinning. "How did you finally manage it?"

"Let him play with my sword," he said.

"Alec!"

She felt a chuckle rumble along his chest. "Nae, I did no'. Bouncing first, I dinna ken what else to do. But then Robert, the eldest, said his mam sang to him. That seemed to work."

Katie's eyes widened. "You sang to a babe?"

"Aye, I did."

"I don't believe it."

And now a shrug was felt.

"Hm, I wouldn't have guessed you would even know any songs."

"I do," he replied. "Aye, but their mostly bawdy or bloody soldiering songs. Changed a few words, he dinna mind."

"I'm impressed. " And she was, with this entire day, and the revelation that was Alec MacBriar. Smiling, and making that quip about the sword, and now revealing that he'd lulled a baby to calmness with song. She faced forward again, a slow and thoughtful smile coming, wondering what other secret and remarkable abilities he might possess.

The animal beneath them leapt across a small dip in the terrain, causing Katie to grab onto Alec's forearm at the same time he tightened his arm around her. When the ground was level again and the ride smooth once more, Katie kept her hand on his arm.

VERY CURIOUS, ALEC thought, how yesterday's heated irritation had been so easily cleaved from his mind, that he was bothered not at all by what danger she'd put herself in, how far she'd travelled by foot and alone, nor by the lingering disturbance that she'd responded so eagerly, so damn bewitchingly to his touch and his kiss but would allow him no more.

All that faded, replaced now, with that image of her holding the Lister bairn.

When Tom had opened the door, finally allowing his sons to return to the chamber, Alec had peered into the room. He'd been rendered mute and motionless at the sight that had greeted him. Katie with that babe in her arms, cooing over him, her voice so musical with joy, her smile so splendid, had overwhelmed him. He couldn't, at the exact moment, know all that gushed through him, was only aware of a warmth and a craving that was not sexual, that came only at the sight of her unbridled happiness, her very delight and how natural she was with that minutes-old babe.

Of course, he'd witnessed smiles and delight in her, mostly centered around her own son, and shown more often since she'd come to Swordmair, but this...this had been remarkable, so pure was her pleasure for these complete strangers and now, this bairn. Alec had thought she was more alive in that innocent and blissful moment than he'd ever been aware. His body had reacted instantly, with open admiration and a suddenly euphoric mood.

He examined this a bit as they rode. He understood that he often responded to her, to the sight or the sound of her, knew reactions to her moods or her words or sometimes just the way she looked. This was somehow different, he decided, wondering if he had felt joy merely at the sight of hers.

Was that possible?

Never mind that the image of her, holding that bairn, had indeed triggered some emotion, unnamed and unknown, to course within him. *Jesu*, if he didn't know better, he'd have called it longing.

His continued musings were interrupted by a long shiver from her.

"Time to retire the shawl, lass," he said. "It'll be your cloak from here on out."

"But not until I mend it yet again," she said over her shoulder.

With that, Alec pulled the loose plaid from over his back, leaving the front yet tucked into his belt. He flapped it out to remove all the folds that it billowed in the wind as they moved, and then drew it forward, around the front of her.

She accepted it eagerly, tucking her slim shoulders inside, and said, "Thank you," just as another shiver wracked her, so that it seemed only a kindness to press himself more closely against her, sharing all his warmth.

"It's late," he said when Swordmair and its fine towers came into view sometime later. He didn't loosen his hold, letting his hand rest yet intimately around her middle. "Right to the hall for supper?"

She shook her head against his chin. "I cannot. Mayhap I'll fetch something later. I was promised to several other people today before we were called away."

"Katie, you have to eat."

Her tone light, she asked, "Do you put aside all the needs must things, only because the hour says it's time to eat?"

Nae, he did not. "Aye, I'll tell mam to put a trencher aside."

With that, he angled toward the village then, and deposited her in front of her cottage.

When they stood beside the huge destrier, and her pouches were now held in one hand by all the different drawstrings, Katie shyly tucked strands of her windblown hair behind her ear. But she faced him, her cheeks heightened with color, her eyes extraordinarily blue under the still-gray sky.

"It was kind of you to stay with me all the day, at the Listers."

"Aye," he accepted and added, thoughtfully. "I'm glad I did."

"Good day, then."

"Aye."

Only now was her smile a wee bit nervous, he thought, before she turned and opened that blue door, disappearing within.

*It's no' finished.*

Whatever it was that lived and breathed between them, whatever warmed his blood and gripped his chest whenever she was near, it wasn't finished.

# Chapter Fourteen

When full dark came, Katie set aside her work and ducked out of her cottage, disappearing into the night. She'd bundled her cloak, linen towel, her nightrail, and a new ball of soap—a gift from the mistress herself, strangely having come with a nodding smile and the admonition, "Ye ken the lads all like their lasses to smell like the heavens, but rose oil and cloves will have to do."

Henry had found her this evening, brimming with his usual excitement, telling her that Malcolm had given permission that he could spend the night in the soldiers' barracks. Katie herself had been inside that part of the keep, which flanked the gate on either side, when she'd tended Simon when he'd had a fever. The barracks were dark and narrow and smelled of sweat and other things she'd not want to inhale all through the night, but they were also relatively neat and there had seemed to be plenty of room, that she could not refuse him.

Thus, she'd decided on a quick bath in the loch, having been assured by Agnes and even her daughters that persons regularly availed themselves to such simplistic luxury, though more often in the summer. She'd been tempted to take a leisurely bath inside her cottage, without having to dunk herself in the same heated water Henry had just used, but found herself too tired once more, lacking the energy for several trips to and from the loch to fill the tub. She'd be quick in the loch, so nervous that someone might stumble upon her, though Agnes had given directions to the entrance to the loch where only the women were allowed, a shallow spot with a good natural entry, had promised her that she'd never encountered a man in that section. She'd purposefully left Boswell in the cottage, that he didn't get up to any nonsense that might only serve to alert any nighttime wanderer of her activities.

She found the location easily enough, and with numerous nervous glances into the nearby darkness, she'd stripped quickly and walked straight into the water. It was much colder than she anticipated, as she'd thought at least it would feel warm in the chilly night air. Only a residual fear of being discovered moved her deeper and deeper into the water, until it covered her up to her neck. She washed speedily, minus those several times she brought the soap to her nose again, so intrigued by the sweet scent.

When the cold began to permeate deeply, Katie finished up with the bath and exited the water. Her bare feet slid on the dewy grass here. She caught herself and dried her body with the thick linen, with less effort to be dry than simply non-dripping that she might don her nightrail. She'd only belatedly thought to bring her shawl, imagining that she'd seem naught but a ghost carousing about, if seen in only her nightclothes.

Her feet rather sloshed inside her boots, being still wet and without hose, that she slid twice while dashing back to her house. Hugging her belongings to her as she rounded the corner, she trimmed her steps lest she find herself on her face in the dirt of the road.

Katie was brought up short, spying a person on the roadway, in the next instant recognizing that Alec MacBriar was approaching her blue door. She'd gone still upon noticing him, only hung back in the shadows near Agnes's house, waiting to see what he was about.

He held something in his hand, she saw, but could not identify it.

Biting her lip, she first frowned and then her eyes widened as she watched. To her astonishment, it seemed he lifted his hand to rap on the door but then stopped himself. He took one long step backward and stood still for several seconds before moving forward again to approach the door. Katie's jaw dropped when she saw him shake his head and then with greater purpose raise his fisted hand to knock at the door.

Of course there would be no answer. Boswell barked from within, but that was all. It didn't dawn on her at that moment to announce her presence—didn't even dawn on her to conceal herself further. She was simply astonished at this uncharacteristic behavior. She wasn't sure why this struck her as so endearing, his hesitation. Honestly, she'd not have ever suspected him to fall prey to any faltering or indecision. He was always so sure of himself. To actually second guess himself or his actions—as he'd just appeared to do—Katie was just stunned.

Rather dazed by this enlightenment, she stepped away from the shadows.

---

HE COULD ONLY IMAGINE that she was yet about some business with a person in need. Where else might she be? Alec acknowledged a large portion of disappointment at her absence from home at this hour. He spun on his heel, resigned to seek her out tomorrow instead.

But there she was, once again behind him, watching him. She stood on the narrow and well-trod road, not directly in front of her own cottage, but the one next to it, as if she'd been surprised to come upon him at her door.

For a moment, they only stared at each other. She'd come from the loch, he surmised easily, her hair wet and loose, the skirts of a gauzy nightrail visible beneath her shawl, which draped only to the top of her thighs, her sturdy boots caked with scrapes of mud. She held her folded, discarded gown in her hands.

Absently, intrigued by the sight of her not-quite-but-almost state of undress, he lifted his hand. His explanation followed rather belatedly while she continued to regard him so inscrutably.

"I'd nearly forgotten—*had* forgotten for a while, that is—that I owed you a gown."

She stepped forward but said nothing. Just one step and then two, a pause.

"I'd meant to give it to you earlier." As if this explained his impolite late night visit.

She moved again, rather rushing past him, pushing open the blue door. She walked straight in, didn't close the door, didn't stand in the threshold, barring him entrance, or intent on seeing the back of him with some genuine but possibly dismissive gratitude.

Boswell came to greet him, tail wagging, sniffing Alec's boots.

He followed her inside.

"You owe me nothing, as well you know," she said, her voice not unpleasant.

He wasn't sure if he concurred with that, thought he had some making up to do yet. She knelt at the hearth, worked to liven the small blaze within, hadn't said thank you and goodnight.

Alec closed the door, leaning his back against it. He thought it best to wait here, not wanting to take any further advantage of the fact that she was not demanding he leave. He let his eyes wander around the house while her back was yet turned to him. The tabletop was crowded, seeming to lodge three or four different projects at once; strips of fabrics including some lace; a few messy piles of seeds and dirt-encrusted roots; what he assumed was a constant, her mending pile; and, directly in the center sat Henry's shoes, soles facing upward, revealing the shredded leather in need of attention.

He'd sent Aymer down shortly after she'd come, had him introduce Ben Carpenter, who'd built her a sturdy work counter on the south side wall. She'd wasted no time putting it to use, the shelves and surface cluttered already. In the far corner, in a similar circumstance to the layout of her previous house, the bed had been set. It was draped now as it had been before, in that earthen wool coverlet. Over the short footboard post hung several different pouches and drawstring bags and on the wall over the middle of the mattress she'd tacked a few hooks, which seemed now to be employed as a drying rack, with several long and unknown plants hanging there, in varying stages of dead and dying.

She bounced up off her haunches, turning as she rose, facing him.

He extended his hand, and the linen wrapped garment.

He thought her quite gracious, unexpectedly so, when she strode easily toward him and accepted it.

"Thank you, but truly, you owe me nothing."

"I dinna ken if it will fit. I charged my mother with getting the thing made, wasn't sure about...the sizing." Much willpower was expended to keep his gaze from raking over her cloak-covered body.

And the shocks just kept on coming though he'd yet to understand why she hadn't requested his departure.

She turned again, setting the package down on the table, shoving the lace and fabric bits aside, and then removed her shawl. Alec hadn't moved from the door that she came close to him, garbed in only that shapeless but very provocative nightgown, and reached up to hang her shawl on the peg hook next to his shoulder.

He didn't turn and ogle her, but the close-up available to his periphery suggested the thing might be near see-through in the right light. She leaned both hands against the wall and toed off her boots, She left him again, leaving the scent of roses and something else he could not name in her wake, moving across the room to fetch something from a pouch hanging from that bedpost, before taking a seat at the table directly in front of him.

She stared at him now, confronted him really. "Why have you come, Alec?"

Yet more shock, wrought by her bluntness, seemingly bereft of any animosity.

He didn't answer quick enough, that she furthered, "We both know the frock might have waited until tomorrow."

And all the words rehearsed in his head fled with dastardly cowardice that he was left to utter what remained at the fore. "It's no' finished."

She nodded, obviously requiring no explanation for *it*, but said nothing.

Alec wanted only to look at her. Instantly, he knew this was his new favorite image of her. He had several already, but just now, she was ethereal and delicate. She sat upon the stool sideways to the table, her gauzy nightrail creamy and covering most of her. Her feet were bare, tucked up onto the wrung of the stool. She held an old bone comb in her hand, which had yet to be used, her hand and the comb laid at rest in her lap. Her hair was wet, darkened and disheveled, the mass of it pulled over one shoulder, the ends curling softly. The generous fire in the hearth cast the entire cottage in shifting shades of a pleasing orange glow, softening everything in its light. Her face was in shadows, the fire at her back. Alec was, honestly, amazed to see no anger or complaint for his untoward presence, only the question. She was still and quiet, her face softened. Her blue-eyed gaze held his, showing no wariness at all. She was breathtakingly lovely just now.

He'd never begged for a thing in his life, not even his life during his captivity, but he thought he might beg now, for her. But no, that wasn't why he'd come. The words returned, heartened by the fact that she'd not thrown him out. Pushing himself away from the door, he stepped further inside.

"I need to apologize for my behavior of yesterday afternoon." He shrugged, ambled over to the hearth, perusing the things set atop it—those cups and bowls he'd known before, char cloth and flint and, three goose feathers—and said, "There's many reasons for it, but none of them seem worthy or justifiable in hindsight." He faced her again, the table between them, thought it wise to make clear, "I dinna rescind my anger that you'd walk off to Loch Oykill on your own. It's a dangerous world, and you ken it well as any. I'd rather you took better precautions." But then, the crux of it was more difficult to put into words. "Still, the other...I needn't have provoked you. Aye, but I ken I did. I'm no' sure what happens whenever you...we...stand so close that I can hear your heart beating, or why it puts me in that frame of mind that I feel the need to prove to you that you do want my kiss." He met her gaze, taking his from where it had sat upon Henry's shoes, saw that she was attentive but yet unreadable, so very still. He sighed. "At any rate—"

"Are you *not* going to kiss me again?"

Flummoxed, Alec stared hard at her. His voice deepened. "Is that you asking me to?"

She nodded.

Irrationally, his response was this: "Christ, Katie, I just—haven't even—finished giving my apology for the way I—"

She stood from the stool and walked around the table. She didn't come very close but stayed at the corner near to him. "You want it to be a choice I make, not one you feel you need to convince me of. I'm making a choice."

*Jesu*, but she was remarkable.

He ignored the why of it, determined he would take nothing for granted. His pulse quickened and all the certainty returned, and all the caution evaporated. "Show me."

---

I AM FEARLESS.

*A leap of faith*, Malcolm had called it when she'd believed what he'd said, that Swordmair would be better for her. He'd been right, and but for her own courage, she'd not have known.

She closed the small space between them.

*There's that fearless Katie Oliver I ken.*

*I am fearless.*

And he is so beautiful, his earlier unease so damnably beguiling—so enlightening. And then so empowering. He wasn't a predator, his emotions unengaged, she believed now. Funny, that she'd denied so much of what she felt, believing that he'd only toyed with her. She wasn't yet ready to explore it all, didn't want to hasten into any false hope of what the future might bring, but she vowed earlier as she'd walked through the door, leaving it open for him to enter as well, that she would go forth courageously, lest something wonderful be left in the wake with her fear. What little she did understand about the way her heart leapt at merely the sight of him, the way her pulse quickened, the delight she'd known from only his kiss suggested she'd be a fool to ignore what else might come.

She stopped in front of him and tilted her head up to him, holding his compelling gaze, her breaths coming rapidly. Finally he moved, lifting his hands to take hers, threading their fingers together. But he made no move to kiss her, didn't take her in his arms, only held her attention with his simmering gaze.

He was either proceeding slowly as to not frighten her or he was giving her the opportunity to change her mind. Neither was necessary. Yet, the boldness was new and her heartbeat was threatening to drown out all else that she simply took the last step and melted into him, laying her head on his chest.

He let go of her hands, now at their sides and she closed her eyes with the bliss that came when his strong arms encircled her. He'd kissed her and touched her but had never simply held her. It was a glorious prelude, his arms powerful and warm, the embrace both gentle and then intoxicating. Katie folded her elbows, resting her hands against him. Beneath his tunic, she felt immediately that his heart was pounding in a pattern similar to her own. Miraculously, this calmed her. He was either excited or nervous, but both suggested he was not immune, not unaffected.

"Ask me again," he said after a while, his chin pressed onto the top of her head.

Of course, she knew what he wanted.

"Kiss me." To her own ears, it sounded like begging. And she didn't care.

He loosened his hold at the same time she lifted her face to him.

His hands settled onto her hips, tightening in the fabric of her gown as he lowered his head to her until her lips met his. This kiss was slow, achingly so, just his mouth moving across hers, until Katie leaned in, lifting her hands from his chest to slide them around his shoulders. She opened her mouth first, gave him her tongue, let him do glorious things to it, to her. It grew, the kiss, until she was clinging to him and her chest was on fire. Blindly, not breaking the kiss, he rid himself of his sword and belt. His arm snaked around her again, lifting her up against him, moving them away from the door. She thought he would lay her down on the bed. Instead, he sat at the edge with Katie in his lap. He arranged her legs so that she straddled him, her knees bent into the thin mattress. And all the while, he continued to ravish her mouth.

His fingers left both sides of her waist at the same time, both hands sliding up between them to cup her breasts through the thin fabric of her nightrail. He lifted her breasts, splayed his fingers around them and they groaned together. She pulled back only so much that his hands were given free rein, the silent offer not ignored that he began to tug at the neckline. The gauzy linen fell away, coaxed down from one shoulder. He played with her nipples but briefly with his fingers, replacing them with his tongue and teeth, that Katie arched her back and reveled in his touch and her own reactions, nipples hardening, toes curling, and a wetness coming between her legs. Alec bared the other breast, which sent her nightgown dropping to her waistline. The house was yet cool but his eyes upon her lit more fires within. He took a moment to hold both breasts in his hands, letting the soft firelight show him the modest display. Katie didn't even care if he liked what he saw, so long as he continued to touch her and tease her.

"Perfect," he said, his breath hot on her naked skin, his lips following his eyes, adoring her breasts once more.

And when he returned to her lips, kissing her greedily, his fingers curved around her bottom, drawing her directly onto his groin. Katie whimpered and tugged at the fabric of her night rail, wanting everything out of the way. His hands found her narrow waist again, grinding her against him, until she did so on her own and his warm hands slid around her back while his mouth found her neck. She liked the feel of his strong hands upon her naked skin, liked very well how he held her so tightly, claimed her, made her ache as she never had before.

"Ask me for more," he demanded.

# THE LOVE OF HER LIFE 223

And oh, how she loved the sound of his voice just then, husky and hungry, breathless and needful.

"Yes, more." *Please don't stop.* She rocked her hips on him. "All of it."

"I need to be inside you." More urgency.

She could stop it now. She need only say, *No, that was enough.*

But it wasn't enough.

"Yes. Alec, please."

"*Jesu.*"

Scooting back, making room for her hand to delve between them, she touched him. She rubbed her hand against his breeches, whimpering at how hard he was for her, for this. She hadn't any idea how his breeches were closed, what held them, but found ties and yanked at them with some determination, wanting so badly to feel the heat of him against her hand. Her mouth found his just as her fingers met with his erection. And for the first time in her life, she was wild with need. She urged herself against him, suckled his tongue, and moved her hand up and down him all the while moving her hips in a motion she craved, but with him inside her, deep inside her. Without any prompting, she moved aside the layers of fabric between him and her. He shifted, lifting himself only to lower his breeches and drawers, and then his fingers gripped the bare skin of her hips. Katie released him and settled her hands on his hard shoulders, positioning herself directly above him until his cock touched her entrance.

She met his gaze, realized his jaw was clenched, holding himself in check. His attention was heavy upon her, the depths of his dark eyes filled with a matching need. His hands flexed, lowering her just as she pushed herself down. Their eyes locked while she slid down onto him, until he was deep inside her. Every nerve in her body screamed and every bone became liquid, but she could make no sound. She closed her eyes, languid and yet aroused, just letting her body feel him. Tentatively, she lifted herself and then pressed down, her nails pressing into his shoulders. Her eyes opened when a rumble of a groan escaped him.

"*Jesu*, Katie, you feel like heaven."

He allowed her to move at her own speed, his hands only set upon her lean hips but not moving her.

But it had been so long, and he was so magnificent, his steady gaze nearly undoing her, that Katie soon began to move to a greater rhythm, propelled by her increasing need. He found her breasts again, lavishing them with attention, his fingers hardening her nipples once more. He pumped upward into her at the same time and slowed only when she cried out, as her release came. It smothered her, overwhelmed her. She sank into him, not yet still, wanting to wrest every bit of this moment, whimpering into his shoulder, quivering as she came.

He continued to move, and then stood, holding her firmly around the waist as he transferred her onto her back on the narrow bed and settled between her legs, burying himself inside her once again. And it started all over, the building desire with each thrust. He kissed her savagely, his hands fisted on either side of her. Katie held his face, returning the brutal and astonishing kiss, hardly able to understand what was happening, how she could be so aroused again. He withdrew, pulling his cock nearly completely out of her and thrust again. And again and again while she lifted her hips to meet each surge, until he stiffened atop her just as another orgasm washed over her. He groaned into the side of her face, his breath hot, and said her name, his tone filled with worship.

She whispered, "Alec" with some wonder, not quite returned to clarity.

She couldn't move, didn't want to, let her mind stay right here, sated and bewitched.

She would be sorry, she knew. But not just yet.

# Chapter Fifteen

He didn't want to move, but to do that again with her. *Bluidy hell*, but she was a wonder. He'd expected passion, to match her fiery eyes, but he hadn't been prepared for the depths of her desire or her willingness to act upon it.

He lifted himself, just enough to glance down at her. Her eyes were closed yet, the fingers of one hand pressed against her lips, as if trying to absorb more sensations yet. Her brow was uncreased and her lashes unmoving upon her cheeks. He raked an admiring gaze over the line of her jaw and her naked shoulder. She was, at this very moment, the most beautiful he'd ever seen her.

Alec pressed his lips to her cheek. She purred and opened her eyes. He tried to read her gaze, but the firelight was behind him and he saw only golden shadows. But then she was Katie and soon enough, he was sure he detected a growing worry in her blinking gaze, even as she tried to smile for him. While he was yet so deep inside her, while his pulse had not even begun to return to anything near normal, he assumed she was already knowing some regret.

"Dinna do that," he pleaded. "No' yet. I know you'll want to give yourself grief, but no' yet." He kissed her again, sent his tongue inside her mouth to stir her, to take back her mind.

She allowed it for a while.

But it couldn't be put off indefinitely, he knew.

With one last lingering kiss, he withdrew from her and settled at her side, laying his arm across her midsection. The slim bed forced him to remain very close to her. They remained clothed, save that all their garments were askew. Hell, he still wore his boots. Her flawless breasts and gorgeous legs were bared to him, as her nightrail was yet bunched around her waist. He would do it better next time, would undress her slowly, and learn and love every inch of her.

After a moment, he asked, "You want to do this now, get it all out?"

She knew very well to what he referred, what he'd already brought up. Still, she asked, "Do what?"

"List all the reasons we shouldn't have done that, or all the reasons you're sorry you did. I'd expect some overlap there."

She gave him no quarrel for how light-hearted his tone was. But then, how could it not be? He'd just enjoyed—nae, lost himself in—some fairly spontaneous and admittedly spectacular lovemaking with her, felt as if he could slay dragons just about now.

But when she didn't respond straight away, he said, "You're afraid or upset. I dinna want—"

"I'm not...anything. Can we not talk about it?"

He rather was hoping to repeat *it*, and soon, so aye, he wanted to talk about it, was keen to settle her.

She sighed then, needing no further urging, but confessed, "I was so in love with life these past few weeks and now...this rather complicates things."

"Complicates?"

"Pardon me, I should have prefaced that with the fact that I *was* willing and very agreeable...and I am not particularly sorry for...the act. But that I hadn't thought past...this." She hesitated, while Alec gently stroked the bare skin of her stomach in a small, circular pattern. "I just didn't want to live this way, didn't want to start this way at Swordmair. I don't want rumors to start. I don't want people's opinion of me to be clouded by this. Good grief, I don't want Henry teased that his mother is a whore. Witch was bad enough."

"*Jesu*, Katie."

She turned in the crook of his shoulder to judge his reaction to this. Her face was alive with regret, or was that pain? Mayhap she only considered what she'd just said, or rather how awfully she'd just expressed her own thoughts.

"I'm sorry. I've not ever done this before—"

"You have a child, Katie, I dinna think you can claim—"

She shook her head. "Haven't ever done it with anyone but my husband, simply for the sake of..."

"Aye, I recall. Coupling merely for the sake of coupling. Like animals." He was wishing he'd not invited her to air her anxieties just now. Trying to control his own reaction to her bluntness, reminding himself this likely was new to her, that she would need time to adjust, Alec lifted himself and leaned over her. "For now, until you come to terms with it—whatever that might need or mean—can you no' just kiss me again? I ken for me, I'm learning that I find a lot of answers in your kiss."

While she digested this, her lips parting in some wonder at his words, and while she gave no indication that she might refuse him now, he kissed her.

"Might not be a bad idea for me to stay with you tonight," he said against her lips after a while, neither unaware nor unaffected by her stiffening beneath him. "No' for this again," he clarified, lifting a brow as he added, "though I'd no deny you. I ken, though, you'll want to push me away now, mayhap blame me for your own misplaced guilt. I will no' have it."

She cleared her throat and said in a level tone, "I don't mean to ruin what was...."

He lifted a brow, but she did not finish. Alec gave an assist, aiming for levity lest she did indeed ruin the entire spectacular affair. "Earthshattering? Mind-blowing? Knee-knocking?"

As hoped for, she grinned a bit and allowed, "Perhaps. Maybe. I might have only said lovely."

"Aye, it was that as well." He kissed her again, his eyes open and on her. And then he whispered against her lips, "Promise me one thing, Katie. Whenever you begin to browbeat yourself, think of this night. Think how bold and fearless and passionate you were. She's always inside you, that lass. I ken sometimes you're afraid to let her live."

She closed her eyes and her mouth moved in such a way to suggest she might cry. She nodded instead and said, "As well you know, I'm...I'm not brave enough to give her full rein. This, what we've done, this is—"

"This is desire," he interjected curtly. "Dinna invent reasons to be angry with either yourself or me. It's desire, same as mine for you. It's no wrong or ugly or sinful. Just desire, a thousand glens full of it on my end. Aye, and we're adults, Katie, and were both willing, that it makes no sense to overthink it. Aye, I wanted you, and aye, I'll want you again, I ken. That dinna make me weak. Christ, lass, I'm more alive because of this need and desire for you than I have been in years."

This tilted her face upward, brought her troubled eyes to his, searching his face to find some guarantee of the truth of his words.

"Let her out," he said. "Let her live."

---

THAT VERY NEXT EVENING, Alec had advised Katie in the hall at supper that he was leaving the next morn and would be gone for two, mayhap three days, about some clan business with his father.

"All right," she'd said with some curiosity for the fact that he seemed to have sought her out simply to disclose this, his attentive expression telling her that her response was important.

She'd spent last night, all of it, in his arms. He'd left her shortly before the sun had climbed over the hills, had kissed her and told her, "This is only the beginning, Katie."

Now, he sent a glance around them, and when assured that no one stood too close, he expounded, "I dinna want you to think I was ignoring or avoiding you."

She understood now. And couldn't withhold a smile for him, for this thoughtfulness. He knew her well, as she supposed she might have done that very thing, wondered if he'd gotten what he wanted and so disappeared.

"Thank you."

"Aye."

She'd been busy enough all day that she had not seen him at all until now. Busy had been a good thing, as it had not granted her time to overthink last night, as he'd supposed she might have.

What rare moments she'd had for reflection had only served to bring the taste and smell and feel of him back to her. Now, she allowed her gaze to fall upon his mouth, memories flooding her and thrilling her, getting lost in her want of his lips on her.

"Dinna do that, lass," his husky voice startled her from her reverie.

He looked as if he was torn between his own powerful, untimely desire and a great pleasure for having caught her experiencing the same.

As innocently as she could, she asked, "Do what?" But good grief, her breathlessness didn't help her cause.

He shook his head at her, his lips pursed with a wee bit of warning, even while his eyes smiled at her. "It's only unknown to all these people for your benefit. I would no' care if Robert Bruce himself and all his army ken, but I ken you dinna want it bandied about. But, Katie Oliver, you keep looking at my mouth like you're wanting to be attached to it, I'm going to make that happen for you."

Her belly flipped and a peculiar heat rose in her chest. She knew he wouldn't disgrace her that way. He just wouldn't. Yet, the promise in his dark eyes prompted her to challenge, "Right here?"

Nodding, he vowed, "Right now." There was something absolutely breathtaking about the light in his eyes just now, indeed in all his face. No shadows, no harshness, no anger, just his regard, warm and filled with promise.

Aye, if she were truly brave....

"Katie Oliver!"

They blinked at the same time, the moment gone, though her heart continued to speed up, even as Alec's father was shouting her name again.

So now, two mornings later, Katie wondered if he were returned, if she might see him soon as she was on her way to the keep, hoping to beg a few candles from either Magdalena or the steward. Inside that narrow assemblage of trees between the village and the castle, Malcolm and Eleanor surprised her, being on foot, coming from the keep.

She called out good morning and received Malcolm's returned greeting. As they stopped directly in front of her, Katie lifted a brow and waited while Malcolm scratched his orange beard with some pretense at detachment while Eleanor heaved a great sigh. This was no casual meeting.

"What? What has happened?" Her heart dropped into the bottom of her stomach.

Eleanor cleared her throat and uttered without preamble, "I think I—I wonder if I may be with child."

Relief rushed through Katie. She pressed her hand to her chest. *Oh, thank God*. Henry and Alec were safe. Katie opened her mouth, but then passed a glance over at Malcolm, who stood very near, his mouth twisted to the right, one brow lifted. To Eleanor, she wondered, "Are you sure you wouldn't rather go back to my cottage—mayhap speak privately?"

The look exchanged between Eleanor and Malcolm explained much, Malcolm's sudden grin meeting Eleanor's eye-roll.

"Oh, my," Katie said, released with her breath.

"Aye," said Eleanor, "he was there when it happened."

Katie smiled wide herself. "Well, then." She cleared her throat. "When did you have your monthly last?"

"'Bout six weeks ago."

"It was no'," Malcolm argued. "Was before the fight near Eddleston. Aye, I remember because I'd wanted to celebrate with a good—"

"Stop speaking," Eleanor instructed him, pointing her finger at him. She turned to Katie. "He may be right though, possibly it's been longer."

Ignoring her own want to giggle at this pair and this most amazing and incredulous circumstance, Katie remained straight-faced and inquired, "Are you typically very regular?"

Malcolm answered, "You can chart the moon by it."

"Say one more word," Eleanor warned without turning toward the father of her child.

"Aye, I'll be quiet, but dinna forget to tell her how your breasts ache now." To Katie, he included, "She will no' even let me touch them."

Sensing he wasn't helping what surely was a mammoth fright for Eleanor, Katie took her hands and pulled her attention to her. "Aye, you are likely with child then." At the face Eleanor pulled—Katie couldn't believe that the woman looked about to cry—Katie insisted, "And as ever, no matter the circumstance, bairns are always welcome, are they not? I'm so thrilled for you, Eleanor. You'll be a wonderful mother."

Eleanor pursed her lips, and gathered all her strength to admit to Katie, "I dinna ken how. What if I'm no'?"

Katie squeezed her hands and said quite earnestly, "But you do know how. You've been at it for weeks with Henry. I can see all the love you have to give. Your circumstance is perfect—you have a home and a man who obviously loves you and a roof over your head and food in your belly. That's the hard part, already done. Love is easy."

"But how to nurse it and dress it, change it—what if it gets sick?"

There was something curiously charming about her insecurities. "First, we'll start with not calling the babe *it*. Next, picture me, alone in that tiny cottage, giving birth to Henry by myself, having to learn by trial and error, making up most of it as I went. My God, Eleanor, if I can do that—*you* can surely conquer anything. And I'm here to help. I adore babies."

"Should have some more of your own," Malcolm supposed.

Both women ignored him. Katie said, "Enjoy the next few months, Eleanor. Embrace it. You will be the mother of great men and women, I vow. It's such a remarkable thing to experience, all of it. Don't ruin it with worry...like I did."

"Aye. Thank you."

Katie accepted the small gratitude but sensed that Eleanor wasn't yet ready to accept it. It would take time, but she would come around, Katie was sure. She'd spoken truth—the way Eleanor interacted with Henry promised she would indeed be a fierce and loving mother.

Just as Katie recognized the sound of a rider approaching, Eleanor looked over Katie's shoulder and grumbled, "Bluidy hell." To Katie, she said, "I dinna want him—anyone—to ken just yet."

*Him* was Alec, who reined in his horse near Malcolm, looking from one to the next, a question in his gaze, as handsome as ever. Her excitement over his return was then clouded by this wee situation. If not for Malcolm and Eleanor, she wondered what her response to his appearance just now might have been.

Would she have happily gone to him? Run to him? "Good day," Katie said, her smile genuine even as she was forced to give him a fib. "We were just discussing Eleanor's scratchy throat. Thankfully, I think it's naught but the change in weather, disrupting her phlegmatic humors."

Malcolm chimed in, too hastily, too loud and stiff, "I dinna ken what that means, but I hope it's no' contagious."

Katie rolled her eyes, much as Eleanor might have, and glared at the captain. "I can promise you, that her condition is *not* contagious."

"Eejit," Elanor grumbled.

"Hm," was all Alec said. He addressed Katie singularly then, "Are you busy then? After this? I need a few minutes of your time as well."

Katie looked to Eleanor, letting her decide. If the woman needed more of her time, more assurance that everything would be well, she would stay with her.

Eleanor nodded, saying, "It'll be fine."

"I promise you it will," Katie said, with some vehemence.

"Verra well."

Eleanor and Malcolm ambled away, Eleanor giving the big man a swat on his shoulder, for what specifically Katie could only guess. Naturally, she would have dwelled on the pair's situation just now, the revelation so startling, but for Alec's presence. She tilted her face up at him, awaiting either a warmer greeting than the stiff one he'd given thus far, or for him to launch into what he might need to discuss.

"Come up with me," he said, directing his destrier closer. He stretched out his hand, bending toward her.

More puzzled than wary, Katie lifted her hand and met his, strong and steady and warm. As was all of him, always.

With little effort, Alec was able to lift her up, and she settled in the small space at the front of the saddle, her legs to the left, nearly sitting atop his powerful thigh. He circled his arms around her to manage the reins and Katie clung to one forearm as he clicked his tongue and sent the beast into a slow jog.

They turned and rode past the village, on the outskirts, behind the outermost cottages and then charged up the hill where the livestock grazed and across the rock and thistle and heather on the other side. Beyond that, they entered a thicker forest of beautiful silver birch, their leaves falling now, the ground awash in color.

Inside these trees, Alec reined in where a small clearing opened, where the sun penetrated and gave light to a large circle of orange and red leafed earth. He swung his leg around the back and slid smoothly off the huge horse and then reached for Katie, his hands finding her waist and pulling her downward until she stood close to him.

And then he kissed her. Not dramatically, or with some effort to have more, just briefly, and followed it with, "Aye, and that's now a proper greeting."

She couldn't help but be amused by this, by his lightness.

He took her hand and led her to the circle of sunlight, stopping her and turning her to face, which felt more or less as if he were positioning her, that she wondered, "Am I to be sacrificed?" Katie lifted her face to the sun before bringing her gaze back to Alec.

He rather winced. "You might want to rethink that question, but after I say what I'm bound to say."

He took a step back, away from her, that Katie's brow fell, curious, and now indeed a wee bit wary.

Alec took a deep breath. "Katie, I...I should no' have dishonored you—that's what I did, insisting it was naught but desire, that it was perfectly fine to act upon it. That remains true, and I canna regret it for my own self, but it occurred to me that it was yet a dishonorable thing to do. I ken women look at it differently."

She wasn't sure if she needed to, or was expected to, respond to this, supposing there was more to come.

He cleared his throat and continued. "And I dinna ken if it's merely that, or if mayhap I'd have gotten around to it anyway—eventually—but having acted dishonorably, I mean to repair that, and therefore, I'll be asking you to wed with me."

Katie blinked several times, trying to fathom his words, their meaning. His scowl, his very earnestness might better lend itself to ordering about his army or taking a tradesman to task for the poor quality of his workmanship. It did not, in any way, connect well with issuing a proposal of marriage.

"You want to wed me...to restore your honor?" Was all she could think to say.

Naturally, he frowned. "And yours," he said. "You were going to tell Gordon Killen that you would wed him, thought he might keep you safe, but I ken there was naught between you and him but pity, mayhap. Many reasons to wed. This makes good sense, I figure. I want very much to...repeat what we did, but I can no', if it means bringing greater dishonor to you. Also, it would give you further protection, bring you into the keep—you and Henry—you'd want for nothing, all your life. Your son would grow as the child of the next laird of Swordmair, his future locked into this house." He shrugged, putting out additional motivation, "We get on well enough, as you do with my parents. That's essential, I ken."

There was some charm in his sudden and apparent sheepishness. She had to wonder if he'd practiced this monologue a bit before approaching her. Still, the substance of his arguments—as far as proposals went—left much to be desired. If she understood it correctly, the essence of it seemed to be that he wanted to marry her for the same reason as her first husband, so that he might make good use of her body, at his leisure.

However, he was correct that she'd been set—determined—to marry Gordon Killen, as old as Swordmair's laird, for her own selfish reasons. Thus, who was she to condemn his?

Admittedly, her heart was gripped immediately by a thrill, but to wed....

She hadn't removed her gaze from him, even as she let her mind skim over...everything. She had feelings for him, she could not deny that, not to herself. Yet, those emotions, desire aside and whatever the whole of them were, had not been deeply investigated yet, and she had not ever, not for one moment, thought that he might suggest they wed.

She knew now—had known for a wee bit—that she craved his kiss and his touch, and she liked his rare smiles, knew that he was a solid man, of figure and honor and morals, she believed.

But to wed....

---

HE WAS BUNGLING IT, he knew. She was staring at him as if he'd sprouted a beak, mayhap feathers as well.

He'd given it thought. Obviously. He'd not just ridden up into that curious scene with Malcom and Elle and Katie and decided he would propose they marry. But this—his actual words—had come just now, without any planning. What he'd thought over the last few days was, *I dinna want any other to touch you. I want all your smiles. I want you as my own. Always.* Yet, having supposed that emotion wouldn't have persuaded his always-wary Katie, he convinced himself that a practical offer, listing all the reasons it would benefit her, was all it would take to not have the thing thrown back at him.

While she stared at him, he realized just now that riding away from Swordmair had been ill-advised. He'd wanted privacy, of course, but now as her silence lengthened, he understood that if she refused him, it was going to be one hell of an uncomfortable ride back to Swordmair.

Finally she spoke. "You keep asking things of me that are so...difficult to say yes to. First to come to Swordmair, then to kiss you, to be...intimate with you. Now to wed. Have you something to beg of me that it might prove easier to say yes?"

Somewhere in there, she'd just hinted either that she really hated to disappoint people, or she was yet conflicted by his attention. *Jesu*, but if the lovemaking hadn't swayed her....

And, he knew, she was stalling.

Vaguely, his mind churning for his next tactic, he said, "But you keep saying aye, so I'll keep asking."

"Well, I..." She began, but this trailed off. She was unconvinced, he could very well see, could not meet his gaze, keeping it on the grass at her feet.

It would be a sorrowful crime if his inept handling of the words produced the wrong result, he knew. So he did what he knew would speak so much more eloquently than he ever could. He moved toward her, caught her lifted gaze and the sharp intake of breath just as he slid his arms all the way around her and joined his lips to hers. She needed to know that this was alive and real and wasn't going anywhere, his want of her.

She returned the kiss eagerly, her initial befuddlement dissolving quickly, her hands finding him, her tongue meeting his. He crushed her to him, sliding his hands down to circle her bottom, pressing her against his groin. She moaned in response, her fingers sliding into his hair, tilting her face to receive his kiss fully.

He whispered against her lips, "Say you'll wed me, Katie Oliver." He didn't even care if she agreed only for this, so long as she was, and remained, his.

Her eyes stayed closed. She dropped her face a bit, that his next kiss was pressed to her forehead while she nodded.

# Chapter Sixteen

"Aye, and you tell me all that," Alexander MacBriar said to his son, "and I can no' find fault with any of it. I ken the lass is good and kind—and we all ken she's clever and would no doubt be a good mistress one day to Swordmair."

"Then I have your approval?" Alec wondered.

They sat inside his mother's solar, two overlarge men fitted poorly into the small furniture, a fire in the hearth to chase away the cold and gloom of the day. At the table between them sat a cup of the vulgar tea Katie insisted his father drink—and which the man did with nary a complaint, though Alec could smell from here how awful it must be.

His father sipped again, the fine teacup, brought from England with his mother decades ago, seeming like naught but a child's toy in his father's large paw. When he set the cup down again, he said, "I only wonder why. Your mam said you were fond of the lass, but I had no' seen any evidence of that."

He shared an open relationship with his father, but Alec wasn't sure he wanted to discuss his feelings with Katie with him at this point, having not identified them beyond his desire for her.

"Were you hoping yet I'd have aligned myself with the Camerons or the MacGowans or the MacGillewies?" It hadn't been mentioned for years, but in his youth, his father had made his wishes clear.

"I'd given up that dream a long time ago," he answered, waving a hand to dismiss this. He folded his hands over his midsection and shrugged, tipping his face to his son. "Might have dodged an arrow with that MacGowan chit. Word has it she'd killed her husband on their wedding night."

"Christ," Alec said.

"Aye, I approve. No reason to deny it. But lad, tell me you have some feeling for her. Swordmair needs a strong chief, no' one constantly embroiled in marital discord because he made the wrong choice. The woman behind ye is as important as the castle and the people before you."

His hackles raised a bit, Alec challenged, "Aye, you say you approve, but I'm no' sensing that, no' wholly."

Alexander pulled his legs off the stool before him and leaned toward his son, his hands resting on his knees. "I canna read ye though, lad. What are ye thinking? What's she mean to ye?" He threw up his hands then. "Closed off, all of ye, never ken what's boiling in that head of yours." At Alec's surprised look, he grumbled, "She's a fine lass, better than some I ken, but she brings nothing to you, no land, no coin, nothing but someone else's whelp."

Alec's jaw clenched. He felt his lip curl. "I dinna need her to *bring* me anything. Swordmair has no need. I dinna want or need land or coin—and Henry is a fine lad. I'd be proud to call him son."

His father scoffed, sitting back again, throwing his hand out dismissively, taking his gaze from his son, as if he couldn't, or wouldn't, be convinced otherwise.

"You dinna ken her at all, do you? You say she's fine but you dinna ken how strong she is or what she's survived, how resilient she is. You think Henry manages to be that exceptional a lad by a woman who was not clever and warm and loving? She puts all needs before her own—*Jesu*, Malcolm said she was laundering in the dark the other night, she hadn't enough time in the day. Brave enough to strike out with us, with nothing but our promise that Swordmair would be better, trying to make something out of nothing for her son."

"Bah!" His father sneered.

Alec thrust himself from the chair. "Are you dotty then? You live with mam all these years yet you can no' see how good she is, how magnificent she is? Did you no' see her at supper tonight? Wanting only to visit and relax but plagued all evening by one after another—this ache, that pain, why is my bluidy piss green?—and she smiles, dinna say nae, gives all her attention and time. And never mind that she's so bluidy beautiful, it'd make you weep or that she wears every fecking emotion on her sleeve even as she tries to avoid them all, so scarred by what life has done to her already—but you can no' see how perfect she is! Are you that blind?" His hands fisted, his disbelief at rather an unholy level. He ground out to his father, "Bluidy land! Coin! I dinna need anything but her. Katie."

And with that his father lifted his merry gaze and a huge smile to his son.

Alec's jaw unclenched. Slowly, until his mouth gaped with confusion.

"Aye, lad. That's all I wanted to ken, that ye were in love with her. Bursting with it, by my reckoning." While Alec continued to gawk at his father for his merciless deception, his sire added with an innocent glint in his eye, "Your mam and I only want you happy."

"Bluidy hell."

---

"YOO-HOO!"

Katie turned, hearing the mistress's airy little voice near.

There was absolutely nothing that she didn't like about Magdalena MacBriar, she thought, as she watched the woman navigate the uneven ground of the trail leading up to the castle. Many parts jiggled as she moved, her chin, her middle, her wiry hair.

"Good day, mistress," Katie greeted.

Maddie flapped one hand in the air, a greeting perhaps, or a steadying arm as her little legs were propelled into speed by the slant of the hill. "Aye, it is, unless ye keep up with that *mistress* bit."

"Apologies, it seems a disrespect to address you by your given name," Katie defended.

"The disrespect comes, lass, when you dinna heed my bidding." She stopped then in front of Katie, needing another few seconds to catch her breath before lifting her button eyes to Katie. "I was just down with Martha," she said, lifting a basket filled with lace. "Three yards lace for naught but the herring and two pounds bacon. Aye and that's a good bargain. Now, what's this I hear you're to wed my son?"

Katie's eyes widened. Alec had said yesterday, in the moments after she'd accepted his proposal, that he'd be telling his mother and father—seeking the laird's permission, as it were—but she'd yet to see him today to know if he had.

"Well, yes," she stammered. "He had asked, and I...I said aye." Quickly, she qualified, "With your husband's approval, of course."

"Aye, they spoke this morning," Maddie said. "Alec dinna want to wait, so the laird sent down for the bishop's signature, and thinks we can make it happen in the next week or so."

This surprised her. Truthfully, she hadn't thought anything about a date being set, hadn't thought much over the past twenty-four hours—hadn't even shared the news with Henry—but that she had said she would wed Alec MacBriar. The very thought since had only brought an equal amount of thrill and uneasiness. The thrill was easy to explain, to acknowledge, as his very presence had done that to her almost from the beginning. The uneasiness, however, she'd only just understood this morning, had only just realized that she was afraid that she might be in love with him, but that he had no corresponding feeling toward her. He liked her, she imagined—no, she truly believed that he did—but she understood there was no greater emotion attached to his proposal. He was an honorable man, and he felt some dutiful responsibility toward her, both because he'd taken her from her home and because they'd lain together. He was a most capable man; he fought bravely and proudly, rode his destrier as if carried by the wind and good grace, could melt hearts with a smile if he but tried, was a good son and friend and practiced compassion likely without even being aware that he did. But love? Katie wasn't sure Alec MacBriar would allow himself to feel something so nebulous as love. Desire? Aye. But love? She just couldn't be sure.

"Of course, you'll have to start spending some time up at the keep," Maddie said. "You'll need to learn all about the management of Swordmair, if you're to be her next mistress." She went on, began to list all the functions and obligations accorded to the mistress of such a great keep.

Katie only listened with half an ear, her mind repeating what she'd convinced herself this morning. It was all right that he didn't love her. She would have the security of the man and his family and Swordmair, so much more than she'd ever allowed herself to imagine she might know in her life. Her child—children?—would never know hunger or cold or fear. She would be pleased to be by his side all the rest of her days. She felt certain she could love him—if she did—and not need to be loved in return, being otherwise so richly rewarded as his wife.

Having decided this, confident in her assessment, Katie gave her full attention to Alec's mom, just in time to hear her say, "Aye, I'm all for it, lass. Haven't had a family wedding in eons. Couldn't be happier."

Katie smiled and was about to give her gratitude to the woman when Maddie stopped and grabbed firmly at Katie's sleeve. "Of course, if you hurt him or bring him pain, I'll have to kill you, lass."

---

HENRY BURST THROUGH the door, holding the handle yet as he called out, "Is it true?"

Katie's hand flew to her chest with a fright for his exploding in like that. "Is what true?"

"Maddie said you and Alec are going to wed."

That was not how she wanted her son to find out. She'd planned to tell him quietly, just here, inside their cottage. She supposed, however, his wide-eyed, grinning façade suggested it didn't matter how he'd learned of it; he seemed well-pleased.

"Aye, it is true, but I'd wanted to tell you myself."

"We're going to live up in the keep? And do I get to call him da'?"

"Come inside, Henry." The whole village didn't need to hear this conversation. She set down the mending she'd been working on, the fantastic new holes Henry had made in his brown breeches.

He did, though he left the door open. He sat at the table with Katie.

"Yes, we are to wed," Katie said, lowering her voice, hoping he would do the same. "And aye, we'll move up to the keep afterward."

"Eleanor said—"

"Good grief. Who else did you talk to about this?"

"Eleanor was there in the kitchen when Maddie told me."

Curious and yet cautious, Katie asked, "What did—did Eleanor say anything?"

Henry shook his head. "She just smiled, but only the funny one. The one that dinna show her teeth."

Eleanor smirked, Katie gathered, finding this amusing and not alarming, as she might have at one time.

Henry continued to jabber, telling her that *Maddie did this* and *Eleanor said that*, all of it quite lovely, until he said, "Maddie said I could stay up at the keep, said I'd have my own room always, that she would fix it up tonight if I want."

Katie was surprised how this clutched at her heart. Both Maddie's kindness to Henry and then whatever it was that tugged at Katie's heart that she asked, "You would leave me here by myself until the wedding?"

"Aw, mam," Henry said, a bit of a wince coming, having detected the disappointment in her tone. With great practicality, making a deal with her so that everyone was pleased, he offered in his small voice, "Mayhap I'll sleep one night there and the next here, and then one night there again, and the one after that here."

She nodded and tried to smile, even as she realized just now that she wasn't ready for all these changes, so many and all coming at once. She could handle Henry gone all day, with friends, up at the keep, with Eleanor, because she had him all to herself every night and morning, just the two of them, as it had been for so long.

That would be taken from her as well, she just realized. She wasn't ready.

Unaware of his mother's sudden dismay, Henry asked, "Can I go back up to the keep?"

She nodded stiffly, her eyes watering, happy for the reprieve that she might cry without him seeing it. Swallowing thickly, she said, "I'll be up shortly for supper."

He was out the door then, quick as he'd come, and Katie put her arms onto the table and buried her head there with her sadness, let the sorrow come.

Aye, he'd leave her eventually, she'd always known. Even now, he'd begun to spread his wings. But she didn't have to like it, and she was sorry that her decision now to marry Alec would speed things along in that regard. And truthfully, there was little consolation in the fact that Henry himself was so enamored with these changes.

"Prospect of a wedding got ye down?"

Katie startled at Eleanor's voice, lifting her face, wiping at her tears with jerky hands. She made to stand but Eleanor waved her to sit and joined her at the table.

In typical Eleanor fashion, she said, "I'd be crying, too."

This made Katie smile and she tried to explain her sudden anguish. "It just dawned on me that my life with Henry will never be the same. It's been just he and I for so long—forever, it seems. And now...now, that'll be done."

Eleanor's straight brows angled downward. "Christ, you really love that lad."

Katie burst out laughing. "Aye, Elle. I do."

"I canna see myself feeling that much...of anything for this one."

Katie could not resist the jibe, "*This one* is not an acceptable replacement for *it*. And of course you will."

Eleanor shrugged and changed the subject. "So why are you marrying Alec?"

Katie drew a deep breath, not having expected the extremely forthright question. "I suppose because he asked."

Now Eleanor lifted a disbelieving brow, tilting her head with some disapproval. "I dinna think so."

Eleanor had shared incredibly personal information with Katie yesterday that she felt now she owed the same to her. She gave her own shrug and admitted, "Of course, I like him and we seem to get on—"

"Aye, and that's all horseshite. I'm wanting to ken if you're doing it simply to make your place all the better here. Because if you've no feeling for the man then tell him you've changed your mind. Do no' wed him. He dinna need that kind of wife, that kind of marriage. You're a decent sort, I ken, but you're no' a simpleton and I ken you have to survive but—"

Katie pushed her hands forward on the table, palms up. "I'll stop you right there, before you kill the friendship with whatever else might spring from your mouth."

"We're no friends if—"

"Aye, we are," Katie said. "Stop being the mean warrior woman because I know you are actually only a warrior woman and not at all mean. And listen to me. I do have feelings for him. I'm not sure...what they are, though. I haven't quite processed it myself, but something happened and then—"

"Did you sleep with him?"

Katie rolled her head back, staring at the ceiling. When she faced Eleanor again, she rather snapped, "Yes, we did, if that's all right with you. So now he feels guilty or something—duty—I'm not sure. But he seemed to like the idea—of marriage—which *he* suggested, and it occurred to me that I...seemed to like the idea as well...so...there you have it."

"So you are in love with him."

Katie almost hated her for dragging out what she'd yet to fully wrap her head around herself. "I might be." She rubbed her hands over her eyes. "I don't know."

"I'm no' surprised though, actually."

Katie put her elbow on the table and her chin in her hand and sighed, resigned that they were going to discuss this fully, until Eleanor was satisfied. "Which part doesn't surprise you?"

"All of it. I've been with the MacBriars for nearly seven years and far as I ken, he's never been with anyone." Eleanor lifted and dropped her broad shoulder again. "Aye, tarts here and there, not often enough to my way of thinking. But they'd come at him left and right, the wedding kind. He dinna care, never saw them. Never made sense to me. Then he sees you and...everything changes. I dinna get it at first. Malcolm was useless, had no insight, just grins, makes me want to slap him."

Katie frowned. "Are you saying I'm not...worthy of him, that you cannot understand what he..." she let it go when Eleanor shook her head so vehemently.

"Nae, no' like that. In some ways, I guess it makes sense. He'd give Malcom the business all the time, *ye can no' save 'em all*, but he's just as bad, needs to be someone's hero, I guess. They think they can save the whole world."

Katie snorted. "So I'm pathetic and that attracts him? Fabulous."

"Aye," Eleanor said, drawing another frown from Katie, until she clarified, "He ken you were, that's what intrigued him, but then he realized you really were no' and to my eye, he was even more intrigued."

"Did you come then, to make sure I am not playing false, or would not—"

"Aye. I'd have to kill ye if you did," Eleanor stated casually, promising, "they'd never find the body."

Completely undaunted, Katie informed her, "You are the second person to threaten my life today, with some fear that I will break his very hard heart." At Eleanor's look of inquiry, Katie explained, "His mother has already promised to cause my death if I bring him any grief."

Eleanor showed no shock at all. "She would, too. She'd cut you like a Yuletide hog."

Katie's eyes did widen at this, but Eleanor continued, "But I dinna actually come here for that, though I'm pleased to ken you and he'll do just fine. I came to ask if...if you...shite...if you can help me—I thought I'd—"

Katie watched with amazement as Eleanor just stopped, pursing her lips and staring hard at Katie, struggling to get all the words said. "Just spit it out," she suggested.

"I want to dress like you," Eleanor blurted.

Katie couldn't help that her eyes remained so huge in her face. She quickly recovered, or hoped she did and laughed nervously, glancing down at her own meager gown, the brown frock, the one Alec had sliced that she'd since repaired. "I don't really think you do, Eleanor."

"I ken I should wear a gown," she said, then supposed, "Maybe. Sometimes."

"But why?"

"Honestly, I dinna even ken."

"Elle, I always imagined you were fairly comfortable in your own skin. Why would you—do you think Malcolm minds that you don't wear frocks?"

Eleanor scoffed. "I dinna give a rat's arse what he thinks. I just, I dinna ken, maybe I miss it sometimes. Being more...feminine. Aye, and mayhap I dinna want my bairn wondering why his mam looks like his da."

Katie supposed, "It *would* likely be easier, the further along you grow with the bairn. And of course, you're gorgeous, you'd be quite striking in, well, probably anything. But is there a market town nearby to purchase readymade wares? My stitches are neat, but I have very limited capabilities in the design of gowns, as you can plainly see." She indicated again her own very simple frock.

"I dinna need anything fancy. Aye, but there is the market over at Carryd."

"Let's go then. I haven't seen a market in years."

"Suppose you'll need a wedding gown anyway, aye?"

"Good heavens, Elle. One thing at a time. I haven't thought that far yet."

Another frown and more unsolicited advice came. "Ye can no' wed the MacBriar in *that*."

"Thank you, Eleanor."

*Oh, what a day!*

---

WHEN KATIE ARRIVED at the hall for supper that night, Maddie flitted by with a tray of candles in her hands.

"Aye, you'll be at the family table tonight, lass. You and Henry." And she disappeared, gone to the kitchens.

Katie would have followed. Of late, she'd gotten into the habit of going directly there, to see what help she might give, usually only charged with delivering platters and trenchers to tables as the meal was served.

But the mistress's words, reflecting her change in circumstance, rather floored her. Stunned, she spit out a short burst of laughter. She really needed to pull her head from the clouds, and give some greater thought to the bigger picture, leave off solely thinking, *I am to wed Alec MacBriar. I can touch him and kiss him and smile at him to my heart's content.*

A happy whoop from behind turned her around just as Malcolm approached, lifting her by the waist in a huge bear hug, spinning her around until she cried out, giggling, and smacked his shoulder. "Put me down, you brute."

He did, but then shocked her by kissing her hard directly on her lips. "Aye, and you're one of us now, truly and always. I've got holes in my belly but you got the future MacBriar, so it's all good, aye?"

He was delightful, for his joy with the situation, and also for not threatening her life.

"Are you waiting on my gratitude then?" She teased.

Malcolm went suddenly very serious and lowered his voice as people began to fill the hall. "Ye deliver me a healthy bairn, see Elle around and through it, I'll consider all debts settled, aye?"

Katie nodded, hardly able to imagine the magnificent creature that was Eleanor would have any trouble carrying or bearing children. She struck out her hand and said, "Fair enough." Malcom took her hand and pumped with enthusiasm and Katie added, "But Malcolm, I do thank you. His scowls alone would never have convinced me to come to Swordmair."

He showed his adorable gap-toothed grin. "Aye and dinna I ken it!" And then serious again and very dear. "You keep smiling at him, lass. Happy is a long time coming for him." With that, he kissed her cheek and was gone.

Alec appeared then, with Henry skipping alongside him, and made straightaway for Katie. Her cheeks warmed under his heated regard while her heart flipped for the very slow and very handsome smile he gave her.

"There's to be an announcement tonight," he said when he stood before her.

"And Maddie said I am to sit next to Edric tonight," Henry said. "And you, too, mam. Up at the big table."

Katie smiled at Henry. "That's quite exciting." She addressed Alec then with a wee accusation in her grin. "There's been a few announcements already, I understand."

He only shrugged. "Swordmair is verra large, but you ken, also verra small."

Henry saw Ronald and Martin then, dashing away to catch up with his friends.

"So it is," she said. "Should I expect more death threats if I prove a poor wife?"

Possibly, her intact grin let him understand that she was more amused than not, even as she still wasn't sure the warnings were not dire.

He grinned briefly before asking, "Do you have plans to be a poor wife, lass?"

It was no hardship at all to give him the truth. "I do not."

"It'll all be good then, aye?"

She didn't suppose he often had moments of doubt, was rather intrigued by his want of assurance, as that wasn't their roles. First, she asked, "Do you have plans to be a good husband?"

Something darkened in his gaze briefly, extinguished quickly, but Katie was sure she saw something.

"I do."

"I think we'll do very well together," she predicted.

He reached out and took her hand, simply twined his fingers but left them low at their thighs, keeping his gaze on her.

"Aye, we will."

# Chapter Seventeen

The shire of Carryd sat snugly in a glen in the shadows of Beinn Arnoch, a curved mountain range hugging the town with gently rolling hills crowded with heather before lifting straight and high, disappearing into the low hanging clouds. The town itself, host to the monthly market, boasted two hostels, a stone-armory which housed a garrison of clan soldiers—MacKenzies, Alec had said—a surfeit of thatched cottages, some two stories high, and in the distance, far outside the town stood a steepled parish church, whose entire north yard was peppered with gravestones.

The market itself ran the length of the main road, which dissected the glen almost perfectly in half. Stalls and tents were erected, fit wherever they might, one atop another. Some local residents sold wares directly from their homes, their window boards ingeniously hinged from the top that only a stout stick or pole was needed to keep the window open that whatever items were being sold could be perused merely by peeking within.

They'd been afoot within the market for nearly half an hour when Katie despaired to Eleanor that she had yet to find any vendor offering readymade frocks.

"We've no' been through but a quarter of the booths," Eleanor reasoned, seemingly unconcerned.

It had not escaped Katie's notice that they—specifically Alec and Malcolm and Eleanor—drew much attention. There were other soldiers about, from near and far the different plaids said, but none of a size with these three. Mostly a path was cleared as they walked about, Eleanor walking in the middle of the aisle that she could examine the offerings on both her left and right, indifferent about the possibility that she might block someone's path or that people were forced to scurry around her if she stopped to inspect anything closely.

At one point Eleanor turned around, walking backwards as she called out to Alec, who with Malcom, walked several paces behind the two women. "I dinna see that smithy yet. Remember him, the one from near Dornoch?"

"Aye," Malcolm replied. "That was some fine metal."

"But first, he needs to find her a wedding gown," Eleanor said, her goading smirk moving from Katie to Alec.

Embarrassed, because she did not want Alec to think she put Eleanor up to that, or that she wanted or needed a gown that she would wear but one day, she was quick to throw over her shoulder at Alec, "That is Eleanor talking and not me. I need nothing. We're here for Eleanor."

"Gotta have a wedding frock, lass," Malcolm said. "Bad omen to wed in everyday things."

Now Katie turned around, though she did not continue to walk as Eleanor had, but stopped so that the two men caught up with her. To Malcolm, she accused, "I think you're making that up." To Alec, she repeated, "I need nothing." She wasn't about to spend her precious coin on a frock.

Alec wasn't persuaded, but by Malcolm. "He's right, though. Bad omen."

She studied his hazel eyes, looking for any sign of lightness, that he might be jesting. "It is not...is it?"

"Aye." He bent his face toward her as Malcolm continued on, catching up with Eleanor. "I dinna come to the market to shop for Elle," Alec said. "I'm here for you. Did you no' have a new frock when you married before?"

"I did not."

"You need no trappings to make you bonny, Katie, but I would no' mind seeing you in finer clothes for the wedding. You ken it'll be a huge feast. The laird's son plans on wedding only once."

There was a lot said just there, a lot of information come her way, but Katie heard first that Alec thought she was pretty, and then, "A huge feast?" She really disliked being the center of attention.

He grinned and took her arm, steering her to follow Malcolm and Eleanor. "Aye, to last for several days. Swordmair is no small keep and the MacBriars have kin in many counties and clans. People will come from all over the highlands."

"Are you serious?" She thought they'd wed before the laird and mistress and the soldiers and the folks of Swordmair, hadn't in her wildest imagination thought it would involve any but those. *Good grief.*

"Aye, and so you'll have your wedding frock, like it or no.'"

She fussed no more. The woman in her, the one who'd been forced by necessity to make gowns and kirtles last for years and years was not about to argue further against something new and fine, certainly if she were to be ogled and judged by so many people.

# THE LOVE OF HER LIFE

Malcolm and Eleanor had stopped at a booth, leaving the middle of the road to crowd into the linen canopied stall. Alec led Katie to their side, using his large size to clear a space for her amongst the eager shoppers. As this booth was so crowded, Katie didn't realize until she stood front and center that this was a baker's booth, the shelves and counter filled with delectable treats.

Eleanor turned, holding a slab of bread, the center of which was filled with raisins and currants and spices. One corner was missing already, and Eleanor was licking her fingers. She shrugged at Katie and spoke around the food in her mouth. "No sense coming to the market if you're no' going to enjoy the fare."

"Ooh," Katie cooed.

"Aye, two," Alec said then to the vendor, pulling coin from a pouch inside his tunic.

Her eyes widened when he pressed a piece into her hands. The meals at Swordmair were always plentiful and tasty, and so much more pleasing than anything Katie had ever known, but Katie had never seen anything like this on her trencher.

Stepping away from the stall that other hungry buyers might find a spot, Katie stopped near Malcolm and Eleanor, finishing off their treats, and took a small bite herself. She closed her eyes and let her shoulders fall in sublime delight. When she opened them, Alec was standing close, enjoying his own fruit bread.

"I like that look on you, Katie." His voice was seductive, causing a stir in her belly that the treat was instantly forgotten. He bent low and said at her cheek, "I can no' imagine I'm going to be able to wait until we're wed to give you that look again myself."

Katie gulped and swallowed, tilting her face to him. Their lips were close. She blinked rapidly and met his gaze, only inches away.

"Aw, c'mon on now," cried Malcolm, a whine to his tone, "ye canna be seducing the lass right here in the market."

Neither Alec nor Katie moved, their eyes locked. Until he grinned, with leisurely charm and so much promise in his hazel eyes and stepped away from her.

Katie released her breath, the forgotten bread held near her waist. She met Eleanor's eye, which she then proceeded to roll when she had Katie's attention.

They browsed yet more, only approaching a few booths, if their interest was piqued enough. It wasn't until another hour had passed that they finally found some clothiers when a thought struck Katie.

She crept up close to Eleanor, who was grimacing as she held up a bright green and yellow woolen fabric.

"Does Alec get a say in my wedding gown?"

Eleanor turned the frown onto Katie. "Why are ye asking me this?"

"Because I don't know the answer."

Dropping the unpleasant fabric, Eleanor held up her hand and clarified, "Nae, I mean why are ye asking *me*? Why would ye ken I might have the answer?"

With a hopeful look, Katie said, "Wishful thinking, I guess."

"Supposing that ye even asked means ye'd given it some thought, so maybe you dinna want his say. Aye, and let's get rid of them anyway for a while," Eleanor said, throwing a glance over her shoulder at Alec and Malcolm. "because if he asks me once more if I feel all right, if I'm tired, or if I should be eating whatever I'm shoving into my mouth, I'll be bringing a fatherless bairn into the world." And with that she pivoted and addressed them. "Go on, then. She dinna want you to see the thing before you need to. Bad omen, anyhow." She waved her hand, shooing them away.

Katie had found a glorious frock in a rich mauve and lifted it up to Eleanor's shoulders from behind when she noticed Alec still hovering outside the booth.

Eleanor saw this as well, wondering to Alec, "Why are you still here?"

"It's crowded, lass," he said, addressing his answer to Katie, shifting his weight onto one hip, his hand familiarly upon the hilt of his sword. "Too many people. I dinna like leaving you—"

"Good grief. Elle's right here."

"Aye, but she's..."

Katie gasped and whispered behind Elle's back. "Did you tell him?"

"I dinna have to. The quacking duck with the orange hair did."

Grinning, Katie called out to Alec. "We're fine. We won't be long."

"Hope he lets ye breathe when you're wed," Eleanor grumbled under her breath.

Alec finally obliged but stepped forward to plunk his coin purse into Elle's hands, saying, "Whatever she wants, but she's to buy her finery for the wedding."

He did then amble away that Katie returned her attention to the gown in her hands. "Elle, look at this. This color would be so amazing with your eyes."

Eleanor glanced around first, likely to be sure not one person witnessed the warrior even considering frilly frocks, before she pulled the skirt toward her. "It's soft," she allowed.

"It'll feel like heaven against your skin, I'm sure."

Frowning over the neckline, which was indeed low, Eleanor made another face. "Drafty. Aye but we're to be finding your togs for the wedding."

"Very well. It has just occurred to me, Elle, that finding the clothiers might have been the easy part. Finding one with something to fit your height is going to be difficult. We may, in the end, be forced to make it ourselves."

---

LEANING AGAINST THE corner of the larger hostel, Alec shifted his jaw and kept his gaze on Katie. She needn't know that he'd stayed near. Markets were notorious for pickpockets and thieves, and worse, drunkards and fools. He couldn't remember a market day where a fight or brawl hadn't broken out, that he felt better keeping her in sight.

Under normal circumstances, he'd trust Elle to handle anything that might happen, but she was compromised now—Christ, he still couldn't imagine Elle, a mother, and hell, Malcolm, father to a child. He'd known previously what they'd been up to but hadn't considered it any of his business since neither of them had ever let it affect their positions as his officers. But he'd thought it had ended last year, hadn't any idea when it had started up again.

Malcolm, less concerned with the lasses than Alec, had entered the hostel, the front pub section, hoping for an ale colder than what these traveling vendors or his own flask could provide. He returned in good time, likewise putting his shoulder into the stone of the building, sipping quietly, his gaze wandering, not at all concentrating on Eleanor and Katie.

Alec turned when Malcolm tapped him on the arm. Following the direction in which Malcolm stared, Alec watched a half dozen soldiers strutting down the road, young and loud and happy to be seen and heard.

"Those Sutherland plaids?" Malcolm wondered.

"Next generation," Alec guessed. "The rest are gone."

Malcolm lifted his brow with some inquiry.

"Aye, had word from Lach Maitland that Iain McEwen had some quarrel with them." He gave a wry chuckle. "And when the Sutherlands went to Berriedale, intent on destruction, our own king happened to be within spitting distance, literally stumbled upon the fight. Wiped 'em out."

"No?"

"Aye. Robert Bruce ambled into the fray."

Malcolm grinned widely, shaking his head at the very thought. "I love that man."

Alec chuckled and nodded, and their attention was returned again to the youths in the Sutherland plaids.

"That's some bollocks, stepping outside Sutherland," Malcolm commented.

"Aye, and making their presence known so freely."

Alec split his gaze between Katie and those lads then, shaking his head when two of the youths began harassing a bonny lass, tugging at her shawl and then at her hair. Another woman, twice the age of the lass, put the girl behind her, and slapped at the boy's hand. Laughing, the group ambled away.

Alec and Malcolm straightened away from the building, but did not immediately step forward, even as they neared the booth where Katie still browsed frocks and kirtles and fabrics, her back to the road. However, poor timing had her turning, searching for Elle, her hands filled with some creamy fabric.

Elle, Alec was happy to see, had already made note of the lads, had one eye on them as they neared, nodding to Katie at the same time, giving her approval it seemed.

Aye, but those Sutherlands had noticed Katie. She was hard to miss. Beauty aside, she seemed to be the only blonde in the general area, her hair uncovered and unbraided, but twisted up into that familiar knot, bright as a beacon. And then she laughed, presumably at Elle's seeming disinterest, that indeed she did draw the attention of those lads.

Alec and Malcolm moved just as one of the Sutherland's smacked the arm of the other and pointed to Katie. They aimed then for the booth, pretending initially to be inspecting the wares.

Elle closed in on them, putting herself directly in their path as they made to get closer to Katie. Casually, Elle put her hands onto her belt. A dark-haired lad, his nose unfortunately long, began to give Elle grief.

The words didn't matter, they were always the same when Elle postured before lesser beings. *What do we have here? Check between her legs! Get home, woman, back to the hearth!*

The beaked-lad flicked his fingers against the fur at Elle's shoulders.

"You dinna want to do that, lad," Alec said in a dangerous voice, directly behind him by now. He caught the unblinking smirk Elle gave the lad.

The youth turned and Alec enjoyed very well how far back he needed to tilt his head to meet Alec's hard eyes. The boy sent his gaze to collect Malcolm's presence, but must have then been buoyed by the fact that they were only two and a woman.

"You and the carrot-head gonna stop us?"

"Just you. Your friends are no' eejits to court this fight."

The lad scoffed.

Alec decided not to make a scene, nor even to waste his time on teaching the arse a lesson. "Move. Away from me. Away from her. And completely out of my sight."

From behind, one of the other Sutherland idiots challenged, "He's no' interested in your hound. He wants the pretty blon—"

His sudden silence suggested Malcolm had quieted him. Alec heard a body hit the ground.

Still holding the gaze of the greater troublemaker, Alec told him, "She's with me as well. And I'm no' sure why you're no' running."

To his credit, his friend falling had only made this one shift his gaze quickly, but now, with these words, he held up his hands with some attempt to project innocence and began to back away.

While they collected their friend from the ground, while he sniveled and held his hand to his bloody nose, Alec and Malcolm and Elle remained still and watchful until the group was out of sight.

"I could've handled those whelps," Elle said, her tone heated.

"Aye, you could have," Alec surmised, glancing around her, to where the wonderfully oblivious Katie had her hands dug into more fabrics and wares, her back to them, blissfully unaware of the near calamity.

Elle shook her head, drawing Alec's frown.

"I ken you would no' have gone far. *Jesu*, you've got it bad."

Alec ignored her but determined he would remain close now.

Within the hour, all the shopping was done, and the four of them walked away from the market to collect their steeds. Alec tucked their few purchases into his saddlebags and lifted Katie up onto his big black. She was getting more comfortable with riding, he knew, pleased with this as he enjoyed very much holding her close while they rode.

"Thank you for bringing me to the market," she said when he'd settled behind her. "I cannot imagine it was high on your list of things-you-love-to-do, which makes me appreciate it all the more."

"Are you happy with your purchases, lass?"

"Aye. Of course, if I were handier with needle and thread, I'd have preferred to make my own gown, but yes, I am satisfied. And I used some of my coin to buy Henry a new pair of shoes. The leather goods in that stall were very well-made."

"Verra good. At his age, I would guess he might outgrow his footwear fairly quickly."

"He outgrows everything fairly quickly."

Malcom and Elle rode ahead, setting a leisurely pace, riding away from Carryd and into the sun.

Alec set his hand against her thigh, the reins held firmly though his arm was relaxed. He liked that she set her hand atop his, lacing her fingers lightly with his. Seemed a very affectionate thing to do. It pleased him greatly.

What pleased him even more was when she turned her head slightly and said, "Henry claims to be sleeping again up at the keep tonight."

Damn, but those words evoked so many emotions. First, her intent to sound only as if she passed on information, as if he should glean no invitation inside her words was quite charming, as subtlety was quite apparently not her forte. Next, the very idea of her alone in that bed both roused him and invoked memories of their lovemaking, vivid enough to stir his blood even now. But lastly, and most sadly, was the news he was compelled to give her now.

"Actually, you've been given a reprieve." He made an attempt at lightness but could not quite keep the disappointment from his tone.

"A reprieve?"

"I'd promised myself I'd no' make love to you again until we were wed proper."

"Why would you do that?" This, he thought, rather burst from her.

Alec chuckled. There was something very endearing about her own displeasure. "I've said, I dinna want to dishonor you further. I want to begin proper with you, wed first."

"Um, it's a little late for that."

"Never too late to undo wrongs, or at least go forward in a better manner."

She was quiet long enough that Alec felt he needed to assert more truths. "Katie, dinna think for one moment, I dinna want you or"—he grinned again—"couldn't easily be persuaded away from my oath. I relive that night way more than I should."

"I think you are a very honorable man, Alec MacBriar," she said, her voice filled with wonder, which faded, replaced by some disgruntlement when she asked, "But how long until we wed?"

Alec pressed a kiss to her hair. "Four days now, lass. Think you can survive it?"

"I have no choice, it seems. I hope your honor doesn't have any other terrible ideas."

Aye, but she was something, his bride-to-be, often quite a revelation.

"We have all the rest of our lives, Katie."

---

KATIE WAS STARTLED awake.

She lifted her head from her arms, where she'd fallen asleep at the table.

First she saw a hand and settled, recognizing Alec's fingers as they gently plucked the threads away from her.

"And where's the needle, lass? You'll be poking your own eye out, you keep up with this, toiling so late in the night." He must have found it and moved these things further away upon the table before scooping Katie from the stool and into his arms.

"No, I need to finish," she protested, but only half-heartedly, barely able to keep her eyes open. She'd been so busy these last couple of days, she felt as if she definitely needed more hours in her day.

"It'll keep 'til morn," he advised, his voice nighttime quiet.

Alec laid her down upon the cozy cot and Katie closed her eyes. But only for a second before they fluttered open again.

Alec stood beside the bed, hands on his hips, staring down at her.

"Why are you about so late?" She thought to ask, knowing when last she was wakeful she assumed it must be getting on to midnight.

"You'd said at dinner you'd be busy tonight so I spent the evening with Malcolm," he said. "Move over."

Katie did, a reflexive action to his softly worded request, but she knew greater wakefulness and a gentle stirring at the very idea.

He dropped his sword and belt where it had rested before, against the crude headboard, and then sat and removed his boots while Katie moved all the way over to the wall. Throwing a glance over his shoulder to gauge the narrow space, he stretched out on his back, lifting his arm in silent invitation. Katie understood immediately, and curled herself into him, settling herself into the crook of his shoulder, laying her hand over his chest.

"I'll stay but a few minutes."

"You haven't kissed me today," she said, still groggy.

"Aye and I'm no' going to. You're exhausted and you ken one kiss will only lead to more."

She snuggled more closely against him, drawing from his warmth and stifled her yawn, just in case he thought or might be convinced to change his mind.

"I'll only have more to do tomorrow, if you won't let me finish tonight."

"You were no' finishing, lass. You were sleeping."

"But I have so much to do yet."

"It'll get done, lass. No' the end of the world if it dinna."

"Says the bridegroom two days before his wedding."

He scratched at his chest a bit then covered Katie's hand with his own and left it there. "Henry was told about Elle's bairn tonight—he was with Malcom and me in the stables until mam called him up to the keep for bed."

"And?"

"Aye, I got the sense he was confused, and then he wondered if Elle would still be a soldier. Seemed he feared he might lose his friend."

"Aw. Of course he won't, but things will definitely change." Poor Henry. He'd just found Eleanor and now might feel, indeed, that he would lose her to her bairn.

"Will they wed, do you think, Malcolm and Elle?" She asked.

"Aye, like as no'. Mam will insist upon it sooner or later."

She let her mind wander to his thoughts about Henry. Sleepily, she told him, "I'd always thought when Henry was older, we'd lease a portion of the fields and he could earn his living with the farming. I'd have preferred him to know a trade—smithing or fletching or carpentry—but I wasn't friendly enough with those persons at Dalserf to inquire about any kind of apprenticeship. Or at least, as he is so young, I hadn't gotten around to it before I left there."

"He'll be a MacBriar now, lass. He'll need to go by the sword."

"I supposed that's to be expected. I won't like it, though."

"Aye, unless he has any interest in the church. Great pride there. Da' would love to send a MacBriar to the church."

She wasn't sure she'd ever given the church thought as an occupation for her son, but she liked very much that Alec would consider Henry a MacBriar when they were wed. "He doesn't read or write, of course."

"Can be taught. Do you, lass? Read or write?"

"Barely. I was never taught. I glean some written things, what Maybeth expected me to know. Very little."

"Maybeth?"

"The woman who taught me the healing arts," she said through a yawn.

"Aye now, I'm pleased for this opening, lass. I'll admit to a rabid curiosity about your past. You're young yet for all the knowledge you have about medicine and healing, and several decades shy of any other healer I've ever known. So I'm curious about how you came into the profession."

"'Tis no great tale," she said. "Mayhap a pitiful one though. I do not recall my parents as they perished when some sickness claimed whatever town I was born into. I'm not sure I have any other family. A woman took me in. I think her name was Isodore, but I canna remember."

"You canna remember the name of the woman who raised you?"

"She didn't. She only took me in for a short period, I'd been told. Then she sold me to the healer, that was Maybeth, when I was about Henry's age."

*Jesu.* "Sold you?"

"It's not as awful as it sounds. The woman had her own bairns and had lost her husband. I guess she couldn't spare more of...well, of anything for a child who was not her own." She was quick to assure Alec, whom she sensed was bristling at this coldness, "Maybeth was...not unkind. And, as you might have guessed, I've been learning the healing arts since I was very young."

"Not unkind leaves a lot to the imagination."

"She didn't...I mean she wasn't as lovely as your own sweet mam. But she was good to me, we got on well enough. She...she just wasn't warm. Everything was a lesson, in regard to life and its mishaps and healing as well. She did not actually teach me anything, didn't say, *now remember this*, just expected me to watch and learn."

"Makes sense," he mused, which turned her toward him once more. "So you have a verra warm, verra loving relationship with your son, make sure he dinna grow up without."

Another shrug and then she admitted, "Do you know that until I actually held Henry in my arms for the very first time, I hadn't any idea that I'd missed out on anything, that something was lacking. Of course, as soon as I did cradle him against me, I was in love and knew then what it was."

"Henry is verra lucky then."

"As am I." She changed the subject then. "Have you siblings? I've heard no mention of such."

"Nae. Apparently, there were many before me who dinna survive, some not until birth, and some not much after."

"How awful for your mother."

"And father, too. I'd always thought they seemed like they would have embraced a large brood."

Quiet then, but comfortably so, until Katie dared to voice something that had been bothering her for quite a while.

"Alec, why do you not hug your mother?"

"What?"

"When I first met you, you'd been gone for a long time from home, but you didn't embrace your mother when we finally reached Swordmair. And...and your mother said you don't hug her."

He didn't respond immediately that Katie bit her lip, wondering if she shouldn't have raised the subject.

When he did react, it was only to ask, "She said as much to you?"

Nearly grimacing, but then determined that if he were to be her husband, they should have no secrets, Katie replied, "She did. Actually, she...well, she blamed in on the time you spent as a prisoner of the English."

"She told you *that*?"

"Was I not to know?"

She felt him shrug and then he was still. Finally, he said, "It doesn't matter. I just...I dinna talk about it."

"But will you? Can you? To me?"

She guessed that all his responses might be slow, while he gave thought to how much he wanted to discuss or to reveal to her.

"It was a long time ago."

This ambiguous response suggested he did not want to share it with her, which was fine, but she wanted to clarify what she understood. "That, as an answer, implies you don't want to talk about it, but then this, coupled with the fact that you cannot or won't embrace your mother, suggests that it still sits unwell with you."

"It sits yet, aye." His tone was cool.

Katie pursued nothing more, having pushed him too far just now, she thought. She closed her eyes and had nearly fallen asleep again as many minutes had passed, when his chin moved against the top of her head as he said, "It...it's just one of those things, it changes you. I left here a green lad, too coddled by them both to ken how ugly the world is."

Roused once more, Katie asked, "Do you blame your parents though? Do you feel they hadn't prepared you better for...atrocities or...?"

"I dinna blame them." He paused before admitting, "They did me no favors, but I ken, they'd buried so many bairns, they...I dinna ken. I love and appreciate both my mam and father. I dinna ever doubt that."

"Maybe that's all that matters."

"Hm."

"I won't force you or push you to disclose more but please give your mother a hug. She misses you."

# Chapter Eighteen

She couldn't believe her own wedding was but a day away. As she walked back to her cottage, she catalogued in her mind everything she hoped to yet get done today. Henry walked beside her, chattering without pause, to which Katie lent only some of her attention. She'd heard this particular story already, earlier when she'd first gone to collect him. But he repeated almost the entire tale, that Alec had brought him to the training field, that Elle had given him some basic instruction in archery.

This afternoon, Katie wanted to spend more time on Elle's dress. When they'd found nothing that suited her at the market, Eleanor had rather dispensed with the idea of wearing a gown to Alec and Katie's wedding, had seemed to lose interest in the entire idea, but Katie hadn't wanted to give up. When they'd returned from the market, she'd put out some of her precious coin to Edric, who was possessed of a vast and varied supply of all sorts of things, but mainly bolts of fabrics.

"But lass, you wait until after the wedding," Edric had said, "and then you dinna have to use your own coin. It'll come from the castle coffers."

"Edric, I rather need it now, and it is for my personal use, so I do not believe the charge should belong to Swordmair."

Having so recently explored so much fabric at the Carryd market, Katie was well aware that Edric was cutting her a very fine deal. She expressed her appreciation eagerly and had started on Eleanor's gown that night. Agnes had leant some aid, being slightly more accustomed to making garments, that at least the design and measurements were set, the latter being rather imagined, as they hadn't anything by which to compare it. Katie wanted to surprise Elle and thus could not ask her outright to sit for a measuring. They'd made adjustments the next day, when Elle had come to Katie's cottage to collect her to tend Aymer, who'd suffered a sprained ankle during training. When Katie had returned almost an hour later, Agnes came scurrying over.

"Longer, lass," she advised when she'd stepped inside and closed the door behind her. "I took note of where Elle stood when she was at your door." She placed her hand against a spot in the top third of the door. "Shoulders were here. Good thing ye dinna cut the skirt pieces yet."

Later today, after she'd made some progress on the sewing, they would return to the keep for dinner. After that, in the early evening, she needed to put some effort into her medicinal supply; she'd rather been forced to abandon her very organized methods of storing, grinding, and blending the seeds and roots that it was taking her longer to treat each person, as so few of the regularly used recipes or ointments were prepared.

When that was done, she needed to address Henry's clothing, what he might possibly wear to the wedding, thinking his best tunic might need some repair.

And then she would have a late night bath, when she'd had time to fetch and heat the water, when Henry was asleep.

"Mam."

# THE LOVE OF HER LIFE

Katie startled, turning. Henry stood at the door to their cottage. She'd walked right past it.

"Good heavens," she said and turned to follow him inside.

"I thought you were going to Agnes's house," Henry said, closing the door behind them.

"I was wool-gathering," she admitted, setting her basket on the table. The well-worn shallow vessel was near overflowing, filled with most of today's payment for services rendered—Ann's father had offered her a wooden bowl and spoon, which he'd said he'd carved himself on some recent rainy nights; Martha, who tatted some very fine lace had asked Katie what she'd like for treating her red and infected eye and left there with an arm's length of lace that would quite easily trim the neckline of Elle's gown; from Ben Carpenter's wife, Sarah, whose infant's bottom was covered in a rash, which Katie had now seen twice, she'd received two crocks of honey, a valuable commodity to her; and from Agnes, whose husband was abed with a purging illness that had turned him milky white, she'd been paid with strips of linen, which she could always use.

Katie unwrapped her shawl and hung it next to the door, sighing with her exhaustion though the day was yet half over. Henry sat at the table with three well-hewn long sticks and plenty of feathers he'd collected all around Swordmair. Elle had provided those arrow shafts and had charged him with fletching the feathers, had told him any good archer must ken how to make his own arrows.

"Elle's going to have a baby," Henry said.

Katie sensed something in his tone, not quite displeasure, but certainly not happiness. "Hm, so I hear."

"She'll probably not be a soldier anymore."

"She may not. But then, she'll be somebody's mam, and that's the most important job of all."

"She dinna want a girl bairn, said boys are easier."

"Aye, that might be true. You certainly were a very easy babe and child to raise." When he gave no response to this, she wondered, "Are you excited for her, to become a mam? I think she's nervous."

Henry screwed up his face but didn't lift it from his task at the table, winding a linen thread around and around to hold the feathers in the nocks. He huffed and unwound the whole thing when one of the feathers had slipped out of place, and then answered Katie. "Elle dinna get nervous. She's verra brave."

"Isn't the fletching usually accomplished with some kind of glue to set the feathers before tying it off?"

"Aye but Elle said when I'm a soldier and need to either repair my arrows in the field, or make my own best I can, I willna have no glue on hand. I need to learn how to do it without glue. She also said I need to hope I dinna run out of arrows."

Katie grinned.

"I hope Elle still is a soldier sometimes," he said then. "I like training with her. Who's going to teach me about the sword fighting and using the daggers like they do?"

Ah, now it made sense.

"Henry, by the time you're old enough to lift a sword, I'd wager Elle's babe will be old enough that his mother might have some time to teach you."

"Everything's changing."

"Aye, it certainly is." After another moment, while he continued to struggle affixing the feathers to the shaft, Katie noted, "I was fairly certain you were pleased with the big change, my wedding Alec."

"Aye. I like Alec—not as much as Elle though. And I like sleeping up in the keep. Maddie is real nice. She's funny, too, but I dinna think she means to be."

He understood Alec's mom pretty well then, for his age.

"Henry, things will change constantly, all your life. Some will be good—like coming to Swordmair. Some might make you sad—like not getting to spend so much time with Elle once she delivers her bairn. Some might be frightening or even unwanted, but we must do the best we can. Always. And you can make your own changes, if a certain one didn't suit you."

"Aye." He dropped his hands, let the linen thread and the feathers rest on the table. "Mam, I always wished da' were here. I dinna like no' having one. But...if he'd been with us at Dalserf, we'd no' have come to Swordmair, would we? Least, that's what Maddie said."

No, they would not have. "That's very possible, Henry. And it doesn't mean you wouldn't want your own da' or that you love him any less because you're happy here."

"Aye, Maddie said that, too."

"But are you...curious or confused about anything else?"

His small shoulders lifted and fell. "Nae, but can I go back to the keep? I canna figure this out. I need Elle to help me."

"Aye. I'll see you at supper then."

She watched him leave, not overly concerned about his short-lived melancholy. Mayhap it had been settled. Henry was usually forthright, would have let her know if something else had been bothering him.

She didn't worry about him. Life was just too good here. He was so enamored of Maddie and Elle, had made good friends with the village lads, had a solid and easy relationship with Alec, and Katie had even come upon Henry and the laird in some cheery conversation the other day.

She pulled herself up from the table and gathered the nearly-finished gown she only hoped would please—and fit—Eleanor.

---

IT RAINED ON HER WEDDING day.

Katie couldn't have cared less.

She stood in the middle of her cottage, clad only in her best chemise. Her feet were bare, and her hair was loose. She stared over at the wedding dress laid across the bed. It was lovely, the cotton soft and smooth, the light sage green and underskirt of ivory more fine and delicate than anything Katie had ever owned. The vendor had called it a cotehardie, which meant nothing to Katie but that she thought it must define the form-fitting style and the breakaway skirt, where the ivory peeked out. Katie especially appreciated the embroidered emerald threads on the fitted sleeves and hem and along the neckline. She thought it was stunning.

She wasn't ready to dress though. Not yet.

She sat once again at the table and finished the last item on her list for today. She'd had neither enough coin or any idea what she might present to Alec as a wedding gift and only last night, when despair had nearly come, had an idea dawned on her. She laid the brooch onto the center of the kerchief she'd embellished near midnight last night, folding the linen all around it. When that was done, she wrapped this inside a sheet of vellum she'd bade Henry beg from Edric first thing this morning and tied the gift with a piece of lace.

A knock sounded at her door and before she could answer Elle stepped inside.

Katie stood just as Eleanor said, not without a whiff of awkwardness, "Mistress said you'd want your friends with ye now. I dinna ken why you need help getting dressed. Same as every other day, put your arms in the sleeves and pull it over your head."

Katie grinned. Eleanor would be no help to settle the anxious bride it seemed, but Katie didn't mind helping to make her feel less awkward. "Elle, I'm glad you're here. I'm feeling a bit nervous, and honestly, a wee bit excited. It's good to share these things with friends, aye?"

"How would I ken?"

Katie shrugged. "I'm not sure. Before now, I've never had any true friends, either, but I suppose it must be that way." She lifted her hands with excitement then. "Oh, Elle. I have something for you." She fetched the linen wrapped surprise from her work counter and approached Eleanor again, hugging the item to her barely clad chest. "Now, you will not hurt my feelings at all if you hate it, or even if you aren't...well, here." She stretched out her hands, thrusting it at Elle.

Her brow crinkling, Elle didn't take the package but said, "Ye dinna give things on yer own wedding. Ye receive them."

Undeterred, Katie pushed it further, explaining, "I was sorry that we didn't find anything at the market for you to wear that would have done justice to your height. But I did not want you to completely give up on wearing a dress again." At Elle's continued frown, Katie said, "I made it."

Eleanor's bottom lip fell. She lifted the frown to Katie. But she knew her friend well, knew Elle wouldn't want any fuss, would be awkward trying to show gratitude, which was unnecessary anyway, so she rushed on, "Honestly, if you're not ready, or you think it's awful, I won't be troubled. I promise."

"You're an arse," Elle accused, but she finally took the package. Gingerly, she unraveled the linen, revealing the dark blue gown. The frown only intensified as she unfurled the folded piece and held it up to her front. "You did this?"

"I did. I had some help." She could hear them now, getting closer.

"But it seems it might fit. You guessed well." So much trepidation in her voice.

"Again, I had some help. From our other friends."

No sooner had these words been put out than the door opened again, and in walked Agnes and two of her daughters, and Ann and Margaret and Sarah. Their hands were filled with more fabrics and flowers, and Sarah held a pair of creamy silk shoes.

Without preamble, Agnes sized up both Elle and the dress she still held against her front, and said, "Aye, we got it right then."

Ann begged Eleanor, "Can I do your hair? Agnes used her age to assert that she should be the one to fix Katie's," she said with some petulance.

Eleanor returned her startled gaze to Katie, who waited with fantastic hope.

Eleanor smiled at her while she answered Ann, "Why the hell no'? If she's brave enough to marry the MacBriar, I ken I might get my hair brushed out."

Katie clapped her hands together with pleasure.

"Come on, lasses, plenty to do," called Agnes with great cheer. "We've a bride to get ready."

---

"DINNA TOUCH IT," ALEC said through gritted teeth. Catching himself, he shooed his mother's hands away from his plaid. "It's fine, mam. Let it go."

"Lad's nervous, bride," said his father, brushing repeatedly and needlessly at the fabric of Alec's sleeve. "Leave him be."

At his side, Malcolm advised, "Hold your breath. Count to ten. First and only bairn they're seeing wed. Let them fuss."

Sighing, Alec closed his eyes and counted to ten. "They're still here," he said when he opened his eyes.

Malcolm chuckled. "Dinna take your own whipped nerves out on your da' and mam."

Completely ignoring Malcolm and Alec's back and forth, Maddie MacBriar said, "Alec, I said that ye needed the boots shined. I told ye to get them to—"

"Mam, stop. I did. They're fine."

Malcolm wondered aloud, "What the feck are ye nervous about anyhow?"

"Language, Malcolm," Maddie cautioned.

"Aye, sorry, ma'am."

"I'm no' nervous."

"Wedding jitters," Maddie said. "The laird had them, too."

"Bah!" Harrumphed the laird. "I was no' nervous. It's just too much waiting, aye, son? Takes all bluidy day and all ye want to do is take your new bride up the stairs and—"

"Aye!" Alec concurred, wishing his father would stop speaking. "Too much bluidy standing around. And where's the cleric? Has he come yet?"

A new voice chimed in from behind the small group. "Christ, he's a mess."

He whirled and found, to his immense delight, both Lachlan Maitland and Iain McEwen standing inside the hall. That had been Iain, giving him grief.

Alec didn't care. He rushed his friends, and all three embraced fondly, as any of them so rarely did with any other person—mayhap save their own wives.

They broke the tight bear hug but kept their heads huddled together, their gazes searching and heartfelt, always.

Lachlan said between them, "We've come to take you away. Arrived just in time I see."

"Take them two away, I'll be fine," Alec assured him, referring to his parents.

"Dinna ever wish that," Iain cautioned.

With his hand still around Iain's neck Alec said, "You ken I would never. I'm glad you've come. Both of you."

"We shouldn't have," Lachlan said. "You dinna come to my wedding."

"Nor mine," Iain said, lifting his brow.

They straightened, releasing each other, but remained close.

"Aye, you talk to Robert Bruce about that."

"Just poking at you," Lachlan said. "First thing your mam said when she came to Hawkmore was, *You ken he'd be here if he could.*"

Iain said, "*Jesu*, when was the last time we were together, all three?"

"Stirling?" Alec guessed.

Lachlan shook his head. "Earnside."

"Could've done without that one."

Alec recalled the actual truth then, sadly correcting them, "England, when Wallace was taken."

Lachlan blew out a rough breath. "Aye, when we met up with MacGregor and Kincaid and MacKenna."

"For all the good it did us," Iain grumbled, "despite having all those numbers."

"No, no, no."

All three turned to find Magdalena MacBriar standing behind them, her hands on her hips, her scowl fierce, even as she was dwarfed by these three men.

"There'll be no talk of war," she dictated. "No mention of king or country or those damn English."

"Language, ma'am," Malcolm called, a chuckle in his voice.

He stepped in to greet the two men he'd known nearly as long as Alec. And then Lach and Iain gave their greetings to Alec's parents, welcomed warmly and showing a matching affection.

Iain said to Alec's mother. "But the king is on his way, Maddie."

"Dinna ye fun with me, Iain McEwen. Ye want the bridegroom's mam in a puddle on the floor, giving me a fright like that?"

One corner of Lachlan's mouth lifted as he threw his thumb over his shoulder, "He was right behind us, Maddie. Should be here any minute."

"Why do you three always want to give her such grief?" Alexander MacBriar huffed. "For decades now, since you were in short pants, always playing games with her."

Iain leaned forward and said in a low voice to Alec, "Aye, but he sends his regards, said if it had been a smaller gathering, he'd have come."

Alec understood. It was a dangerous time to be king. To Iain, he said, "I heard he gave away your bride."

"He did."

Alec grinned. "That when he stumbled into your fight?"

"Aye, did you hear that? I still think about that, most unbelievable thing I'd ever seen."

"*Jesu*, where's my head?" Alec exclaimed. "Where are your wives?"

"Aye, they're coming in," Lachlan said. "We met up with Iain about an hour ago. The lasses immediately threw over their husbands to ride together in the carriage."

"Carriage now?" Alec lifted a brow, impressed.

"You ken my mother will not travel by horseback or even by cart," Lachlan said with a grin. "Hope it was worth it though. She will no' get a word in between Maggie and Mari."

"Christ," Alec said, pulling them in for another embrace. "I'm seriously so pleased to see you both."

Malcolm interrupted. "Aye, c'mon then, Alec. Time to get to the church."

"Aye, give me one second." He broke away from Lach and Iain and jogged after his mother, who was on her way to the kitchens. "Mother," he called just as she'd turned into the corridor.

She didn't wait for him, but kept on, waving a hand over her shoulder. "Go on, son. Get to the church. I'll be along with Edric and Corliss, just want to check on the—"

He stopped in the dimly lit passageway. "Mam," he called again, a bit forcefully, and then nearly chuckled when there appeared a jump in her step, as if he'd startled her.

She did turn now. "Alec, what? You've got to get to the...."

He strode with purpose toward her and pulled his mother into his arms. He'd forgotten how tiny and frail she truly was, how his arms could enfold her so easily. It felt good though, felt right. She was warm and so familiar. He whispered at her ear, "You're a beautiful person, mam. I love you."

Her initial shock gave way to weeping. He felt her shaking against him. Nothing more than some *ohs* and *oh my* could be ascertained from her voice and her words, pressed into his chest.

Alec rubbed her back. He was a lucky man, to have a mother like her.

Malcolm was calling him from the hall, but his mother wouldn't let him go, sniffling and still speaking into his tunic and plaid, though he still couldn't understand any of it.

"Mam," he prodded, grinning for how tight she was holding him now. Pulling her arms from around him, he kissed her tear-stained cheek. "See you at the church."

Her delighted and airy little sigh of, "Oh, Alec," followed him back into the hall.

# Chapter Nineteen

The images of the day would forever be forged into his memory. The sun fought hard to show itself, winning the battle long enough that the first part of the ceremony, outside the doors of the village church, was dry. He was surrounded by great friends and a loving family, and his bride was absolutely breathtaking.

Henry stood at his side, waiting for her arrival. The entire village and dozens of people from near and far gathered outside the church. She'd walked over the small rise from the middle of the village, her hand tucked into Alexander MacBriar's elbow. His father had beamed, nearly as much as days before, when Katie had asked him to give her away, saying, *You are my father now, too*, which had sufficiently watered the laird's eyes at the time.

Neither slashing rain or deafening thunder, not marauding armies or the good Lord himself come to witness the nuptials, could have torn Alec's gaze from her. He would just have to get used to it, that she only became more beautiful to him. The gown she'd purchased at the market was finely made and hugged her lean body with adoration; her hair had been arranged as he'd never seen it before, rolled and curled up into many intricate knots and threaded with autumn blooms of pink and orange and yellow, verbena and rudbeckia, he thought he recognized, among others. He caught sight of a delicate pair of ivory slippers, peeking from beneath the hem as she moved, but couldn't imagine where she might have acquired them.

But it was her face, her expression, which tightened his chest and filled him with pride and overwhelming joy. No shyness, even as she was indeed the grand center of attention, shadowed her features. No hesitation slackened her walk toward him. She was smiling, wide and bonny, her face lit with happiness, her gaze only for him.

She was simply radiant. And she was his.

The ceremony was nice, he thought, even as he had some hope that none begged that he recall any of it. Save for Katie standing next to him, he knew little else.

Later, the hall was more crowded than he could ever remember, and Alec realized he didn't even know all of the guests, only supposed his parents did. He introduced Katie to Lach and Iain, the most important persons in attendance in his mind, after all the Swordmair kin and folk. It had dawned on him too late to have given Katie warning about Lach's scars, but damn if she hadn't done him proud by barely blinking, smiling fondly as his friends shared their good wishes. And both he and Katie had met their wives, Mari and Maggie—nice lasses, though neither possessed the poise and beauty of Katie, Alec had thought with even greater pride. Mari and Maggie had pulled Katie away from their husbands, engaging her in quiet chatter, which pleased Alec for their overt friendliness.

Katie, in turn, had caught a woman's hand as she walked by the threesome. Alec had blinked and scowled, though was able to refrain from rubbing his eyes to clear them. It was Elle. In a gown. Looking...amazingly feminine. Christ, how the hell had that happened? How the hell had he not noticed this earlier? He recalled then having woken Katie at the short table in her house, when she'd fallen asleep. She'd had needle and thread in her hands, and the fabric he'd pushed out of the way had been the exact same blue as what Elle now wore. Admittedly, he ignored Lach and Iain just then, watching to see how Elle handled herself—in this new persona and amid these three very petite, very graceful women. Like she was born to it, was the answer, he realized, grinning, as Katie dragged her into their circle, keeping hold of her hand, including her in the conversation with Mari and Maggie. Elle showed not one ounce of unease but laughed and joined the conversation as easily as Katie had.

"Christ, is that Elle?" Lach wondered.

Quite regularly, any of the three men had sent their gazes, if only briefly, over to where the girls chatted.

"Aye, I guess it is," Alec said, a small chuckle of lingering disbelief emerging.

"How the hell'd that happen?" Iain wondered.

"Katie, I'm sure," was all he could figure.

"Losing a good officer, there," Lach predicted.

"Likely." She was lost to him anyway as a soldier, he knew. A bairn and now a gown. Aye, but it was as it should be.

Sometime later, Alec and Katie were ushered back to the head table, having occupied the two head seats earlier for the meal. Now, they were made to stand behind the raised table while a line of people passed before them, each person depositing a bannock upon the table in front of them, one on top of another.

"What is this?" Katie asked of him, her eyes alight with joy.

"They stack 'em high as they can, until they can no more. Whatever height that is, they'll want us to kiss over the top of it. If we can no' or we topple it, 'tis a bad omen."

"And if we do?"

"Prosperity and a happy life," he told her.

She joined her hand with his and smiled up at him. "We can do this."

Alec returned her smile. "Aye, we can."

They did. Even Lach and Iain's attempt at finer engineering to maintain a straight tower of buns couldn't see it any higher than Alec's head that all he had to do was lift Katie into his arms and kiss her for all to see.

So, it was a magnificent shame then that when the newly wedded couple were finally hastened up the stairs and to his chambers which they would share for now and evermore, that she'd begged one moment to tuck Henry in, had taken her hand from Alec's and had swept gracefully down the hall to her son's new chambers.

Alec had, at first, leaned against the wall in the corridor, content to allow her a few moments with Henry, but damn, so eager to get her naked. But she'd been gone into that room for much longer than he'd have suspected that he walked down the hall, hoping nothing was amiss, that Henry hadn't developed any sudden or worrying dislike of this new circumstance.

Their voices, soft and quiet inside that room, drowned out by the ongoing merriment in the hall, had forced him to move closer, to hover in the doorway, listening.

"But is he my da' then?"

"Henry, Alec will be a father figure to you, and likely a very good one. But of course, no one can replace your true da', as he was a very great man. All your intelligence and bravery and even your long legs come from your father. You must always honor that."

"What did I get from you, though?"

Lightheartedly, she told him, "Your good looks and your charming personality."

Still serious, Henry had asked, "But do you have to stop loving da' now? Should I?"

"Of course not. He should remain always in your heart," she'd answered softly but firmly.

*I've had already my life's love.*

Her words, from so long ago, crashed into him with all the force of a massive sword strike, straight through his heart.

Stunned, and so many other things he couldn't define just now, Alec strode back to his chambers. Blindly, he removed his plaid and belt and sword. He sat, or rather fell into the chair before the hearth. It wasn't anything he hadn't known. He hadn't forgotten that she'd been wed before, hadn't forgotten at all that she'd apparently loved that man, the one who came before him, beyond reason. He'd simply chosen to not think about it. But, Christ, that was a punch in the gut, ill-timed and unrelenting.

The harm done, though, by that sobering memory slapping him in the face, was what shocked him most. He knew a deep and unexpected anguish, his lip curling with the strangeness of it. He thought he should crush her in his arms when she came to him, and demand that she say it wasn't true, make her tell him there wasn't room in her heart for any but him.

A muscle moved convulsively in his throat while he waited her. The day had been perfect, he thought with some emotion he recognized belatedly as bittersweet pain. She'd been so impossibly gorgeous, had smiled so prettily at him, had been rightly in love with the merriment and kind to his dear friends. His current condition—stark bitterness—had him uncharitably wondering how much of it had been a lie.

Yet something nagged at him, some other memory, of her telling him that she'd not ever known love until she'd held Henry in her arms, had only understood it at that moment. At the time of this revelation, he'd frowned over this, trying to impose that statement with her previous one, *I've had already my life's love.*

He shook his head, trying to make sense of everything, more so his reaction than to understanding what her truth was. He reminded himself they'd made no vows of love, reminded himself further that he'd asked her to wed him for sensible reasons. Neither had made any declarations of greater emotions.

Cold and lifeless reason prevailed.

Resolutely, he convinced himself that it didn't matter. He'd known of her undying affection for Henry's father when he'd met her, and when he'd pursued her, and when he'd made love to her. She'd promised him nothing more than to be a good wife. The only thing that would change, then, he decided, was how much he ultimately allowed her to mean to him. Already, it was very much.

When finally she entered their chambers, Alec straightened, making his back rigid but caught himself enough to unfurl his fists from the arms of the chair.

Katie closed the door and leaned against it, smiling at him. More playacting?

With a wee bit of shyness and a rising blush that he cynically refused to find endearing, she watched him.

Ten minutes.

That was what laid between the jubilant expectation he'd known walking up the stairs with her, knowing what he would have tonight and always, and the heavy emptiness that gripped his chest right now.

Ten bluidy minutes.

"Alec?" She pushed away from the door, went to her knees at his feet. Ten minutes ago, he would have adored her hands so familiarly upon his thighs, might have grabbed hold of them and moved them further, up between his legs.

"Aye."

She gave a nervous giggle. "Are you...are you tired or...?"

"Verra."

She was undeterred. "I'm very sorry to hear that, husband. I'm going to have to insist that you consummate this marriage."

Oh, he would.

But damn....

*Just ask her. Get it all out.*

"Katie," he said. *Jesu, do I want it fecking verified, by her own lips and to my face?*

With a curious tilt of her face, she returned with some playfulness, "Alec."

Shaking his head, he reached for her, taking her by the arms, lifting her to her feet to stand between his thighs. He settled his hands on her hips and stared at her waist, where the light green cotton fabric of the skirts was split in two, revealing the embroidered ivory beneath. She touched his shoulders. Possibly she sensed his mood now, guessed it might be more than weariness that had turned him to stone.

Decisively, he stood and crushed her lips in a punishing kiss, savage as was the riot inside himself. He said nothing, whispered no sweet words to her, didn't bother to gentle his touch or even his racing heart. He didn't scoop her up into loving arms but walked her back toward his bed. They rather fell onto it, Alec landing on top of her. He let his hands wander, mumbled impatiently, "Get this off," when the tight bodice refused to bow to his want of access.

She pulled her arms free, sent the gown and chemise down to her waist, reminiscent of their previous tumble. And while she did, her gaze sat uneasily upon him, surely so many questions in her blue eyes. He couldn't be sure, though, wouldn't look at her.

*Bluidy hell.* She didn't deserve this, not some fumbling, impersonal coupling on her wedding night. She couldn't help that she still loved Henry's father any more than Alec could force himself not to be so damn enamored of her. He closed his eyes and brought himself under control.

"Alec?"

When he opened his eyes, her breasts were bared to him, his for the taking. Pinked tipped, silken skin, beckoning him.

She raised her hand and touched his cheek. He did not meet her gaze but kissed her again. The same pride that wouldn't allow him to confront her with the fears inside his head also demanded that he not come up short against a ghost in regard to pleasuring her. It wasn't difficult, in reality, to gentle his touch or his kiss. His own pleasure would only be heightened by hers, he knew.

He opened her mouth with his own, his tongue driving inside, reveling in her response, eager and filled with a similar longing. His hands cupped her breasts, rousing her nipples into tightness before he lowered himself and replaced his hands with his mouth.

He felt her hands in his hair and then on his shoulders, moving down his arms. "Get this off," she whispered, trying to pull his tunic away, using his own words to have her way.

Alec obliged, sitting up but briefly to yank it over his head. When he returned to her breasts, she caressed him, sending her soft hands around his back.

"Alec?" Alarm tinted her voice now.

She'd discovered his scars.

"Gifts from the English," he explained mildly, but thought to add emphatically, "and no' something we're going to discuss right now." Wait until she saw the mess they'd made slicing up his legs.

She'd lifted her hands, held them around him yet, but only hovering above his back, when she'd first noticed them. But now she returned them to the carved and scarred skin, her touch gentle. She'd learn soon enough there were few places on his body that her hands might *not* encounter any remnants of the English's hospitality.

He sensed her distraction then, supposed her mind was whirring with some misplaced sympathy for what she'd discovered. Alec didn't want her pity. He wanted her body. He coaxed the skirts down off her hips until she kicked them off her legs while he explored her soft and warm skin with his hands, over her naked hip and up her ribs, across her breast and still-hard nipples and down again, until his fingers delved between her legs, into a triangle of hair several shades darker than the blonde waves around her head, loosened and mussed already.

A breathy gasp spilled from her as he slid his fingers over her, his touch deliberately light and teasing. She was patient, breathing rapidly, but did not raise her hips to his fingers. Alec swayed his fingers gently back and forth over the hair and not until she was writhing, begging, "Alec, please," did he actually touch her fully, opening her, sliding his fingers over the most sensitive part of her with aching slowness, back and forth. She whimpered, and his erection surged, hardening yet more when he finally, satisfyingly slipped one and then two fingers inside her. And now her hips moved, answering his touch.

"I want you inside me," she moaned, her neck and back arched, her skin golden silk in the firelight. "Please."

Needing no further urging, he complied, rising quickly to slip off his breeches and drawers. He spared a glance at her complete nakedness, unable to renounce her beauty or the lure of her innocently seductive pose; elbow bent and her fingers languidly resting just above her breast; her legs closed and tilted toward the right in some display of modesty; her small breasts glistening where his tongue had loved them. He joined her again, his cock made rigid when he laid himself on her, when she opened her legs so willingly to him. Alec kissed her wildly then, teasing her by pressing his erection against her but not inside. But she moved against him, rocking her hips back and forth, tormenting him that he growled and surged deep within. They gasped together at this, still for a moment, until he began to move, hungrily stroking her again and again until she cried out, clutching the bunched muscles of his shoulders. Moments later, with one final plunge, Alec gave a hoarse cry of his own and joined her in that perfect oblivion.

He waited only long enough that it didn't seem an outright rebuff, and then withdrew from her, falling heavily onto the bed beside her. He'd flopped on his stomach, facing the window and the darkness, wondering if making love to her wasn't so damn amazing if it would disturb him less that she cared naught for him.

She turned, folding herself against his side, and one arm slid across his back. She pressed a kiss onto his arm and sighed.

Alec closed his eyes.

---

MORNING HAD COME.

She watched him for a while. She'd opened her eyes to find him already awake, lying on his back, thoughtful, one hand idly scratching his chest, his jaw tight. Tentatively, she'd reached for him, set her hand upon his warm, hard skin. He startled, must have been so lost in thought, but then did not return Katie's cautious smile. Instead, he nearly leapt from the bed and had begun to dress.

"Good morning, husband," she said. More as a test, to see what his response might be.

"Aye."

Just that, nothing else.

She sat up, let the blanket fall away. And watched him covertly as he moved about the room, retrieving his clothes. He bent to pluck his tunic from the floor and Katie was offered a full, unobstructed view of his backside. It was as she imagined, as her hands had discovered last night, riddled with scars, large and small, deep and not, and then covered as he pulled his tunic over his head and it dropped over his back, shrouding the marks at the top of his hard buttocks. Her eyes enlarged when her gaze fell on his massive thighs, which were lined with marks of a similar size, one after another, four or five inches long, from just beneath his buttocks all the way down to his calves. These were not, had not been, superficial flesh marks. These had been carved deep enough to leave raised and thick welts yet, even after so many years.

Was this then the reason for his remoteness on their wedding night and now, this morning? Something was terribly, undeniably wrong. Throughout the day he had been unquestionably charming and solicitous, had smiled at her and teased her, had seemed to enjoy the festivities as much as she had. And yet, last night when she'd first come to their chambers, he'd been so detached. When he'd kissed her, she'd sensed a harshness about him that had no place inside a kiss between them. Even their lovemaking, initially, had been lukewarm. It had heated, that was certain, but Katie had been left not only sated but befuddled. Was it the scars she'd discovered? Was he shamed by them? Did he think she would have been disgusted or appalled by them? She didn't dare ask, recalling his stoic, grave reaction the last time she'd mentioned his captivity.

But she could show him that they didn't matter to her, wouldn't need to remind him that the scars were part of him, had forged him in some ways, had shaped him into the man he was today. She would show him. He would realize they mattered not, would not be so aloof again with her.

"You should show yourself belowstairs soon," he said while pulling on his breeches. "We've guests to visit with."

Katie was torn, having a hard time believing Alec MacBriar was made uncomfortable—with her—by his scars. Was there something else?

"Alec, what...what has changed? I don't understand why you're—"

"Changed?" He lifted his gaze though did not pause in the action of arranging his plaid over his shoulder. His brow furrowed. "Nothing has changed."

"But you're so....you're treating me so coolly."

He continued to work on his plaid, positioning the pleats neatly and evenly but lifted his broad shoulders in a negligent shrug. "Dinna seem too cool last night."

Aye, but it was, certainly if this were to be his behavior afterward.

Good Lord, had she misread any emotion in him? Had it only been fleeting, or worse, fabricated, employed merely to coerce her acceptance of his proposal. It didn't make sense though. She was no coveted bride, she knew, had no coin or land or connections to bring to him. Was it as she had originally believed, she wondered, assaulted by some thought that he'd married her out of some misplaced sense of pity or duty, that he coupled with her out of necessity—though freely now, as he was her husband—that all her life, there might be no other emotion that tied them together?

Katie sighed, but her dismay only grew when he was fully dressed, boots and sword and all, and did not kiss her before he left the room, only said, "I'll likely be gone most the day with Lach and Iain."

She didn't move for several minutes, having concluded that Alec was incurably hard-hearted, unlikely ever to change. This caused her no amount of heartache, but the larger part of her was infused with anger. She felt as if she'd been tricked. The man who had made love to her the first time in her cottage, the man who had so sweetly and ridiculously asked her to wed, and the man who had lain inside that narrow cot with her and said that he genuinely loved his parents was not the same man who had shared her marriage bed last night or walked out on her just now.

# Chapter Twenty

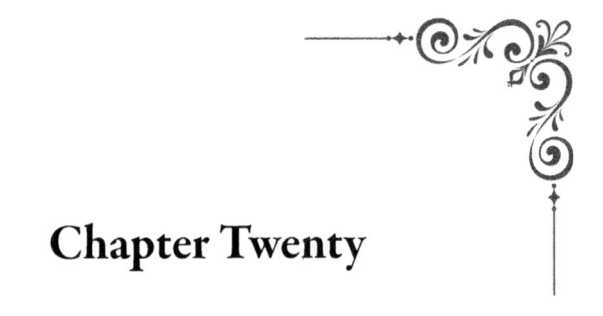

"Your son is darling, Katie."

Katie blinked and forced a smile, turning it upon Mari Maitland. "Thank you."

These ladies, whom she imagined she might know all her life, due in part to Alec's friendship with their husbands, were truly very charming, very gracious. She needed to thrust away the plaguing worry over Alec and concentrate on them. They'd traveled far to see two people, previously unknown to them, wed. She owed them greater courtesy than what she'd been able to manage as of yet today. Luckily, when Maddie had suggested she and Mari and Maggie might enjoy a visit inside her solar, the first quarter of an hour had required only that she smile and nod while they discussed the events of yesterday, confirming to Katie that it really had been magical, the sweet ceremony, the festive reception, the unruly dancing, the delicious feast—all beyond anything she might have hoped for.

Attempting then to pay greater attention to her guests, Katie watched as Maggie McEwen, with her striking green eyes and that glorious red-blonde hair, leaned forward and said, "Mari, I have to ask: what is the history between Lachlan's mother and Swordmair's steward? They appeared quite cozy yesterday."

Edric? Katie hadn't noticed, but then she'd had eyes only for Alec.

Mari flipped her long dark hair off her shoulder and her blue eyes flashed. She, too, bent forward, as if divulging secrets. "Months ago, Diana had very casually made mention that Swordmair's steward was sweet on her, often sent her gifts—mostly the most incredible fabrics and laces. But then yesterday," she went on and lent her gaze strictly to Maggie for a moment, "before we met up with you, she was a bundle of nerves inside the carriage. I badgered her about the cause until she admitted that she was nervous to see him again after so long." Mari pressed her hand to her heart. "It was so sweet, she acted twenty years younger. Anyway, I kept on until I had the whole story—which is more tragic than not. Seems they were smitten with each other when they were younger, but her father married her off to someone else. And then," she continued, her eyes widening, "when Lachlan's father died, she thought she might reach out to Edric, but she'd been married off again, as the Scottish nobles loyal to Edward didn't want Hawkmore falling into the wrong hands—essentially Lachlan's, as he was nearly of age but was known for his fierce loyalty to Scotland."

"How sad," Maggie said, her slim shoulders falling.

"It was," Mari agreed. "But now it's not." Her pretty smile grew, and she looked to Katie. "I fear Swordmair is about to lose its steward to Hawkmore."

Katie gasped with pleasure. "How charming."

"Never too old to find love—or recover it, I suppose," Maggie concluded.

They remained in the solar for nearly an hour, not once even pretending to be about any chore such as mending or embroidery, gave all their attention to the conversation, which moved with lightning speed from one topic to the next. Katie liked them very much.

"Your friend Eleanor is amazing," Maggie said. "Is she really a soldier?"

"She is, as able and brave as any man. She's quite remarkable. And Henry adores her, as do I. And wasn't she absolutely splendid yesterday? Outshone the bride, I daresay."

"She's just so..." Mari began, searching for words, "I don't know, how do you describe someone so unexpected? She's gorgeous and so enviously tall—"

"And her eyes!" Maggie added.

"And her hair! And her...I don't know, her command of the room, of attention. I know I couldn't keep my eyes off her."

"You're lucky to have a female friend in your midst, Katie," said Maggie. "I adore Iain's mother, but there's nothing like a bosom companion—of your own age—to trade secrets and worries and come what may."

"I am indeed blessed to call her friend."

The door was pushed open. "They say you've only yourself to blame if you dinna like what ye hear through doors," said Eleanor as she entered, returned once more to her breeches and tunic, though her long hair was braid free, neatly knotted at her nape. She met Katie's eyes. "That bit there did me no harm, though."

"I'm here if you need me, Elle," Katie quipped. "Anytime your ego needs feeding. Are you joining us?"

"Say you will," Mari encouraged.

Elle shook her head. "Nae, they're wanting you out of doors."

"Me?" Katie wondered.

"All of ye. Men being men, they want to have some games, make use of the larger crowd, receive all the adulation and whatnot."

Maggie rolled her eyes and grinned. "Speaking of ego feeding."

They all laughed but then Mari said as she got to her feet, "Well, egos aside, ladies, I'm not about to squander a chance to gawk at my husband while he's about some manly play."

"Good point," Maggie said, and she stood as well.

Katie's eyes widened at their open admiration for their spouses while Elle lifted her brow, her expression suggesting a new appreciation for these two women.

Twenty minutes later, the entire household, including the dozens of guests had moved outside the yard and across the bridge to the wide meadow. A few chairs had been carted out, where the laird and Maddie and several of their contemporaries sat on the sidelines.

"Oh, I know this game," Mari said excitedly, clapping her hands together as about twenty men broke off into two groups on the open field. "It's called *shinty* if I recall. Now, there's two teams and they'll use those curved sticks to try and get the ball past that man at each end. It's silly, as they only get points for each goal and not a cake or sweet bread, but they're men, so I understand it's all about the winning, the competition of it—apparently that's the prize."

Katie and Maggie exchanged grins at this, and they all watched while one group of men began to remove their tunics. Alec was within that group, surprising Katie that he showed no reticence to be bare-backed, exposing his scars to one and all.

"I like it already," Maggie said, with a pretty blush as Iain McEwen, within Alec's group, also discarded his tunic, balling it up and tossing it to the side.

Katie gasped. His back was similar to Alec's, equally and as grotesquely disfigured. Neither of the scarred visages could rightly compare to Lachlan's face, worn every day for all to see, but she now understood their bond, what drew and held them together.

Rather out of the blue, Mari said, "I've often wondered what they were about, those English bastards." Obviously, she'd taken note of both Alec and Iain's backs as well.

"Evil is what they were about," Katie said absently.

"But why the different tactics? Did they grow bored with one form of torture and then move onto another? Lach said several of those prisoners were burned, he was the only one to survive it."

"Mayhap that's the answer," Maggie said, her voice small and sorrowful. "If they all died, so would their...fun, whatever it was. So they used other methods to bring pain, to humiliate them."

Mari blew out her frustration in a short burst of breath. "I'd like to get my hands on just one of them."

"No," Maggie shook her head. "You wouldn't. Iain has worked too hard to put it behind him—he has so few nightmares now, he can talk more freely about it. I say leave it in the past, bury it further."

Katie was stunned, first by the revelation that Iain, built as solid and as large as Alec, struggled with night terrors. And then, because their wives talked so freely amongst themselves about it. Not a man out on that field, likely none of the older folk too, could claim to be without any scars. Alec and Lachlan and Iain, of course, could not hide from them, Lachlan least of all. But there they were, running around shirtless, laughing, playing, as if they'd struggled with no trauma at all.

"Alec doesn't like to talk about it," she confessed. "Should I...try to get him to, so that he might one day be able to leave it behind?"

Both women agreed. "No," Mari said, while Maggie shook her head. "Of course, if he brings it up, then he's given you leave to engage, and you should, or might want to."

"For me, with Iain," Maggie said, "I guess I just try to love him as best I can, never give him reason to doubt it, which there isn't. He knows he can tell me anything, knows as well that my love is sure and strong and not going anywhere. I think he hid his pain well, pushed it all down as deep as he could, but I'd like to think, I honestly believe that since we married, he truly is happier."

"Of course he is," Mari insisted. "Lach was just so flummoxed that I saw past the scars so quickly—but honestly, how could I not? I mean look at him. He always seemed to be fighting a greater battle with himself than with any mere mortal. It's no exaggeration, though, he was fearsome and inflexible and frankly, often quite terrifying." And with a simple shrug and a bonny grin, she said, "And now he's not. I won't take all the credit, though. Lach is very good at loving and showing love and I think letting himself do that, be that man, has allowed him to recognize what's important. And then, what's not."

Katie acknowledged the small rising bit of envy creeping around inside her. What little interaction she'd witnessed between the two couples showed that Lachlan Maitland and Iain McEwen quite obviously adored their wives. And Mari and Maggie felt the same, she was sure. These then, aside from the laird of Swordmair and his bride, would be marked as the only spousal relationships she was aware of that were genuinely happy. She'd never known another.

But she knew she wanted that with Alec.

If only she knew what had turned him so cold last night and this morning.

---

THREE DAYS LATER ALL of Swordmair was returned to normal, the last of the guests taking their leave. The Maitlands and the McEwens had left yesterday, and Katie was very sorry to see Mari and Maggie leave, having enjoyed their company enormously. She'd been particularly enamored with the news Mari had shared, that she was expecting a babe. Lachlan was over the moon, she'd said, and while Katie's joy had been tremendous as well, she felt very privileged that Mari had shared it with her, as they'd only just met.

They would meet again, Alec had told her, when she became a little weepy waving them off. She was sad to see them go, thought maybe only Mari and Maggie had kept her sane over the last few days.

Alec's mood had not improved. He was polite, but didn't seek her out; he made love to her each night, bringing her to glorying heights of pleasure, but remained aloof, seemed to be holding himself back even as he was giving her so much joy; he sought her out not at all on his own, and when Lachlan and Iain's desire for their wives company had brought them to their side, they'd each unabashedly kissed their wives while Alec only stood silent at her side. It had almost been embarrassing, and she couldn't believe the distance he'd kept from her had gone unnoticed, certainly not when *she* began to notice that Lachlan and Iain subsequently expressed themselves lesser and lesser to Mari and Maggie the longer they remained at Swordmair, as if they were uncomfortable causing her so much discomfort.

She wanted to rail at him, wanted to force the truth out of him, but knew he wouldn't respond well to that. She realized then that the departure of all the guests, most especially Lach and Iain, was likely a very good thing, as they'd taken up so much of his time. He was all hers now, she could begin to show him love. Soon, everything would be well.

She'd spent the morning in the kitchen with Maddie and Corliss, the mistress wanting her to learn more about the management of Swordmair.

"I'm ready to put my feet up, lass," Maddie had said. She wouldn't, of course, Katie knew. Likely Alec's desire to always be busy, always be about some chore, had been gotten from his mother. Katie couldn't recall even one instance, outside supper in the hall, that Maddie sat in any form of leisure.

When she'd been released from those duties for the day, Katie purposefully sought out Alec, the task made easier by his business inside the stable. She waited for him to finish his conversation with the stable master, smiling when he finally did and found her waiting just outside.

Her husband did not return her smile, nor show any great pleasure at seeing her. Instead, he asked, "What do you need?" as if she were but one more task he must contend with.

Katie let go a nervous laugh. "I need my husband," she said. "Or rather, I'd like some of his time. I thought we might—"

"Katie, I've got thirty-three things yet to do today," he said. "Can we talk at supper? Would that be all right?" His tone hinted that he wasn't actually asking her opinion.

She began to nod, her disappointment swift and aching, and Alec began to walk away.

"Actually, that is not all right."

He faced her again, his frown deepening.

"I'm sorry. Is it asking too much for your wife to want some of your time? Really, do you not have an hour to spare me?"

He seemed to temper whatever hardness had bit him with her challenge. Still, his hazel eyes were narrow upon her. "An hour for what?"

"For anything. Will you come to the loch with me or can I help you with anything? Can we just ride somewhere, just the two of us? Maybe we could—"

"We can, just no' today. As I've said, I've—"

She interrupted him now, her ire rising. "You're not making it very easy to be your wife. And it seems you're doing it purposefully and I don't understand what has happened, but I'll tell you right now, if you continue with this behavior—whatever the bluidy hell it is—I can't imagine I'll continue to be so accommodating inside our chambers each night." *Good Lord*, this is what she was reduced to! How dreadful.

He bore down on her, taking three long strides to stand very close to her. His lip was curled, and his eyes glittered with fantastic menace, so reminiscent of the very first time she'd met him, when he'd likewise frightened the bejesus out of her at her cottage at Dalserf.

Katie held her ground, clamping her lips, breathing her anger out her nose.

"You dinna want to go that route, wife," he warned in a dangerous tone.

"But as you've chosen this strange path, you've left me with little choice," she returned tartly. She eased her tone then, didn't mind pleading, "Alec, I just want us to—"

"Aye, you've said what you want, and I've said I've matters to attend that cannot be put off."

She nodded tightly, giving him a good glare for his implacable attitude. "Very well."

She pivoted quickly and walked away, keen to hide the threatening tears, quivering with the heartache that came. She could not ignore the very sad truth, that they had—somehow, for some reason—circled fully around, back to what they were when they met, when he frightened her and scowled at her and cared not one iota for her.

---

HE GROUND HIS TEETH, which moved his jaw left and then right, watching her walk away, her angry strides and swinging arms harking back to when he first met her.

This current annoyance was self-directed, hating himself for not even trying to be agreeable. There went the result of his own infantile snit, that she was returned again to that angry woman he'd first met, the one he truly hadn't seen in some time now. Swordmair had been good for her. The regular pinched look about her had disappeared. *Jesu*, she smiled and laughed now, had friends to call her own. Or rather, she *had* smiled and laughed for weeks and weeks, until they'd wed, until he'd managed to take that away from her.

She didn't love him, mayhap never would, but she was a good person, had proven to him already that he was lucky to have her as a wife. He'd known it immediately, on the very day of their wedding. She'd charmed his friends by way of her quick and easy friendship with Mari and Maggie. It hadn't only been Lach and Iain's heads turned when their sparkling laughter had drifted toward them. Before their wedding night, before everything had changed, he'd watched her with great satisfaction and no small amount of affection. Katie was perfect, open and friendly, managing her role as bride and hostess with rather impressive aplomb. True, she'd spent the majority of the days after the wedding with Mari and Maggie, but she'd also made time for their other guests. When Horace McGreevy had learned that she was a healer, the old man had bent her ear for nigh on an hour about his *unaligned humors*. She'd sat and listened, hadn't rebuffed him or made excuses, hadn't hastened away, had charmed the man enough that Alec's father later reported that the three hundred acres he'd been badgering McGreevy for years to sell was, suddenly, available for purchase. His father had winked at Alec, said, "Ask her to get on Annand—I need to get that price down for the grain."

She'd met and conversed easily with aged matrons and crusty old lairds, and had evidently charmed Lach's mother, Diana. Before she'd departed with her son and daughter-in-law, Diana had said quietly to Alec, "I'm so pleased for you, Alec. She's a wonderful woman. Your mam says already, she's had a true and extraordinary effect on you." She'd kissed his cheek. "You always reminded me so much of Lach that I worried excessively about you as well. I can rest now, that you both are so wonderfully settled."

His mood souring further, Alec thought of the wedding present Katie had given him. Possibly she would have presented it to him on their wedding night, mayhap after he'd made love to her for the first time as her husband, if he'd bothered to hold her close afterward. Mayhap she'd have reached over and retrieved the small, wrapped token and laid it upon his bare chest.

She hadn't, of course.

He'd come into their chambers the next night, while Katie was sitting before the fire. He'd met her gaze but briefly before beginning to undress for bed, tired and yet restless. When he'd stood in only his breeches and hose, she'd approached him, not without a fair amount of hesitation, had offered up the vellum wrapped and linen tied gift.

"I'd...forgotten to give you this last night," she'd said.

Awkwardly, he'd plucked the gift from her hands, her gold wedding band then exposed, shining softly.

She'd dropped her hands, had said, "I didn't know what to get you." Her face was still, her gaze on the package as he'd slowly untied and unwrapped it.

Inside the sheepskin paper was a creamy cotton kerchief, embroidered quite expertly with thistle and pine cones in threads of blue and black and beige, the colors of the MacBriars. When he'd unfolded that completely, he found an inexpensive but finely tooled brooch of pewter. It was half the size of his palm and circular in shape, the metal worked into a filigree pattern, the letter M forged into the center of it.

"You had this made?" He'd asked, a bit overwhelmed by the gesture.

Katie had shaken her head. "No, this was mine. Or, I was told it was mine. I've...I've just always had it. Maybeth supposed it had belonged to my parents, thought my birth name, my surname that is, must have begun with an M." She'd glanced up at him. "It's not costly, I'm afraid, but...but I wanted you to have it."

"It's very fine. Thank you." In turn, he'd fetched the gift he'd gotten her, having actually forgotten about it until then. And the truth of it was that he'd tasked his mother with procuring it. That had not been done with any disinterest in what he might give her for the occasion of their wedding, but only with some hope that his mother would have a better notion about such things, as he'd certainly not had any idea.

He'd been just as surprised as her, then, when she'd opened the small wooden box to reveal a star-shaped brooch in cast bronze, which he supposed would effectively hold her cloak together sometimes. She'd smiled sweetly and had thanked him prettily, but without any great emotion.

Now as he watched Katie walk away, he wondered what kind of fool tossed away his entire coin purse simply because of the upset caused by being robbed of naught but a farthing or two.

He sighed, more frustrated with his own disappointment than anything else. He'd allowed himself to feel for her, to have hope for something he'd not ever known. Christ, who was he kidding? He'd fallen in love with Katie and was naught but a petulant child now, knowing that she wouldn't ever return the sentiment.

He walked off, left the yard and headed for the bonemaker's cottage, needing a new blowing horn for the training field. Mayhap he'd request a comb for Katie and offer it up as a truce, or as a token of apology for being such an unmitigated arse.

They would be fine, he decided. He'd come to terms with it. He'd come around eventually, they'd have a decent life. He wasn't so large an arse that he would forsake all that she did offer him.

# Chapter Twenty-One

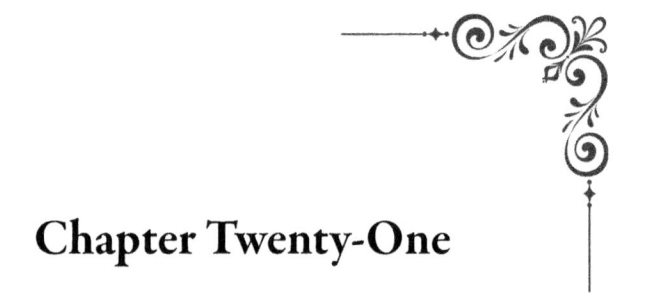

Katie chased Boswell out of Agnes's garden as she passed, scolding him to mind his manners, and headed back to the keep. She wasn't too concerned with Ann's fever, but would keep an eye on it, and the rest of the village, knowing very well how quickly and effectively one illness could wipe out an entire close knit group of people. She squinted up against the sun, spying Henry ambling toward her.

"I thought you'd be the entire day with Malcolm," she said, though was pleased to have his company.

"Nae, we only stayed with the smithy all morn." He turned and walked with her, swatting playfully at Boswell as the hound sprinted past. "The metal stuff is kind of boring. I dinna care how the swords or daggers are made. I want to learn how to use them."

"All in good time, I'm sure."

He grumbled. "That's what Alec said."

"I'm headed out and around the loch, on the far side for a bit of foraging. Want to traipse about the woods with me?"

"I guess so. Ronald and Martin are stuck helping their da' with stuff."

"To the keep first, though," she directed them. "I want to change into my boots."

Alec was inside the hall, at the head table with the laird and Edric, stacks of ledgers splayed out on the table between them. She greeted them with a smile and responded to Alec's lifted brow without breaking stride, "Henry and I are headed out to the loch, foraging and whatnot."

Without waiting his response, she turned into the corridor and found her way upstairs to don her heavier boots and soon rejoined Henry in the hall, smiling politely at the men once again before she and Henry took their leave.

Yesterday's little scuffle with Alec had faded, to some degree at any rate. Or rather, she refused to give it leave to dampen her spirits yet more. And then last night he'd made love to her with greater tenderness than previously shown, had seduced and pleasured her masterfully, had actually held her throughout the night, that she knew—she was sure—they were going to be all right. She woke today with a thought that consoled her. He may not love her, but he had chosen her. That was as good a beginning as any.

Katie and Henry caroused around the north side of the loch for nearly an hour. Despite her need of certain plants and roots, she found herself easily distracted by Henry's play, helping him turn over a huge rock to discover what might be discovered beneath, making a face when critters scurried out from under the rock. They investigated a thicket close by then, deciding the red deer might regularly nest here, the grass flattened in so many spots. She held Henry's hand then, while he walked across a long and thick fallen pine, again and again until he could do it without slipping off, and faster and faster.

They paused briefly, watching a lone rider approach Swordmair, his pace furious. They turned to follow his progress, Katie shielding her gaze from the sun, as he sped by the opposite end of the loch and over the bridge. No alarm was sounded, and no soldiers spilled from the keep to meet him that Katie supposed he was naught but a speedy messenger. She'd given Alec her direction, should he in fact be someone in need of medical attention.

Eventually, she did get around to plucking plants and roots, filling her basket, while Henry and Boswell continued to frolic, so easily entertained by everything that might be discovered near and around the water.

But she and Henry both jumped to their feet when their names were shouted. Katie stepped out from the brush at the shore to see Alec racing furiously toward them on his massive destrier.

"*Jesu*, Katie, you scared the shite out of me," he growled when he was close and had brought the horse to an abrupt stop. "You said by the loch!"

"I—we are by the loch," she defended. "Alec, what has happened? What is it?"

Alec shook his head, and gave a sharp whistle, which brought Boswell 'round again. "Get back to the keep now."

She nodded obediently, didn't even bother to grab her basket, but reached for Henry's hand and they sprinted after Alec, who'd charged away as feverishly as he'd come.

Breathless by the time they reached the keep, Katie paused inside the now-bustling hall only long enough to inquire of the laird where Alec was.

"Above stairs, lass," the laird said, quickly returning his attention to the soldiers gathered around him.

Henry had left her, insinuated himself in that circle of men, that Katie bounded up the steps and burst into their chambers.

# THE LOVE OF HER LIFE

Alec was pulling things from the trunk at the end of the bed, tossing items onto the mattress.

"What has happened?"

"A thousand English just ran through Ardmore," he said without turning around.

Katie's hand covered her mouth and her gasp. "But...that's not very close to Swordmair."

"Too close for my liking," he said, removing his plaid and tunic and breeches.

Katie began to shake her head. "What are you doing?"

"I'm leaving, Katie," he said curtly, as if the question was offensive to him, as if she should have known. "Bound to intercept them, as they're headed north."

She couldn't stop him, of course, wouldn't dare ask this warrior to not go, to leave the defense of his beloved Scotland to another.

She needed to be brave. "Tell me what to do."

"Da' will hold down Swordmair, as well you ken. Dinna stray, keep Henry close."

That wasn't what she meant. "No, what to do for you right now. What do you need?"

He shook his head. "I dinna need anything. All the logistics are being handled below stairs right now."

Wanting—needing—to do something, Katie recovered his plaid from the bed while he donned fresh hose and his heavier wool breeches. She'd yet to learn how to properly affix the beautiful plaid to his person but she'd watched him enough that she began to fashion the pleats in one end.

Her hands shook and when he turned, dressed and ready for his plaid, she only handed it to him, could not place it over his shoulder. He didn't care, arranged the tartan wool capably himself and then glanced around the room, chewing his lips, likely cataloging that he had all he would need.

Alec faced her then.

Katie didn't move. She wouldn't force an embrace on him, wasn't sure he would welcome it. But then he strode forward and pulled her into his arms that she sagged against him. His lips touched the top of her head, his arms crushed her to him.

Katie tipped her face up to him and Alec covered her mouth with his. It was the first time he'd kissed her without the intention of making love to her. She was as heartened by this boon as she was dismayed by his imminent leave-taking.

Impulsively, she wrapped her arms around his middle and tucked her face into his shoulder. "Please be safe," she cried. "Please come back to me."

"Aye, it'll be fine, Katie." Only one of his hands touched her, low and still on her back.

Until it moved forward, likely about to push her away. Katie closed her eyes and squeezed him tighter, tears falling for her worry, not prepared for this farewell.

"I love you," she said. She couldn't let him leave without giving him these words.

Alec said nothing. His fingers circled one of her arms, meant to drag her off him. Katie straightened and looked up at him. "I love you, Alec."

His jaw shifted, a muscle ticked in his cheek. "Aye, I heard. I have to go."

A world of pain exploded inside her. He couldn't be that cold, that cruel. He just couldn't. She couldn't have been so utterly and completely wrong about him.

# THE LOVE OF HER LIFE

"That's it? *I heard*. Fare thee well? And off you go."

He turned a ferocious scowl on her. "I'll no' fall. I'll be back, Katie. You needn't...say things you dinna mean, that aren't true, simply to make this seem—"

"Things I don't mean? Alec, I am in love with you. I've wanted to tell you for some time, but you've been so..."

"Aye, you've mentioned. I'm cold, aloof, and what else is beyond my ken." The expression on her face must have perfectly matched her utter desolation, her complete shock at both his abruptness and his scathing words, that he tempered what sounded like a fairly decent rising fury to say, "I have to go now. We'll talk when I get back." He clamped his mouth while her lips trembled. Finally, he said, "Katie...I heard you talking to Henry about his father."

Katie blinked. *And?* "I talk to Henry all the time about his father. I always have."

As if she hadn't spoken, he continued, "I ken you loved him greatly, that your heart...." She made to jump in, had so much to say, to correct. Alec held up his hand. "It dinna matter and that's your business, but you have to ken, I will no'—"

"No," she whispered. Katie stared at him, aghast. She began to shake her head. "No, you misunderstand."

"Katie, I—"

"No," she said, bolder now. "It was all a lie. Every word, everything I've ever said to Henry about his father." *Oh, thank God.* She could fix this so easily.

Alec frowned, unwilling to listen. Or to believe.

Katie pounced on him, grabbing his sleeve. "Alec, I lied to him. His father was a wastrel, useless in so many regards, that I suffered no tears when he died...but for what trouble it caused me, being alone then. Afraid."

His arm went completely rigid under her fingers. "You do yourself no favors—neither of us, for these untruths now. And you do Henry's father an injustice. We get on well enough, you and I, mostly enjoy each other, there's no need to invent tales to make this anything more than what it is. There were reasons for us to wed, sound reasons. We needn't have love when we have other things."

She went slack jawed, her hands falling away from him. "Alec, I...oh." The dawning of understanding came with an entirely new wrenching pain. "You don't love me."

"As I've said, we've a good marriage, better than most, I would wager. One could say—"

She shook her head, stiffly and painfully, and straightened her spine. Lifting her chin, she said, "It's fine." Her hands fisted in front of her, her face void of any emotion.

"Katie."

Lowering her gaze to the floor, she gave an unexpected and nervous laugh. "How humiliating. Pardon me for troubling you." She cleared her throat. "I wish you Godspeed, Alec. Truly."

She turned on her heel and left their chambers, ignoring his call to come back. She had no fear that he'd follow, possibly trying to placate her with some feeble, parting words. He had a war to get to.

A quarter hour later, she watched from the nearly empty battlements as the bulk of the MacBriar army rode away from Swordmair. Alec and Malcolm led them, followed immediately by the flag-bearer, and then the rest of Alec's officers and the remainder of the many units. Alec was tall and proud in the saddle, his short hair bouncing a bit with the jog of the horse, his shoulders broad and square. He didn't turn at all, didn't seek any last glimpse of Swordmair or his parents or even his wife. Katie didn't see Elle, for which she was thankful, imagining someone—Malcolm?—must have had a hell of a time convincing her she could not join this fight, not now. Tucked behind the crenellated merlons, Katie said a quick prayer for Alec's safe return.

She didn't stay long, didn't watch until they were no longer in sight. She needed to find Henry, needed to be sure he grasped what was happening, that he understood they were, here at Swordmair, safe.

---

BEFORE HE LED HIS ARMY into the trees, which would effectively remove Swordmair from sight, Alec turned and cast a glance over his shoulder. He'd waited too long, though, was too far now, couldn't see the yard at this lower elevation. He ran his gaze along the ramparts. No blonde hair swayed in the wind, no bright eyes followed him.

'Twas no more than he deserved. *Jesu*, why would she have lied to Henry about his own father? Or, as he suspected was more likely, why would she have lied to him now? A better parting was all he could think. People generally liked to clear the air before they said farewells.

Generally speaking, though that had not been what he'd been about.

*Bluidy hell*, but every word he'd uttered, each lie he'd spewed, had burned as it left his body.

His jaw clenched repeatedly, yet tormented by her crestfallen expression, at his own unwillingness to admit what was in his heart, what he couldn't deny to himself, but which he would disavow to her, for the sake of his goddamn pride.

Years of training and years of warring had not been futile so that after a while, eventually, he was able to purge his mind of the matter of Katie. For now.

They met up with the Maitlands and McEwens after two hours, where the messenger had said to find them. Two other clan armies joined them. Immediately they compared numbers, needing to get a handle on what they could bring to the fight.

"Iain and I have two-fifty, give or take," Lach said. "Cameron brings another hundred and Chalmers adds fifty. Alec?"

"One-twenty."

Iain said, "MacGregor and Kincaid are waiting on us, straight west of Inesfree. Us or the English, whomever they meet first."

"We'd better move then," Alec suggested. "MacKenna coming?"

Lach shook his head. "No response from Aviemore."

"Where's the king?" The young Chalmers laird asked.

"North," Lach said. "Mayhap out on Skye."

They discussed only a bare strategy, knowing they did need to move quickly. And the next several hours saw a united Highland band of over five-hundred soldiers galloping wildly across the craigs and meadows and hills, leaving thunderous clouds of noise and dust in their wake.

They met up with Conall MacGregor and Gregor Kincaid, which added several hundred to their numbers then. Alec had spent time with Kincaid in the spring though hadn't seen MacGregor in years. But if he were going into battle, *Jesu*, but these were solid men and armies to have at his side.

They greeted each other sparingly, knowing the longer they rested, the more ground the English would gain. Conall informed them, "We'd had some intelligence in the last few weeks they might try to make headway up north, so we'd put some scouts around, half dozen here and there."

Gregor Kincaid added, "This Edward is no Longshanks, tucked tail and skittered on back to England fairly quickly, so we imagine they're only testing the water, so to speak."

"Aye," said Lach, "but let's no' give them any ground lest they decide to stay. They take one castle large enough, you ken it'll only invite more."

"As it is," Conall continued, "scouts put them last at Ardmore, as you ken. But that was yesterday. They could be further north."

"Split in two," Alec suggested. "Come at 'em from both sides. They'll want to stay by water, but from Ardmore they have to go through the glen between Ardgay and Kincardine."

Iain nodded. "That's half a day to get through there with a thousand men. They can't have advanced further so soon."

"Aye, we thought the same," Gregor said. "No hardship to get behind them while they meet half of us straight on north at Ardgay."

Lachlan advised, "We'll go 'round to the south end, near Kincardine. Even if we dinna catch them in the glen, we simply keep moving south."

They sent Chalmers then with MacGregor and Kincaid and the armies moved once again, riding south with all due haste. After another hour, the many armies separated into two factions, with Alec and Lach and Iain pushing their units still at a furious pace to get around the south side of the glen, while Conall and Gregor and Chalmers sped directly for the northern end.

But all their plans and conjecture and want of speed were for naught. The English army had indeed moved northward from Ardmore but now only made camp in the forest very close to the small town of Kincardine. But too close to that town to act upon yet, as none wanted to send any fleeing English units through that vulnerable community. They needed to wait until they moved further away from Kincardine so that Alec and Lach and Iain could position their armies behind them.

They were forced to wait three days, the English either in no hurry to move, or waiting on directives or worse, reinforcements. When they did move, none of the watchful Scotsmen could say why, as no more forces joined those English tucked into the trees, and no messenger was seen coming or going.

Only the endless landscape of green and brown and gray, so remarkable for its vastness, made that army of nearly a thousand men seem small when they finally left the forest and moved deliberately along the gleaming blue water of the Dornoch Firth.

Alec and Lach and Iain were patient, watching from a rugged beinn west of the advancing intruders. They waited until the English had begun to climb the rising land, which would then level out before lowering them into that glen.

When the time came, when nearly half the English had disappeared over that rise, they finally moved. Alec unsheathed his sword and set the head of his axe into the top of his boot. Lach sent the archers of these three armies to the front. They would need to move fast, once the English were beyond the hillock, and set up to await their inevitable retreat when those at the fore met with MacGregor and Kincaid and Chalmers.

As with so many fights that Alec had seen over the years, after their initial encroachment, things progressed with lightning speed. The English retreat was swift, trying to gain the hillock again, finding it blocked, first by those archers, reining down more terror, and then by the mounted force, charging down from the rise and into the fray.

Any retreat was always more desperate and hence, more dangerous when you met it head on. Those bolting had nothing to lose, would cull strength and courage and whatever they thought might save them, from recesses they'd not even known they'd possessed until this moment. It was then, a ruthless and brutal melee. These numbers, in their entirety, were but a quarter the size of the armies that had met at either Falkirk or Stirling but Christ, it got bloody fast. The narrow space didn't help, too many bodies and horses and weapons moving about inside a hundred foot wide valley, reminding Alec of Glen Trool only months ago. He hacked and cleaved and dodged and parried, one after another but they just kept coming that Alec was sure MacGregor and Kincaid were bluidy merciless at the other end.

He saw Aymer take a sword from behind, right through the middle of his back, and topple from his steed.

"Son of a bitch." Alec jerked on the reins, turning his destrier toward the fallen Aymer, having to battle several more English to reach him. Malcolm was near, his booming war cries unmistakable. Alec finally reached Aymer, who was groaning on the ground, lifted only onto his elbow.

"Aymer!" He called his attention, leaning low in the saddle for his hand.

Aymer stretched, their fingers touched, but only for the space of a second before Alec was thrust away, in the opposite direction by an arrow to his side. "Christ Almighty," he seethed, straightening just enough to see the tip and several inches of the shaft protruding from the right side of his breastplate, in the middle of his chest. He let out a strangled and vicious howl for this frustration but righted himself that he reached again for Aymer.

Aymer screamed wildly, just enough of a warning that Alec shifted, catching sight of an attack coming at his left flank. He couldn't turn quick enough but dug his heels into the horse's flanks. He was jerked forward but not quickly enough to escape the full force of the Englishman's blow that a sword glanced off his shoulder, slicing down the back of his arm.

"Alec!" Malcolm was shouting, close but yet too far.

Alec's steed kept moving and he was carried away from any further danger from that braw Englishman. He blew short, even breaths through his mouth and lifted his head but only to search for Malcolm, when another blow came, walloping him upside the head, tipping him off his horse.

He hit the ground hard, struggling to draw in breath, and fell forward onto his face. He felt nothing even as his body spasmed when another haphazard arrow struck his thigh. All the gruesome noises dulled, and light faded as he closed his eyes.

When he opened his eyes, he was on his back. Malcolm's face came into view when he was able to focus.

"Hang on now," Malcolm urged roughly.

"Straight to Swordmair, then. We'll follow directly." That was Iain. Or mayhap Lach. He couldn't be sure.

He was jostled and lifted, sensing several held him by his limbs, moved him off the battlefield.

He recognized the sounds of a battle finished, could hear captains and officers shouting out orders and the wounded groaning, but no steel clanged and the shuffling sounds and cacophony of men and animals moving that were always the backdrop to any skirmish were unheard. He must have been out for quite a while.

Alec lifted his hand, fisting his fingers into Malcolm's sleeve, dragging him near.

"Get me to Swordmair...get me to Katie."

"Aye, Alec," Malcolm said, his hand firm upon Alec's shoulder. "We're going, moving like the wind, my friend."

"Katie will save me."

He watched the sky overhead, even as it began to blur. He thought it might be tears that clouded his vision, couldn't be sure, couldn't feel...anything. He was laid into a cart, he thought, felt his body being heaved up onto a hard and flat surface that soon began to move as well. The wagon was set immediately into motion, jostled along quickly over the uneven trail, and he knew somehow he hadn't much time.

"I should have told her," he mumbled. *Jesu, I should have told her.*

# Chapter Twenty-Two

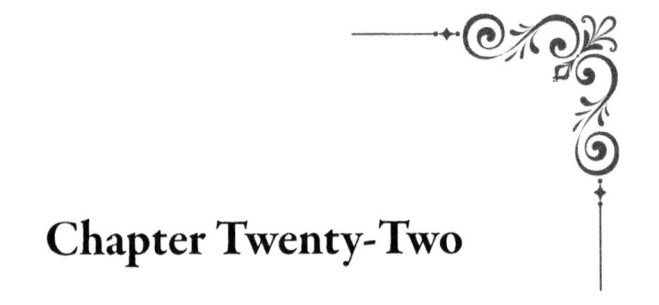

"Will ye sit already?"

"Nae, I will not," Katie snapped, throwing Elle a scowl. "And I do not know how you can."

"Ye bend yer legs and—"

The next glower Katie sent her way effectively silenced her, and Katie continued to pace back and forth across the hall. Good heavens, but how had the laird and Maddie handled this for seven months? It had only been three days and she was beside herself, of no use to anyone. But then, thank God for Elle, for being so stalwart, for keeping Henry engaged and unworried.

*I need to calm down.* But she just couldn't. The first two days had not been so awful, she'd managed to keep herself busy, her mind occupied as much as was possible. However, this morning, she'd woken with an awful feeling of doom. She hadn't dreamed, hadn't had any vision or intuitive notion that Alec was harmed....or worse. She'd only been imbued with this calamitous and heavy sense of catastrophe that she had yet to figure out how to dispel.

Eventually, she did sit with Elle and Henry at the trestle table closest to the head table, where they'd spent much of the last few days. Presently, Henry worked on those silly feathers and that arrow shaft, but was pleased to do so with Elle so near for continued instruction.

Maddie was inside the kitchens, was wise and brave enough to tackle industry to keep herself from fretting. The laird only moved about the castle and keep, sitting mostly silently, currently in his chair at the family's table, his chin in his hand, his gaze blind upon the door of the hall.

When a few more minutes had past, noise from outside disturbed the uneasy quiet within.

Katie and Elle jumped to their feet, the laird rising as well only a second later.

"Rider coming fast!" Was shouted from atop the curtain wall.

Katie was the first out the door. The gate was yet closed that she lifted her skirts and dashed across the yard and into the gatehouse, taking the stairs to the battlements. Elle was right behind her. By the time they'd reached the wall, the rider was across the meadow and crossing the bridge.

Only one.

Katie lifted her gaze beyond him, to the trees, watching for more, for the rest of the army.

But no more came. The gate below was cranked upward, creaking loudly with a groan.

She left the wall, as did Elle, skittering back down the stairs to see what news came.

It was Simon, his youthful face flushed and anxious, the hair at his forehead damp with perspiration. He charged through the gate and leapt from his lathered horse. The laird stood directly in front of him, Maddie at his side, waiting, but Simon's gaze searched the yard, landing on Katie as she emerged from the gatehouse.

And she knew right then what news he brought.

"What?" The laird shouted. "Jesus, Mary, and Joseph, lad! What?"

Simon swallowed visibly. Katie had reached him, and Alec's parents. Simon's gaze stayed with Katie. He began to shake his head even before he spoke. "It's bad. They're bringing him in, but..."

Maddie wailed and collapsed to her knees, her skirts ballooning until they settled around her. She braced one hand against her husband's leg and dropped her head into her chest.

Elle went to her, hugged the mistress tight.

Katie stood motionless. He was alive, was all she heard.

"How far out?" The laird wanted to know, his voice breaking.

"Half hour, no more."

"How many?"

"Just him. The rest—Aymer, John, Robert, they're gone, dinna survive the drive home. Others injured, but...not so gravely."

Katie's lips trembled, but she managed to nod. Swallowing her fear, she began to give orders. "Put up several kettles of water to boil. I'll need many ewers and cloths inside our chambers. I need all the pouches brought up from the workroom..." she continued to list items she might need, all the while keeping her gaze on Simon until she could no more bear the mournful shaking of his head. "Don't you dare give up on him, Simon. And don't you dare tell me there's no hope."

A minute later, another mounted rider came through the gate.

Lachlan Maitland.

He spoke even before he dismounted. "Ten minutes out, sir."

Alexander MacBriar nodded stoically and finally thought to address his wife, weeping yet at his feet. He bent and lifted her by her arms. Elle helped her to stand. The laird whispered to his bride, though his large voice carried still. "It's the same as last time, bride, same as any other time. Until he's gone, he lives yet."

Her head shook convulsively, and she clung to her husband.

Lachlan pulled Katie aside, his deep blue eyes steady upon her. "Sword to the shoulder, plenty of blood lost. Arrow to his thigh, we left that intact." He pointed to the right side of his chest, straight across from his heart. "Pierced here, struggling to breathe. Broke the arrow when he fell from his horse, but it's still lodged."

She nodded and whimpered. "Is there more?"

Lachlan shook his head, concern etched harshly upon his scarred visage. "Took the side of a blade to his head, knocked him out, but no bleeding there." He put his hand firmly onto Katie's arm and instructed sternly, "Put the fear aside. No time for that now. You make him better, wail and weep when that's done."

Nodding shakily, she watched Lachlan lift his head, listening. "Here he comes." He held her arm still, walked her toward the door to the hall. "Go on up. I'll bring him myself."

At her continued, wretched nodding, he left her, striding toward the gate.

Katie remained only long enough to see that Iain and Malcolm rode directly in front of the cart, their expressions grim. Malcolm's face was a blotchy red and she thought he must have wept, or cried still.

Composing herself, forcing deep and even breaths, she didn't wait to see him. She turned and entered the keep, walked stiffly up the stairs and to their chambers. She left the door wide and arranged the two pillows on top of each other in the middle of the bed. She lit three candles at the bedside table with unsteady and uncooperative hands and then waited, her head bowed, as she heard them coming.

She closed her eyes only long enough to pray for strength and when she opened them, Lach was carrying Alec into the room. She bit back her instant fright at the sight of him and felt her body begin to quiver uncontrollably.

He was not awake, his face dropped into Lach's chest, his pallor grave. His legs swung limply with each step Lachlan took. From his chest, she could see the splintered and cracked remains of one arrow. Another, with feathers yet attached, was wedged deep into the outside of his thigh. Blood caked so many parts of him, most notably his entire left arm and shoulder. Curiously, because he was unconscious, Katie noted that one hand was fisted tight.

Iain appeared directly behind, and Malcolm followed him. As Lach went to one side of the bed, Iain and Malcolm took positions on the other, reaching for Alec so that he was not dropped onto the mattress.

Inhaling deeply, Katie noticed Elle in the doorway. "I need that boiled water. Now."

"Aye." Elle said, her eyes red and watery. And she darted away.

Katie stepped forward. The three men standing around the bed shuffled out of her way, but kept their eyes trained on her.

"Cut it all off," she instructed as she stopped near the head of the bed. She lifted Alec's eyelids, noted that his pupils were only slightly dilated but, as suspected, unresponsive.

Iain promptly withdrew a knife from his waistband and began slicing at Alec's breastplate. Katie stopped him only long enough to press her ear to the right side of Alec's chest, her chin above the remnant of that offensive arrow. She closed her eyes but heard no sounds.

"The shaft," Lach cautioned Iain as Katie stepped away again. It took all three men to remove Alec's padded armor and tunic, trying not to cause any further disturbance to the protruding arrow, splintered and jutting yet six inches above his chest.

"Is this the beginning or the end of it?" She asked about that most damaging dart just as Simon appeared, his hands laden with all her medicines and tools.

"Back to front," Malcolm answered.

She feared it had struck the lower portion of his lung, which subsequently had collapsed the entire thing, and would account for his labored breathing but no sounds from within on that side. "We'll sheer off the end and push it through then when I'm ready." She needed to prepare everything first before she began to treat all the wounds.

A muffled cry brought her gaze to the door, where the laird stood with his arm around his wife, who was sniffling into her sleeve, her teary-eyed gaze on Alec's unmoving form.

Katie found Iain's gaze on her, a question asked by his lifted brow.

"Two minutes," she mouthed to him. She could not deny his parents seeing their son, and she had another minute or so of work at the cupboard where usually sat only the ewer and basin.

It was paramount that she concentrate and not lose herself to fear or anxiety or any sort of melodrama, that she forced herself to tune out the sound of Maddie's tearful pleading for Alec to wake.

Elle returned then, squeezing into the crowded room with a steaming kettle of water. Malcolm leapt forward and relieved her of the weight, setting the iron kettle onto the bedside table, which Lachlan moved closer, pushing the candles toward one end.

"Keep them coming, Elle," Katie said over her shoulder. They would need plenty. She pivoted and stretched out her hand to Lachlan, who stood closest to her. Without question or hesitation, he accepted the spoons and different sized knives, the bone needles and her pliers. "Into the kettle."

The laird and Maddie were shuffled out of the room by Iain and Malcolm, with promises they'd be allowed to return as soon as possible. Malcolm ushered them out, leaving as well to fetch more kettles himself.

They worked together over the next hour, Katie and Lachlan and Iain, while Elle and Malcolm and Simon managed all the running and fetching. Katie was open with them, sharing with them her suspicions and estimations, and plenty of instructions, with which any one of them were happy to comply. She used Iain's strength to wrest the arrow tip from the bone, and Lachlan's steady hands on the spoons so that she could better assess the damage done to Alec's thigh. The wound at the back of his arm was easiest, requiring naught but a good cleaning and a long length of silk for stitching.

After an hour, Alec was completely naked by necessity, a linen sheet draped over his middle for his own modesty, even though he'd roused not at all.

"You're no' going to sew the chest there?" Iain asked.

Katie shook her head, her hands on her hips while she surveyed Alec, mindful and a wee bit anxious for his paleness yet. "Despite the trauma to the immediate area, the entry and exit spots are so small." She narrowed her eyes and lifted Alec's hand, still fisted despite all the rearranging and jostling they'd put him through in the past hour. She pulled at his fingers, but they wouldn't budge. Some instinct made her lean forward, bending his elbow as she did. She leaned very close to his face and whispered, "Open your hand, Alec." He did not but when she tried again to pry his fingers open, she found success. Inside his palm, squeezed and flattened to the size of a walnut was the linen kerchief she'd wrapped the brooch in, her wedding gift to him. Startled by this, that he'd not only kept this small token, but that he'd held it so dear, hadn't given it up, Katie felt her first tears in almost an hour.

Only Lachlan's question of, "What now?" kept her from throwing herself at Alec and begging him to please live long enough that she might convince him that she loved him.

"Let's put one more pillow under him, to aid his breathing," she said instead, using the back of her hand to wipe at her tears.

When this was done, she spelled out what else they would need to do to keep him alive.

"He needs to be kept in this state," she said. "I know we want him to wake, would find great relief in that, but it won't help him. His breathing is compromised, as his right lung is not working. It can heal itself from the inside, but it won't be helped if he wakes and struggles to breathe."

"Aye," Lachlan said. "But how do we do that? Keep him sleeping?"

"By giving him a mixture of herbs...and other things."

"Other? What other?" Ian frowned.

Katie held her hands up, thinking out loud really. "I've never used it, never had cause, but I'm familiar with a mixture—Maybeth, the healer who was my teacher—used it occasionally. She called it dwale, said it was employed quite commonly in England." With a bit of a grimace, she informed them, "She also insisted on including the bile of a barrow swine, but I could never imagine any medicinal properties in such, that I think we might leave off adding that."

"What do you need then?"

"Mulberry juice, henbane, bryony—the wild neep—but I haven't come upon any of that around Swordmair. And a few other things I do have here."

Lachlan and Iain exchanged glances. "Either Cameron or MacGregor might have it," Lach supposed.

"Aye," Iain concurred. "Isla Cameron is skilled." He shrugged. "Send 'em down to both places, no harm to have excess."

"What else?" Lach asked.

"And prayers." Was all she could imagine.

---

ALEC HAD BEEN RETURNED for two full days before Katie would leave him. She still resisted but had now come up against the insistence of not only Maddie and Lachlan, who'd suggested as much regularly, but Iain and Elle and even Henry.

"You dinna look verra good, mam."

She forced a smile for her son. Elle had brought him up, which Katie did not mind. Henry had known sickness and death since his infancy, as she'd never once left her son to tend another person, so she wasn't afeared that he might not be able to process the circumstance or that he might find it disturbing. He'd asked only when Alec would wake as he'd gingerly touched one finger to the back of Alec's hand.

"I'm fine, Henry. Tired, is all."

"Ye always say to all the people ye tend, *take care of the caretaker*."

She nodded, knowing he was right, and lifted her gaze across the bed to Lachlan and Malcolm, and especially Elle, all of whom were giving her an expectant look.

"Mayhap I wouldn't mind a quick bath," she thought out loud. She'd eaten, as Maddie kept the room and all its constant occupants well-fed. She'd slept, curled up next to her husband in their big bed, wanting to be near should there be any changes.

"Aye, we can make that happen," Elle said. She took Henry's hand and they departed.

"Dinna make it quick, lass," Iain said. "The lad's right—learned from his wise mother—you're no good to Alec if you run your own self down."

"Aye," Lachlan concurred, "so you'll be off then, and we will no' allow you back until after supper."

"Before supper," she cajoled, which was still too long gone from his side.

Lachlan nodded, conceding. He took her arm and bade her stand from the chair. "Go on then—"

"But you'll fetch me straight away if—"

"Ye ken we will," Iain said as he propelled her toward the door.

She allowed him to close it after her, not all the way, that she hovered, torn, not really wanting to leave him.

After a moment, just about when she shifted one foot to turn away, she heard Lach's voice.

"I'll kill him myself if he lets this be the end—done off by a fecking ragtag band of weak-kneed fops."

"*Jesu*," Iain breathed, a shaky laugh bursting out. "I ken the same thing. You mean to tell me he survived Falkirk and the seven months after and all the shite since and he's gonna be felled by some wee skirmish that will no' even be given a name, it was over so quick."

"All those years, living only for the next battle—*Jesu*, how he loved the fight. Sought it out, I ken. Now he's got her...might finally ken some peace and.... Christ, I'll kill him."

She stayed no longer, needed to hear no more. Her husband was in good hands. His friends loved him, as he did them.

---

SHE BEGAN TO TALK TO him on the third day. Not out of fear that he was slipping away or out of boredom for the long quiet hours she spent at his side. But with some hope that he might hear her and that he didn't worry himself that he couldn't wake yet.

Katie didn't mind if any others heard, didn't let the presence of his father or mother or Lachlan or Iain keep her from chatting away. She only talked trivialities at first, letting him know who was there and what others were doing, how the battle had ended in their favor, according to Iain, whom she'd thought to question at some point.

"Your mother was here this morning, as she has been every other morning, which you might well know," she said to him on the fourth day. Yesterday, she'd asked Lach and Iain to shift Alec's resting form a bit to the right of the bed, that there might be more room for her on the left side of the mattress. So she sat there now, crossed legged at his side, unconcerned with the impropriety of her position as it allowed her to be closer and not turned so awkwardly. She held his hand, rubbed her fingers along the back of it. "We bathed you again and she quite enjoyed combing your hair, was about it for quite some time. Then she was off, but I was very proud of her—she lasted nearly an hour without tears today. She'd stay all day if you needed her, of course, but you understand she's just so much better off moving and busy tending things and people." She laughed a bit. "Though your father did suggest that when it's time for you to wake, we might sit her right down and let her chatter non-stop until you roused and begged her cease." She turned his hand over, tracing the lines of his palm, pleased that his skin was warm, but not overly much. "Malcolm came by, stoked the fire a bit, and shuffled his feet. I sent him off after a bit, on a frivolous errand, as his staring so eagerly at you even makes me nervous. And I'd explained to him already—twice now—that you are sleeping at my behest, and with the help of the herb recipe, so that you can heal properly." Katie turned, staring off out the slim window a bit, until she thought of more to share with him. "I cannot say enough, or convey with any amount of perfection, how grateful I am for

Lachlan and Iain's presence. Alec, those are two very remarkable friends you have and how blessed you are. They love you so much, have cried and prayed and jumped to do all my bidding, all for you. What a wonderful thing, to have such friends. You truly are very blessed. Lach said they might send for Mari and Maggie, which I'm not against at all, if it makes them feel better to have their wives near. Yes, they already did send off word that they were safe, advising of the situation here, that neither Mari nor Maggie was left to fret over their husbands."

The door to their chambers was always open now, save for at night when Katie slept beside him. Katie turned now, sensing a presence. Lachlan had returned, one broad shoulder leaned against the doorjamb, his arms crossed over his chest as if he'd been there a while.

He entered when she noticed him.

"Will Mari and Maggie come then?" She asked, assuming he'd heard.

"Aye, Murdoch and Archie and a dozen more'll bring 'em up."

She nodded, but then kept talking to Alec. "More friends coming, which will bring more prayers."

Her shoulders sat low, but only because she was very weary. It wasn't even past noon yet, she thought.

"Katie," Lachlan drew her attention to where he sat, in the chair, which had been moved to the other side of the bed, "I ken you want him still for the healing but are you sure this is working?"

This came as no great surprise to her, someone questioning her methods. Truth be told, she questioned every day if she'd made the right choices, if this were what he needed to live, if she weren't causing him more harm. In the end, always her conclusion was the same. She was certain of one thing: Alec would not die.

"I love my husband. I want him—"

"Do you?"

Her initial, spontaneous and internal response to this shock was, *I take back all the kind words I'd spoken about this man.* Her dander rose, along with her shoulders. She could only stare at him.

"I've never heard or seen this method practiced. I'm only thinking of Alec."

"By questioning my love for him?"

His big shoulders lifted and fell, his hands folded together in front of him, elbows on the arms of the chair. "I was at the wedding. And I was here for a few days after."

She didn't need to ask to what he referred. Alec's coolness instantly came to mind.

Deciding she didn't need to explain all the particulars to him, she said pertly, "When Alec wakes, you can ask him yourself exactly how big an arse he was in those days."

He seemed to accept this or chose not to pursue the topic. Mayhap her gaze, suddenly and annoyingly filled with tears, staved off any pursuit of this line of questioning. After a moment, something else occurred to her—that mayhap at some point, Alec had spoken with Lachlan about the state of, or the reasons for, their marriage. A bit awkwardly then, she said in a small voice, "I love my husband. I-I cannot...that is, I know he does not feel the same, but I do. I would rather see harm done to me than—"

"Dinna love *you*?" Lachlan frowned, which intensified every line and mark and crease in the scars on his face. "*Jesu*, lass. Make him better and get the truth from him. If he says nae, tell him he's a liar. That was your name on his lips anytime he was wakeful enough to speak. *Get me to Katie*, over and over."

She was quiet, a bit unnerved by the dark intensity of Lachlan Maitland, who at this very moment made Alec's frowns seem rather tame in comparison.

Considering his words though, Katie turned her attention back to Alec, still holding his hand.

Lachlan interrupted whatever musings she might have lent to his surprising words. "He ever talk about being a prisoner?"

Katie shook her head, startled by the question. "But once." She thought she should add, "He shared no details though." While Lachlan nodded, Katie dared to ask, "What are the marks on his legs from? They're all the same size, evenly spaced, one after another."

He pushed his lips out with the distaste the memory brought to him. A long silence filled the space between them before he answered. "John of Knolles had been marking the wall, one strike carved with a stone for each day we were held. Every day, someone would ask, *how long? how many days now?*" He shook his head. "I never ken why they cared. John died and Alec...he assumed that role—among others. Iain could barely move, his back so shredded, bleeding, infected, so forth. I was...no help to any for weeks, couldn't see out one eye, too busy praying for death. When the English found the marks on the wall, they decided to start marking the days on Alec instead, one slice every morning. He used to smirk at them—*Jesu*, he was a hard-bitten son of a bitch. "

"They were monsters."

"We all are, were. War is...it turns people ugly."

"That's not true. Alec wouldn't have treated any prisoner like that. You wouldn't have. The laird—" Katie broke off, as Lachlan had thrown her a narrow-eyed scowl. "What?"

He only shook his head. "Turns people ugly, lass. All of us."

She shook her head. No, that wasn't true.

And then, rather out of the blue, he asked, "Why do you boil the utensils?"

She blinked, wondering if Lachlan Maitland actually had an agenda, of things he wanted to know, bouncing around as he was. "I'm not exactly sure," she admitted. "But over the years, I'd noticed that minor scrapes and cuts on Henry, when kept clean, or on a part of the body that was less exposed to dirt or debris of any kind, seemed to heal better and faster. Cuts on the fingers or his face—parts that a young boy quite often got dirty—tended to, more often than not, become infected, or at the very least, take longer to heal." She shrugged. "I'm not sure it means anything, but I'd always thought it couldn't hurt."

He only nodded and requested, "Swear to me, Katie. Tell me he'll be fine."

Oh, how she wanted to. She believed it with all her heart. She wept. "He must be. He has to be."

# Chapter Twenty-Three

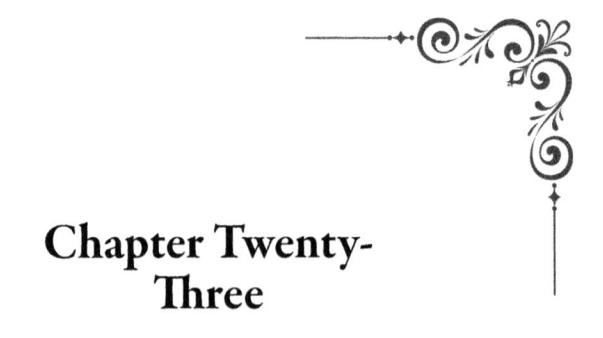

They developed quite a system for the caretaking of Alec. Though he slept mostly peacefully, he needed to be roused several times a day and forced to ingest both sustenance and the medicine. This chore required the strength of Lach or Iain or Malcolm, and usually involved his father nearby, his booming voice scolding his son to comply. It was messy and not always successful, sometimes requiring that Katie squeeze his cheeks to open his mouth, and all of them hoping he didn't choke on any of the liquids.

He was bathed every other day, and a kettle of water was kept constantly at the hearth, where Simon and Malcolm had rigged up a spit of sorts, a long metal rod suspended over the fire from which hung the pot. She should expect his mother every morning, shortly after sunrise, and his father several times a day, though he adhered to no schedule it seemed. Elle was in and out, sometimes with Henry, and usually fussing after Katie to take care of herself. One day, they'd sat together, Katie on the bed with Alec and Elle in the chair, while they tried to figure out how to make dressing gowns for the bairn Elle would deliver in the spring. Lachlan and Iain came every day around noon and then again in the evening, when they forced Katie away from her husband for as long as she could stand it.

She rarely found herself alone with him, save for at night, when she laid on her side and lightly set her hand on him, just to know he was warm and still yet. Everyday, she listened to his chest with her ear over the shrinking hole that had pierced his lung.

She continued to talk to him and had observed that several others had begun to do so as well. Henry had happily told him of the fish he'd caught in the loch with Ronald and Martin, her son being so dear that he'd lifted his voice and leaned close to Alec, as if his ears were stuffed with cloth and this was Alec's only deficiency now. She'd returned one evening an hour after Lach and Iain had sent her off, pleased that her presence didn't silence the two, as they'd been reminiscing about their youth, many summers spent here at Swordmair, training with the laird. She held no grudge for Lachlan, didn't think ill of him for the concern he'd shown for his friend. And she enjoyed their lightness this evening, laughing together over some trouble they'd gotten into with Alec's father way back when.

"He was right pissed," Iain said. "Face all blotchy red, spittle flying with each word he roared."

"Aye, but first, remember that look? He wanted to laugh, I swear to God."

"What had you done?" Katie asked, taking her usual spot on the bed.

Iain's eyes were bright with merriment. "The laird convened a meeting of northern nobles, when Balliol was first chosen. Naturally, he trots out all the accoutrements, good food and imported wine—back then it was easier to come by. Has the proud and righteous MacBriar banners slung over the wall, three of them." He stopped, laughing so hard he couldn't finish, pinching his eyes with his thumb and middle finger.

Lachlan picked up where Iain had left off. "We thought we'd add our own banners, but first we had to make them. We tried filching some linen from the laundress, but she wasn't having it, so we stole three pairs of the laird's drawers—"

"And turmeric and onions and our own piss to make a yellow paint," Iain was able to add, his voice still ringing with laughter.

"We drew—and I use that term loosely—our crests onto his drawers and flapped them over the wall just in time for the approaching nobles to see," Lachlan's shoulders shook, his eyes crinkling at the edges.

Katie covered her mouth with her hand, stifling her shock and laughter.

"He gave us hell for three days when they'd all gone," Iain said.

"One of the many times we put him through his paces," Lachlan concluded.

*But then he saved you*, she thought, recalling that Laird MacBriar had been the one to see the release of these three, and others from the godawful English prison.

When they left an hour later, having shared more stories from their youth and even adulthood, Katie once more laid beside Alec, holding his hand near her thigh.

"I love you," she told him in the quiet room. She said it again and again until she fell asleep.

# THE LOVE OF HER LIFE

WHEN A WEEK HAD GONE by, Katie put her ear to Alec's chest first thing in the morning. Out of habit, having heard so little in the last seven days from his right lung, she made to pull away after only a cursory attempt, supposing nothing had changed. But it had. She flattened her cheek and ear against him once more and heard the faint, but unmistakable sounds of the lung at work.

Disbelieving, she listened for quite a while, closing her eyes in splendid joy for this progress. When she was satisfied that she hadn't imagined it, she ran to the door and pulled it open, shouting out for Maddie and Lachlan and Elle, knowing the rest would come as well at her happy cries.

They came quickly and heard the good news.

"We can stop the sleeping draught," she advised, which enlivened the group even more. "He will wake then."

But he did not, not that morning and not that afternoon.

And when the evening grew old and he still did not wake, Katie now contended with worry over other things. Was there an infection somewhere inside that produced no fever? Had she over-medicated him that he might not ever wake?

Her own anxiety making her distraught, she thought to distract herself once again by talking to her husband. "I've been meaning to take you to task for the way you left me. Honestly, it peeved me enough that I cannot believe I'd put it off until now. And no, sir, your current condition will not see you off the hook for your shoddy behavior." She'd yet to change into her bedclothes that she only sat next to him, as she had for countless hours over the last seven days, legs crossed beneath her and his hand in hers. "You shouldn't have confessed that to me only minutes before your departure. That was ill done and unfair to me. What if you *had* been...hadn't returned? I would have had to live all my life with that agony, that you'd misunderstood that, that you didn't know I loved you. Only you. But then to throw my words back at me, say I lied. I won't forgive you for that. Not ever." There was no truth to this last part, but she watched his eyes, the closed lids. They moved not at all. If these incendiary words had not roused him, she feared nothing would.

Katie sighed and confessed again, "I lied to Henry. I'm not sure why, or even how it started. His father was no great man." She felt she needed to clarify. "He wasn't mean at all, rarely struck me, or likely I'd never want to speak of him at all. But I was there to serve a purpose, wash his clothes, make his supper, be available to his needs. It-it wasn't awful, I never thought that. It was just—I mean, he provided well, saw that we mostly had the makings for bread, game was supplied fairly often, I had a roof over my head." She paused, thoughtful for a while. "I don't know why I started telling those fabulous stories to Henry. Wishful thinking, mayhap. It gave him something to dream on, to aspire to. Seemed to bring no harm. I just wanted him to have a history, have a family, as I never did." With a sigh, she continued, "But he was...he was simply Henry's father, more so that than my husband, and then so much less...so irrelevant when compared to you. He wasn't beautiful or wise. He carried not the weight of great honor, struck no chord in me of desire or want or need. He wasn't...you. I love you." She cringed though, for how inadequate those little words were, for how pitiful they sounded compared to what it felt like. "That's...that's not right. The words are too simple, they diminish it. I cannot whittle it down to a simple *I love you*. It's so much more. I don't even know yet what all of it is. I only know that I want to be wherever you are, for as long as you'll have me. And I don't care if you don't love me in return. Just let me love you, I'll be happy."

"Think he can hear ye, lass?"

Katie lifted her head and swiped at her tears.

Laird MacBriar stood in the doorway, his beloved and familiar hazel gaze watery as well.

Matter-of-factly, she told him, "I believe he can. Some parts are broken, but he's still here. He's *right* here. I *have* to believe he can hear me."

The laird nodded and stepped slowly into the room.

Katie composed herself, what little she could, and rose from the bed.

"Ye take a break now, go say goodnight to the lad. I want to talk to my son."

She nodded. She did not at all want to leave him, but he had more right to Alec than she did.

---

"AYE, AND WE ALL KEN she'd be perfect for you, and that's the truth," Alexander MacBriar said, moving the chair a wee bit closer to the bed before sitting down. His mouth moved, emotions nearly overwhelming him, for several seconds until he was able to speak again. "Aye, and she's right, the words dinna do it justice. But Alec, you've given me so much pride and brought so much joy—enough for all the bairns we lost and more, so help me God. Your poor mam cried for a week before your third birthday. That was the longest any child had lived—that was Benjamin, had him for nearly three years. Nice boy, sparkling eyes. Christ! How they shone. She was so afeared that was it, that your end was nigh. But then we get another week, and another month, and another year, and we only loved you. Now, it's true, ye weren't always easy and ye canna go blaming that entirely on us, but I ken...you just wanted to be your own man and we...well, we just wanted you here. With us. Always. So aye, it was hard to let you live free, I ken. Lach and Iain coming in your twelfth year, that was good. Got ye trained, made ye some friends—and thank God for that, aye?—but still kept you close to us." He talked more, told his son how watching him ride away from Swordmair to fight at Falkirk was the hardest thing he'd ever had to do. "And I ken you can no' forgive me for what I'd done at Hawick House. I canna explain it, cannot even recall making the decision. It was wrong and aye, that's my cross to bear now, my mercy to beg from God when I meet Him." He lowered his chin to his chest and wept. "But lad, dinna hate me because I loved you, because I couldn't...let it go without answering...what they'd done to you." He cried more, said nothing else for a long while.

When he next spoke, his voice was clear once again. "That's on me, those Englishmen dead. That was by my hand, no' yours. I killed them, killed those innocent men same as they'd done to ours, but mostly, for what they'd done to you." He sniffled, wiped angrily at his nose. "And I never really did recover my boy, which seemed to double the crime, then. But there ye have it, and that's why I dinna fight no more. Couldn't trust myself. I'd never ken blind fury like that, never wanted to meet it again. Dinna fight, blamed it on my age, my knees, whatever else anyone might believe. Shame is what it was."

He sat quietly then, content to have these minutes with his son, however long the good Lord allowed him. And then Alexander MacBriar nearly jumped out of his chair when Alec's lips moved. Didn't just move, but put words out.

"Say it again, lad," Alexander demanded, clumsily falling to his knees at the side of the bed. "Say it again. I dinna hear ye."

"I dinna hate you. No' ever." His voice was low and scratchy, but the words were clear.

The laird could form no thoughts, could do naught but touch his son, his huge hand gentle against Alec's face, while his cheeks were streaked with tears. Alec opened his eyes, blinked several times, struggling to focus, it seemed. His lids were heavy, shrouding half his eyes.

"I ken why you did it." Alec needed time to draw breath between sentences, sometimes between words. "I dinna like it...that it was done because of... me. But I never...dinna love you, da."

Alexander nodded, the tightness in his chest, his constant companion for so many years, eased.

"I need Katie," Alec murmured, closing his eyes again. "Where is Katie?"

Alexander MacBriar, bless his soul, turned his head, still very close to his just-wakened and very weak son, and bellowed for all the keep to hear, "Katie!"

---

SHE CAME RUNNING, BURSTING into their chambers, her hand held at the doorjamb, her gaze stark with fear.

But she came not alone, followed by Elle and then his mother and soon after, Malcolm. He thought he spied Lach's big frame and Iain, too, standing behind them all. But his gaze was only for her.

She hadn't moved, not since she'd appeared in the doorway, not since she found him awake. None could enter then, until she did, as she blocked the entrance.

His mother wouldn't or couldn't wait for Katie to recover but pushed at the arm stretched across the doorway and burst inside. His father remained where he was so that his mam came to the other side of the bed, falling onto him, taking his cheeks in her hands, kissing him repeatedly.

His poor, dear mam.

They all fussed over him.

"Bluidy lucky son of a bitch," Elle murmured.

"Aye, and I dinna have to kill you now," Lach said.

"He did threaten as much," Iain confirmed, "if you were no' going to wake."

He allowed it, gave them several minutes to enjoy what his mother had just called his resurrection, was thankful for them, nodding and trying to smile, his gaze straying every other second to Katie. She hung back yet, those moody blue eyes he loved so well bright with tears and joy, but then filled with caution as well. He barely spoke, realized with only those few words to his father that it was a chore, that it taxed what little strength he had. He needed to save it for Katie. He didn't need to ask what happened, as his mother proceeded to recount all seven days in glorious and unnecessary detail.

When he could bear it no more, he found Lachlan's eye, inclined his head just enough that his friend came near. Christ, Alec could barely lift his hand, he was so weak. He could do no more than tip his head back on the pillows. Lach understood and bent low.

Alec whispered, his voice rusty yet, "I need to talk to Katie."

Lach said only, "Aye," patting Alec's shoulder and then straightened to make that happen. "C'mon, Maddie. Your lad's hungry. Let's get down to the kitchens and fix him a feast."

"Oh, aye," said Alec's mother, pushing off from the mattress, still holding Alec's hand though. "We had the pork tonight, love. Would that suit? Or I can make you the beef with the mushrooms if—"

Lachlan herded her away. "He'll eat shoe leather, Maddie, if that's what you've got. He hasn't eaten in a week."

Elle and Malcolm caught on, that Lachlan was trying to clear the room. Iain nudged the laird's elbow and inclined his head toward the door when the MacBriar faced him. "Aye, aye, right." Iain helped the laird to his feet.

And then it was only Katie and him.

She stood near to the door still, one hand clenching and wrinkling the fabric of her bodice. She was tired and pale, and even thinner mayhap. Her hair was untidy, falling from a sloppy knot at her nape. He thought her lips might be trembling.

"Sit with me," he said.

Her lips parted. She moved without haste and claimed the spot his mother had vacated, surprising him by pulling her legs up underneath her on the mattress. She didn't, or wouldn't, lift her gaze to him. But she took his hand, held it lightly within hers. One tear slid away from the corner of her eye, marked a trail down her cheek.

He drew a deep breath to say it properly, without hesitation. "I am so in love with you."

She didn't lift her eyes from his hand, indeed, she dropped her chin onto her chest and cried more.

"Dinna cry, Katie," he begged, closing his eyes, his strength sapped already. But he squeezed the fingers that held his. "Unless you cry because I'm an arse....Which I am.... Still, I love you."

Now, she lifted her magnificent blue eyes to him.

"And you're right," he continued, "*I love you* doesn't...say it all."

"You heard?"

"Aye, some. Maybe more. I dinna ken...right now."

She nodded.

"I feel as if...I've been trampled by...all of Swordmair's horses."

"Aye. Your breathing will improve, I'm sure, with rest and time."

"But seven days?"

She rather winced. "In all probability, you'd have woken sooner. I gave you something to keep you sleeping and still."

He wouldn't question it, somehow knew he lived because of her.

"Lie down with me. I need to feel you." He wouldn't force her to admit just now what he had once so carelessly, so cruelly, flung back in her face.

"I don't want to...ruin anything or...hurt you."

"Katie, love, will you please come closer? I ken a good healer. It'll be fine."

She first left the bed, walking around to the other side. She climbed in again and settled herself gently against his left side.

Alec moved the hand that lay between them, searching for hers. When their fingers folded around each other, he closed his eyes again, knowing a breathtaking sense of peace.

But it wasn't finished.

"I need to ken if I've killed it, Katie?"

"Killed...what? Alec, what are you—"

"I love you," he said raggedly. "But you haven't...do you no' feel it still?"

It was a long time before she answered.

"I feel it. I just didn't know if you only...said that because you felt bad for how you left."

"What have I done? *Have* I killed it? Ruined it?" He could do nothing about the raw heartbreak in his voice. "Do you no' trust your heart with me now?" *Jesu*, could he blame her?

"I..."

Ah, but he'd made a muddle of it. He needed to go about it differently. He'd been a fool to doubt her, when it had been written so plainly upon her face, the anguish she'd shown at his departure. She should doubt him not at all. It should be known, and live in her, and just always be there for her. He did not deserve her if he couldn't convince her.

Alec closed his eyes and spoke slowly and with great conviction. "I love the sound of your voice, especially when you talk non-stop, hoping I might wake. I love the way your eyes wrinkle at the corners when your laugh comes full. I like that my presence calms you when you're afraid. Aye, and ye ken, I like the way you mother Henry; I enjoy the relationship you and he have. I like that you and Elle are friends—no' sure how you did it, but it impresses me. I like how you minister, efficient and so damn clever. I like your hands, they're soft and fine but I ken, verra strong. And I'll no' lie, I like that I disturb you, because you ken, you do the same to me."

"Oh." More than likely, she'd not have suspected such detailed honesty from him, may have expected not much more than some mention that she was bonny, and he liked her kiss.

"Katie, I swear I can hear your heart beating now."

And his brave and fierce Katie said the most remarkable thing. She said, "I was trying to figure out exactly when I might have fallen in love with you."

Alec blinked, but otherwise remained completely still, his heart bursting with relief.

She moved her thumb along his palm, back and forth. "Of course, I'm sure it wasn't when you first crashed through the door at Dalserf." She swallowed. "And I honestly don't even think it was behind that tree when you decided you might want to kiss me. Maybe it was when I saw you holding the Lister babe so beautifully. I cannot be sure." She shook her head. "No, I do believe it was when I came upon you at my cottage, after my bath, before you made love to me."

"Why? Why then?"

Against his shoulder, she lifted her gaze to him, her eyes shiny, so beloved.

"Because you were so unsure. Which I have to believe is something you have never in your life wrestled with. But then you stepped forward and knocked on the door anyway."

When he said nothing, only waited for more to come—surely his nerves of that night had not made her fall in love with him—she explained her reasoning.

"Because it was important to you, so you faced it, pushed through the unease."

"I wanted—needed—to apologize to you."

She tilted her head at him.

"Fine," he admitted. "It was as I'd said then—it was no' finished."

"No, it was not. I love you, Alec. More than reason, mayhap. More than anything."

*Thank God.* "Just the beginning."

# Epilogue

*Summary, 1308*

———∽∾———

"I'M SO EXCITED, ALEC."

"Aye, I ken you are. I like when your eyes shine like that."

"Aren't you excited?"

"Aye, and truth be told, probably more on this occasion than any other time I was bound to see Lach and Iain."

She sidled a bit closer, so very pleased to have her husband so at peace.

"I apologize for falling asleep so early last night." She put her hand on his thigh. "I'd wanted you to make love to me, but then I couldn't keep my eyes open. Why didn't you wake me?"

Alec shifted just slightly to place a kiss on her forehead, leaned into him. "I ken you were tired. You had a busy day with Eleanor and her bairn."

"But that's all settled, her struggles with the feeding. I wouldn't have been able to leave her today if it weren't."

"Aye, but Mam says you will be verra tired for the first few months then it will taper off. Anyway, I dinna have the heart to wake you. But I did sit a while and stare."

Smiling, wrapping her hand around his upper arm, she said, "I'm expecting a babe, Alec, and do not need to be treated as if I'm fragile. You know I adore your mother, but please don't let her dictate our lovemaking schedule."

Alec chuckled, the sound surely comparable to the heavens rejoicing. "I can pull off the trail right here, love. Show you what you missed last night."

She pressed her blush into the sleeve of his tunic. "Your parents and Henry are in the wagon directly behind us."

"You think my parents never took a little—"

Laughing, she straightened and covered her ears. "Please stop speaking."

"You dinna want those images in your head?"

"Do *you*?"

"I dinna. But I canna lie to you. I've been thinking all week about taking you down to the beach at Hawkmore, making love to you under the stars."

"Yes, please," she said unabashedly. With a contented sigh, she asked, "Can we name our daughter Magdalena?"

"Aye," he answered promptly and then ruined it by qualifying, "when we have one. But Henry and I have decided this child is a boy—we'll accept no substitutes—and he's to be named Robert."

"You'll be eating crow when my daughter is born," Katie teased, "and I've just now decided I will name her whatever I please."

"Our daughter." He was quiet for a moment and then said, "I still cannot believe it. I ken I believe it, I understand that's what happens with all that lovemaking. But Katie, I'm going to be a father. Someone's da."

This warmed her heart, his overdone joy. She recalled the expression on his face when she'd given him the news. She'd never, not once, been witness to anything that remotely resembled tears from this man. He hadn't rushed into her arms, hadn't cried out with joy, hadn't even smiled, she recalled. He'd sat down and lowered his head. Katie had watched, and waited, until he'd lifted his face to her, his eyes watering, speechless, just absolutely overcome with the splendor of it.

Her own joy was boundless now, had been for so long she could scarce recall before Alec, before love. None of it mattered, save that it put her where she was and made her who she was, that he could know her and love her.

They arrived at Hawkmore just after noon, greeted by waves from the battlements and an open gate.

Lachlan and Mari waited inside, near the keep, with Diana and Edric and another dozen happy souls gathered in the bailey. Katie's eyes lit on Mari, who was covering her mouth with her hands, hardly able to contain her excitement. Katie waved her arm wildly with her own delight. They'd visited last just before the snow fell. It had been a long winter without seeing her friends.

"If you leap from this cart before I've stopped it fully," Alec warned her, his tone suggesting he did not tease, "I swear to God, I'll tan your hide."

"I love you, too. I will wait for your assistance, husband, lest you have fits."

"I'm just asking you to be careful, mindful of the babe."

Not in a thousand years would she tease him about his concern. It had taken her three days to convince him that they could still enjoy lovemaking during her pregnancy. Actually, she hadn't convinced him at all. She'd set Malcolm to the task, which in turn had resulted in a scolding from her husband, that she'd discussed so private a matter with his captain.

"It was either him or your mother," she'd told him then.

But he'd made love to her splendidly that night. And all the ones before, and all the ones after.

---

HE LOVED THE BEACH at Hawkmore. He thought he should make a point to visit more often.

Loved particularly this view just now, his gaze set so happily upon Katie while she frolicked with Mari and Maggie and Henry and several others. Possibly, she wasn't aware of his scrutiny, as he'd come from the dunes further down, content to sit inside the tall grass, unobserved. He sat on the small slope, his legs bent before him, his hands locked over his knees.

He liked best when her hair was loose, as it was now, likely encouraged by Mari and Maggie as neither of them had wound their manes into any serviceable knots. The soft blonde shone brighter under the midday sun, swinging around behind her when she lifted her skirts and dodged away from the incoming waves. Her laughter reached him, so damn bewitching, hearty and infectious.

A noise behind him turned his head.

Lach and Iain came quietly and joined him.

"It's a good view, aye?" Lachlan asked, sitting next to him.

"Never gets old," Alec said, instinctively knowing that Lachlan referred to the people and not the gorgeous sea.

Iain slapped Alec on the shoulder and sat as well. "How'd we get so lucky?"

"I dinna ken about you," Alec challenged with a grin, "but I had to work fairly hard to get this."

"Aye, and you'd do it again. And again and again."

"Aye."

Henry was down there by the sea with them, equally at ease in the company of soldiers and lads his own age and with family. Alec hoped he stayed that way, hoped he didn't go through any stages that brought his mother grief, as Alec was sure he'd done to his own.

"We were some cocky lads, eh?"

None could deny it.

Iain dared, "Got that kicked out of us in bluidy fine fashion, aye?" They didn't often discuss their time as captives of the English. Sometimes they'd reference it, *aye, that was before Falkirk*, or *you recall so-and-so who was kept with us at Hawick House*, but they rarely, if ever, discussed any particulars, and certainly not the residual effects.

But then Lachlan said, "Alec, if your mam said it once, she's said it a hundred times to me—everything happens for a reason. Never sat well with me. I thought it trite, thought your mam only dinna ken how or what to say to explain the why of it. Why us. Why we suffered. Why we lived, why they died."

Sensing that he was going somewhere further, Alec prompted, "And?"

"Sometimes I get to thinking I'd no' have...if that hadn't happened, if I'd never been scarred, if I'd kept on as we had as lads—arrogant, selfish, oblivious to so much—I'd no' have appreciated, no' have been *able* to appreciate Mari."

Iain and Alec nodded, contemplating, though they said nothing, that Lachlan expounded, "What she is, how good she is"—he shook his head, trying to figure it out internally—"why I need her."

As youths, if any one of them had spoken so openly, so emotionally, they'd have ripped into him, have jibed and mocked him ceaselessly for showing such weakness.

They didn't now, of course. Alec said, "Christ, I'd like to think I'd have ken Katie was meant for me, even without...all that."

Iain admitted, "I dinna ken. You're right, though, Lach. We were different people back then, our trajectory different, our heads mostly up our own arses." He shrugged.

They were quiet for a few minutes, all eyes on the group near the water. Mari was shouting something out to Lachlan's captain, Murdoch, whiling away in a dinghy close to shore. Maggie and Henry had their heads together, both on their knees near the water's edge, bent over whatever had caught their attention. Katie stood near, one hand on her hip while the other shielded her eyes from the sun as she talked with Diana and Edric now. She laughed at whatever Edric said, the sound carrying magnificently across the sand and sky.

"Aye," said Alec. "used to be, I dinna want to see you, either of you. Dinna want to resurrect those memories, and that's what being around you did. I understood the connection, the bond wrought by that time, but it was hard to escape it, if I spent too much time around you. But I dinna ken, today it's different."

It had been different before that even. Since Katie.

"That's peace," Lachlan surmised.

"Aye, a wee critical something come to save you."

*The End*

*The Highlander Heroes Series*
The Touch of Her Hand
The Memory of Her Kiss
The Shadow of Her Smile
The Depths of Her Soul
The Truth of Her Heart
The Love of Her Life
Highlander Heroes Collection, Books 1-3
Highlander Heroes Collection, Books 4-6

Other Books by Rebecca Ruger
*Highlander: The Legends*
The Beast of Lismore Abbey
The Lion of Blacklaw Tower
The Scoundrel of Beauly Glen
The Wolf of Carnoch Cross

---

*Far From Home: A Scottish Time-Travel Romance*
And Be My Love
Eternal Summer
Crazy In Love
Beyond Dreams
Only The Brave
When & Where

---

*Heart of a Highlander Series*
Heart of Shadows
Heart of Stone

Heart of Fire
Heart of Iron
Heart of Winter
Heart of Ice

———∽———

rebeccaruger.com

Printed in Great Britain
by Amazon